THE TIME TRIALS

BOOK I

By
Jon and Dayna McConnell

TinyFox
PRESS

A Tiny Fox Press Book

Cover art by Christian Bentulan

Library of Congress Control Number: 2021931553

ISBN: 978-1-946501-34-9

Tiny Fox Press LLC
North Port, FL

For Declan and Ezra

CHAPTER 1
THE UNFORTUNATE

Finn Mallory's tie felt like a fancy, expensive noose. As he climbed the steps of Wharton Academy, an exclusive school that serviced the elite who could afford its hefty tuition, he loosened it with one hand and pushed open the doors to the school secretary's office with the other. His battered sneakers squeaked on the pristine marble floor almost in protest as he made his way to a chair that was more decorative than functional. A gramophone in the corner played light, classical music that bounced delicately off the dark, wooden paneling of the room.

Finn's eyes swept the room, falling on the secretary's trash can of all things. It looked like some kind of priceless artifact. Her *trash* can. He shook his head, laughing on the inside; that antique trash can looked like it never got used.

Rich people did that: they collected stuff they never used. They had cars they never drove, kitchens they never cooked in, and pools they never swam in. Wharton Academy was a boarding school...

Finn frowned; rich people had kids they didn't raise.

The rich, he concluded, were weird.

The secretary offered him a polite, tightlipped smile full of thinly veiled condescension. Finn didn't belong at Wharton Academy any more than he belonged in its uncomfortable school uniform. He was a publicity stunt, and she and everyone knew it. He was, after all, an "Unfortunate."

Wharton Academy accepted one or two students per year on full scholarship as part of its "Good Fortunes" community outreach program. These scholarships were always awarded to students who would provide good fodder for photo ops, and in light of Finn's recent tragic circumstances, he certainly checked that box. His parents, along with thousands of others desperate to give their children a Wharton Academy education, had filled out a Good Fortunes Scholarship application.

Then they died.

With their untimely deaths, Finn earned the title of "orphan," and Wharton Academy had granted him a full scholarship. When he had received his letter of acceptance at his foster home, he hadn't wanted to open it, but in some way, it felt like rejecting this opportunity was also a rejection of his parents' last gift to him, so he reluctantly accepted.

"The headmaster will see you now." The secretary's voice interrupted Finn's thoughts. He pried his eyes away from the unreasonably elegant trash can, drew himself to his feet, and smoothed the fabric of his new uniform over his legs before he was ushered into the headmaster's office.

Headmaster Bruce, a middle-aged man with a military haircut who looked like he could have been a P.E. teacher at some point, smiled and rose from his leather executive chair. His even, white teeth reminded Finn of a toothpaste commercial.

"Mr. Mallory." The headmaster pumped Finn's hand hard enough to dislocate his shoulder. "I hope you've gotten a chance to see our school." He reseated himself and motioned for Finn to sit as well.

"I've seen a little of it," Finn lowered himself into his chair, "but there's a lot to see."

"Yes," laughed Headmaster Bruce. "It can be a little intimidating at first. Do you have all your classes in order?"

"I think so," replied Finn, before muttering, "I can't believe you guys have an observatory. My old school barely had a gym."

Chuckling, the headmaster flashed his toothpaste-commercial-worthy smile as Finn glanced across the desk at his folded hands; he sported a large class ring on one finger, and his right wrist boasted what appeared to be a very expensive watch.

"Well," he smiled, "You're not in your old school anymore." Headmaster Bruce leaned back in his chair, lacing his hands behind his head. "I love the Good Fortunes Scholarship. It shakes things up around here."

Finn tried to suppress a smirk as he looked at the floor. After a brief pause, the headmaster softened his voice to add, "I want you to know that your story...it really touched us all. I'm glad the committee picked you, Finn." Finn couldn't tell if the headmaster's comment was sincere or if it was something he said to every scholarship recipient who came through his office. His eyes briefly rose from the floor and then lowered again.

"Well, Finn, let me tell you," Headmaster Bruce changed the subject, leaning forward and clapping his hands together, "you're going to fit right in here!" Finn winced as the man shot him playfully with double pistol fingers.

Yep. *That* happened.

In reality, Finn had received a cold welcome on his first day. The other students were well aware of who belonged at Wharton Academy and who had received the Good Fortunes Scholarship. They were sons and daughters of CEOs, the titans of industry, and powerful politicians—the children of people who pulled the strings behind the curtains of society. Money made you different. Finn knew he could adjust his blue tie all he wanted, but in the end, this uniform was only a costume.

It was also a student tradition that recipients of the Good Fortunes Scholarship were nicknamed "Unfortunates" because it always seemed as if some unfortunate situation led to winning one. "Unfortunates" were charity cases, and a top-notch Wharton Academy education would never change the fact that they simply didn't belong.

"Thank you, sir." Finn forced out the words as he made a study of his feet, his scuffed shoes contrasting sharply with the extravagance of the plush Oriental rug beneath them. "I'll do my best to prove myself here."

There were unspoken rules to being an Unfortunate. The academy would never acknowledge this, of course, but Finn knew that it was the unspoken rules that meant the most. Unfortunates kept their heads down. They were constantly expected to prove their worth. To earn their keep.

The headmaster laughed again. "You don't have to 'prove yourself,' Finn. But in order to keep the Good Fortunes program running, we do need to let the community know that it's worth our, er, *your*, while. We need to make sure we have you...involved in something. Something that shows that attending Wharton Academy is truly enriching your life. It has to be something...." The headmaster paused and glanced up at the ceiling as if the word he was looking for would appear above his head.

"...something...visible?" Finn fought to sound less cynical than he felt.

The headmaster threw him a rueful smile. "You could say that. Something that shows that your stay here benefits your future as well as the future of the community."

A dog and pony show.

Headmaster Bruce's face brightened, both eyebrows jumping as if pulled by invisible strings. "So, what are you into, Finn? Sports?" His eyes scanned Finn from head to toe, and he quickly changed course. "No. Debate?" He snapped his fingers. "I almost forgot: Professor Moskowitz has you tagged for his Young

Historians Club. In fact, you have Mordecai—I mean, Professor Moskowitz—for your next class. Professor Moskowitz is one of our oldest and most highly esteemed faculty members. You'll get along well, I'm sure."

"Yeah. Okay." Finn brushed a stray lock of coffee-colored hair out of his eyes. "Sure. Young Historians. Could be cool." Finn had never considered himself to be much of a history buff unless you counted the history of 90s music from the Pacific Northwest, but he wasn't in the position to argue.

Beggars can't be choosers.

Don't mess this up.

This is what they wanted.

This is for them.

The headmaster drew himself to his feet, walked across his office, and placed his hand on the doorknob. "I'll walk you to your next class."

Finn trailed him down the corridor, hands in his stiff, poplin pockets. Legacy photographs and lacrosse trophies filled glass display cases. As he eyed the wrought iron lamps and heavy mahogany doors, he couldn't help but suck in his breath in awe, impressed despite himself. It really was a beautiful place—the type of place he never imagined he'd be.

As they reached the second to last door on the right, Headmaster Bruce clapped a hand on his shoulder. "Well, this is where I leave you. Enjoy your class, Mr. Mallory. And again, welcome to Wharton Academy."

Finn offered him the barest of smiles.

As he was about to push open the door, Headmaster Bruce added, "Oh, and you'll want to do something about that hair. There's a great barber up the way."

He winked as Finn ran a self-conscious right hand over his shaggy mop of brown hair. With a flash of blinding white teeth, Headmaster Bruce turned on his heel and strode back down the corridor toward his office.

9

Chapter 2
History Lesson

Twenty-five sets of eyes flicked upward as Finn entered the room and tracked him as he approached Professor Mordecai Moskowitz, the teacher of Perspectives on World History.

Professor Moskowitz was a slight man who looked at Finn over a pair of small, chrome spectacles. He was incredibly old, with skin like a relief map and silver hair that was neatly combed straight back, and he wore a tweed vest with a brass stopwatch stowed in the front pocket. He extended a weathered hand to Finn, who felt immediately reassured despite the critical eyes he could feel burrowing into his back.

"You must be Finn Mallory." The old man's voice was gentle, comforting, like a shirt straight out of the dryer. "We've been looking forward to having you join us."

"I'm glad to be here," Finn mustered, trying to pretend he didn't feel like some exotic safari animal being watched through binoculars by a throng of eager tourists. Perhaps sensing his discomfort, Professor Moskowitz raised a merciful finger and pointed to the third desk in the row closest to the window. "Take a seat, Mr. Mallory, and we can speak after class."

Finn wove through the desks to his seat, acutely aware of the way the other students leaned back in their chairs as he passed them, seeking as much distance from him as possible, as if accidentally brushing against him or even feeling the breeze that he left in his wake might dirty them somehow.

Two muscular boys sat on the left side of the room; or they sprawled, rather, seeming to have no qualms about taking up space. Their uniforms featured conspicuous patches that read "WHARTON ACADEMY LACROSSE." They laughed derisively as Finn passed.

"Tellerville Trash," the biggest of them muttered out of the side of his mouth. With perfectly styled brown hair and blue eyes, he looked like he belonged in a Ralph Lauren ad or something. Finn didn't look at him for long enough to see much else other than his shit-eating grin before he cast his eyes away.

He sat gratefully, feeling as if the walk from the door to his chair had been hours rather than seconds. He was glad to be out of the spotlight—and yet he *wasn't* out of it—not really. He felt the stares follow and rest on him, and now he could hear whispers permeating the room like a cold wind. One particular word was very clear: "Unfortunate." Finn narrowed his eyes, trying to discern who had said it, but he couldn't—the word was coming from more than one source, the many whispers blending as one.

Four girls whispered into each other's ears behind cupped hands in the front of the room. A high-pitched giggle that resembled a bird call escaped one's mouth before she clapped her hand over it. The girl in the center of the hive pushed a curtain of silvery-blonde hair out of her face and turned to look at Finn.

For a moment, their eyes locked, and Finn felt as if he'd been gut-punched. Her eyes were liquid green. Piercing. Even through this haze of embarrassment, he could recognize that this girl was unreasonably beautiful—the kind of beautiful that almost hurt to look at. Apparently, it hurt to look at him, too; her green eyes widened and blinked before they dropped to the floor.

"So, Mr. Mallory," the professor's voice jolted Finn out of his spell, "perhaps you can weigh in on a little chat we're having."

Finn's heart began to hammer like a kickdrum. He had hoped to try to blend in a little longer, but clearly that wasn't happening.

"Why is history important?" The professor's eyes smiled behind the lenses of his spectacles.

"Why is history...important?" Finn repeated the question, stalling in order to buy some time. This seemed like a trap. "I don't know." His eyes darted from side to side as one of his hands rose to his neck to loosen his tie. Some muffled snickering began to bubble up from the class as the new "Unfortunate" struggled to answer what seemed like a simple question, and the professor politely waited with a slight smile.

"Well," the professor tilted his head to the side, "it seems like an important question, no?" He straightened, his eyes sweeping the room. "Perhaps one of you has an answer?"

The class went silent. Where many teachers would be frustrated by this silence, this old man didn't seem to mind. Feeling the heat of the spotlight leave him, the kick drum in Finn's chest began to slow.

"It's an important question because if you can't answer it, you simply won't learn anything in this class," the professor continued in a quiet, conversational voice. "My goodness," he laughed, "is there any value in what I teach?"

He paused for a painfully long moment, palms raised, waiting to see if any student would provide an answer.

"Well." He clapped his weathered hands together when no one did. "Perhaps we should change the question. What *is* history?"

A few hands shot up, and Professor Moskowitz picked one. "Important dates?" answered the student hesitantly.

"Yes." The old man's chin rose and fell in a slow nod. "Dates are important to remember, although I'm assuming you mean

12

dates of significant historical events and not awkward hand-holding in the movies, my dear." The class tittered with nervous laughter. "But dates are not an important part of my class." The professor held up an atrophied forefinger. "Don't get me wrong—precision in history is important. Very important. But that is not why we study history. Remembering the date that something important happened is not as important as remembering *why* it happened."

The professor drew his palms together and looked at the class over clasped hands. "Now, I might be a bit biased, but I believe that history is the most important class you can take here at Wharton Academy, or at any school for that matter. History makes us who we are, and it dictates who we will be. Those are two powerful statements. Take a moment to think about what they mean."

He took a few steps into the sea of desks before him, and Finn watched the class become statues as if moving might draw attention to themselves and prompt the old man to call on them.

"History makes us who we are," Professor Moskowitz continued. "Luckily, my brain still works—for the most part." His old eyes sparkled under his glasses as he paused to throw a sly look at the green-eyed girl in the front of the room, who smiled. "But I do have old friends whose minds have been slowly sanded away by time and I have seen what happens when a person loses their history." The professor unclasped his hands and used them to illustrate his point. "But perhaps more importantly, history has the ability to influence the future. Few things in life wield that type of power. If we learn from the mistakes of the past, we alter the course of our future. We become better than those before us, as we should, for we hold the advantage of being able to learn from their decisions."

The professor turned to Finn and addressed the class through him. "That is why history is important, Mr. Mallory. It makes us who we are and tells us who we can be."

The bell rang then, making Finn wonder if this old professor had somehow timed his last statement with it. Students gathered their things and filed out of the classroom in a blue and grey argyle flood. Finn alone remained seated.

When the room had cleared, and the noise of student footsteps had subsided, Professor Moskowitz leaned against the desk in front of the room and looked Finn over, face stretching into a warm smile. "So, Mr. Mallory, I'm guessing our esteemed headmaster has spoken to you about the expected extracurriculars for our Good Fortunes Scholarship recipients."

"He mentioned it." Finn blew an errant lock of hair out of his face. "Can't get something for nothing."

"Indeed," laughed Professor Moskowitz. "I'm guessing you won't be joining our lacrosse team?"

Finn's lip curled before he could stop himself, and Professor Moskowitz raised his grey eyebrows. "I also assume the headmaster told you about our Young Historians Club?"

Finn nodded, looking at the floor. "He didn't say much about it."

"Well, he doesn't *know* much about it." The old professor's reply was swift, and Finn's eyes darted up from the floor. "Not many of our students take an interest in the most important subject at Wharton Academy. There are only three of us, actually, and we need four to make a team."

"A team?"

"Four players." There was a spark of excitement in the professor's voice. "It's in the rules."

"Is it like, some sort of academic decathlon or something?"

Professor Moskowitz smiled again. "Something like that."

CHAPTER 3
FORGET IT

They came into the room like a storm making landfall—Liam Fillery and Nick Dain screaming and hooting at some vulgar joke, Lacy Locatelli, Amanda Ayers, and Janelle Burr tossing their hair around and giggling like maniacs. But if this group was a storm, Everly Caldwell was the eye: still, silent, placid.

Everly smoothed the wool of her pencil skirt behind her before she lowered herself onto her bench at the table closest to the window in Wharton Academy's banquet hall, across from Nick, Liam, and Lacy, and next to Amanda and Janelle. Lacy ceased her chatter long enough to blow a bubble with her watermelon-scented gum. Everly watched as the pink orb grew more translucent as it increased in size, her ears full of the hum of Janelle and Amanda's voices—like the buzz of a colony of bees—the colony of which Everly was the reluctant queen. They were talking about Fall Fling; it was a conversation Everly should be paying attention to—a conversation she should care about, considering she was Wharton's Social Chair. But she hardly heard a word as she looked past Lacy's huge, pink bubble at the lone figure seated at one of the banquet tables across the room, a dark shock of hair falling into his broody eyes.

The Unfortunate.

"Everly. *Everly!*" Janelle's needy invocation coincided with the moment Lacy's bubble burst.

Everly flinched with her whole body. "What?" The startled look on Janelle's face told her that her tone had been sharper than she'd intended.

Lacy pried the gum off her lips with the tip of her tongue and rolled it back into her mouth, pulverizing it with her jaws once more, eyebrow raised. "We're talking about the color palette for the Fall Fling," she said between chews.

"Amber, silver, and plum are always safe choices for autumn," Everly murmured, trying to feign interest, but her gaze was still trained on the new kid across the room. His right leg was jiggling under the table, like he was nervous, but he had a strange expression on his face—equal parts uncomfortable and sardonically amused. What was his name again?

Finn.

Janelle, Amanda, and Lacy were still talking—something about table linens—and Liam and Nick hadn't stopped howling about something wildly inappropriate, but Everly tuned them out as she rose to her feet.

"Everly? Where are you going?"

Everly didn't turn at the sound of Amanda's voice. Her Prada mary janes clicked on the marble floor as she crossed the room. "Just...give me a minute."

Finn speared a piece of diced carrot with his fork and kept his eyes down. Wharton Academy's banquet hall was a far cry from the cafeteria at his old high school, with its faded linoleum floor and beat-up, foldable tables, their tops etched with obscenities and their undersides caked with chewing gum. He remembered the artery-clogging, vomit-inducing fare that students had been served at Tellerville High School: limp, greasy pork chops, canned fruit cocktail, or mysterious casseroles drowning in about two inches of grease, the contents of which were anyone's guess. Here, there was a dizzying array of high-end, seasonal, sustainably grown choices.

Kale and lobster bisque. Pear, kale, and brie finger sandwiches. Finn had chuckled to himself as he served himself a glass of lavender-infused water and a scoop of "autumnal vegetable melange"—which also featured kale.

Rich people. They love their kale.

Finn had picked a seat at an empty table in the furthest corner of the room. He was already an island at this school; he may as well look the part.

He tried in earnest to avoid looking at the table closest to the window, inhabited by four girls and two boys—the girls who had been sitting in front during history class and the boys who had called him "Tellerville Trash." They'd made no shortage of noise as they'd entered, carrying themselves with a sense of ownership and authority as they claimed a long banquet table near the window. The boys hadn't seemed to notice or care that they smacked several people with their lacrosse gear on the way to their seats, and no one had seemed willing to risk calling them out on it.

Although she was the quietest of the lot, the nucleus of the group was the silvery-blonde girl. Finn remembered her green eyes as they had fixed on him. She'd been the only person to make eye contact with him all day—and that counted Headmaster Bruce; even with his painted-on smile and carefully-crafted speech full of empty, condescending positivity, the headmaster hadn't actually allowed his eyes to rest on Finn's even once. He'd looked just above Finn's head, or to the right or left of him—anywhere but at his actual eyes.

Yes, the girl had made eye contact, but she'd also looked away, as if the sight of him had been painful. Now, he looked away from her table and stared down at his autumnal vegetable melange. He pushed a piece of butternut squash around on his plate with his fork, the tines of which were tangled in a piece of sautéed kale.

He could avoid looking at the table of teen models, but he couldn't avoid hearing them; a leggy brunette with hoop earrings was talking around a thick wad of chewing gum, loud enough to be heard in the observatory across campus. Something about a color palette. For a dance. Finn rolled his eyes. The girl's words were punctuated by the deafening guffaws of the lacrosse players, who slapped the top of the mahogany table as they slung their crass, obnoxious banter across it.

Grade A douches.

Finn skewered a piece of sweet potato with his fork and brought it to his mouth as he thought of the professor's cryptic words, the twinkle in his eye, as he'd talked about the Young Historians Club.

"Is it, like, some sort of academic decathlon or something?"

"Something like that."

For a history club, the old man sure made it seem like it was steeped in mystery. Weird. Whatever this club turned out to be, Finn took comfort in the fact that it likely wouldn't involve any lacrosse players.

A sudden hush fell over the room, and Finn looked up from his tray to find the table of teen models staring at him, eyes agog. But one was missing now: the green-eyed blonde.

Between the sudden heat in his cheeks and the prick of their stares, he felt like some sad ant on a hot sidewalk under a kid's magnifying glass.

Do I have something on my face?

He ran his hand over his chin and mouth. Nope, nothing.

Someone cleared their throat softly, and Finn shifted his eyes to find the blonde standing in front of him, behind the bench across his table. Almost as if staring into the sun, he squinted up at her, the full force of her formidable beauty hitting him hard at such close range. In the classroom, he'd been able to register that she was attractive—in a celestial, otherworldly sort of way. But now that she was standing, he was able to fully appreciate all of her attributes—and there was a lot to appreciate.

The blue, argyle pencil skirt that was part of Wharton's uniform flattered her in a way that it didn't any of the other girls. This girl would probably be capable of making a burlap sack look good; her miniscule waist flared out into perfectly rounded hips, and her long legs ended in... a pair of expensive-looking shoes.

Yep, those shoes probably cost more than either of his parents had made in a week.

The realization shook Finn back to reality.

Okay, she's hot, but she's also a snob.

He glanced back at her table of friends, who still stared at them from across the room, whispering.

Her friends, who less than an hour ago, had been laughing at him.

She's one of them.

So, what does she want with me?

Finn felt his inner walls rise as she slid onto the bench opposite him and extended a well-manicured hand. He stared at it for a beat before reluctantly accepting it. An involuntary tremor coursed through him at her touch; her hands were warm and smooth, her fingertips soft—a sharp contrast to his own, which were hardened, callused from years of feverish guitar playing.

"Everly Caldwell." The girl's lips lifted into a smile, her green eyes somehow soft and piercing at the same time. "You're Finn."

Finn opened his mouth to speak but closed it. After fumbling for words for a few awkward moments of silence, he finally managed, "I saw you in Moskowitz's class."

He set his mouth, reminding himself not to be distracted by how pretty she was.

Remember: hot snob.

And what kind of name was Everly, anyway? It sounded like something you'd call a gated community or something.

He bristled, throwing another bitter look at the table where Everly had come from. "Those your friends?"

Everly's companions were still boring holes into both of them with their eyes. The biggest lacrosse player—the one with the shit-eating grin from history class—was pointing now, scowling and elbowing his friend. Finn felt resentment build inside him like steam in a pressure cooker as he returned his attention to the girl sitting across from him. She still hadn't answered the question. Instead, she looked down at her hands, biting a full bottom lip.

"You don't have to do this, you know." Finn spat out the words as if trying to reject a bad taste from his mouth. The girls at the teen model table stared at Everly with horror from across the room, wagging their heads, hands over their mouths, the way people do when watching a tragedy unfold.

Everly looked up, green eyes blinking once. "Do what?" Her expression was innocent, the tone of her voice guileless, but Finn couldn't change course now.

"This." He gestured a line between the two of them. "This is a joke. Right?"

Everly looked briefly wounded before her pretty features hardened. Her chin lifted, making her look regal, haughty, like a queen regarding a lowly serf.

"Look, I'm not a project, okay?" Finn was shocked at the vitriol in his own voice, yet he couldn't stop the flow of his words—a day's worth of pent-up frustration over having to play a role he hadn't auditioned for. "I'm wearing the stupid uniform, and I'm getting the stupid haircut. What else do you people want?"

Everly narrowed her eyes and drew herself to her feet in one fluid motion, smoothing the wool of her skirt on her knees. As she made to walk away, she stopped and turned her head slightly.

"Forget it." She said it over her shoulder in an almost imperceptible murmur before she breezed across the banquet hall,

Prada mary janes clicking against the marble floor. Heads turned as she left, and the heavy door of the banquet hall thudded behind her.

CHAPTER 4
REWIND

As Finn trudged across Wharton grounds toward the dormitories, he pictured Everly Caldwell sitting across from him, poised, like a young Grace Kelly in a schoolgirl uniform, trying, apparently, to be his friend.

He sighed, dragging a hand down the side of his face. He'd tried to justify his behavior to himself, but he knew he had stepped in it.

Her friends called me trash.

But then he remembered the look on her face, that flash of hurt in her eyes, before she had turned to stone and stalked off. The moment he'd seen it, he'd realized his error, but it had been too late. No, Everly hadn't been toying with him. She had been sincere, and Finn had been, well, an asshole.

This sucked.

He passed through Wharton Gardens, which were located to the right of the classroom corridors. A sprawling green lawn dotted with topiaries ran adjacent to a courtyard with an ivy-covered gazebo in the center. Rose bushes lined the perimeter.

Finn climbed the brick steps of his dormitory—a modest, brick square of a building. Like everything at Wharton Academy, it was well-kept; the white porch appeared to have been freshly painted and looked like it was swept several times a day. But living in Aion Hall was like flying coach, as the simplicity of the building might suggest. The "first class" equivalents were across the Wharton Gardens, on the other side of the Promenade, Wharton's social hub. It was bookended with an elegant gazebo painted in stark white on one side and a tiered fountain on the far end, which looked like a giant, stone wedding cake.

He paused at the steps of Aion Hall and looked back at the Gardens, bustling with students that all dressed and acted exactly the same. They all seemed to have a certain sheen to them—a sheen he figured came from money. For all its grandeur, the Gardens were really just a fancy buffer zone separating the "haves" from the "have-mores."

Raine Manor and Kingsley Tower, the elite dormitories, rose up across that rolling courtyard, imposing their supremacy with size alone. It was fitting, really; if you looked at Aion Hall at the right time of day, like right now, it literally sat in the shadow of the dramatic spires of Raine Manor and Kingsley Tower, a detail that Finn decided had probably been carefully planned out.

As he fumbled in his uniform pocket for the key to his room, he wondered who he would encounter inside. At least he'd likely be safe from lacrosse players; those self-important douchebags would never slum it in a place as comparatively unremarkable as Aion Hall. His hand found the key, and he let himself in.

He found his dorm room up a flight of stairs, the second door on the right. It was utilitarian, plain, with two loft beds flanking both ends of the room. Under each bed was a desk area and a chest of drawers, and the wall closest to the door was almost entirely taken up by a long closet.

Finn's eyes scanned the room for signs of life. At first, he assumed his roommate wasn't home. Then he heard a soft exhale, followed by a snort. A head was nestled into the pillow of the loft bed on the right side of the room. Finn proceeded toward the other bed, taking slow, careful steps so as not to make the floorboards squeak. He didn't want to wake up his roommate; enough people hated him here already. He remembered Everly's green eyes in the banquet hall, the school secretary's patronizing smile, and the lacrosse player's predatory glare.

The room was cold, and Finn realized the window was slightly ajar. As noiselessly as possible, he moved across the room and closed it.

An acoustic guitar sat on the ground, propped against his desk: his guitar. At the sight of it, a warmth spread through him. It had seen better days; the body was dented in areas from being faithfully toted around by its owner, and adhesive marred the surface from an old Pixies sticker that had long worn off. The pickguard was discolored, and the excess strings curled away from the headstock like tendrils on a vine. But Finn couldn't help but smile when he imagined the pride in his father's face as he said, "It's a Martin. Same kind played by Kurt Cobain in *Unplugged*!"

Finn picked up the guitar, eased its strap around his neck, and as he ran his callused fingers along the strings, they issued a faint squeak. He threw a look across the room at the snoring figure, remembering he was supposed to be quiet, and set the guitar back down again. He turned his attention to a cardboard Converse shoebox on his chest of drawers.

A Walkman was inside, the headphones' cord wrapped around it, carefully and intentionally stuffed inside several layers of socks and a pair of boxer shorts to avoid being confiscated under Wharton's technology ban.

The antiquated feel of Wharton Academy did not only come from the palpable age of the buildings; it was carefully manufactured by the rules themselves. The school adhered to a strict ban of anything technological, as if the ring of an iPhone or the flicker of a flat-screen television might break some unspoken spell and cause the weathered walls to crumble on the spot. Modern technology was simply not the Wharton way.

A mixtape labeled "Summer '96" in electric blue marker, carefully curated by Finn's dad, kept the Walkman company within the confines of the shoebox. Finn pictured his dad pressing rewind to listen to Pearl Jam's "Yellow Ledbetter" one more time as he drove Finn to school in their 1980s Volvo station wagon, laughing as he did his best Eddie Vedder impression. The car's bumper had been nearly obscured by stickers honoring his dad's favorite record labels and grunge bands.

Finn clicked the tape into the Walkman's cassette chamber and pulled on his headphones, climbed onto his loft bed, and pressed play. The first chords of "Time" by Hootie and the Blowfish began, and Finn's heart raced as he fumbled to press the "stop" button with shaky fingers.

His grief was like the tide. Usually, it just lapped at his feet as he went about his business. But other times, it crested into a wave and smashed into him from behind when he least expected it, taking his feet out from under him and threatening to drag him under, leaving him gasping for air. It usually happened at night, when the noise of the day had subsided and he was left alone with his own thoughts and memories, which emerged from the shadows of his mind, kind of like cockroaches that come out when the lights are switched off.

Screeching tires. Shattering glass. Blinding headlights getting closer and closer. This was all Finn Mallory remembered of the night his parents died.

He could almost feel his father ruffling his hair, his fingertips as callused as his own, calling him "Shark Finn" with that easy, whiskered smile dancing on his lips. A smattering of freckles decorating the bridge of his mother's nose. Pancakes on Sunday mornings, with Alice in Chains blaring in the background, his father hopping around on one foot, playing air guitar, singing into the spatula. His mother's laugh, pealing like bells through their modest, rented duplex unit. Finn smiled as he remembered getting up in the middle of the night for a glass of water and finding his parents slow-dancing to Mazzy Star, bathed in the light of the open microwave.

The Mallorys had had little; there were no trips to Disney World, no trendy toys, no back to school shopping trips to Macy's, but Finn's parents had mastered the skill of making the simplest things feel special, and it was due to this that their son never sensed their lack of means.

Trent and Sarah Mallory were young parents, as Sarah had given birth to Finn at the age of seventeen. They were disappointments to their own parents—embarrassments who were promptly disowned and sent packing to reckon with adulthood on their own. Trent's big dream of making it as a musician never panned out and he had to work three jobs to support his new and unexpected family. He played in a series of cover bands, working weddings, Bar Mitzvahs, and proms, but work wasn't steady, and his "big break" never came. Sarah waitressed at the Coffee Pot and cleaned hotels on weekends to make ends meet.

No, the Mallorys were not a success story; not if you define success in the traditional way, at least.

It took years for Finn to realize that they were poor. He remembered nights sitting cross-legged on the living room rug, his family sharing a box of mac and cheese by candlelight, the three of them laughing, joking, and making shadow puppets against the living room wall. At the age of eight, this was an adventure, but by twelve Finn had learned that nights like this happened because the electricity bill hadn't been paid and they didn't have money for groceries. Yet even after this epiphany, he struggled to think of anything he truly needed or wanted that he didn't have.

Things changed on a grey December day, when Finn was fourteen. He burst through the doors of the Mallory's duplex unit clutching a piece of paper, pulled off the bulletin board at Guitar Haven.

"Birds Eye View!" he sputtered, waving the paper in his mother's tired face. Sarah Mallory was between cleaning shifts, feet elevated on a stack of pillows propped up on their chipped, laminate coffee table. She looked a bit older than her thirty-one years, with lines of fatigue etched into her forehead, a result of working long hours waiting tables and spending tedious nights scrubbing toilets, vacuuming floors, and laundering sheets. A few wisps of silver had already crept into her long, reddish hair.

Bird's Eye View was Finn's favorite band. He'd become instantly obsessed with their music when he first heard them on the car radio last year, and now they were going to be playing in Greely, a few towns over. Trent whipped his head around the kitchen door frame, smiling as he wiped his wet hands on his flannel shirt.

"What's up, Shark Finn?" He plucked the show flier out of Finn's hands and crimped an eye. "Bird's Eye View, huh?" The smile vanished from his face as his gaze fell to the bottom of the paper. He sucked his breath in sharply through his teeth. "Tickets are $60 each. That's a little...steep." He pushed a hand through his sandy brown hair. "I don't know if we can swing that. For the three of us, that's..." His voice trailed off, his eyes finding his wife's over Finn's head.

"We don't all three have to go," Finn blurted. "I can go alone." He anticipated his mother's rebuttal and turned to face her. "I can handle it. The subway, I mean. That way it would only be the cost of one ticket."

"Honey, that's...no. We can't have you ride the subway alone. Not yet," Finn's mother said gently. "At least one of us needs to go with you."

In a single instant of injustice, Finn felt the disadvantages of his station in life for the first time and the words poured out of his mouth like water from a busted pipe.

"Can't I ever have...anything?" He faced his father again, surprising himself with the pent-up resentment that he hadn't even known he had. "It isn't fair. Just because we're—"

Finn didn't say the last word in the sentence, but he didn't have to; the damage had already been done. Trent looked like he'd been slapped. His eyes met his wife's again, and the room grew silent but for the rumble of the washing machine.

"I'm sorry," Finn stammered. "What I said...I didn't mean it. I don't have to go to the concert. It's not a big deal."

"No." Trent cleared his throat as if to rally himself. "You're right. It *isn't* fair. You deserve to go." Finn watched the wordless exchange that unfolded between his parents through eye contact alone.

"I can pick up a few extra shifts at the Coffee Pot, maybe do an extra weekend at the hotel this month. We'll make it happen." Sarah's smile was weary but reassuring. "I mean, it *is* Bird's Eye View."

"No, really, forget it." Finn ran his hands over his face, embarrassed at his outburst and guilt-ridden at having wounded his parents. They worked hard—to the bone—to support a child they never meant to have, and now they were going to work harder just so he could go to some stupid concert.

"Don't worry, Shark Finn." Finn's father wiggled his eyebrows. "Get excited. You're going to Bird's Eye View."

That night Finn could hear the hushed voices of his parents as they talked at the kitchen table. He couldn't make out every word, but he could hear the tone—tense and strained—and words like "opportunities" and "future."

In the morning, Finn's parents were less animated than usual. There was no air guitar, no Soundgarden blasting in the background. His parents waited at the table in their eat-in kitchen, each holding a cup of coffee. The coffee pot, nearly empty, sat on a trivet on the table, evidence that they'd been up for a while.

"Finn, sit down." Finn's mother slid a mug of hot chocolate across the table. "We've been thinking." She threw a look at her husband.

"We talked about some stuff last night," Finn's father said, sipping at the dregs of his coffee. "Things you don't have. Things you deserve. Things you may never have if we don't..." he ran a hand over his whiskers, "...make some changes."

"Dad, I'm sorry," Finn slid into his chair, hooking his fingers through the mug's handle but making no move to drink. "Seriously. I didn't mean it. If this is about Bird's Eye View, I told you—"

"It's not just about the concert, Finn." Trent pinched the bridge of his nose and closed his eyes. "It's about a lot more than that. It's about...opportunities. Opportunities that you deserve but you won't get because of—" he made a sweeping gesture with his hand toward the living area with its chintzy, sun-bleached curtains, stained carpets, water-damaged ceiling, and sparse furnishings, "—this."

Finn's parents proceeded to explain that they had entered his name to be considered for Wharton Academy's Good Fortunes program. Finn had heard of Wharton Academy—everyone had—but he'd never paid much attention. Why should he? Like so many things, a school like that wasn't in the cards for him and never would be.

"Look, Finn." The absence of his father's usual playful smile put a cold pit in Finn's stomach that even his hot chocolate couldn't thaw. "I need to do right by you. I made some choices earlier in life that put us here, but maybe...maybe this Wharton thing can make it right. Maybe this will open some doors."

It was only a few weeks later that the Mallorys piled into their 1980s station wagon for what would be the last time. Head-on collision, they said. Drunk driver. Finn remembered the lights, the screech of the brakes, the shattering glass, but nothing else except waking up in the hospital with two drawn faces hovering over him that he didn't recognize. He'd been lucky, the nurse had told him, to come away from such a nasty crash with nothing but a broken clavicle and some facial lacerations.

"Your parents likely died instantly and without pain," the doctor had said. "They probably never saw it coming."

None of this was any comfort to Finn.

They shouldn't have even been there.

They were there because of me...

They're dead *because of me.*

Now, Finn pressed fast forward on the Walkman, wishing it would also push him past the memories of that horrific night. But what he really wanted to do was press rewind.

"Hey. HEY!" A voice. Loud. Toneless. Insistent.

Finn jolted upright and pulled the headphones from his ears. "What?"

"Two and a half inches. Didn't you hear me?"

Finn snorted. "Uhh...*what's* two and a half inches?"

"I said it four times, and you didn't answer. I *said* it has to be exactly two and a half inches."

Finn pushed his Walkman away from him, shoving it under the pillow before he scrambled down the ladder from his loft.

"Oh. Hi, sorry. Guess I didn't hear you." He extended a hand to who was quite obviously his now very awake roommate—a pale kid with thick, black, square-framed glasses.

"You can't close it." The roommate ignored his outstretched hand. "It has to be open two and a half inches." His voice had a robotic quality to it—a kind of dissonance Finn had never heard before.

Finn opened his mouth to ask what he was talking about, but then he recognized that the guy was gesturing indignantly toward the window—the one Finn had closed when he had entered the room.

"Sorry." Finn stuffed his hands into the pockets of his uniform. "It was sort of freezing in here."

"Every night, the window needs to be opened exactly two and a half inches." By now, the roommate had begun to pace back and forth in front of him. "The only exception is if it's raining." He threw another wild gesture toward the window. "Do *you* see any precipitation?"

"Uh, yeah, no, sorry." Finn didn't know what else to say; obviously this kid was pretty passionate about ventilation.

He tried to introduce himself again. "I'm Finn. Finn Mallory." But the roommate offered him nothing but a blank stare.

"Do you...have a name?" Finn shifted uncomfortably under the roommate's unflinching gaze.

"Edison," the roommate said flatly, arms crossed.

Finn smiled. "So, do people call you Ed?"

Edison's expression didn't change. "No." He pushed his thick glasses up further on the bridge of his nose with his index finger.

Finn was beginning to sense that Edison was a very different sort of person, even beyond his rigid preferences and the flatness of his tone. This felt like talking to an alien.

"Okay. Edison it is, then. Like, the guy who invented the lightbulb. Right? Pretty...*bright* guy, huh?" The terrible joke escaped Finn's mouth before he could stop it, and he died a little inside.

"Technically, Thomas Alva Edison did not invent the lightbulb," Edison responded in a deadpan voice. "He invented the lightbulb *filament*. There is a difference."

Finn nodded, and not knowing what else to say, began pulling his weekend clothes out of his suitcase and putting them away in the closet. He could feel Edison's eyes burning into his back as he slung his worn-in flannels and jeans onto hangers and hooked them over the rod. As Finn loosened his shitty Wharton tie, Edison continued to rattle on about the invention of the lightbulb filament.

"Did you know that over twenty different inventors tried to invent the lightbulb before Thomas Alva Edison created the filament that made it successful?" Then, suddenly, his eyes bulged behind his glasses. "Wait! What are you doing? You can't put that there."

Edison lunged forward and began frantically pushing Finn's clothing to the right side of the closet. Finn noticed Edison's clothing, meticulously organized by what appeared to be color, hanging on the left.

"Okay, okay, sorry." He displayed his palms in apology. Clearly, he'd crossed a line.

Finn soon learned that there were several idiosyncratic "rules" that he would have to abide by if he were going to successfully cohabit with Edison, who, without shame or embarrassment, rattled off his rules of conduct as if they were standard norms of behavior:

1) No visitors without clearing it with Edison first.

2) No loud chewing.

3) All hair or other personal hygiene products in the room must be unscented.

4) Don't touch Edison's banana chips.

"Can you adhere to this?" Edison asked formally as if he were the president of an HOA, explaining the rules of yard maintenance to a new homeowner.

Finn ran a hand through his hair, his loose tie still draped around his neck. "Yeah, I think I can do that. Sure."

"Good." For the first time in their bizarre interaction, a restrained smile flitted across Edison's face. "Finn Mallory, we are now friends."

CHAPTER 5
THE YOUNG HISTORIANS CLUB

Four seats, arranged in a semicircle, faced Professor Moskowitz's desk. Finn and Edison had just arrived for their first official meeting of the Young Historians Club. When Finn had initially attended Professor Moskowitz's class, he hadn't noticed how heavily embellished this classroom really was; there were shelves thrown up on many levels of the four walls, each one packed with antiquities of all shapes, sizes, and origins. Meticulously carved wooden dolls stood watch over the classroom next to some worn, clay tablets, which were engraved in some ancient language. Terra cotta pots, many of which were chipped and broken, were lined up next to Viking drinking horns and battered stone carvings. A series of masks from various tribes and time periods hung at the back of the classroom, the expressions on their wooden faces ranging from emotionless to truly dreadful. A pair of heavy, ivory tusks wreathed the collection of masks, the stares of which made the nearly empty classroom feel like it had a ghostly audience.

Finn felt his face grow warm as he noticed Everly, the fair-haired goddess from the banquet hall that he'd last seen in a huff, apparently the third member of this club, sitting in the seat closest to the far wall. He looked away, but too late—she saw him, pursed her lips and redirected her gaze to the windows. He muttered under his breath as he lowered himself into his chair, bracing himself for how inevitably awkward this meeting would be. He could still hear her angry footsteps echoing out of the banquet hall in the ear of his mind.

Edison took the seat closest to the door, forcing Finn to sit only a seat away from the girl he had insulted just yesterday.

Terrific.

Professor Moskowitz leaned against his desk, sketching a meditative smile as he took in the three new members of the Young Historians Club and patiently waited for the fourth.

As if on cue, a brunette with well-defined calves breezed through the door and took the last seat next to Everly, out of breath. She wore a "Wharton Athletics" sweatshirt over her uniform, and her hair was pulled up in an impossibly high ponytail.

Edison looked at her impassively. "You are two minutes late."

As Ponytail Girl narrowed her eyes at Edison, Finn sat back further in his chair to avoid the glare, but it only exposed him to Everly, whose green eyes settled upon him briefly before she again cast them away with a disgusted sigh.

"I'm glad to have you join us, Ms. Konrad," Professor Moskowitz threw an amused look at Edison as he spoke to Ponytail Girl, "even if you *are* a few minutes tardy, as has been so astutely observed."

'Ms. Konrad' kept her eyes locked on the kid in the glasses, unflinching, but he didn't blink either—he simply stared back at her.

"Welcome, my young historians and friends!" Professor Moskowitz clapped his hands together. "I'm pleased to have such an interesting group, as this is a particularly exciting year to be a Young Historian."

"Professor," Ponytail Girl began, "you might have already gone over this because I was a few minutes late—"

"Two minutes," interrupted Edison monotonously.

Ponytail Girl gave him a once-over. "I've seen you around, but I didn't catch your name."

"That's because I never told you." Edison adjusted his glasses. "Edison Pellegrin. But I'm rarely called that. People usually call me 'weirdo' or other variations of that. I prefer 'eccentric.'"

An amused smile played over the girl's lips. "I like you, Edison. You don't mince words."

Edison looked at her without expression. "I don't know if I like you yet."

It was Everly's turn to smile, and at the sight of it, Finn felt a little weight come off his shoulders. The ice seemed to be softening, and it was due to the thaw of Edison's dry wit. He secretly gave thanks for the eccentric kid in the square glasses.

Professor Moskowitz, who had also been quietly enjoying this awkward exchange, sensed a moment to restart. "Ms. Konrad, perhaps I can guess at your question. This club is not what you think it is. It is exclusive, and it is special. You might have noticed that the Young Historians are not advertised on the campus bulletin board." A smile spread across his wizened face, a trace of mischief in it. "It is certainly not what Headmaster Bruce thinks it is."

Finn leaned forward in his chair. Things were getting interesting.

"The Young Historians Club is part of a larger society of historians. There are many schools who participate, and as you can imagine, they are schools comparable to Wharton."

"You mean *rich* schools." Finn blurted it before he realized he'd spoken. He felt Everly's eyes on him, but he pretended not to notice.

Professor Moskowitz nodded. "That's one way of putting it. In any case, privilege is not without perks, and the chance to participate in the Young Historians Club is one of those perks. It's a once in a lifetime chance to be a part of something truly amazing."

"I've never heard you talk about the Young Historians Club like this before." Everly propped her elbow on her desk and rested her chin in her palm. "I always figured it was just a boring club where you drone on about history...no offense."

Finn watched the way Everly interacted with the professor with interest; something about their banter felt comfortable. Familial.

"It's never been bland. How dare you!" The old professor feigned outrage, hand flying to his chest. "And yes, these clubs are very private. I could never tell you the truth before because I was sworn to secrecy, my dear. If you accept this challenge, you will all be sworn to secrecy as well."

Ponytail Girl leaned back, arms crossed, head cocked. "Well, *this* all feels very cloak and dagger."

"It can be," admitted Professor Moskowitz. "As your mentor in this program, it will be my job to prepare you for the challenges that lie ahead." He wandered to one of his many shelves, picked up an hourglass full of black sand, and turned it over musingly.

"What types of challenges?" Everly's perfectly symmetrical face clouded with suspicion. "I think you owe us at least an explanation."

"I can tell you about it," answered the old professor, watching the black sands trickle from one end of the hourglass to the other. "But showing you is not possible until you have signed a contract."

Finn's face scrunched up.

Who has to sign a contract for a history club?

"A contract?" repeated Ponytail, as if echoing his thoughts.

"A contract." The professor restored the hourglass to its place and folded his hands in front of him. "It's mostly a confidentiality thing. And there's a little liability."

"Liability?" Ponytail arched an eyebrow.

"Yes." The professor offered a nonchalant shrug. "The Young Historians are not without risks." Finn dragged his eyes from the professor's face to Ponytail as he tracked the back and forth.

"*Risks?*"

"My dear, this would go a lot faster if you would let me explain and stop repeating the last word of all my sentences." The professor smiled. "What I'm about to disclose will be a bit of a shock and I'm not sure how you will all take it." He pressed his lips together. "It requires...a leap of faith."

"This would go a lot faster if you just said it," stated Edison in his robotic voice. He'd begun to rock back and forth a bit, something Finn had seen him do more than once back at the dorm. One of his many quirks.

"See?" Ponytail smirked. "Not a word mincer. I like him."

Edison stared at her for a beat without a hint of expression before returning his attention to the professor.

"Very well." The old man released a long sigh. "I shall not mince words then." He walked to the window. "The Young Historians Club requires that the four of you, should you accept, participate in a competition of sorts." He ran a wrinkled finger along the window pane, which drew a faint squeak. "It's a series of events, actually, called the Time Trials. Each one has its different challenges and tribulations. Its own *dangers*. It is exclusive and by invitation only. Wharton has not participated in the Time Trials for twenty years."

"Uh, this doesn't sound like pop quizzes and field trips." Finn's eyes darted from side to side, a defensive laugh escaping his mouth.

Dangers?

"Not quite," confirmed Professor Moskowitz, turning to face the team again. "There *are* field trips...of a sort. But you will not be traveling in a Wharton Academy van." He drew in a deep breath and narrowed his eyes as if trying to inhale courage. "You will be traveling in a time machine."

All four students went silent, frozen in their chairs as the professor's words took hold, sure they'd heard wrong. For nearly a full minute, one could have heard a pin drop in Professor Moskowitz's classroom.

Finn smiled, arms crossed, assuming the professor was playing an elaborate hoax and waiting for him to reveal it. Forgetting he was trying not to, he looked to Everly, who had knotted her brow as she stared at Professor Moskowitz. Ponytail scanned the room to gauge the reaction of her peers. Only Edison, who had stopped his rhythmic rocking, showed not the slightest change in his expressionless face as he waited patiently for clarification.

"A...*time* machine..." Everly drew out the words slowly as if attempting to encourage the professor to elaborate.

"Well," the old man displayed his palms, "it isn't actually called that—it is called a Time Bender. But they are essentially the same thing." He waited a few seconds before continuing. "It's a machine that creates a bend in the force that we call 'time.' This bend allows those within the vehicle to travel the opposite way and punch through to a different period of time."

Finn's lip curled. This guy wasn't joking. Was he crazy? Maybe; he was definitely old enough to have dementia or something.

"Hold on." Ponytail threw up a hand. "Even if that were true, it would be ridiculously dangerous. Couldn't we inadvertently affect the future...or the present?"

Finn shifted in his chair to face her. "What do you mean?"

"She's talking about the butterfly effect," answered Everly quickly, leaning around Ponytail. "If time travel was even possible, any changes you make in the past would be magnified in the future."

"Go on." There was pride in the professor's eyes as he watched Everly. He cupped an elbow in one of his palms, resting his chin on his fist.

Everly sighed, green eyes raised to the ceiling as if searching for a way to explain. "Well, let's say you go back in the past and get bit by a mosquito and kill it."

"So?" Finn shrugged, ignoring the striking way her long, dark lashes contrasted with the alabaster hue of her skin. "Mosquitoes suck, and there are millions of them. What's the big deal?"

"Well," a hint of impatience bled into Everly's voice, "you're not just killing one mosquito. You're also killing every mosquito that this mosquito would ever make if it reproduced, and all of the mosquitoes that *those* baby mosquitoes would have produced. In the end, you're killing millions, maybe even billions, of mosquitoes over the course of time."

"Like I said...," Finn knew his tone was combative, yet he couldn't seem to stop it, "not the worst thing, right?"

Everly rolled her eyes. "But what if one of those potentially billions of mosquitoes you just killed was one that carried a disease like malaria and had killed some settler in the Virginia Colonies?" She held up a hand to stop Finn's point before he made it, and Ponytail shrank back in her chair, stuck between them. "It sounds like that's a good thing because now this settler is alive, but if that settler doesn't die, they go on to have kids, and those kids have kids, and all of a sudden killing one little mosquito might change who the president of the United States is hundreds of years later." She shrugged. "Or maybe there *isn't* a United States. All I'm saying is that little changes or decisions in the past could have huge consequences for the future."

Finn pictured that Bird's Eye View flier in his fourteen-year-old hands.

Little decisions, big consequences.

"That actually makes a lot of sense." 'Ms. Konrad' nodded, her ponytail bobbing its assent.

"The bad reputation of mosquitoes is undeserved." Edison twisted his fingers together on the surface of his desk. "Most of them are actually vegetarian and help pollinate flowers." He was rocking in his seat again, but with less intensity than before.

"But those are just the bad things." Finn ignored Edison's defense of mosquitoes. "Can you imagine the good that time travel could do?"

For the first time, he allowed himself to consider what it might mean if Professor Moskowitz wasn't crazy—if somehow time travel were possible. His heart quickened at the notion. "Think of the things we could change for the better. Think about the things we could...undo." His eyes met Everly's. He held her gaze for a moment until the professor's voice drew his focus away.

"I had a good feeling about this team," beamed the old man, who had been trying to hide his excitement as he watched the back and forth. "But there are some clarifications that need to be made."

All four students straightened.

"First off, the present is not affected by the past, as strange as that sounds. We can learn from the past, and what we learn can help to dictate what choices we make in the present, but changing things in the past does *not* affect the present." He raised his eyes to the ceiling and used his hands as he spoke. "Think of time like a book with an unlimited number of pages. As time unfolds, our stories are printed into this book, which constantly turns the pages. If you go back to a past page, scratch parts out and write in changes to this book, would that magically change what happens on the next page?"

Everly looked to Ponytail, who shrugged. The professor continued. "Say I just read 'Goldilocks and the Three Bears' and I want to change it. I turn back to the page where Goldilocks breaks into the house of those poor, unsuspecting bears, and I scratch that part out and rewrite that she minds her own business in that forest and walks on her way. When I turn the page, Goldilocks is still in the house eating porridge, and nothing I wrote on the prior page matters. It's the same with time—any changes you make to the past during time travel are not permanent, and thus they do not affect the present."

"Okay." Everly leaned forward on her elbows and spoke through her hands. "So, real changes can't be made to the past. But what about the competition? What does *that* entail?"

"The Time Trials are a series of challenges put on by the Historians Society," answered Professor Moskowitz. He bit the inside of his cheek and looked off to the side. "The challenges vary. Scavenger hunts are a possibility. At times they will ask you to change a major historical event. There are other times when the Historians' Society will enter a time period prior to an event and fundamentally alter it in some way to make it more of a challenge. There will be four challenges throughout the year, and the school which acquires the most points in that time will win this most secret and prestigious competition." He smiled as he said those last words, eyes raising to the ceiling as if at a pleasant recollection.

Edison, who had been quietly listening, suddenly stood straight up, arms pressed flat to his sides. "Professor, if we die in the past, what happens?"

Professor Moskowitz released a deep exhale and looked at the ground. "If you turn back to change the beginning of the book and accidentally snap your pencil, is it still broken when you flip the book back to where you were?" He dragged his eyes up from his feet, the mirth in his voice gone. "As much as it pains me to say, Edison, if you die in the past, you die in the present."

Edison sat. "That is unfortunate."

The room was silent, the professor's words hanging in the air like the echo of a gunshot.

"It is true—the Time Trials are not without risk." When the old man spoke again, his voice was hushed. "I do not offer this to you lightly. But there are advantages that come with this inherent risk." As his eyes swept the team, they lingered on Everly. "I've seen the Trials change people for the better. They will expose you to profound moments and incredible experiences, some of which will be beautiful and some of which will be terrifying. But all of them will offer you the chance to become a better version of yourself."

The old man's voice contained a note of entreaty now, as if he were a lawyer wrapping up an important case to a grand jury. "These trials will unmask strength you didn't dream to possess." His voice faltered slightly. "I can only offer the choice—one that is yours alone to make." He cleared his throat. "The first of four competitions begins in one month, and if Wharton Academy intends to accept the invitation to compete, we must let the Historians' Society know soon. It will also give us time to prepare for whatever the first challenge might be."

He drew a manila envelope out of his desk drawer and handed it to Everly, who accepted it gingerly as if it were a bomb with a lit fuse. "I will leave the contracts with you. Should you decide to sign them, our next meeting is in this room on Wednesday." He took the time to look at each student individually in the eyes. "Perhaps I will see you then."

The old man issued a light pat to Everly's cheek with a weathered hand before leaving the teammates with their own scrambled thoughts and four unsigned contracts.

CHAPTER 6
EVERLY

Everly watched the new "Unfortunate" leave her grandfather's classroom, tie slightly askew, shirttail untucked, messenger bag slung over his arm.

After what she'd just heard her grandfather say during the first meeting of the Young Historians Club—that they would be engaging in competitive *time* travel—Everly knew she should be thrown. She should be reeling from those revelations, mulling it all over. Doubting their validity and even her own grandfather's sanity. But instead, all she could think of was Finn Mallory and what might be written on the outsole of his beat-up sneakers.

He broke off toward Aion Hall, hands in his pockets, Edison loping beside him. Everly knew who Finn was—*what* he was: dead parents, foster care. She had heard the whole sad story before he'd even arrived at Wharton. She also knew what this place did to those deemed "Unfortunates"—it ridiculed them, ostracized them, never let them forget their place. Everly had known Finn's reception here wouldn't necessarily be a warm one, and for that she was sorry.

Just the same, Everly wasn't used to being brushed off, which was exactly what Finn had done. The experience had been one that was completely foreign to her, and she didn't like it one bit. When she'd sat across from Finn in the banquet hall, she had thought he would be grateful—grateful for one kindred spirit in this new place. But he hadn't been—instead, he'd just been brusque. Rude. Judgmental.

Now, as Everly walked through Wharton Gardens toward Raine Manor, her footsteps almost angry as she stalked through the grass, she remembered his rough fingertips on hers as she'd shaken his hand. She remembered his eyes, accusing and wary. The edge of his voice.

"I'm not a project."

When she'd seen him show up to her grandfather's classroom for a meeting of the Young Historians, she'd considered just getting up and leaving. She was already Social Chair and the head of Young Philanthropists—she could stand to drop a club, even if her grandfather balked a bit. But she'd stopped herself; why should Everly Caldwell, who'd performed in front of hundreds of people for countless piano recitals and spelling bees, and recited from the Torah more fluidly than anyone else at her Bat Mitzvah (her grandfather had wiped away actual tears), be afraid to sit in the same room as some new kid with a sloppy tie and messy hair?

She breezed into Raine Manor, past the grand piano, and up the spiral staircase, pausing on the landing to look out the picture windows. Across the sprawling green, past the Wharton Gardens, she could see the squat outline of Aion Hall.

She charged to her room, picturing Finn's worn sneakers. There had been words written on the white, rubber outsoles in pen. She'd noticed in history class but hadn't been close enough to see what they were. She might have asked him if he'd given her a chance.

She sat at the edge of her four-poster bed and pried off her Prada mary janes, feeling the heat of embarrassment wash over her; she was wearing close to a thousand dollars on her feet, and had thousands more worth stowed away in her walk-in closet, all carefully tucked into the boxes they came in. Finn thought she was just another self-absorbed, rich airhead. She was just a stereotype to him—an idea.

Everly moved to the mirror and looked at herself. Her hair, flaxen and shiny, took little effort to maintain, framing a perfectly symmetrical, alabaster face with deep, green eyes. She looked cool and composed even now, when she didn't feel that way. When Everly walked into a room, people were drawn to her in the same way flowers turn to face the sun. It was as if they believed her beauty, grace, and reputation would somehow rub off on them if they got close enough.

Everly and Finn both had eyes on them. But it was different for Finn—she knew that. People recoiled from him the same way they leaned toward Everly, as if getting too close to the new "Unfortunate" would infect them somehow.

"Those your friends?"

Finn's eyes had looked equal parts accusing and wounded as he'd asked the question.

"Friends." Were they? Yes and no; at Wharton Academy, Everly was Helen of Troy, the reluctant queen in her hive of worker bees—Lacy Locatelli, long-legged captain of the dance team, Amanda Ayers, materialistic and loud-mouthed, and Janelle Burr, aptly named, who was, in fact, stuck to Everly like a burr on a hiker's sock: irritating and difficult to shake. Everly had grown used to it, just as she'd grown used to the feel of eyes on her everywhere she went. She didn't enjoy hanging around with a bunch of vapid, obsequious fawners, but she found herself resigned to it. The other girls looked at her with expectation. Everly's word was law...usually.

A thrill worked its way through her as she remembered how Finn had challenged her in the meeting today. She couldn't remember the last time anyone had dared do that. Even the staff of

Wharton bent to her will; perhaps they figured if they stayed in her good graces, she'd donate a new wing to the school or something someday.

Barefoot, she moved to her ensuite, stopped up the sink, and turned the knob. She watched as it began to fill, steam rising and clouding the mirror above, casting a blurry filter over her own face. She was the spitting image of her father.

The only daughter of Sam Caldwell and Selah Moskowitz, two of Wharton Academy's most renowned alumni, Everly had always been fated for this place. She was never alone, and yet she was *always* alone. Surrounded at any given time by a throng of admiring "friends," one assumed she led a charmed life.

Within Wharton's walls is where Everly's story began, as this was where her parents had met as students in the 1990s. The halls of Wharton Academy were lined with pictures of Everly's parents, showcasing their accomplishments. Pictures of dark-haired, fiery Selah Moskowitz leading the debate team. Pictures of Sam Caldwell leading the lacrosse team to victory. Pictures of the two of them, arm in arm, at Wharton Academy's Achievement Ball. In each picture, Selah stared directly into the camera, confident and self-assured, her dark, kinky locks spilling over her shoulders.

Everly was born shortly after Wharton's power couple was married. The Caldwells enjoyed successful careers. Selah became a public defender. It satisfied a deep need she had to make a difference in the world. Her father, Mordecai Moskowitz, had raised her to be a changemaker, to be extraordinary. This was, in fact, where Everly derived her penchant for activism. Sam Caldwell inherited the position of CEO of Caldwell Acquisitions. Their home life was lively and comfortable. But when the words *"brain tumor, malignant, inoperable"* were uttered, their lives were changed forever. Selah, a complete force of a woman, reduced to a frail invalid in a hospital gown. Her wild, untamed hair, once her defining physical feature, was replaced in those last days with a colorful cotton scarf, and this is the way Everly remembered her mother.

The cancer took Selah quickly, shattering Sam. On a grey October day, Sam brought Everly to the Moskowitz home with a single suitcase. He needed to "take care of something important," he'd said. Whatever it was must have been truly pressing because he never returned. After a year with no signs of Everly's father and no prospects on where he might be, Sam Caldwell was assumed dead.

Everly grew up quickly, a physical copy of her father with the spirit of her mother. Loss at a young age has a way of squeezing every bit of "child" out of a person, and Everly knew that firsthand.

She knew her family history afforded her a certain reputation that made her life very comfortable here, and she was not ungrateful for that. But in spite of her station as school royalty, Everly felt like an island. She had been quietly looking forward to the arrival of the new Unfortunate. Despite appearances, their lives were not entirely different. Everly had felt something well up inside her when she'd seen him in her grandfather's history class— something confusing and indefinable. It wasn't pity but rather a sort of protective instinct.

Everly turned off the water and plucked a white washcloth from the bathroom shelf. She lowered it into the sink, allowing it to saturate and drop to the bottom before she plunged her hand beneath the water's surface and pulled it out, dripping.

She wrung it out and pressed it to her face. Her cheeks. Her lips. Her eyes. Her *father's* eyes.

Finn's eyes had borne something that Everly recognized, and it had drawn her in and made her want to look away all at once. It was the same look she'd seen in her own, reflected back at her in her bedroom mirror at the age of seven: tormented, lost, in search of a safe harbor.

Now, Everly narrowed her own eyes at herself in the mirror, ten years later. That look was still there.

Why do you want to know him so badly?
Who cares what's written on his outsoles??

She turned away from her own reflection, damp and bare of makeup. Who was she kidding? She knew why: the things people admired about Everly—the things that drew them to her—those were the things that made Finn judge her. *Recoil* from her. And that intrigued her.

Truth be told, Everly's motivation in speaking to Finn Mallory wasn't solely to make his time at Wharton easier; it was to make hers easier, as well.

Everly stalked out of her en suite and stared down at her expensive mary janes, side by side like identical twins at the foot of her bed. She hooked her finger through their straps, stood in the doorway of her walk-in closet, and tossed them janes unceremoniously to the floor, not even bothering to put them back in the box they came in.

CHAPTER 7
WONDERWALL

It was past midnight. Edison's chest rose and fell in sleep, his breathing deep and rhythmic, with a snort on the inhale and a whistle on the exhale. He'd been out cold since 8:30 under a weighted blanket, an open bag of banana chips next to him on the bed, and the window, open a precise two and a half inches, permitted a stream of freezing air into the room. Finn couldn't sleep. He'd have to request a couple of extra blankets from housekeeping if he was going to live with Edison.

He crept down the brick steps of Aion Hall, hands stuffed into his sweatshirt pocket, where his Walkman was carefully stowed out of view. Truthfully, cold wasn't the only thing keeping Finn awake tonight.

One thing was on his mind: the contract. To sign, or not to sign? Did Finn even believe Professor Moskowitz? A time machine? The Time Trials? How *could* he believe him? It seemed like the plot of a science fiction movie. Maybe the old man was simply out of his gourd. And even if it was all true, was it worth the risks? Edison's robotic voice sounded in Finn's mind: "Professor, if we die in the past, what happens?" followed by the professor's solemn reply, "If you die in the past, you die in the present."

And why him? Why was he, Finn Mallory, one of four people tasked with this? Throughout history, soldiers who were put on the frontlines had often been poor orphans—"Unfortunates." Maybe people figured they'd never be missed if they didn't come home. Is that why he was picked? Because no one would miss him if he disappeared?

He shook his head at himself, throwing a look across the green at Raine Manor and Kingsley Tower.

You're overthinking it.

"Ponytail" Konrad wasn't poor, and Everly Caldwell certainly wasn't either. Even eccentric, cerebral Edison was from an affluent family. If they'd been tagged for this club, there had to be some other criteria by which they'd been chosen.

Overthinking was what had gotten Finn into trouble in the banquet hall, too. It's what had made him snap at Everly, a girl who could have been an ally, even a friend. That was the second thing keeping Finn up tonight. He pictured Everly's green eyes and the way they'd gone from warm to arctic in only a couple of moments. It put a chill in him that had little to do with the cold outside. And to make matters worse, the unofficial queen of Wharton Academy, who now undoubtedly hated him, was clearly some sort of relative to his history professor. Their familiar and easy banter had made that pretty evident.

Finn threw a furtive glance around himself as he pulled on his sweatshirt hood and made his way through the Wharton gardens. He'd have to try to be as inconspicuous as possible, as he was out way past curfew. He waited until he knew he was alone to put on his headphones. All was quiet, all was still, but for a few yellowed leaves that skittered across the ground in the night breeze.

Finn ran his hands over the shell of his Walkman in his sweatshirt pocket, letting his fingers find the "play" button. He'd clear his head by filling it with music.

As the first riff of Oasis' "Wonderwall" began to play, he glanced around once more to make sure he was alone before he sat, back against the gazebo wall. It was a murky night. A convenient blanket of fog hung in the air, further obscuring him. He took the Walkman out of his pocket and watched the tape reels spin in the sparse light that emitted from a nearby streetlamp. A few moths danced in its glow.

It took a few moments for Finn to notice the slim figure that was suddenly in front of him, spectral in the mist and low light. She wore a black pea coat, her blonde hair long and loose.

Finn hadn't seen her coming in time to hide his contraband, but he lowered his hood, pulled the headphones off his ears, and dropped them around his neck, callused fingertips fumbling for the "stop" button.

"So, I guess I'm not the only one with insomnia." Everly's voice was soft as she stood over him, devoid of that edge with which she'd spoken to him earlier.

Finn's eyes dragged up from her feet, which were curiously covered in a pair of ordinary-looking flats, replacing the expensive pair of mary janes she'd donned earlier. "Hey," he managed.

Everly lowered herself to the ground next to him, closer than he'd expected her to. Her eyes darted from the headphones around his neck to the Walkman in his hand.

"Old-school. I like it." The corners of her lips turned up, and Finn felt relief course through him, like the warmth that spreads through you when you sip a hot drink on a cold day. Someone who hates you doesn't smile like that.

Everly drew her knees up to her chest and hugged them. "Also totally against school rules, but your secret's safe with me."

Finn studied her profile in the scant light. Now was his chance to clean up the mess he'd made earlier. He'd certainly practiced this speech enough times in his head already.

"Listen," he started. "About what I said yesterday in the banquet hall. I was an—"

"I know." Everly cut him off mid-sentence. "I get it: you spent the day being judged, so you turned around and did the same thing to me." She looked almost amused as she flicked at a button on her pea coat, her voice barely above a whisper. "It's okay." After a brief pause, she raised her eyes to his, voice growing a bit louder as she asked a weird question: "Can I see your shoe?"

Finn's laugh came out in a short burst. "My *shoe?*" He dropped his gaze to his Chucks. "Uh, yeah, I guess. Which one?"

"The one with writing on it." Everly kept hugging her knees, her unflinching green eyes on his face, expectant. "Come on; if you didn't want someone to ask you about it, you would've written on the insole."

"Oh." Finn had forgotten about the writing on his shoe. Music was in his very blood and marrow, and he thought in song lyrics most of the time. He scrawled them on just about everything he owned—notebooks, the insides of textbooks...shoes. Frankly, he didn't even remember what was written on his sneaker. Hopefully, it wasn't anything too stupid.

He drew his leg up toward himself to display the white rubber outsole, and Everly squinted down at it in the dark, her nose wrinkling a bit as she did. Finn's breath caught in his throat as he watched her face.

God, she's pretty.

"'Oysters, no pearls.'" Everly shrugged. "What does it mean?"

Finn felt heat rise to his face, and he looked away, extending his leg back to where it had been. "Nothing. Reminds me of a song. Counting Crows." He shook his head. "I was in a bad mood when I wrote it. Back at my..."

Foster home.

Back at my foster home.

"...Back when things weren't going great. It's stupid. No big deal." He searched for a way to change the subject. The silence in the garden had become deafening, and he could see the lingering questions hanging in the air between them. Questions he wasn't sure he was ready to answer.

As if reading his thoughts, Everly flicked her chin at the headphones around his neck and raised her eyebrows in silent entreaty, as if to ask, "Can I?"

Finn nodded. Restoring one headphone speaker to his own ear, he bent the other one back for Everly, who leaned in to listen, inadvertently leaning into Finn in doing so. He was acutely aware of her shoulder against his, and the smell her hair—clean, with a trace of tartness, like an apple mixed with Ivory soap. He could feel his heart accelerate in his chest as Liam Gallagher crooned about winding roads, blinding lights, and things too difficult to say.

They let the song finish, silent as the tape reels spun. Before the next track began, Finn fumbled for the "stop" button, suddenly uncomfortable with how close she was, with the confessional quality of the lyrics—with the staccato beat of his own heart.

"So." He cleared his throat and dropped the headphones back around the back of his neck. "You're related to Moskowitz?"

"He's my grandfather." Everly nodded beside him. "He's also my legal guardian." She watched his face intently, as if searching for a reaction. Finn was caught off guard—it didn't fit the image he'd had of her life. *Legal guardian.* The words implied a death, or abandonment, or some combination of the two that led to orphanship, a thing he knew a thing or two about. He wondered what had happened to her parents, but it didn't seem appropriate to ask.

"You don't look like him," Finn mused. His right arm was warm against hers, their shoulders still pressed together from sharing the same set of headphones.

Everly smiled down at her hands. Her nails were polished—clear with white tips. Classic, not flashy. "Everyone says I favor my dad in looks." A trace of bitterness crossed her face as she said it, so quickly one could miss it.

"Is your grandfather, like, okay? Mentally, I mean?" Finn felt remorseful as soon as he'd asked.

Stupid.

Rude, and stupid.

But Everly giggled, the wrinkle of her nose making her look for a moment like the sixteen-year-old girl she was rather than some inaccessible goddess. "Sometimes, I wonder." Then, more seriously, she added, "I know all this time machine stuff sounds pretty...bogus. But if I know my grandfather, there's something to this."

"You're going to sign the contract then?" Finn allowed himself to look Everly directly in the eyes, feeling again that freshly gut-punched sensation that he'd had the first time he'd seen her. Those things—her eyes—were a weapon; they seemed to see through you. *Into* you. He hoped he didn't look as affected as he felt.

"I *think* so?" Everly's shoulders jumped. "I mean, I don't know." She shook her head as she looked out into the darkness of the gardens, the topiaries dark shadows through the mist. "It seems like it's worth a conversation. You know, with the four of us."

"Maybe we can meet in the library. Tomorrow, after history. If you tell Ponytail, I'll tell Edison."

Everly laughed. "Ponytail?"

Finn shrugged. "Didn't catch her name."

"It's Valerie." Everly smiled and rose to her feet. "Yeah. I'll tell her."

As the glow of the streetlamp lit her from behind, it seemed to radiate from her, and the fair hair that wreathed her face shone like a halo. Finn's breath caught in his throat. She was the sun in the middle of the night.

She glanced into the distance, toward Raine Manor. "I guess I should, you know..."

Finn nodded. Cleared his throat. "Yeah, I mean, it's late." There was an awkward pause before he issued a small, two-fingered wave.

"Hey, Finn?" Everly stopped halfway across the lawn, a shadow half obscured by mist. Finn peered into the darkness as he drew his hood back up. "Yeah?"

"I hope you find a pearl." She smiled that inward smile of hers before she turned, her shoes making squelching sounds in the grass as she left. Finn exhaled, realizing only now that he'd been holding his breath a little bit throughout the entire exchange.

As Wharton Academy's charity case walked back to his dorm that night, he felt a bit less unfortunate.

Chapter 8
Stegosaurus

Finn and Edison were early. After Edison had pointed out Valerie's lateness with shocking scrupulosity at the last meeting, there was a certain pressure to be punctual. Evidently, Finn was not the only one who felt this need, as they arrived to find Valerie and Everly already seated at one of the long tables in the far corner of the library. Edison and Finn slid into the bench across from them and an awkward silence ensued as they all pulled out their contracts. Everly threw a small smile at Finn over the edge of hers, and he returned it nervously.

"Okay." Valerie clapped her hands together, taking the lead with no sign of reluctance. "Did we all get a chance to read these...contracts?"

When everyone nodded, Valerie continued, tucking a damp strand of hair behind her ear. "It seems pretty legally binding." She lowered her voice, staring at them from under lowered brows. "It's crazy that we're even talking about this, right?" She glanced at each of their faces in turn. "Do we even believe that this is...possible?"

The group sat in silence for a moment before Everly spoke. "My mother was a lawyer, and I've seen plenty of legal contracts. This one seems pretty serious. As far as whether I 'believe' in this or not, I don't know. But I do believe in my grandfather. He's not the pranking type."

"Well, if I'm being completely honest, part of me hopes this *is* a joke, because it sounds insane," returned Valerie. "For the sake of argument, let's just assume your grandfather is being completely real with us...that we *can* travel through time to compete in some crazy competition. Shouldn't they be using this technology to kill Hitler or something?"

"What would that accomplish?" asked Everly. "Remember, my grandfather said what we do in the past doesn't affect the present."

"Except we can die," stated Edison.

The group lapsed back into silence.

"We can die," repeated Edison loudly, misreading the quiet as not having been heard.

"We know," reassured Finn, looking at his roommate out of the corners of his eyes. "If we die in the past, we die in the present." He ran his finger along his contract. "Did you guys read that part? If one of us dies in the past we just get left there and everybody is legally bound to keep quiet about it. We become kids on a milk carton."

"I saw it," confirmed Valerie. "We have to sign a waiver in polo, too—it releases the school from liability if we break our ankles and stuff like that. But there's also a 'death clause' in there if you read the fine print."

"Think about it." Finn's voice grew quiet. "If my face goes on a milk carton, nobody's going to come looking. But you guys...you have people who will." He averted his eyes to the shelves of books that rose up around them.

"That isn't fair," whispered Everly.

"No," Finn heard a bit of bite creep into his voice, "I guess it's not, but it's true. You guys don't want your parents to spend their entire lives wondering what happened to you. It's probably worse not knowing."

Now it was Everly who looked away. Finn registered that something he'd said had struck a nerve, but he didn't know what, and the others didn't seem to notice. He grasped for a way to change the subject, but Edison did it first.

"I want to see a stegosaurus." His fingertips wove together on the tabletop in that frenetic way they often did. "The stegosaurus is a dinosaur."

Valerie laughed. "I think we know what a stegosaurus is."

"I have seen them in books," continued Edison, "but artists are only guessing what they looked like because we only have fossils to go by, and they lived 163 million years ago. I'd like to see a real one."

"It's a good choice of dinosaur, Edison." Everly seemed to have recovered and looked thankful for Edison's flat, yet impassioned observation.

"Thank you." Edison offered a hint of a smile. "I do not want to die. But I do want to see a stegosaurus."

"Edison makes a good point." Valerie laid her contract flat on the table and smoothed her palms over it. "When I was ten, my family went to Africa and saw lions on a safari. We could have died *then*. Hell, you could die walking to the grocery store."

"Or from playing polo," offered Finn sarcastically. He stretched his legs out under the table but pulled them back and reddened when he brushed toes with Everly.

"Well, maybe someone on the other team," Valerie said with bravado, ponytail swinging. "You've never seen me play. The point that Edison's making is that we risk our lives every day. If we're going to believe that this whole thing is possible, isn't it worth the risk?"

"It depends on where we're going," decided Edison.

"Honestly, does it matter where we go?" Everly toyed with the chain on the green banker's lamp beside her. "People pay to ride roller coasters every day. How many people get to take a ride through time?"

"Think of the places that these challenges might allow us to travel to." Valerie nodded vigorously, feeding off the excitement that was brewing at the table. "We could see the Colosseum in ancient Rome...or we could see the pyramids of Giza being built...we could see what the Wild West was like—"

"Look, I don't want to be a downer here," interjected Finn, "but the great events in history books are more romantic than in reality. They fed Christians to lions in the Colosseum. And the Great Pyramids? Those were built by enslaving an entire race of people. The West was won by massacring a nation of Native Americans. History is bloody, and we'll get front row seats." There was a silence as the four of them mulled over what Finn had just said.

"Finn has a point." As Finn secretly reeled the way he did every time he heard his name come out of her mouth, Everly flipped through her contract, which was heavily highlighted and covered in notes and annotations. "These events could be really dangerous, and if you look at the third clause of the fourth page of this contract, it pretty much says that if we agree to this tournament, we're legally required to finish it."

The four of them flipped over to the clause and went quiet as they read it to themselves.

Once contestants have agreed to the terms of the Time Trials, they are required to complete all four subsequent challenges presented by the Time Trials Committee of the Historians' Society. Contestants who do not wish to finish the challenge or the Time Trials are in strict violation of said agreement and will be met with consequences.

"'Consequences.'" Everly drummed her manicured fingertips over the tabletop. "That could mean anything."

"Pretty vague," agreed Finn. "What do you think it means?"

"This society has the ability to travel through time," Everly said. "Imagine what else people like that could do."

"It's a huge leap of faith," admitted Valerie, echoing what Professor Moskowitz had said the previous day. She looked to Everly. "But do you think your grandfather would sign us up for something that was...over our heads? Do you think he would sign you up for something dangerous?"

"I don't think so." Everly bit her lower lip. "I trust him. But he's my family; it would make sense for you guys to feel differently."

"Guys and *girl*," corrected Edison. "Valerie is not a guy."

"I'm glad somebody noticed," Valerie said, clapping a hand on his shoulder. Edison stared at her hand until she retracted it and turned back to Everly. "Look, I know he's your family, but I think we all trust the professor." She glanced at each of their faces as if to gauge whether they concurred. "I get that there's risk—but I think the risk might be worth it. I'll sign, but only if you guys -" she smiled at Edison, "—and *girl*, sign it too."

Edison issued a curt nod. "I will sign the contract as well."

Everly and Finn looked at each other searchingly before Everly took a deep breath. "I trust my grandfather. With my life." Then she added, "This might sound crazy, but I feel like I trust you, too."

Finn held Everly's stare for a lingering moment before running his hands through his shaggy hair. "Fine. I'll sign."

A nervous apprehension gnawed away at his stomach, and his mind teemed with reasons why he shouldn't sign this contract, but a stupid smile still forced its way onto his face.

CHAPTER 9
TIME WILL TELL

Mordecai Moskowitz paused in the corridor on the way to his classroom, where he would wait with eager anticipation to see if any of his four prospective Young Historians arrived with signed contracts.

The decision he had thrust upon these kids—upon his own granddaughter—was a big one, and it weighed upon him heavily. It had been twenty years, but Moskowitz remembered how utterly ruthless and dangerous the Time Trials could be. The Historians' Society took precautions, of course—they were not in the business of losing children—but it happened.

And yet for all its peril, Professor Moskowitz knew how *amazing* the tournament could be. Seeing old worlds in new ways was, of course, incredible in itself, but the Time Trials also had a way of eliciting the best from its competitors. Participants grew into better versions of themselves. How could he not offer them this chance?

In truth, the old professor had spent the last few nights arguing with himself about whether or not he wanted the four of them to walk through that door. He had tried to imagine how he might feel in either scenario and found himself both disappointed and relieved with either option. When he imagined the four of them handing him back unsigned contracts, he felt a weight lift. They could assume it was a joke or even that the old man had lost touch with reality. There was a comfort in the idea of it all just going away.

Yet, as he relished in how easy that would be, a nagging disappointment crept into the back of his mind and scratched away like some incessant insect. This competition was a rare opportunity that hadn't presented itself in two decades and might never present itself again. His granddaughter deserved the choice. They all did.

He frowned; or, was he presenting them this choice for himself? Was he putting children at risk so that *he* might be a part of something extraordinary?

Whatever the result might be, Professor Moskowitz was sure of one outcome: that he would be confused tonight when he sorted it all out before falling asleep.

Slowly, Professor Moskowitz approached one of the glass display cases that lined the corridor and indulged himself with a rare peek inside. Although he passed these display cases several times a day, he didn't often stop to look; it was usually too painful, even after all this time.

A father isn't supposed to outlive his daughter—it's against the natural order of things.

Selah.

She smiled back at him from the picture, mid-laugh, her dark curls a voluminous mane around her shoulders. His only child. Mordecai's fingers raised and touch the glass, remembering how if you gently pulled one of those spiral curls, it would bounce back into place like a spring.

Selah was sixteen here, the same age Everly was now, although mother and daughter didn't look much alike. It was only in Everly's expressions that Mordecai could find Selah—the fierce, sarcastic eyebrow that shot up when he said something stodgy or out-of-touch, the wrinkle of the nose when she laughed.

No, that wasn't true—Selah was also very much alive in Everly's bold, determined spirit, although Everly wore her boldness in a quieter, more refined way than her mother had. There had been nothing quiet about Selah. Mordecai and his wife had always joked about the irony of the name they'd chosen for her; Selah was a Hebrew word, a nod to their Ashkenazi Jewish heritage—a musical term, actually, that meant "to pause or take a breath." Their daughter never seemed to do either of those things— she said what she thought without filter or apology.

Yes, Everly was much more reserved than her mother. She carried herself with an almost practiced detachment that bordered on aloofness, a quality which Mordecai knew only loss at a young age could bring. Even at ten, she'd been an old soul, never spoiled, regardless of the heaps of her father's money that she'd had at her disposal. Her one indulgence seemed to be designer shoes and accessories, a thing that amused the old man, but beyond that, she never seemed taken by most of the frivolities of youth. Sometimes her seriousness worried Mordecai. Sometimes he wished his stunning granddaughter would skip her weekend philanthropy and go to the theatre with friends or ask to miss Temple to go out on a date with one of the many young men who tripped over themselves at the sight of her. But that wasn't Everly's way.

Since his wife had died, it had just been the two of them: the old man with the tweed overcoat and his breathtakingly beautiful granddaughter, sitting side-by-side at Temple or reading the newspaper quietly opposite each other in a coffee shop. While Mordecai often claimed it was teaching that kept him young and staved off his sorrows, he knew deep down that the unexpected bequeathment of his seven-year-old granddaughter at his doorstep by his grief-stricken son-in-law had even more to do with it. He shuddered to think what would have become of him by now if not for the little green-eyed girl left in his charge.

Mordecai's eyes shifted from his daughter's sixteen-year-old face to the boy's next to her in the picture. Blonde. Green-eyed. Oozing charisma.

Sam Caldwell.

A blend of emotions sluiced through the professor at the sight of his son-in-law—fondness and disappointment whipped up into one strange brew. Fathers often have complicated relationships with their daughter's husbands, and this was no different. And yet it was; Sam had worshipped the very ground Selah walked on, even beyond the day she no longer walked at all. He would've followed her anywhere, which was typically a good thing—what man in their right mind wouldn't want a son-in-law with such unflinching devotion to his only daughter?

Mordecai shook his head as if to dispel the mystery that was Sam Caldwell. This road was a dead-end. Yes, it was complicated—a matter that could tie one's mind into knots. The issue of his son-in-law was one that Mordecai refused to allow his aged mind to settle upon for too long. This made it easier to avoid the inevitable questions that his beloved granddaughter continued to hurl at him about her father, even after nearly ten years. Some questions were better left unanswered.

For this same reason, Professor Moskowitz had never divulged to his granddaughter that her parents had been part of Wharton Academy's first and only Time Team, twenty years ago—and he didn't plan to. There were no pictures of the original team here in the display cases, of course; the Time Trials had been as secret back then as they were today, for obvious reasons.

Mordecai's own reflection came into focus in the glass of the display case, superseding the pictures behind it.

Twenty years.

Mordecai had been in his fifties back then. Silver had begun to overtake the black in his hair, and he had grown bored with the minutiae of daily life—truly, he had been on the edge of burnout when the first Time Trials had come along, bringing with them untold danger, excitement, and the promise of being part of something extraordinary. And the Trials had delivered on those promises. So, when Mordecai hadn't been invited back, even after his team had won, he'd quietly stewed about it, ruminated on it, and waited with eager anticipation to be invited again.

In retrospect, perhaps it was for the best; Mordecai was tasked with choosing the recruits for the team, and when he scoured his mind for students he'd had over the past two decades who would have made worthy members of a time team, he came up empty. This year, the very year his own granddaughter was a junior and eligible to compete, he had them: four individuals with the qualities that might blend together as seamlessly as the original team's had.

He shuffled down the corridor and unlocked the door to his classroom—the only classroom he'd ever taught in for the whole of his tenure. With considerable effort, his slight body dragged four desks to the front of the room and arranged them in a crescent before he sat behind his own desk, hands folded in front of him.

As he looked at each of the chairs, he imagined the student that may or may not arrive to sit in it today with a signed contract in hand. Each of them had admirable qualities to bring to the table, but each of them lacked certain attributes, as well—qualities that he hoped the Trials would develop or draw out of them.

Everly had been the most obvious choice as a member of Wharton's second time team. Besides being his own blood and the daughter of two of Wharton's original time travelers, she was intelligent, cool-headed, and approached every task with all the dogged persistence of a blood-hound and the energy of a worker bee, be it practicing for a piano recital, planning a benefit gala, or acing a test. But Everly's spark was fading, this year especially. It had pained Moskowitz to watch it happen, but he'd known it would; no granddaughter of his would ever be content as Social

Chair, planning party decorations and testing out punch recipes. She was meant for bigger, grander things, and she deserved this opportunity. Her parents would have agreed; Mordecai liked to think so, at least.

Next was Edison Pellegrin. The old professor had watched the boy flounder for the past three years, either targeted as the butt of cruel jokes or ignored altogether. He'd helped him gather his spilled books from the corridor floor more than once and even fished his glasses out of a toilet after those petulant, empty-headed lacrosse players had grown bored and used him for entertainment. The boy had a remarkable mind, but few bothered to look beyond his unusual mannerisms and bizarre social behaviors to appreciate it. His unmatched skills would be seldom recognized if not for a chance like the Time Trials.

Then there was Valerie Konrad. She was a take-charge powerhouse, born to lead and hungry for competition. But he'd seen her in class when she'd received an A- rather than an A; she'd all but crumbled in front of him. The professor knew that when Valerie had been late to their meeting, it had been on purpose: it was a power move. By being fashionably late, she forced people to wait for her before they could start. Valerie tried to involve herself in as many clubs as possible. It looked good on transcripts and it allowed her to be the president many times over. She had already established herself as the undisputed captain of the Women's Polo Team and planned to do the same for the tennis team when the season started. Much like his own granddaughter, this was a girl who would benefit from letting her hair down. She needed to learn to fail, to relinquish control, to improvise...

...which brought him to the wildcard of the lot, Finn Mallory. Professor Moskowitz had chosen Finn without having ever laid eyes on him. He'd read his file, learned his story, and promptly concluded that a student with this background would likely possess a finely-tuned ability to think on his feet and make do with little. He also assumed a high propensity for empathy in the new

"Unfortunate," which could be either a hindrance or a help in a game like this.

Yes, Professor Moskowitz was sure that the unique notes and flavors that these four brought to the table would blend together to create something truly great, like a fine wine.

But would they sign the contracts?

Would they take the risk?

He drew in a deep breath and glanced at the clock, then at the door, drumming his restless fingers on the top of his desk.

Only time would tell.

CHAPTER 10
DODGEBALL

Walking behind Everly, Finn watched her graceful stride, her long curtain of hair swaying behind her like a hypnotic pendulum. Her hair wasn't the only thing that swayed hypnotically, but he tried to keep his eyes above her waist out of respect. She clutched a manila envelope under her arm, which contained four signed contracts.

When Everly pushed open the door to her grandfather's classroom, the team found Professor Moskowitz already seated at his desk, hands clasped before him. His head snapped up as they entered.

"So." He seemed to be trying to force an air of casualness into his voice. "Do we have a verdict?"

Everly produced the manila envelope, and the four of them took their seats. The professor rose to his feet, staring down at the folder in his hands. Patting it lightly on his leg, he didn't look up for a lingering moment.

"We'd like to hear the details that signing these contracts entitles us to," said Valerie in a no-nonsense tone.

"Of course, you do." The old professor's voice was soft as he continued to stare at the envelope in his hands. He shook his head slightly and raised it with a smile. "And you will. You've earned that."

"You said that we have a month to get ready," Valerie continued. "That isn't much time. I think we'd like to get started immediately."

Professor Moskowitz drew in a deep breath. "Yes. There is much to learn and little time to learn it. We will be at a disadvantage because two of the other three teams have competed in the Trials before and know what to expect."

"Well, I don't like to lose." Valerie looked to her teammates before her gaze swung back to Professor Moskowitz. "What do we know about our competition?"

"Vale Academy is the winning school from last year." The professor stood, plucked a piece of chalk off the ledge beneath his chalkboard, and scrawled "Vale" in all caps. "They are ambitious, resourceful, and cutthroat." He underlined Vale's name with a dramatic flourish.

"*They* sound like fun," Finn muttered under his breath, stuffing his hands into his pockets. Everly leaned forward in her chair and looked around Edison at him, scrunching up her face in a playful wince.

"As the winning team, they were brought back for the next year of competition, as is the custom," continued the professor, chalk still pinched between his thumb and forefinger. "A team that loses might also be invited back if they distinguish themselves in some way or impress enough Society members. The Halls of Ivy Prep is one such team; they were invited back after a very strong performance last year, even though they didn't win. While Vale Academy was able to eventually win the competition, their tactics were controversial."

Valerie and Everly exchanged a wary look as the professor barreled on, scrawling "Halls of Ivy Prep—strong second" across the chalkboard in his looping, slightly tremulous script.

"The last school in the Trials this year is Wilmington School. As it is their first year being accepted to this competition, I'm afraid not much is known about them. But don't make the mistake of underestimating them." The professor paused to scribble "Wilmington—?" across the board before dropping his piece of chalk on the ledge beneath and dusting his hands.

"It sounds like Vale Academy might need to be watched carefully." Everly, who had been furiously scribbling in a small notebook, raised her head and bit the end of her pen. "Are we allowed to make alliances? I wonder if the Halls of Ivy Prep would work with us, seeing as how they were the victims of 'questionable tactics' in the Trials last year."

The old professor cocked his head to one side, a proud smile on his lips. "It has never been done before, but there are no rules against it. It would require trust, a thing that is very difficult to come by in a game like this, even amongst teammates. In any case, the opportunity might never present itself. It's rare that all four teams would compete at once, but it is possible. You will get to meet the other teams during the Summit of Selection."

"The Summit of Selection?" Valerie cocked an eyebrow.

"It's a rather formal ceremony followed by an even more formal dinner—the Feast of Yesterday; quite a festive occasion, if memory serves." Professor Moskowitz eased himself back into his chair. "You will get a chance to meet your fellow competitors and listen to a rather wordy speech delivered by Grand Timekeeper Garridan, who takes his job as the head of these games very seriously." His eyes raised to the ceiling before he returned them to the faces of his team. "At any rate, it is during this time that the types of games will be selected at random."

"So, we get these games selected at random," Finn interjected, "but what types of 'games' are we talking about, professor? I doubt we'll go back to ancient Roman times and play dodgeball, right?"

"Actually," laughed Professor Moskowitz, "dodgeball *is* one of the options. The challenges of the Trials are named after traditional children's games. The challenges are obviously much more complicated than the games they are named for, but when you draw for the competition at the Summit of Selection, which will be held at the headquarters of the Historians' Society, the name of the game will likely be familiar to you."

"Can you give us an example?" Valerie looked dubious.

"If you draw 'Capture the Flag,' for example, each team will be sent back in time and assigned a coveted item to retrieve—perhaps the crown jewels or some treasured item belonging to a pharaoh." The professor waved his hand in the air. "Whatever the object is, it won't be easy to get."

Everly didn't look up as she scribbled some more in her notebook. "Does each team go after the same object?"

"There are some challenges where the Historians' Society will select different historical events for each team, but there are also some challenges which will include all teams in one time period at once. It really depends on what fate selects for us."

"So, there's Capture the Flag." Valerie folded her arms across her "Wharton Athletics" sweatshirt, a look of impatience flaring across her face. "What other games might we look forward to?"

The professor took a deep breath and expelled it slowly, tilting his head as if trying to recollect the full list of games. "There is King of the Mountain, which is much like Capture the Flag, except that all of the teams are sent to the same time period and compete for the same object in order to win. Then there is Simon Says, where the Grand Timekeeper will give you a moment in time which he wants you to change in some specified way, using whatever means you see fit. A more complicated version of this is Cat's Cradle, where it would be your job to convince or coerce someone in history to change a major decision in some way while you 'pull the strings' from behind the curtain."

He set his mouth and lowered his voice, his tone changing from energized to grave. "Then, of course, there is Hide and Seek, where you are sent to a very dangerous moment in history and must survive for as long as you can before you are extracted. This is the worst of them and has the highest fatality rate. There are many calling for it to be removed from the Trials entirely, but their voices have not yet proven louder than tradition."

There was a brief, heavy pause before the professor held up a hand, eyes closed. "Please, be assured that the likelihood of Hide and Seek being drawn is a small one, especially with it having been drawn last year. The Historians' Society prefers to avoid repeats of challenges whenever possible for novelty's sake." Seeming uncomfortable, he quickly surged forward. "There is Marco Polo, where you are sent to an undisclosed location and given a challenge on the spot. This is a very difficult one to prepare for, obviously, but remember that the opposing teams will be at the same disadvantage."

Everly's pen danced across the page of her notebook as she attempted to keep up with her grandfather, lower lip wedged between her teeth in concentration.

"One of my personal favorites is Red Rover, where each team selects one member from the other teams, and the four of them are sent into a challenge to compete against each other. There is Pop the Whip, Ring Around the Rosy, Musical Chairs, and Duck Duck Goose." The professor laughed, hand to chest, making a show of being out of breath. "Frankly, there are too many games for me to explain right now, and it does us no good to worry about them until they have been selected. Our first job will be to get used to the equipment we will be using."

"You mean the time machine, right?" Finn tried to keep the skepticism out of his voice. While he was inclined to trust Everly's judgement, and she trusted her grandfather, none of this could be real to him until he saw a time machine.

The professor smiled. "That's clearly a very important piece, but there are other tools that the time traveler must learn to employ. The Summit of Selection is in a month, so we can't do any research yet, but during a given challenge, we will all have roles to fill, and we can begin to prepare for those roles." He took a step forward and braced his hands on the edge of his desk. "There is an old barn past the lacrosse practice fields on the west end of the grounds. Let's meet there tomorrow at noon, and we can begin."

He stared at the team a moment longer, eyes replete with youthful excitement behind his spectacles before he abruptly left the room. There was a palpable silence in his wake, like a stillness after a storm.

"Does anyone else feel like this might actually all be true?" Valerie's voice was hushed as she glanced at the door.

"I was hoping for some proof tonight," admitted Everly, capping her pen and tossing it into her Prada handbag, "but my grandfather enjoys taking his time with important information." She rolled her eyes. "He always has."

"I have decided that I believe him," stated Edison plainly.

"What do *you* think?" Everly leaned forward again on her elbows and looked past Edison, studying Finn's face.

Finn looked at her out of the corners of his eyes. "I don't know," he said almost apologetically. He sighed. "I guess we'll find out tomorrow."

CHAPTER 11
SCRAP

Finn felt smaller than he ever had as he walked past the hulking, grunting, prototypical members of Wharton Lacrosse. A swell of anger crested in him as he recognized the teen model who had referred to him as "Tellerville Trash" on his first day. By now, like everyone else on campus, Finn knew his name: Nick Dain. Nick spun gracefully around a would-be defender, gave his wrist a powerful flick, and the solid rubber ball found the back of the net. As he smirked behind the faceguard of his helmet, the always-present Liam Fillery celebrated for him by lifting him into the air, the other teammates surrounding him, hooting, howling, and cussing.

Finn kept his eyes on the ground as he passed. Nick didn't celebrate—his team celebrated *for* him. He was effortlessly cool. Everly and Valerie walked ahead, whispering excitedly to each other, no doubt about what might be in the barn, but it seemed impossible that they hadn't noticed Nick's casual excellence.

The celebratory commotion cut abruptly as they passed, and Finn's eyes raised to see Nick and the lacrosse team staring at him with undisguised disdain. Liam whispered something to the team behind a cupped hand, elbowing one of his teammates as they burst out in boisterous laughter.

Though he couldn't hear the comment, he knew what it was about, why they were laughing. It must have been comical, he, this piece of "Tellerville Trash" and Edison, two misfits that simply didn't belong, trailing behind Everly Caldwell and Valerie Konrad. Finn's face flushed.

He threw a look at Edison, who stared ahead blankly through his thick, square glasses seemingly oblivious to the lacrosse team's laughter. Finn envied that.

They finally reached the old barn on the far west side of the school grounds. It was in decent shape and only slightly weathered but stood out starkly against the ornate backdrop of the prestigious Wharton Academy. The side barn door was slightly ajar.

Valerie leaned forward, a thread of excitement in her voice. "So, do you think there's really a time machine in here?"

Edison took off his glasses, squinting as he shined the lenses on his sleeve before restoring them to his face. "I do."

"I'm kind of hoping there isn't." Finn stuffed his hands into his pockets. "Can you imagine if this is all real?"

"Well," Everly raised an eyebrow, "there's only one way to find out, right?" She pushed the barn door open, and the four teammates tentatively proceeded inside.

It took a moment for their eyes to adjust to the dim light of the barn. The floating dust in the air became an iridescent silver as it wandered into the pathways of sunlight that filtered through the cracks in the walls.

Professor Moskowitz sat on an industrial stool, wearing a leather carpenter's apron over his customary tweed vest. His white sleeves were rolled up to his elbows, and his hands were folded in his lap as if he'd been watching the door in eager anticipation of their arrival. Behind him, a heavy canvas tarp obscured a large circular object. Whatever it was must have been at least ten feet tall and just as wide. A light mechanical hum buzzed beneath the heavy tarp, and dull, yellow light leaked through the fabric in certain areas. The team exchanged an apprehensive glance.

What lay underneath that tarp? And could it actually take someone through time?

"Welcome to our first real lesson," said the professor over the soft electric purring. "Before I unveil the Bender, I should preface it by assuring you that there will be no time travel today. This device is always on, so you will see that lights and parts of it will be functional, but the actual bending of time is controlled at the Historians' Society Headquarters for precautionary measures. Joyrides through time are strictly forbidden. We can, however, review the basic mechanics and familiarize ourselves with the functions of this machine."

"Can we see it already?" There was impatience and perhaps a bit of desperation in Valerie's voice.

The professor smiled. "If you will help me with the tarp..." He rose stiffly to his feet and handed Valerie one end of a frayed, old rope. Grinning, she began to pull it with both hands. It tightened, snaking up to the top of the barn and becoming lost in a series of wooden pulleys, which creaked in complaint. The tarp began to lift, exposing the metal legs of the machine, and Finn and Everly joined Valerie at the rope, the three of them tugging and heaving until the tarp dangled limply above.

The four teammates stepped back and took in the contraption before them. It wasn't sleek, polished, or modernistic. It didn't look advanced or precise; in fact, it appeared to be rusting in some areas, and parts of it looked haphazard, as if they had been slapped together. The circular machine rested on three firm and stubby mechanical legs.

The entrance was surrounded by a bright façade, which appeared to be a polished brass, a stark juxtaposition to the tarnished outer shell. This facade was made even brighter by a series of circular inlaid lights which dispensed a warm pop of luminescence, making it difficult to see inside. A smaller, circular platform opened from the front entrance like a brass drawbridge, and served as a ramp into the vehicle.

"This," said the professor proudly, "will be your primary tool: a Time Bender. It's an older model, but that simply means it is tested and reliable." He gave the side of the machine an affectionate pat and it emitted a hollow ring. Finn raised his eyebrows and scratched his head as he took it all in. Beside him, Everly released a soft exhale.

"Why is it called a Time Bender?" Valerie walked the perimeter of the machine, hands clasped behind her back, attempting to sound as casual as possible.

The professor crossed his arms, still smiling. "It bends time."

Valerie knuckled her hands at her hips. "I'm not sure I understand what that means."

"It's complicated." The professor's shoulders rose and fell in a shrug. "Perhaps my description of time as a book is not fully accurate. Time is more like..." he wiggled his fingers, as if grappling for the right words, "...a continuous sheet of paper, eternally expanding into space. The Time Bender allows us to very precisely fold that sheet of paper until our present time and space overlaps with that of which we wish to visit. At that point, the Time Bender becomes more like a drill of sorts, which uses a tremendous burst of energy to burn a hole through the space-time continuum—or that sheet of paper—plopping us out onto the other side."

"Can we go inside?" asked Edison in his even, robotic tone which made every request sound like a demand.

"I should hope so. You will be using it in less than a month!"

To the surprise of everyone, Edison sprinted to the machine and squeezed through the small, brass porthole. It was obvious that he had been exercising incredible patience during the entire conversation as he waited to go inside that machine.

"What are we waiting for?" Valerie followed suit, dashing to the machine and disappearing behind the glowing lights that surrounded the entrance.

Finn and Everly exchanged a nervous smile as they approached the Time Bender. They both took a step towards the small porthole at the same time and stopped, laughing.

"After you...sorry," mumbled Finn, having remembered to be chivalrous a moment too late. "Ladies first, right?"

"You don't have to be sorry." Everly pushed some blonde hair away from her green eyes. "It's the twenty-first century, you know." She smiled. "For now." Finn felt momentarily dizzy as she brushed against him and vanished into the porthole of the humming machine. He took a deep breath and followed her in.

The inside of the Bender was no more than ten square feet and lit by a series of round yellow lights. Brass piping ran haphazardly around the bends of the circular walls, and there was some exposed circuitry in spots where the oxidized and rusted piping were thin, as well as a tangle of various wires, coils, brass wheel handles, and mysterious valves. The entire machine interior smelled like a wooden chest full of old, forgotten pennies.

Most of the room in the tiny space was taken up by four chairs, which looked like they belonged in an old-time barbershop. They had dark leather harnesses built into them, encrusted with an assortment of brass buckles.

A colossal horde of bronze gears was attached to the domed ceiling. The gears ranged in size from a few as large as ceiling fans with monstrous mechanical teeth, to the smaller ones layered on top, which were the size of frisbees, small saucer cups, and Christmas wreaths. Interspersed among them, if one looked carefully, were the tiniest gears, some as small as quarters and dimes.

Somehow, this ruffled blanket of bronze connected like a complicated puzzle. And it moved; the interlocked gears were turning. The movement of the larger ones underneath was barely perceptible, but some of the smaller gears up front were turning quite quickly to keep up with their enormous siblings.

Edison, having already strapped himself into a seat in the back, stared up at the ceiling, mouth ajar. Valerie ran her index finger along some of the rusted piping, eyebrow raised. Everly turned around too quickly, colliding with Finn, who let out an involuntary gasp.

"Sorry." Everly threw him a sheepish smile and eased herself down into one of the front seats, her face taking on a slight blush.

"There isn't much space in a Time Bender, I'm afraid," called the professor's voice from outside the polished, brass porthole as Finn took a seat next to Everly. "This machine is mostly there to get you where you are going. Once it punches through time it is pretty much immobile until you are ready to come back." He had to shout over the clatter of the busy ceiling. "One of you will take the command post for each mission and run the team from the Time Bender."

Finn's eyes roved over the interior walls, overwhelmed by how busy this space was. The pipes wrapped and wound their way through and around each other. His eyes caught a shape tucked away into the piping. Curious, he reached out to touch it.

Suddenly, the shape began to move, little puffs of steam shooting out from its joints. With what appeared to be tiny mechanical arms, the thing began to emerge from a nest of cords and bronze piping. It made a series of rapid clicks and soft beeps as it popped out of its crevice in the wall, clattering to the floor.

Finn panicked, hopped over Everly, and dove out of the brass porthole, eyes wild. Everly and Valerie instinctively followed, both trying to squeeze out of the small hole at once. They hit the concrete floor of the barn and retreated by scooting themselves away frantically, all the while screaming.

"What?" Valerie demanded of Finn through heavy breaths. "What happened?"

Finn ran both hands through his hair. "Something... something *moved*!"

"Goodness gracious!" Professor Moskowitz pressed his hand to his chest. "The only thing alive in there is Edison—if he didn't just suffer a heart attack from all your screaming!"

It was then that the mechanical monster emerged from the Time Bender. In truth, the "monster" was about the size of a desk lamp and seemed to be almost shy as it peeked its brass head around the corner of the Time Bender entrance. Its head looked similar to an old, brass diving helmet, but behind the thick glass faceplate, a soft, yellow light flickered nervously.

The professor shook his head. "All of that just for SCRAP? I assure you, Mr. Mallory, SCRAP is more afraid of you than you are of—" He stopped. Smirked. "Well, I assure you, he is harmless."

The robot's body looked clunky and heavy, but its movements were smooth and effortless. It fidgeted with its robotic fingers as it advanced down the brass walkway, the yellow light that pulsed behind the faceplate of the polished diver's helmet intensifying as it stared up at the new faces of the time team.

"SCRAP stands for Strategic Chronological Robotic Automation Prototype," explained the professor, "but old SCRAP hasn't been a prototype for years; he's older than I am. He is programmed to make needed repairs to the Time Bender. He can also be loaded with research for competitions, and he can run numbers for you."

The little robot advanced a few steps and extended a hand to Everly, who bent over to shake it. She laughed, and the robot answered her with a series of clicks and beeps. "He also makes a good friend," added Professor Moskowitz.

"Will we be able to communicate with it?" Valerie tilted her head to the side, watching the mechanical creature.

"SCRAP is an older model." The professor watched the small robot with a fond smile. "We could have replaced it with one of the newer ones that has voice capabilities built-in..."

The robot turned its head and looked up at the professor with an ominous series of beeps as its faceplate grew dim.

"...but it didn't seem right. SCRAP has always served his time teams faithfully and I think that counts for something. Now, as to how we communicate with SCRAP, there is a special app built into this pocket watch, and I will give it to whoever wants the responsibility. It will allow you to read and translate SCRAP's thoughts."

"I would like it!" Edison's words exploded from the porthole of the Time Bender with a volume to his voice that Finn had never heard. He emerged, eagerly gathered the silver pocket watch and chain into his hands, and snapped it open to reveal two circular touchscreens, technology which stood out against the antiquated shape of the watch.

Edison knelt down in front of SCRAP and shook its robotic hand. "SCRAP, I am Edison. I hope very much that we can be friends."

As the little robot looked up at Edison, it sent out a series of friendly clicks and beeps, the light in its faceplate warming.

CHAPTER 12
WETSUITS & POCKET WATCHES

Retreating to the Time Bender, Edison began to speak softly with SCRAP, translating the robot's responses on his new pocket watch. The professor didn't attempt to hide his grin as he watched them. "I *thought* those two might get along."

"I'm still not convinced that any of this is real," Valerie said, hand on hip. "But if it is, I'm not sure how we would even complete a mission anyway."

"What do you mean?" The professor blinked rapidly behind his chrome spectacles, seeming to take slight umbrage at her bluntness.

"I mean, I took French through junior high, and I think I might know how to ask 'What time is it?' and 'Where is the bathroom?.' If we get sent to France during the middle ages, my French skills definitely aren't getting us into Charlemagne's high court. It probably won't even get us into the bathroom."

"And some ancient languages are incredibly complex," Everly chimed in, easing herself down onto a crate and crossing her legs.

"Ancient Egyptian would be impossible because it evolved over time, taking influences from Arabic and Hebrew, meaning that we would have to tailor any language lessons we take to the specific time period...if we could even learn it that quickly."

"Not to mention the accents." Finn leaned against the barn wall, eyes fixed on one of the pendants suspended from the ceiling. "A bad pronunciation or accent would probably give us away—not that we wouldn't stand out anyway in ancient Egypt." He grimaced down at his hands, the skin of which leaned toward the fair side.

The professor walked slowly to the far side of the barn and wheeled back a mobile coat rack with four black bodysuits on hangers, and a few briefcases stashed below. "I was hoping," he said, voice laced with excitement, "that you would ask that question. Ms. Konrad, I cannot demonstrate the Time Bender for you right now, but we can begin to practice with these." He opened one of the briefcases and withdrew a round, silver collar.

Valerie crossed her arms and lifted her eyebrows. "You want me to practice being a dog."

"Put it on, if you will." The professor pulled his pocket watch out of his carpenter's apron and began to fiddle with it.

With reluctance, Valerie accepted the silver collar, holding it in front of her with two fingers. She looked to her teammates, who shrugged, before rolling her eyes and placing the collar around her neck.

"*¿Qué quieres que haga?*" She spoke in an authentic Spanish accent. Her eyes went wide, and Finn and Everly exchanged a look of disbelief. It was Valerie's voice, but the words flowed out of her in a language not her own, and they didn't quite match her lips, as if she were in a dubbed foreign film.

"*¡Ay, Dios mío!*" she shrieked. "*¡Estoy hablando Español!*"

The professor issued a soft chuckle and touched his pocket watch again.

"*Kore wa dono yō ni kanōdesu ka?*" spat out Valerie in crisp Japanese. She clamped a hand over her mouth, as if doing so might prevent the foreign words from escaping. She pulled the collar from around her neck and looked down at it in amazement before raising her eyes to the professor.

"It's called an Articulator," the old man bragged, hands tucked into the front pocket of his leather apron. "It is programmed with every language that has ever been spoken. Typically, you will be wearing an earpiece that connects to it, which will translate both your speech and that of others into the language and time period of your choice. To you it will sound like everyone is speaking Generation Z English. It will also account for accents, vernacular, slang...it will even auto-correct for you."

"Autocorrect?" laughed Everly, nose wrinkling.

"Yes," nodded the professor. "The programming is quite intuitive. If you use modern slang, it will correct it to the term that is equivalent to time and place."

The professor opened a case and handed Everly an Articulator. "You probably noticed that it didn't change your lips, so you need to be careful about that. Keep your sentences brief and purposeful. Most people don't look at a person's mouth when they speak, but it has been noticed before." He opened another briefcase and withdrew a silver pocket watch with ornate moldings etched into the outer shell. It was attached to a long, silver chain with a metallic clasp at the end. It was nearly identical to the one that he had given to Edison.

"This," the professor held the pocket watch up for display, cupped in the palm of his hand, chain trailing down his forearm, "is a pocket watch." He looked at Valerie as if waiting for her to make a snarky comment, but she remained silent. "If you press the button, it will open for you." He did this, and the small contraption snapped open, revealing a ticking watch face with Roman numerals prominently displayed in pearl against a background of a series of oil-rubbed gears, all which jerked in unison like a mechanized heartbeat.

Valerie, Finn, and Everly drew closer to observe it, heads bent low. "However," the professor beamed up into their faces, "when you click the button twice..." he did so and the numbers vanished instantly, revealing a blank touchscreen, "...it essentially becomes the time traveler's iPhone. It will allow you to communicate to each other, access notes, and even acts as a GPS of sorts."

The professor stopped and looked at the teammates with a more serious expression. "There is one other function of the pocket watch which you need to be aware of. If you find yourself in inescapable danger and require extraction, pulling on this watch chain three times will trigger a distress call, and the Historians' Society will run a rescue mission as soon as they can. In the heat of the moment, it is easy to forget about this feature, so take great care in remembering it, as pulling on that chain might very well save your life."

Finn's gaze snagged on Everly's, whose eyes flared.

"Be advised that if you do pull it," Professor Moskowitz added, "you and your team will automatically forfeit the challenge."

After a beat, the professor's smile sprang back to his weathered face. "There is one additional tool to show you," he held up a hand, "if you are up for it, that is. I've given you a lot to think about today, and I do not wish to overwhelm you."

"I think we can take one more," Valerie stated for the group.

The professor gestured to the coat rack. "In that case, I will need you to change into these bodysuits."

Finn shoved his hands into his pockets and dropped his gaze to the barn floor. "Those look sort of...tight." He tried not to look at Everly, but he could feel her eyes on his face.

"Oh, come now." The professor was unable to hide his amusement. "You are teammates. Your lives will be in each other's hands. What do you expect to accomplish if you can't even do this?" He threw Finn an indulgent smile. "There are small supply closets in the back corners of the barn. Girls to the left, boys to the right." He cupped his hands around his mouth. "And Edison!"

Edison popped his head out of the Time Bender.

"You are not excused from this one."

Edison looked at the professor without expression from behind his thick glasses, whispered something to SCRAP and begrudgingly emerged from the Time Bender to join the group.

"I almost forgot," the old man handed off a sleek, black bodysuit to each member of the team, "No undergarments. Just you and the suit."

SCRAP made a series of clicks and beeps, his faceplate pulsing with light. Edison looked down at his pocket watch for a translation as he followed Finn to the back of the barn. "It *is* degrading."

In a few minutes' time, the new members of Wharton Academy's Time Team emerged from the supply closets. Their reveal was slow and self-conscious, as if they were children whose clothes had been stolen from the edge of the swimming hole who must now emerge from the water to seek help.

Finn sank to a crouch on the barn floor, knees drawn up to his chest, scowling and averting his eyes to avoid looking at the girls out of a sense of respect. Only Edison stood proudly, hands on his hips. His pose in this ridiculous bodysuit made him look like a cross between a superhero and a near-sighted ninja.

SCRAP made an indiscernible comment in his robotic language, and Edison glanced at his pocket watch. "Thank you." He issued a curt nod to the small robot.

"Please take out your pocket watches and press the button twice," Professor Moskowitz said to the heavens above.

The students followed his orders eagerly, their silver antiques quickly shifting to state-of-the-art gadgetry.

"Swipe downwards until you see the needle and thread icon," commanded the old professor, still admiring the craftsmanship of the ceiling.

The team swiped through a few icons before they came to the needle and thread. Both sides of the pocket watches contained a circular touch screen, and when an icon was swiped it would pass from the top screen to the lower screen and then disappear with the next downward swipe.

"Now select the icon and press the question mark."

The team followed this direction, and, as if by magic, they were all wearing clothing. They cried out in surprise, eyes wide. Upon hearing their shock, the professor lowered his gaze, a tickled smile touching his lips.

"The question mark icon is a random selector." He tucked his pocket watch back into his carpenter's apron and lowered himself onto his industrial stool. "These are called wetsuits. They produce holographic images of period-appropriate attire."

Finn permitted himself a glance at Everly again, who was now clothed in a dramatic blue dress from the Victorian era. It was form-fitting up top with long, embroidered sleeves, and it ballooned below into a cascading fountain of silken fabric, which pooled realistically at her feet. The dress was stunning.

She was stunning.

Finn tore his eyes away from her curves, which the dress accentuated quite well, hoping she hadn't noticed him looking. He looked instead to his own clothes.

He wore a crisp, white, collared shirt under a grey, woolen vest and matching overcoat. His neck was encircled with a thick, green tie and his head donned a dark grey driver's cap. But when he raised his hand to grab the hat, his fingers passed through the brim.

"The hologram will present some give." The professor's eyes shone behind his spectacles. "It will move with you, fold like natural clothing would, and, if you poke it, the fabric will flex, crinkle and bend. It just can't process when your hands go all the way through it."

Finn stifled a snort of laughter as he turned to look at Valerie, who now wore a peach calico dress in a floral pattern with a matching bonnet, a white apron, and an expression of unfiltered repugnance.

She curled her upper lip as she stared down at her pocket watch screen. "Lucky me: 'Early American Pioneer Fashion: Mid-Nineteenth Century.'" She rolled her eyes. "I feel like someone's about to ask me if I'd like to ford the river, take a ferry, or caulk the wagons and float."

It was an odd sensation to look so heavily dressed and yet feel so light and free at the same time. Finn took a few tentative steps, watching in amazement as the fabric of his clothing moved with him in such a realistic way. As his heavy wool coat moved, it somehow even replicated the sound of the fabric brushing against itself. The top screen of Finn's pocket watch read "1930-1935: Standard New York Fashion," and the bottom screen showed his very ensemble, even offering a small color wheel. As he dragged his finger along it, his green tie shifted to various other shades.

"Not bad, Finn," Everly said as she watched him change the hue of his tie. "It's a good look on you. You look...dapper." She smiled as she posed in her massive Victorian ball gown.

"You can change the color," said Finn quickly, embarrassed at her compliment and suddenly finding it difficult to string a sentence together. As he showed her how to manipulate the color wheel on her pocket watch, he wondered if it was possible for her to hear his heartbeat.

Everly began to hum "Once Upon a Dream" from *Sleeping Beauty* while spinning in place, allowing the train of her dress to swirl around her as she used her pocket watch to flash it from blue to pink and back again.

Finn watched her, mesmerized until SCRAP began to emit an enthusiastic series of clicks and beeps. His small, mechanical hands came together in excited applause. Everly, Finn, and Valerie directed their attention towards the object of the little robot's admiration.

Edison stood, arms akimbo and legs planted wide apart, draped in an elegantly embroidered matador outfit. It was a bright, silken red, arrayed with golden tassels and adornments. A black montera rested atop his head, spilling out on either side. He stared back at the group without expression.

As SCRAP clicked and beeped, Edison moved his silken cape out of the way of his pocket watch to read his message.

"I know."

CHAPTER 13
SUMMIT OF SELECTION

Finn had never been on an airplane before, nor was he particularly fond of heights. This was the day of the Summit of Selection, which would take place at the Historians' Society Headquarters. The Historians' Society provided each of the four competing schools with a private jet that would take them to the ceremony. The jet was clean and white, the back displaying the insignia of the Historians' Society, painted in a sleek black—an owl clasping an hourglass.

Finn blew some air out of the side of his mouth as he climbed the steps.

History sure paid well.

He sat beside Everly in one of the six leather chairs inside. Her green eyes were hidden behind a pair of rounded Chanel sunglasses. Looking like a socialite en route to an impromptu trip to the Hamptons, she was in her element; the thought of Everly Caldwell flying on a commercial airliner clashed sharply with the natural order of things.

Valerie was forced to sit next to the professor, as the seat beside Edison had been claimed by SCRAP, who Edison insisted be allowed to travel with the team. SCRAP wasn't tall enough to get into one of the seats alone, so Valerie reluctantly picked him up and set him into the high back chair. As soon as she walked away, the little robot began clicking and beeping. Valerie rolled her eyes, stormed back to his chair, and fastened his seatbelt.

As the jet began to rumble and vibrate, Finn felt his stomach drop.

"Nervous?" Everly looked at him over her sunglasses, which she'd pulled down on the bridge of her nose.

"I guess," Finn managed, realizing he'd been holding his breath. "First time flying." Truthfully, his nervousness had as much to do with Everly's hand unconsciously touching his on the armrest as the prospect of being thousands of feet in the air.

Everly's lips lifted in a reassuring smile. "Here. Take the window seat."

"But won't that, like, make it worse?"

"I don't know." Everly rolled her shoulders. "I guess I kind of feel like if something freaks you out you should just...you know, look at it. Face it."

Finn issued a slow nod, eyes on hers until she pushed her sunglasses back into place and stood. The two slid past each other as they moved into their new places, and Finn spent several minutes trying to will the blood back to his head after having been pressed against her for mere seconds. He turned to the small, round window and watched the airport grow blurry as the jet began to taxi and pick up speed. The nose of the jet lifted into the air, and the world in the window became smaller and smaller.

Just look at it.

Face it.

Professor Moskowitz turned his chair to face the group. "The accommodations are excellent, but we must not lose sight of why we are here. The Summit of Selection is not just a chance to select the game to be played—it is a chance to get to know our competition."

Valerie leaned forward in her seat intently, elbows on her knees.

"If individual challenges are selected, knowing the competition is less important," continued the professor, "but in group games like King of the Mountain or Red Rover, it provides distinct advantages."

"We already know that Vale and Halls of Ivy Prep don't like each other," remembered Valerie. "That seems like an advantage to the rest of us."

"It might very well be," admitted the professor. "But don't count on anyone who isn't wearing Wharton colors."

"Earlier you mentioned that Vale Academy and the Halls of Ivy Prep have an edge over us because they've done this before," mentioned Everly. "Maybe that could work in our favor."

"What do you mean, my dear?" Professor Moskowitz cocked his head to the side.

"Our inexperience makes us less of a target. If we play nice with everyone, we seem weak. We can pretend to be more innocent than we really are. Make them underestimate us."

The professor nodded. "It might work. But let's not return the favor and underestimate *them*. Vale Academy is smart. Their captains are Emily and Elden Neil. They are twins, and it's almost as if they share one mind...a dangerous one. This will be the third straight set of Time Trials in which they will be participating. They have a nose for weakness and a knack for exploiting it."

Finn watched as Everly's small notebook appeared from her purse, and she began to furiously scribble into it.

"Halls of Ivy Prep is led by Kade Davis," the professor went on. "They were close to victory last year but lost a teammate during a particularly brutal game of Hide and Seek." The old man's jaw clenched, his voice taking on a harder tone. "They were sent back to the Revolutionary War to survive the Battle of Trenton for as long as possible. Kade found them a strategic place to hide and they were on their way to putting up an impressive time, but one of his team members was lost during the battle and Kade was forced to pull his chain and evacuate."

"Was he shot?" Finn winced at the thought of how much damage a lead musket ball could do.

"No." The professor shook his head sadly. "*She* died of hypothermia. The wetsuits can make you look like you are warm, but in the end, they are just a thin piece of holo-cloth. By the time Kade realized she was unresponsive it was too late."

As the professor looked down at his hands, Everly's pen grew still. "The Neil twins at Vale Academy did what they could to torture and blame the boy. They said terrible things...made him feel responsible. Kade lost his confidence and Halls of Ivy Prep lost the remainder of the competitions." The professor stared into his lap for a moment longer before he spoke again. He looked up and addressed his granddaughter. "Trying to outsmart Vale Academy is a terrific notion, but more often than not, it is a failing proposition. They are simply willing to do anything in order to win. Unless you are truly willing to do the same, they will always have the advantage."

"We want to win," Valerie assured the professor, hands capped over her knees, eyes hungry.

"Believe me, my dear, I want you to win, too. But if you wanted to win as much as Vale Academy does, you would not have been selected for this team."

The captain of the private jet announced over the loudspeaker that they were approaching their destination, and Finn turned to look out the window again. Private jets, time machines, secret societies...what would the headquarters for such an establishment look like?

Finn wasn't sure what he'd been expecting, but this definitely wasn't it; the landscape was parched and desolate, with a few large warehouses in what almost looked like some forgotten airfield, making the establishment look like an abandoned compound. A high, chain-link fence surrounded the perimeter. From the air, Finn could just make out that the top of the fence was woven with spirals of razor wire. There were only two details which hinted that this barren, unremarkable compound was more than it seemed: the first was three other private jets, identical to the one that had taken them here, their clean, sleek bodies standing out sharply against the dilapidation surrounding them. The second thing that caught Finn's eye was a set of black satellite dishes on the top of one of the buildings.

The jet touched down, and Wharton's Time Team stepped out into the hot, dusty air. The entire place felt harsh. Unforgiving. The last place one would expect this plush private jet to touch down in. A van waited to take them to their next destination, bearing the same owl and hourglass insignia that was stamped onto their jet.

"This is...interesting." Valerie's voice held a hint of scorn as they climbed into the van. She curled her lip in disgust, wiping away some dust that had settled on the shoulder of her navy blue cardigan.

"What did you expect, my dear?" The corners of Professor Moskowitz's mouth turned up into a sly smile. "A secret chamber inside Big Ben?"

"London would have been fine by me," Valerie fired back as the driver, a silent man in a black bowler hat, started the engine.

"There are too many eyes in London." The professor looked at Valerie over the chrome rims of his spectacles. "The timekeepers brought the Historians' Society out to this location precisely because it doesn't look like a place you would expect big things to happen."

"Area 51 looks a lot like this place." Edison pushed his square glasses up, staring out the window into the deserted landscape. "They don't fool me."

The van came to a stop in front of a large warehouse, and the driver got out to open the door for the team. As they emerged, they were greeted by a man wearing a leather top hat which looked like it belonged to another era. At the base of this curious hat were a pair of strange, round goggles, the frames of which were made from unpolished brass. The lenses of this contraption were dark, and a number of smaller, clear, round lenses of various sizes fanned out on either side. Despite the dry heat, the man wore an antiquated suit, the heavy suede overcoat of which ran over a dark, wine-red vest. He removed his top hat and issued a deep bow.

Finn tried not to stare. There was something strangely dissonant about this man; he had a full head of hair and didn't look a day over thirty, yet his slicked-back tresses were white. His skin was flawless—devoid of even a single wrinkle, freckle or mole. He almost looked as if he were made of wax.

"Many greetings to Wharton Academy." The man spoke with a formality so often lost in these times. "I am Grand Timekeeper Garridan, and I am most pleased to meet you all." He shook Professor Moskowitz's hand eagerly, pulling the slight man into a near embrace. "And I don't have to tell you again how pleased I am to have *you* return to the Trials after all these years, old friend. You've been sorely missed."

Professor Moskowitz sketched a polite smile as he extricated himself from the Grand Timekeeper's embrace. Grand Timekeeper Garridan was a full head taller than the professor, though he wore high leather boots with a ridiculous number of straps and a very generous heel.

"I should hope that the flight was comfortable." The timekeeper gestured to the warehouse behind them. "I'm sure that our facilities seem strange to you; we find it best that we don't call attention to ourselves."

As Finn shook the man's extended hand, the timekeeper looked into his eyes probingly. "Finn Mallory. I can't wait to see what *you* will bring to the Trials this year." Finn threw him a tremulous smile as the odd man moved on to shake Everly's hand.

After finishing his introductions, the Grand Timekeeper strode back toward the open doors to the warehouse. "We had best get on with the show, as the other three schools have already arrived and are waiting for us," he said behind him to the team, mid-stride. He paused then, a twinkle in his eyes. "*Time* is of the essence." He threw his head back in laughter. Everly bit her lower lip and stole a glance at Finn, who raised his eyebrows, reminded of the bad jokes he had endured from Headmaster Bruce.

The Grand Timekeeper led the group inside and it took a moment for their eyes to adjust to the scant light. Massive chandeliers hung from the overhead tresses, composed of clusters of large electric bulbs, which dangled haphazardly from enormous, rusted gears. A number of high wooden shelves rose against the industrial walls, housing an assortment of old tools and strange mechanical curiosities.

The team made their way past a large wooden printing press into a generous space where four Time Benders waited. Each one was slightly different, but all bore a resemblance to the one that Professor Moskowitz kept in the barn at Wharton. Finn raised his eyes to see a banner above each machine, suspended by long, black cords out of which vintage light bulbs sprouted like electric flowers.

The first banner displayed Wharton's classic, calligraphic "W," painted in thick, royal blue against the tattered and discolored canvas. A sharp and narrow "V" in deep scarlet hung over the next Time Bender, which, Finn assumed, meant that they would be seated next to the infamous Vale Academy. Next to Vale Academy's banner hung a series of bold green letters—"HIP"—which must have stood for Halls of Ivy Prep. The letters were a dark and deep emerald with a vibrant, lighter green encircling some areas in the shape of English Ivy, which seemed to be growing around and up the letters. Another "W" was suspended over the last Time Bender, but this one was checkered in black and white—the insignia of the mysterious Wilmington Prep.

The hanging banners, combined with the industrial ambiance of the Historians' Society, created a strange atmosphere which was both medieval and mechanical.

Long, wooden tables were positioned in front of each Time Bender, and three of them were already populated by the other competing teams. Finn's eyes instinctively drifted to Vale Academy's table, only to find them already watching him.

The twins weren't difficult to pick out; Emily and Elden Neil glared at him with perverse smirks. Both had long, straight hair, parted down the middle. Emily could have been almost pretty if not for the perpetual pinched look on her face, which gave the impression that she had just smelled something foul. Had it not been for the maroon lip color that Emily wore, it would be difficult to tell her apart from Elden. Finn quickly cast his eyes away.

Valerie led the group to their designated table and planted herself in the seat nearest the contentious twins, putting a welcomed barrier between Finn and the frigid looks they were sending his way. Elden snorted as she casually adjusted her seat.

"Nice of Wharton to show up," Emily whispered, leaning forward on her elbows, voice dripping thickly with condescension.

"Nice of you to wait." Valerie issued a saucy smile, keeping her eyes straight ahead.

Everly and Finn exchanged a glance, both of them stifling laughter. It was good to have Valerie on your side. At the end of the row, Edison waited patiently for things to begin, with SCRAP sitting on his lap. The professor joined a curious-looking crowd who were flanking the Time Benders on both sides. A long table draped with a clean, white tablecloth stood directly in front of them.

An explosion of light from the crowd drew Finn's attention away from the table. A small contingent of reporters dressed like they were from the early Hollywood era furiously scribbled notes onto little pads of paper. Around them, flashbulbs from accordion-style cameras that had been slightly modified with rusty accoutrements popped like a volley of musket fire.

Momentarily blinded, Finn rubbed his eyes. When he opened them and stopped seeing spots, he noticed a short, portly man in a feathered fedora, whose gaze darted eagerly from Vale Academy's table to Wharton's, looking like a shark that smelled blood in the water.

Grand Timekeeper Garridan strode to the main table and took a seat beside three others, who observed the teams with quiet fascination. Dressed as oddly as Garridan was, they wore strange old suits from another age, their heads sporting a series of bowler hats and low-rise top hats, the sole woman wearing a felt cloche hat which was tipped to one side of her head. All of their bizarre hats were topped with strange goggles similar to the ones that Grand Timekeeper Garridan wore on his own eccentric headpiece. They all had the same unblemished skin, as if their features had been sanded down.

As the Grand Timekeeper removed his hat, the other three mirrored the action, almost in unison.

White hair.

Bone-white.

They *all* had it. Finn made brief eye contact with Everly.

The Grand Timekeeper pulled his high back chair out and took a seat, the rest of the crowd following suit. There were actually five seats at the table, leaving one spot curiously vacant. The overhead light from the industrial chandeliers draped the council's faces with intimidating shadows.

The friendly quality of Garridan's voice eroded into a detached and business-like tone, though his words still poured out smoothly. "May I present the esteemed High Council of the Society." He made a sweeping gesture to the three other members sitting on either side of him. As he said their names they rose and gave a slight bow. "Mr. Keenan Wakefield, Mr. Maverick Doherty, and Ms. Philomena Vandecraft." The woman smiled and nodded, looking over the teams with electric, grey eyes, as if judging livestock.

"The Historians' Society has long lived by the saying: 'Veritas Filia Temporis.'" Upon hearing this, the small crowd of strangely dressed people lightly applauded to show their approval.

"It is in understanding the past that we are able to prepare for the future," continued the Grand Timekeeper, his voice echoing off the rusted metal walls. "The Time Trials are our way to learn from the past. To connect to the past. To be *part* of the past. Today, we salute the sixteen young historians who have elected to join this lifelong journey in the pursuit of the past."

The crowd erupted into another round of light applause. "This is no easy task that you are about to embark on." The Grand Timekeeper spoke directly to the four tables of students now. "It is one which is fraught with danger and could easily cost you the highest price. Thank you for being willing to take such risk."

The professor had apprised the team of the risks involved in the Time Trials, and Finn had signed a contract accepting them, but even so, the words put an uneasy feeling in his gut. He glanced beside him at Everly again to find her already looking at him. Her expression appeared composed, but Finn felt like he could detect a trace of trepidation in her green eyes. He dragged his gaze away from her and found the professor across the room, his small form nearly engulfed within the curiously-dressed crowd with the other mentors. The professor's stare caught on Finn's and he threw him a reassuring smile.

A long moment of silence followed before the Grand Timekeeper continued. "And now, to business. Each team's mentor will select a game for the Trials at random. Of the games selected, fate will choose what will be played as the first challenge of this year's Time Trials. The High Council will convene in private to determine where and when in history each team will compete."

As the energy in the Grand Timekeeper's voice reached a crescendo, Finn felt some of his anxiety contort into excitement. If the articulators, pocket watches, and wetsuits hadn't made this feel real, this speech certainly did. He watched as several men, clad in black suits and bowler hats, brought an assortment of old clocks of all shapes and sizes out to the center table.

"Each team will be given their specific assignment one week prior to the competition in order to prepare a strategy under the guidance of their mentor," Grand Timekeeper Garridan went on, "and on the day of the first Trial, you will be flown out to Headquarters to complete your challenge in the very Time Benders that you see behind you." In one fluid motion, the sixteen contestants turned in their seats to admire the four machines that waited behind them like sleeping giants.

"And now the time has come for selection." Grand Timekeeper Garridan's face lit up in a Cheshire cat smile. "Will the mentor for each esteemed school come up to select the fate for their team?"

Professor Moskowitz rose stiffly from his chair and made his way through the crowd and up to the center table, which was spread with the eclectic collection of clocks. Three other mentors joined him, each of them selecting a clock from the table before placing it before the Grand Timekeeper.

Grand Timekeeper Garridan paused for a moment for dramatic effect before choosing one. He closed his eyes, raised his hands, and trilled his fingers before laying his palms on the very timepiece that Professor Moskowitz had brought him—a dark, wood tambour clock with a brass filigree face. The Grand Timekeeper opened the clock crystal and used two fingers to withdraw a small slip of dirty paper that had been wedged under the minute hand.

He held the paper up for the crowd to see, nearly quivering with excitement. "And the first official Trial is..." he basked in another moment of dramatic silence as the crowd held its collective breath before booming, "...Marbles!"

A gasp rose from the mass of onlookers, followed by a fresh eruption of wild applause. The throng of photographers in the press box unleashed a new salvo of loud, bright flashes from their bizarre cameras hoping to catch candid reactions to the news.

Finn shaded his eyes and found the professor again in the roaring crowd. In the midst of the commotion, the old man stared at the floor in silence, hands clasped behind his back, head bowed.

CHAPTER 14
THE FEAST OF YESTERDAY

Finn was afforded no time to consider the implications of Professor Moskowitz's stricken expression before the warehouse full of young historians and strangely dressed timekeepers, observers, and mentors were ushered into an adjoining room by an ecstatic Grand Timekeeper Garridan. According to the Grand Timekeeper, it was time for the highly-anticipated annual Feast of Yesterday— an event that was the highlight of his year. In a whirlwind of noise and activity, the time teams were herded in one direction and the mentors in another, allowing Finn only a brief glimpse of Professor Moskowitz, who offered him a brittle smile before everyone was seated.

Wharton's time team was seated together on one side of a long banquet table. As Finn's stomach growled, he threw a look at Everly beside him, hoping she hadn't heard it. He hadn't even realized until now that he was hungry; he'd been so nervous before boarding the jet that he'd lost his appetite, and he hadn't eaten since yesterday. He wondered what was hiding under the polished silver domes that sat in front of each guest.

An army of well-dressed butlers removed the silver domes from the porcelain plates in unison, and a sweet smell saturated the room in a burst of steam. Finn waved the steam away and stared down at a small, curved piece of cooked meat that looked like a mix between chicken and clam.

"Not entirely sure what this is, but I'm too hungry to care," he whispered out of the side of his mouth.

Everly's face wore a look of subtle amusement as she watched him struggle with the ridiculous assemblage of silverware that fanned out from his plate. Finn shrugged and lifted a small silver fork between two fingers.

He was about to dive into the curious entree, but Everly cleared her throat, looking at him out of the corners of her eyes. His fork froze in midair. A tall chef with a strange mechanical arm had walked to the head of the table and stared at him expectantly, eyebrow raised, mouth twisted up into a wry smile. Finn moved to restore his tiny fork to its place, but his fingers fumbled, sending it down to his plate with an embarrassingly loud clatter. Everly stifled a laugh with her knuckle.

"Honorary members of the High Council...," the chef turned, issuing a deep bow to a large table behind him where Grand Timekeeper Garridan and his fellow timekeepers sat, "...esteemed mentors...," he nodded to another table at the head of the room where the four mentors waited patiently. He spun on his heel and made a sweeping gesture to the long banquet table where the teams were seated, "...and venerated competitors of this year's Time Trials. May I present your first course of the Feast of Yesterday. Considered a delicacy of the highest order in Ancient Rome, reserved for the Roman elite, I bring you braised flamingo tongue."

The chef's face was a mask of pride and satisfaction in equal measure as soft sounds of delight emanated from the High Council's table.

As he stared down at the plate in front of him, Finn tried to quell a surge of nausea that coursed its way through him.

"I think I just threw up a little in my mouth," Valerie muttered, as if reading his thoughts.

"I highly doubt it's kosher," Everly breathed.

"This bird was a symbol of wealth and procured at great expense," the chef bellowed. "We have cooked it as they did, in traditional Roman fashion: the meat is served with a garnish of garum, as was the custom of the time." The man bowed again and disappeared into the double doors at the far end of the room.

"Garum?" Finn repeated.

"It's the ketchup of Ancient Rome." Everly prodded the contents of her plate with her fork, lip curled in disgust.

"Do I want to know what's in it?"

"Fermented fish guts." Everly shrugged. "I guess having a grandfather who's a history professor finally paid off."

Finn's stomach complained again as he looked down at his food. Shouldn't have asked.

Edison leaned across Valerie and stared at Finn with intent. "Are you going to eat that?" As Finn shook his head, Edison reached over and stabbed his flamingo tongue with a tiny fork.

A deep chuckle sounded from down the table. "Someone's got an adventurous palate." A boy with dreadlocks smiled in Edison's direction, with pale eyes that stood out against tawny skin.

Edison paused for a moment, his mouth full of tongue. "Tasthes like chicken," he mumbled, shoveling in another bite.

"Kade Davis." The dreadlocked stranger flashed a brilliant smile and extended a hand across the table.

Finn clasped it. "Finn Mallory."

Where had he heard Kade's name before?

"I remember what this meal was like last year," Kade mused. "I think they served calf's foot jelly. Victorian specialty."

"No chance of mac-and-cheese?" Finn gave him a sarcastic smile. "Maybe a pb&j?"

Kade shrugged. "We can only hope."

"You're good at that, aren't you, Kade Davis?" Emily Neil exchanged a smirk with her twin brother. "Hoping, I mean. But hoping and praying only gets you so far, doesn't it?" She pouted her lips into a simpering smile that made Finn's gut turn over.

Kade's smile faded, but Emily wasn't through with him. "Don't worry, Kade; at least our first trial is Marbles and not Hide and Seek, right? We wouldn't want Halls of Ivy Prep getting *cold feet* or anything, would we?"

Kade Davis.

Finn suddenly remembered where he'd heard the name before. He could see Professor Moskowitz's wizened face and the sad expression it had worn in the eye of his mind. Hide and Seek. Revolutionary War. Battle of Trenton. Hypothermia.

He swallowed hard. Kade had made a study of his own hands, which were folded, trembling, in his lap.

Valerie leaned forward on her elbows. "Shut up and eat your tongue," she hissed at Emily, ice in her voice. "Maybe the next course will be roasted snake-assholes or something and you can get a taste of home."

Emily narrowed her eyes but kept them on Finn. Disconcerted, he looked away.

"Technically, snakes do not have anuses; they have an orifice called a vent." Edison shoveled another forkful of food into his mouth, seemingly unaware of the tension at the table.

"Shut up, Edison," Valerie whispered.

A series of clicks and beeps sounded from beneath the table and Edison checked his pocket-watch. "I know," he said to SCRAP, gathering the robot into his lap. "You can't roast an orifice."

A raven-haired girl with perfect posture tried to change the subject. "That's a cute little robot."

"Thank you." Edison issued a proud pat to the diver's helmet that was SCRAP's head.

"Prana Kapoor." The dark-haired girl extended her hand to him. "I'm the team leader of Wilmington's Time Team."

Edison lost interest and completely ignored her, leaving Prana's hand awkwardly extended across the table. She tilted her head, a bemused expression on her face.

Finn swept in on Edison's behalf. "Finn Mallory," he took her outstretched hand, "from Wharton Academy."

"Well," Prana said with a smile, pumping Finn's hand across the table, "looks like we're the new hands here, Finn—Wilmington and Wharton, I mean. You and your team are lucky to have Mordecai Moskowitz as your mentor. He's well-regarded by ours." Her dark eyes scanned the row of Wharton students across from her. "Who's the team leader for Wharton? You?"

Finn felt himself flush. He looked at Everly, who was whispering into Valerie's ear behind a cupped hand. She was probably trying to talk Valerie down, who was still glowering in Emily's direction, murder in her eyes.

Finn turned back to Prana. "No, it's not me. I mean, we don't really...have one yet." Prana angle her head to one side, confusion playing over her face.

"I guess we didn't know we needed one?"

Across the table, Kade continued to stare into his lap in silence. He was the leader of Halls of Ivy Prep's Time Team, and he'd seen the loss of a team member as a personal failing. It had torn him up, and clearly, if the look on his face was any indication, he hadn't quite put himself back together again.

Nope; Finn would take a hard pass on the title of "leader."

"Hey kid, care to comment?" The words came at Finn fast, like those spoken by an auctioneer. He turned in his seat to find the small man with the feathered fedora holding out some strange type of recording device. "Felix Winkler of the Temporis Times. Glad to meetcha. People wanna know, howzit feel?"

Finn released a short, nervous laugh. "How does *what* feel?"

"Inquiring minds wanna know, Finn, howzit feel to be lucky enough to land Wharton's Good Fortunes Scholarship *and* a spot on the Wharton Time Team? Is it intimidatin'? Do ya feel outta place?" Finn recoiled as the small man shoved the strange device further into his face. He attempted to scoot his chair back, but there was nowhere to go.

"Uhhh..." As Finn spoke, the machine screeched with feedback. "Yeah. I mean, I guess..."

"Whaddaya think your parents would think about you competin' in the Trials?"

His parents.

The mere mention of them made the tide of Finn's grief rush in across the sands of his mind and pull at him with sudden force. His hand rose to his tie to loosen it, as it suddenly felt like there wasn't enough air in the room. The little man studied him with black eyes, pulling his fleshy lips back to expose a row of pointed teeth.

Everly swiveled in her chair, eyes tapered to slits. Her voice cut like hot shears. "Excuse me." Her hand rested itself on Finn's shoulder in a sort of protective stance. Typically, her touch would have elicited something from Finn, but the mention of his parents coming out of the mouth of this audacious stranger still had him reeling enough for him to barely notice it.

Felix's smile vanished, his eyes falling upon Everly's hand which was still at rest on Finn's shoulder. "Sorry, Miss Caldwell—very sorry. But inquiring minds wanna know—Miss Caldwell, do ya think *your* parents would be proud?" The pointed smile returned to his face. Felix raised a thick palm and swept his open hand through the air as if reading an invisible marquee, "The daughter of Wharton's famous power-couple teamin' up with 'The Unfortunate!'"

As Everly reddened, her hand retracted from Finn's shoulder as if suddenly realizing she had been touching a hot iron.

Felix wiggled his eyebrows, which were like two fat, lounging caterpillars. "I'm sensin' a little heat here, amiright? Whaddaya think, Miss Caldwell—am I lookin' at a case of uptown girl, downtown boy?"

For a moment, Everly looked stunned. Then her lips set and the frustration in her face melted away and froze into a mask of cool condescension. She lifted her chin and folded her arms, looking down her nose at Felix as if he were but a mildly annoying insect. "No comment." She spun around and turned her attention to more important things.

"I can assure you that Finn's temperature is normal," Edison directed to Felix, pushing his glasses further up on the bridge of his nose.

The little man raised his hands defensively before he slunk away, his bright feather bobbing above the surface of the table like a periscope, no doubt in search of his next helping of steaming hot scoop to deliver to "inquiring minds."

Finn slumped back in his chair, dabbing his face with his cloth napkin as the chef returned to the head of the table and waited for silence. "Our next course will be Anfu ham, originally eaten by members of the Qin Dynasty of Imperial China..."

Sensing Edison's blank stare, Finn turned to face him. Edison blinked behind his thick glasses, his plate picked clean. "Your temperature *is* normal, isn't it, Finn? Are you sick? You *look* sick."

CHAPTER 15
MARBLES

The four teammates filed into class and took their seats, waiting in quiet expectation for the professor to begin. Everly bit her lower lip and twisted the hem of her cardigan. They'd been awash in curiosity as to what Marbles would entail; they had asked no questions on the flight back to Wharton from Historians' Society Headquarters yesterday, deterred by the professor's pensive silence and drawn face. Today, her grandfather seemed to have rallied.

"Marbles." He stood and rocked on his heels, hands clasped behind his back. "It's a dangerous game in which you will be dispatched to a dangerous historical event, and tasked with saving as many 'past people' as possible. The total saved will be divided by the total lost in history, and the result will determine the winner."

"Do we know what 'our tragedy' is?" Valerie ventured.

"Not yet," replied the professor. "But this," he held up the large, flat envelope, "will give us the clues and details that we need to prepare for the challenge."

"No use wasting time, then." Valerie cracked her knuckles and crossed her arms.

"Indeed." The professor broke the red seal to the envelope, and though he smiled, Everly swore she saw his lower lip tremble.

He shook out the record and handed the empty sleeve to Finn.

As the professor fumbled with his ancient gramophone, Finn studied the crest that was printed on the record sleeve, which depicted a massive, horned owl clutching a tilted hourglass in its talons. Below it were the words "Veritas Filia Temporis," written in looping calligraphy.

Finn handed the sleeve to Everly. "What does that mean?" he whispered, forefinger gliding over the words.

"It's Latin," she whispered back readily, having taken it all through grade school and junior high. "It means 'truth is the daughter of time.'"

"Oh." Finn's chin dipped in a slow nod before he turned to face the front of the room again, but Everly's eyes felt stuck to him, like magnets to a steel surface.

Her attention was only pulled away when Professor Moskowitz finally fit the record onto the turntable and as it began to spin, the needle drew sound out of the black disk. The smooth voice of Timekeeper Garridan poured out into the room, interrupted occasionally by a series of pops and imperfections.

"Greetings, Wharton Academy, and welcome to your first Trial!"

The timekeeper's voice attempted to sound upbeat, but there was a formality to it which bled through this attempt easily.

"The Time Trials is steeped in tradition and you should consider it a great honor that your school was selected. History affords us the chance to truly see ourselves—and this game, though perilous, will give you just that chance. Listen to your mentor, listen to each other, and may the best team win.

"The first competition selected is Marbles. Marbles is perhaps one of the most universal games in history. They have been found

in Ancient Egyptian tombs, the ashes of Pompeii, and have even been used by various Native American tribes. The rules might vary, but the goal is always to win as many of your opponent's marbles as possible by knocking them out of a ring. Marbles has always been a gambling game and this is not untrue in the Time Trials.

"Unfortunately, history is rife with tragedy. How often have we told ourselves that we could have done it better? How often have we questioned if we could have survived? Perhaps you will find the answer. Marbles is no easy game. Your task is to save as many lives as you can within your provided scenario.

"What scenario, then, has been selected for you? The Historians' Society is pleased to announce that we have tasked Wharton Academy with a true historical gem. The RMS Titanic was the biggest ocean liner that the world had ever seen. Launched on May 31st in 1911, she famously sank on her maiden voyage in the freezing waters of the North Atlantic on the 14th of April, 1912 after she struck an iceberg at 11:40 at night, according to the ship's log. She sank at 2:20 am, two hours and forty minutes after the initial contact. That night 1,503 souls were lost to the ocean. Only 705 survived."

Everly snuck a look at the her grandfather, who stared at the floor as the record spun. The old man flinched slightly when he heard the numbers spoken aloud.

"You will be placed in a storage compartment at the stern of the boat at precisely 11:10 in the evening. The more people you save, the higher your score will be. The RMS Titanic is one of the most famous ships in the history of mankind, and this event is an exciting one to explore. Please take precautions, and remember that although the Trials are important, safety should come first at all times. Again, welcome to the Time Trials, and I wish you only the best of luck!"

The voice abruptly disappeared, and the only sound in the room was the deep cracking and popping of the spinning record.

Professor Moskowitz fumbled with the needle and turned the machine off as the team looked at each other in silence.

It was certainly easy to be excited about the prospect of traveling back in time, but now that they had a specific destination and a daunting task set before them, things felt a bit more real and a lot more dangerous.

The professor looked up at the team and smiled, but his eyes betrayed his true feelings. "Marbles is always a dangerous game to play." He dragged his chair from behind his desk to face them. "I am only your mentor in all of this. The decisions that you must make are ultimately yours alone."

"You're not going to tell us what to do?" stammered Everly. Her grandfather had always been fairly hands-off in regard to raising her–supportive, available, but never smothering–so she shouldn't have been surprised at his uninvolved approach. And yet, she was.

Apparently, Finn shared her surprise. He scoffed and raised an eyebrow. "Seriously. None of us have exactly done this before."

The professor was silent for a long moment before he spoke. "I can't do this for you. It's not because I don't want to help—it's because it gives you the best chance to survive."

"How does you not telling us what to do help our chances?" Valerie's voice had an edge to it.

"Because I will not be out there with you, my dear." The professor released a deep exhale. "The difficult thing about developing a game plan for any challenge is that nothing ever goes the way you think it will."

Everly conceded a nod, his statement bringing a whole slew of things to the surface of her mind.

"Well, not always. But if I have too strong a hand in developing this plan it will limit you. You are all smart and you were chosen for a reason." The professor nodded emphatically, and Everly wondered if it was to remind himself of the point he'd just made. "If I help develop a plan with you it will only hinder you. I've seen it before—teams that rely too heavily on their mentor. If something changes or goes wrong in the throes of the challenge I will not be there. It's not fair for me to come up with a plan of action but not assume the risk. And if I suggest something, it will be considered more heavily by the group simply because I am your mentor." The professor offered a wry smile and added swiftly, "And because I am old."

The group laughed in spite of itself.

"It is not my opinion that matters, it is yours," the professor continued. "The four of you have an equal say in how this is to be accomplished. One person must stay back in the Time Bender and run command. The rest is up to you." He rose from his seat. "I would, however, like to leave you with a few tips, if I may."

The group nodded and waited for him to continue. "I have seen these games before, and it is always the challenges which seem the easiest that prove to be the most difficult. The Historians' Society will have gone back to the ship in prior days and taken measurements. They will have run tests. The sinking of this ship is a major moment in history, and they will want to make it special."

"Listen to each other," he implored. "You will only do well if you work together. Develop a plan by constantly considering what might go wrong. When you do develop your strategy, don't get attached to it. Don't be 'proud' of it. And when you get on that ship, trust your instincts."

The professor moved to the door but stopped. When he turned around, his face looked different; it was harder. "There is one more thing." His tone, too, had hardened. "These marbles—the people that you are trying to save—they are not going to live happy lives when you turn the page. They still will have drowned in the icy waters of an unforgiving ocean one hundred years ago, no matter what you accomplish in the challenge. They are already dead." As he looked each teammate in turn, Everly felt the strange sense of looking into the eyes of a stranger, and a tremor passed through her. "Don't risk your lives any more than you have to, because you all have quite a few pages left to turn."

CHAPTER 16
54%

Wharton Academy's library was the crowning achievement of P.H. Wharton, the founder of the school. Although it was said in jest, it was theorized that he might have created the school for the sole purpose of building that library. Devoid of technology, with the exception of a dated microfiche reader, it was symbolic of Wharton itself, believing that no worthwhile thing could come without good, old fashioned work.

Finn stopped in the doorway and took in the room. This library was enormous: two floors of ancient books framed the central study area, connected by a quartet of elegant, spiraling, wooden staircases. The books rose up, row after row, on dark, walnut shelves, and a number of ladders granted access to some of the harder to reach titles. It was in the central area of study that the four teammates congregated amongst a stack of old books, plotting, debating, and thinking. They had received their assignment for their very first challenge of the Time Trials, with only a week to prepare and they didn't intend to waste a moment.

Valerie pulled her hair up into a ponytail and secured it with an elastic band that she wore around her wrist. "So, this isn't going to be as easy as telling the captain to turn the ship to the left." She seized a book from the stack of weighty tomes in front of her and began to flip through the pages until she reached the index. Her forefinger ran down the page, stopping at the letter "T."

"I don't think so," Everly agreed. "They wouldn't give us an event like this and make it so simple. You heard what my grandfather said—if it seems straightforward, it probably isn't."

"He said they will have gone in and done 'measurements.'" Finn turned to face her. "Does that mean timing things out?"

"It sounds like it." Everly tapped her pen against the edge of the table. "I figure they will have studied the ship's timetable from launch to sinking."

"The *Titanic* was 883 feet long and 92 feet wide," Edison chimed in flatly, not lifting his eyes from the page of the book in front of him. "That is equivalent to approximately three football fields."

"Sounds like a lot of ground to cover." Finn lifted his hand from the table, which had grown warm under the heat of the green, antique banker's lamp beside him and dragged it through his hair.

Valerie tapped her index finger against her forehead. "Not to mention that the ship had nine decks, and it will be full of stairs, doors...people. Would we even be able to *find* the captain in thirty minutes?"

"They would have timed it all out," Everly said again, more to herself than the group, head bent over a printed cross-section of the *Titanic*. She drew a polished finger from one end of the ship to the other. "The record said we'd be dropped in a storage compartment, but we aren't sure which one. By the time we find our way out and figure out where we are, we might not have enough *time* to reach the captain."

"That's true," Valerie agreed. "What if he isn't on the bridge? What if he's walking down a hallway...or in the bathroom? We can't rely on finding one man. It narrows our options too much."

"We could just go for the wheel." Finn raised and lowered one shoulder. "The captain might be anywhere, but the wheel of the ship is in one spot. If we hurry, we might be able to get to it in time."

"Makes sense." Everly's eyes were brilliant beside the green glow of the banker's lamp.

Valerie shook her head. "Too much sense. This is a trap. It can't be that easy."

"We also have to think about how we get back to the present." Everly lowered her voice as a horde of argyle-clad students passed by, books tucked under their arms. "Finn, if you break into the wheelhouse, you might very well save the lives of everyone on that ship. But *they* won't know that's what you're doing. What if you get in trouble?"

Finn let his breath out slowly. This was more complicated than he'd thought it would be. He stretched his legs out under the table. "Okay, then do we go after the lookouts? We could get to them faster, because we'd know where to find them. But they would never stop the boat just because we told them to." He leaned backward in his chair and looked up at the spiraling staircases that wound toward the upper level of the library. "How do we save everyone?"

"We don't." Valerie's voice was surprisingly frosty, and the hair on Finn's arms stood straight up.

He righted himself to face her. "What do you mean?"

"We *don't* save everyone." Valerie crossed her arms and leveled his stare. "We just save the ones we can."

"The *RMS Titanic* had twenty lifeboats." Edison read from an open book. "They could accommodate 1,178 people."

"Yeah, well, there were over 2,200 people on that ship." Finn gripped the edge of the table, beginning to feel the heat of indignation set in.

"True." Valerie's tone was irritatingly flip. "But there's no way to save all of them. That's what makes this challenge so difficult. They dangle that obvious solution in front of us, but that doesn't mean we have to bite. If we just fill those boats to capacity—"

"Then the poor people all die." Finn spoke louder than he'd meant to, and Everly's eyes widened beside him. Edison began to dry wash his hands over his book.

"Those people are dead anyway." Valerie closed her book with a thud of finality. "The professor's last bit of advice was to remind us that these people are already dead. I think that's what makes this scenario so dangerous. The Historians' Society is counting on us to be controlled by our emotions and try to save them all."

"The first lifeboat only had twenty-eight people in it," admitted Everly, almost apologetically. "What a waste." Finn could feel her eyes on his face, but he avoided looking at her, refusing to be sidetracked. He mirrored Valerie, crossing his arms over his chest.

"If we fill those lifeboats up to capacity, we save half of the passengers and crew." Valerie's tone had warmed up a bit now, and Finn knew an attempt was being made to pacify him. He issued a slight scoff.

"Fifty-four percent of the passengers and crew," specified Edison, who had begun his rhythmic rocking over his open book.

"Right." Valerie nodded. "That's a lot better than—"

"Thirty-two percent of the passengers and crew," finished Edison.

"Still," Finn cut in. "Most of the victims are going to be the steerage passengers. The third-class ones." He could hear the bitterness in his own voice. "It isn't fair."

Valerie drew in a deep breath, uncrossed her arms, and lowered her palms to the table. "Look, Finn—I understand why you're upset. And you're right...sort of."

Finn felt the inevitable "but" coming, and he braced himself for it.

"But," Valerie continued, "maybe we can work this out in our favor. Part of the reason so many of the poor died that night was that they were too calm...too obedient."

"Wait, what?" Finn's face scrunched up. "Too *calm?*" He glanced around him and lowered his voice, remembering again that they were in a library. "They locked the third-class passengers up down there! They wrote them off." He threw an exasperated look at each of his teammates. "*You* guys might not get why that's so disturbing..."

"Don't get salty, Finn." Valerie rolled her eyes. "Just because you're at Wharton on scholarship doesn't mean you get to play that card." She pursed her lips. "Besides, they didn't even lock the gates down in third class—that's a myth. Totally James Cameron."

Finn looked to Everly for support but found her staring at the floor. "It's true." Her voice was feather-soft, still laced with a hint of apology. "There's no evidence that any gates were locked, and even if they were, they were waist high." She raised her eyes to Finn's, and he felt himself deescalate under her conciliatory gaze. "The third class stayed down below because they were told to, and maybe because the language barrier kept some of them from understanding what was going on. But they weren't locked in."

Finn looked from Valerie to Everly and back again. Edison watched the exchange without a hint of expression, his rocking having slowed to a gentle sway.

"Everly and I—we did some research last night." Valerie shrugged, took another deep breath and tried again in a more sympathetic tone. "Finn, I get it. You feel compassion for these people in third class, and it pisses you off that nobody else did."

Finn thawed a bit more and Valerie seized the opportunity. "There was one first class child who died that night, next to fifty-two third class children. Hell, more first-class men survived than third class children." Finn saw Everly wince down at her hands beside him. "Everly and I looked at the schematics for the ship last night to try to get a head-start on guessing which cargo hold the

Historians' Society might send us during the challenge, and what we found was that...well, the ship was definitely built to keep the poor in their place."

"What do you mean?" Finn muttered, reaching up to loosen his tie.

"I mean that another one of the reasons so many third-class passengers died that night is that they literally couldn't find their way out." Valerie leaned across the table and traced her finger over the cross-section of the *Titanic* that was spread in front of Everly. "The first- and second-class cabins were easy to access and they're close to the upper decks. But the third-class cabins were spread out; there was no direct route to the upper decks from steerage. It's like a steel maze down there." She looked up and met Finn's gaze. "They didn't want the third class on the upper decks, so they purposely made it confusing."

"Maybe that's why the Timekeepers chose to place us in the bottom part of the ship," Edison said.

Everly nodded. "The confusion in the lower decks would make it even more impossible to find the captain or the wheelhouse."

"Saving all of them is ideal, obviously," Valerie assured Finn, "but they know that we'll try to do that. If we let the iceberg hit and focus on helping more people find the lifeboats, we can save more lives. The third class stayed below and waited patiently because they assumed that they would eventually be helped, but they never were; when some of them finally found their way to the upper decks, there were no lifeboats left." Her voice softened. "So, let's change that."

Finn's anger, which had already begun to ebb, finally rushed out completely. "Isn't the boat sinking a pretty dangerous option, too, though...for us?" he mused through a deep exhale.

"It took two hours and forty minutes for the ship to sink," Edison recalled flatly.

"That's a pretty good chunk of time," Everly said. "The timekeeper said that we would be dropped in the back storage compartments. Only the first five bulkheads flooded when the ship made initial contact and after that they poured over one by one. We would be safe from harm for a while..."

"We can play it safe." Valerie stood, leaning across the table and jabbing her finger at the lower part of the cross-section. "We'll create a panic in steerage to get the third class to come to the upper decks sooner. It won't take two hours to do that. We should be back to the Time Bender in plenty of time before the ship goes down." She drew back and looked intently at Finn, Everly, and finally Edison. "Who wants to be in the Time Bender as Command for this challenge?"

Edison remained silent, and Finn felt himself scoot his chair back, as if to exempt himself.

Everly smiled. "I'll do it." She settled her eyes on Valerie. "We'll need your assertiveness in action if we're going to rouse the third class to rebellion. No one says no to Valerie Konrad."

Valerie returned Everly's smile as Edison handed her a stack of books. "Let's start learning more about these lifeboats and how they work."

CHAPTER 17
TELLERVILLE

Finn ran his fingers over the top screen of his pocket watch, frantically searching for the correct function. He swiped to the needle and thread icon but hit the question mark by accident—the "random" function. He muttered under his breath as crimson slats of armor pushed their way out of the black holo-cloth of his wetsuit and clattered into place. A hooded red helmet closed over his head and two black horns shot up from either side as a faceguard folded over his nose and mouth.

As he fumbled to make the lifelike projection vanish, he could hear Valerie's sigh of frustration from across the barn. "We need you to find your Titanic presets, Finn, not look like a samurai!"

Finn located the erase button and his armor quickly folded away, leaving him in nothing but his skin-tight, black wetsuit. By some miracle, he managed to press the correct sequence the next time, and a navy-blue uniform materialized, a row of polished brass buttons blooming down the center of his chest in a straight line.

"Time?" Valerie shouted to Edison, who stood behind her, pocket watch in hand.

Edison looked up, studying Finn behind his thick glasses. "8.56 seconds."

Valerie rubbed her eyes and pinched the bridge of her nose. "That's not good enough, Finn." She crossed her arms and set her mouth. "Again."

Finn shook his head in frustration. "This is hopeless."

Valerie eased herself down on a crate in the old barn. "Your last attempt was..."

"...10.32 seconds," finished Edison.

"This isn't hopeless, Finn. This is progress." Valerie stood and whipped out her pocket watch, fingers dancing over the controls with confidence. Her wetsuit activated and a starched White Star Line maid's outfit spilled out of the holo-cloth of her wetsuit. A clean, white apron ballooned down into place, its hem kissing a pair of pointed, black boots.

"2.34 seconds," Edison chimed in from behind her.

Valerie looked down at her outfit and sighed. "How did I do that, Finn?"

Finn rolled his eyes. "Because you're awesome." He offered a sarcastic thumbs-up.

"You're damn right I am, but no. The answer is practice. This is just like hitting a tennis ball or swinging a golf club. Muscle memory. Repetition. *Practice.*"

Finn kicked at the dusty barn floor as Valerie narrowed her eyes. "What did you spend your time doing last night?" she asked, still looking like she was ready to offer someone a cup of Earl Grey in her dated, black dress and white apron.

Finn shrugged.

"He played his guitar," answered Edison without taking his eyes off his pocket watch screen.

"Thought so. You're a talented musician, Finn. As good as Jimi Hendrix, even."

"Yeah right," Finn mumbled. He knew she was working him—she'd never even heard him play—but he was beginning to feel his mood lift anyhow at the thought of his guitar. He *was* pretty talented.

"All those strings and frets or whatever seem...complicated. How'd you get so good?"

Finn suppressed the smile that tugged at the corners of his mouth. "Practice."

Valerie deactivated her wetsuit and the uniform sucked back into the holo-cloth. "Exactly."

"He's not as good as Jimi Hendrix," Edison added.

Finn had no chance to retort before Everly's voice came in through their earpieces from inside the Time Bender. "Let's run through it a few more times and then we can study the schematics of the ship some more. I'm sick of being stuck in the machine as Command all the time."

Finn took a deep breath and tried to relax. At least Everly was in the Time Bender and couldn't see how stupid he looked fumbling around and making a fool of himself. To make matters worse, he'd begrudgingly complied with Headmaster Bruce's demand that he cut his hair, and now the back of his neck felt naked, his ears exposed.

He couldn't shake the feeling that he didn't belong. Everly was effortlessly smart (not to mention impossibly good-looking), Valerie crushed everything she did, and Edison had a mind like a computer. Why had the professor put *him* on this team? What did he possibly have to offer?

He furrowed his brow in concentration and ran his fingers over the controls of his pocket watch once more. His finger swiped left instead of right. He frantically tried to correct the mistake, but it was too late: he watched in helpless frustration as the sleeves of his wetsuit expanded into dramatic cuffs, and unpolished brass buttons popped out from a quickly-forming wool coat. A tricorne hat edged in gold appeared atop his head.

Finn groaned. He was dressed like a pirate.

Valerie slapped her forehead and sat back down.

As Everly emerged from the porthole in the Time Bender, she bit her lower lip to conceal a smile. "Well. At least you look like you belong on the sea."

"5.25 seconds," Edison said, still looking down at his pocket watch.

Finn didn't feel like walking with the rest of the group this time. The quiet voice that whispered that he didn't belong had become a scream. He walked briskly away from the barn in the direction of Aion Hall, leaving his teammates behind him.

Before he could react, a solid rubber ball slammed into his shin. He cursed to himself and hopped on one foot, rubbing the spot where the ball had hit.

"Sorry about that, Tellerville." Nick Dain jogged over, lacrosse stick in hand.

"Don't worry about it." Finn stared at the freshly cut grass as his feet, hoping to avoid looking at the lacrosse captain at all costs.

He hadn't forgotten his first glimpse of Nick Dain in history class. Blue eyes, contemptuous smile. *Tellerville Trash.*

But the unexpected image of Everly's face beside him on the jet graced his mind next, round sunglasses pulled down on the edge of her nose, green eyes probing his.

"I guess I kind of feel like if something freaks you out you should just...you know, look at it. Face it."

Nick stooped over to pick up the ball. Smirking, he tossed it back to the team behind him.

Just look at him.

Face him.

Finn raised his gaze from the turf and leveled his eyes with Nick's blue ones. Nick flashed a perfect smile. "I'd ask you to play, but I'm guessing you're not really a sports guy." His eyes roved over Finn from head to toe.

"Good guess." Finn turned to walk away, in no mood to make small talk, but Liam Fillery jogged over to join them. "Hey, Tellerville. Didn't know they let Unfortunates on this part of campus. You helping the janitor or something?"

Nick slapped his lacrosse stick against his shoe to knock some mud loose. "He's part of that stupid nerd club. Archaeology or something weird like that." He jerked his thumb toward the barn. "You practice over there, right?" His voice switched from condescending to contentious. "With *Everly*." His face hardened as he said her name, and the sinews in his neck went taut, like really thick guitar strings. Finn felt his resolve start to falter, and he let his eyes drop to the turf.

"You look at me when I talk to you, Tellerville." Nick poked Finn in the chest with his lacrosse stick.

Finn stumbled but managed to stay on his feet, narrowing his eyes and raising them again to meet Nick's. He willed fortitude into his legs, but he could feel them start to go languid, like a pair of cooked noodles.

"It's the least you can do, you little publicity stunt; my tuition helps pay for your Wharton education. Don't forget that."

The rest of the Wharton Lacrosse Team had begun to swarm around them now, like vehicles that slow on the road to get a look at a car accident, eager to watch their fearless captain in action.

Seemingly emboldened by his audience, Nick drew more volume into his voice. "Without us, you'd be stuck at whatever garbage public school you crawled out of when Bruce picked your name from a list."

"You know what?" Finn mumbled. "I didn't even want to come here."

He turned to leave, but Nick handed his lacrosse stick to Liam and took a step forward, giving Finn a violent shove that dropped him to the ground. "So, you're ungrateful, too, huh? What'd I say about looking me in the eye? Get up!"

The team exploded in excitement and Finn made no effort to rise from the ground. His eyes darted between the brutish faces that surrounded him, feeling like a brush rabbit surrounded by hungry wolves. He wished Nick would just get it over with—beat the shit out of him or whatever it was that he planned to do.

Look at him.

Face him.

He forced his eyes back to the lacrosse captain's, whose hands had balled up into fists at his sides, and locked them there, trying to sell eye contact as confidence. Somehow it made sitting in wet grass feel the tiniest bit less humiliating.

Nick's grimace faded and his eyes widened as approaching footsteps began to squelch loudly in the wet grass. A figure approached, long blonde hair billowing up from her shoulders with each angry step.

Everly.

Finn felt embarrassment pump out of his heart like hydrochloric acid.

Go away.

This couldn't get any worse. Being thrown on the grass surrounded by a bunch of aggressive cretins was bad enough without *her* seeing it.

Everly cut a hole through the pack of lacrosse players and swept up to Nick, who seemed to shrink in her presence despite being several inches taller than her.

"What the hell are you doing?" Everly's voice was cold but eerily composed. The team around her bowed their heads like kids caught with their hands in the cookie jar, many of them slinking off at the first sight of her lethal stare.

"He started it." Liam pointed down at Finn, who was still sitting back on his hands in the grass. "You know what they're like, Everly."

Everly threw Liam a look that could curdle milk and he backed his way into the crowd without another word. She redirected her polar gaze to Nick.

"Everly, come on. He's a piece of trash," Nick sputtered. "I don't get it. I don't get why you—"

Everly stepped toward the lacrosse captain, her nose level with his chest, drawing up to him the way prizefighters face off in center ring before a bout. Her voice was low and hard. "Get out of here, Nick."

"Fine." Nick issued a short, nervous laugh, backing away from her as he threw up his hands. "Whatever. I know how much you like a charity project. That's what I like about you, Ev—you're such a philanderer." He cupped his hands around his mouth. "Practice is over, boys," he shouted before lumbering off with his team of mutants, leaving Everly standing over Finn.

She waited until the team was gone before she extended a hand. "Are you...okay?"

Finn dodged her outstretched hand and pulled himself to his feet. "I'm fine," he muttered, wiping the dirt from the thighs of his uniform and stuffing his hands into his pockets.

"Look, I've known those guys a long time, and...let's just say money can't buy brain cells. The whole team has about five between them." Everly stepped closer and began plucking grass off the front of Finn's sweater. "The stuff they said—"

"I've got it." Finn stepped back. He began to walk away but stopped and turned. "I had it back there, too. You don't have to keep saving me like that." He waited for Everly to meet his eyes. Hers had the strange ability to be piercing and soft at the same time, but right now they were just soft. Finn sanded down the rough edges of his voice to match them. "Alright?"

Everly issued a reluctant nod. "Alright."

She watched him disappear toward Aion Hall, hands in his pockets, grass still clinging to his pants.

CHAPTER 18
STUPID THINGS, LITTLE THINGS…

The Wharton Gardens were beginning to die. Fall was not quite in full effect yet, but the trees were beginning to brown, and the many fragrant flowers were shedding their petals, leaving a colorful carpet on the garden walkways. The night mist crept over the gardens, making the light from the high street lamps seem blurry and subdued. It was past midnight, and Finn needed to clear his head.

The team would officially play Marbles tomorrow, their first challenge in the Time Trials. The last week had been a whirlwind of strategy and study. Using the ample resources of Wharton's extraordinary library, the teammates had spent long nights studying the schematics of the *Titanic*, scrutinizing old photographs of the ship, and learning what they could about the passengers and crew.

It was a surreal feeling to study old images and know you were days away from seeing them in person. When Finn looked at the photograph of the *Titanic* sailing away on her first and last voyage, he imagined how the black exhaust smelled as it was belched out of her proud smokestacks. When he saw pictures of the ship's empty dining rooms he imagined what it smelled and sounded like when families used it for the first time; the scents of the kitchen wafted up and mingled with the smell of salt, which saturated everything on the ship. In Finn's mind, he could hear the sounds of children laughing as their parents stared off into the horizon, enjoying the luxury of it all and dreaming of new places, adventures, and opportunities.

The *Titanic* burned 825 tons of coal a day. There were 10,000 lightbulbs on the ship, give or take, and there were thirteen honeymooning couples celebrating on her maiden voyage. Finn knew all this because Valerie had made flash cards for the group, and they hadn't been optional. Included were photos of rooms, random facts, and even pictures and biographies of some of the more prominent guests aboard the ship. Should Finn run into any of these passengers, he would be able to tell them if they lived or died.

He leaned back against the gazebo wall, finger on the "play" button of his Walkman, which was obscured within the folds of his green army jacket.

"Can't sleep either?" Everly's voice came softly through the mist as she emerged into view. She brushed some blonde hair out of her face and hooked it behind her ears, easing herself down next to him.

Finn shook his head as he looked off into the misty black outlines of Wharton Gardens. "Just nerves, I guess." He could smell her—that clean scent—and he felt the warmth of her shoulder against his, but he couldn't bring himself to look at her face tonight. Not after the incident on the lacrosse field, where she'd swept in like Wonder Woman and pulled his soggy, grass-stained ass up off the turf.

"We have a solid plan," Everly reassured him. Feeling the heat of her eyes on his face, he finally looked her way. She seemed to know not to bring up today, and he was silently grateful.

"I know you have your reservations about it." Everly looked down at her hands and then back up at Finn's face. "Valerie's right, though; we can't get that ship to turn around in time. If we had an hour, maybe..."

Finn heard his tone harden. "But those *people*..."

Everly held his gaze for a moment. "I know."

"I know they're dead already. But they won't be dead tomorrow."

"It's dangerous to think like that, Finn."

"I don't care if it is." Finn repositioned himself to face her. "I know this is stupid. I get that. But I want to save *all* of them. All of them, Everly." In the heat of his impassioned speech, he'd taken hold of both her hands without even knowing he'd done it. Everly didn't pull away; she simply stared down at his hands holding hers until he let them drop, feeling his cheeks burn.

"They're going to die whether we save them tomorrow or not," Everly murmured. To Finn, it sounded like she was saying it more to convince herself than him.

"Look." Finn searched for the right words. "If we turn the page and this terrible thing has still happened a hundred years ago or whatever, I can live with that, but don't you want to give them a better ending, even if just for tomorrow? Save them while we can?" They were both sitting cross-legged now, knees touching.

Everly nodded. "Do you..." she drew in a deep breath and tapered her eyes, as if searching for the courage to ask her next question. "Do you ever think about using the Time Bender to see them again?"

Finn looked away and paused before he tried to answer, trying to swallow the lump in his throat that had materialized out of nowhere. He pressed his lips together.

"I'm sorry," Everly said quickly. "That was stupid. *I'm* stupid."

"No." Finn smiled dryly into the darkness. "It's fine. I thought about it the moment the professor told us he had a time machine."

Everly went silent, as if encouraging him to continue, and Finn made sure the lump in his throat had fully dissolved before he did.

"I remember such normal things about them." He dropped his eyes to the edge of his army jacket and fiddled with a loose thread. "I remember my mom working at this diner, and how she always came home smelling like stale coffee and burger grease...my dad messing around on his guitar." He felt a warmth course through him at the images that filled his head—images he rarely allowed to grace the chamber of his mind. "I remember them taking out the trash and sitting at the kitchen table stressing over bills, which was pretty much the only time my dad didn't smile."

He looked up into Everly's liquid green eyes, which had taken on a certain sheen while he'd been talking. "It's weird, but it's the boring stuff I miss the most. They're stupid things, little things, but they're also sort of...everything."

Everly's smile was contemplative. Her chin rose and fell in a slow nod of understanding. "I can remember my mother practicing her opening and closing remarks to the jury in our living room." Her laugh was soft. Musical. "She set up twelve of my stuffed animals as the jurors and gave me a meat tenderizer so I could be the judge."

A corner of Finn's mouth lifted into a smile as he waited for more. Not wanting to overstep, he hadn't asked her about her parents, but he'd been curious. Now it looked like some of his questions might be answered. The light of the streetlamp shined off Everly's hair, giving it that silvery look.

"She got sick when I was seven," Everly said to her hands. "It didn't last long."

It stunned Finn how matter-of-factly she said it—as if she were talking about a bout of rain or a power outage, rather than a terminal illness. Maybe this is how it was after a while. Maybe grief just...settled.

"Do you know one of the worst things about someone you love getting cancer?" Everly looked up at Finn's face but didn't wait for a reply. "You can only remember what they looked like when they were sick. When I think of my mom now," she shook her head. "It's always her without her hair. I...I can hardly remember anything before."

As Finn resisted the urge to reach out and grab her hands again, he couldn't help but notice that she still hadn't mentioned her father. He was intensely curious, but he stopped himself from asking. Something about this omission seemed purposeful, and Finn could sense that now wasn't the time to force the issue.

"I'm sorry." It was a weak reply, and Finn reached within himself for something better, but came up empty.

Everly smiled. "You know, I haven't thought about my mom delivering a speech to those stuffed animals in a long time. I'm really glad we talked about this. And thank you, by the way."

"For what?" Finn arched an eyebrow.

"For not saying 'everything happens for a reason' or 'she's in a better place' or something trite like that."

Finn's knowing scoff raked the air. "I've heard those lines myself a few times more than I'd like to remember." He absentmindedly twisted the cord of his headphones around his index finger.

As they lapsed into silence, Finn took a breath, unsure if he truly wanted to say what was on the tip of his tongue. It was as if the words had been boiling within him all this time, building pressure and steam, and now he was some kind of whistling teapot, shuddering and spitting on a burner.

"It was my fault." He said it quietly—quickly, before he had a chance to change his mind.

Everly studied his face in the dark, her green eyes probing into his brown ones. "What was?"

"Everything. All of it. The accident, them dying...it was my fault." He'd never spoken the words out loud before, but in the quiet confessional of the gardens, it just spilled out of him. The teapot went quiet now. He felt a bit of weight come off him—a sense of relief, as if he'd just removed a pair of shoes that were too tight.

Now it was Everly who took Finn's hands in hers. "Finn, you can't really think that. That's not possible. You couldn't have prevented—"

"They died because they were trying to do something for me—give me something I wanted." Finn's voice was all hard edges now. He gently withdrew his hands from hers but held her stare. "I put them there that night. If we hadn't been on the road, they'd still be alive."

He watched Everly's face; her green eyes had gone wide. She opened her mouth to speak, but closed it, as if at a loss for words.

"You were right—it's best to just look at it. Face it. See things for what they are." Finn threw her a rueful smile and drew himself to his feet. When he spoke, the serrated edges of his voice had been filed smooth again. "We should get some rest for tomorrow. Valerie has us on a curfew."

Everly nodded slowly from the ground before she stood, making her way across the lawn toward Raine Manor, but as Finn started back toward Aion Hall, her voice stopped him. "Finn."

He turned around to face her.

Her eyes were suddenly intense in the dark. "I want to save them too."

CHAPTER 19
LAUNCH

Everly drew in a deep breath as she faced her reflection in a mirror in the medical bay at Historians' Society Headquarters. The team had practiced basic procedures for weeks, so much that Everly could activate her pocket watch and run through the features without even looking at it. Now it was time for their very first challenge of the Time Trials, and she held the position of Command.

The Historians' Society prep team had taken the team's vitals multiple times, scanning them with strange devices and triple checking that their equipment was fully functional. They had even tried to update SCRAP's programming, but the feisty little robot wouldn't allow it.

As Command, Everly was tasked with coordinating the mission, and the responsibility weighed upon her heavily. She would be responsible for making changes should the unexpected arise, which her grandfather had assured them was inevitable. She was responsible for getting the team home safely. She was responsible for their *lives*.

A few months ago, Everly might have complained about the responsibilities of planning the Fall Fling with the Social Committee. That had been important to her...once. But everything had changed now, and she fully understood that if the team made it back from this mission, nothing would ever be the same.

She always appeared composed, as if she had the answers before the questions were even asked. That's what it meant to be Everly Caldwell. But it was in these little, tense moments of quiet right before the big ones came that she felt doubt overtake her. It never lasted long, but it made her feel like an imposter—like she was a lie that everyone wanted to believe.

She couldn't stop thinking about what Finn had said to her last night: *Don't you want to give them a better ending? Save them while we can?* She realized that she was nervous that they themselves might die, but she was afraid of watching these poor passengers die, too, even if, as the professor had said, they were already dead. The idea of saving them, even if it was only temporary, was beautiful.

And then there was that other thing Finn had said.

His admission last night had shaken her, but it had also given her new insight into the dark-haired, cynical new kid and what lay beneath his defensive surface. She was afraid of what watching these people die could do to him; to Finn, this challenge couldn't be anything other than real. He would feel responsible—he would blame himself—for each and every life lost to the ocean. When he'd bared his soul to her last night in the glow of the streetlamp, Everly's mind had connected the dots. His indignant face in the library, facing off with Valerie to insist that they had to save them all? It suddenly made perfect sense. Saving everyone on the *Titanic* was about so many things for Finn; it wasn't just about the social class of most of the victims—yes, that was part of it, but it wasn't all of it.

This was about making amends. This was about redemption.

She threw a look at Finn now; his leg jiggled nervously as he listened to Edison rattle off facts about who knows what. Edison always did this, but today he did it in an especially frenetic way, twisting his fingers together as he rocked back and forth. Everly smiled, watching Finn nod as Edison prattled on, throwing in a "Really?" or a "Wow" here and there to let their myopic teammate know he was listening. Maybe he understood that this was Edison's way to be nervous.

All four team members were in their wetsuits, which clung to their bodies like second skins. The team was getting used to wearing these by now; most of the mortification they had felt at having their goods put on display had waned for the most part. The wetsuits contained millions of sensors and micro-cameras, which helped them to create stable and believable holographic images of clothing. If it was windy, for instance, the sensors would pick that up and react appropriately, even making adjustments for the type of clothing being worn. Silk, for example, reacts much differently to wind than denim, and the wetsuit would account for that. These micro-cameras also went both ways; hence, if one were to wear an article of holo-clothing that revealed skin—say a pair of shorts—it would accurately project a scar on your left leg through the wetsuit. Finally, these cameras allowed those in attendance at the Historians' Society Headquarters to watch the challenges as they unfolded from the safety of the present. Illegal betting on the results was frowned upon, but it was known to happen. How many people would bet on Wharton today?

The door to the prep room swung open and an arbitrator entered. Dressed in black suits and matching black bowler hats, arbitrators were similar to referees. They ensured that rules and regulations were followed and kept the challenges running smoothly. On the lapel of their dark suits, they donned a small, official cluster of gears which distinguished them as official arbitrators of the Time Trials. The arbitrator nodded to the prep team, which quickly packed their things and vacated the room.

"Two minutes," he warned, and promptly shut the door.

Despite Everly's designation as Command, the team instinctively looked to Valerie, who paced in front of them as if this was the locker room and she was about to give a pregame speech.

"We all know the plan," she said, using her hands for emphasis. "We get to the rooms, get people out, and create panic early. Remember—the problem was that they were convinced that they couldn't sink. Let's fix that. The first lifeboats were barely full because they were playing music and serving refreshments, but a few panicked White Star Line employees will change that quick. We time the pandemonium with the ship's contact and the momentum of it will take care of itself." She stopped pacing and looked directly at Finn. "Remember—they're already dead."

"We can do this," Everly chimed in, remembering it was her who was meant to take the lead. "You need to trust me. Look at me." She paused and looked at each of her teammate's faces. "We can do this."

"I can't swim," stated Edison suddenly, without a hint of fear in his voice.

They were interrupted by the stern voice of the arbitrator, who stood in the doorway with folded arms. "It's time."

Valerie looked back at the group. "I'm just as nervous as you are, but when we walk to that Time Bender we do it as a team, and we do it with our heads high."

The teammates walked out of the room in single file, Valerie in the lead, followed by Edison, SCRAP, Finn, and finally, Everly. The small crowd applauded as the team made their way to the Time Bender, the High Council nodding in approval as they passed their table. The Grand Timekeeper leaned forward eagerly in his chair, as if about to dive into a sumptuous meal.

Everly searched the crowd for her grandfather and found him sitting in the front row, his hands folded and a warm smile on his face. He might have been watching her at a piano recital.

Everly took a deep breath and turned her eyes forward. Her insecurities faded away and left her rock-solid. Her eyes narrowed as she ducked into the brass porthole of the Time Bender.

SCRAP contorted his robotic body and melted into the wall in the spot where Finn had touched him so many weeks ago, and Everly's three teammates secured themselves into their seats with their leather restraints. Everly, from her Command spot in the rear, pressed a few glowing buttons on the wall and flipped a couple rounded metal switches. The machine responded by lifting the small, brass entry door with a mechanical groan.

No going back now.

"Inner door secure." Everly pressed another sequence of buttons and the large, circular door, which usually hovered over the entrance like a glass visor, began its slow, smooth descent. It slid into place, and a series of inner locks clicked into position, echoing through the walls of the device while unseen hydraulics hissed.

"Outer shell secure."

Finn, who was seated in front of Everly, turned around and threw her a half-smile. Everly raised her eyebrows at him and smiled back, feeling her stomach somersault. He always smiled that way—a lopsided grin that made him look slightly dopey but also sort of...

Oh my God, stop, Everly scolded herself.

Nerves. You have...nerves.

She straightened her posture, checked the security of her restraints and returned her focus to the business of the launch.

"Receiver check," she commanded to the group. They all complied, activating the small receivers in their ears which would allow them to communicate to each other. As Command, Everly's pocket watch was the only one that could activate the distress call should anything go wrong. These receivers would help her to make that important decision if the need arose. The team gave a thumbs up to report that the receivers were all working.

Everly switched the frequency to speak with the launch team in the building. "Launch, we are secure and ready, awaiting your coordinates."

These Time Benders had to be entered with chronological coordinates from the launch team at the headquarters. No joyrides. Everly watched as the coordinates appeared on a small screen on the curved wall to her right. "Coordinates received. Launch, we are ready to begin the bend."

Outside, the society members adjourned to the nearby viewing room where a projector would relay the team's progress. Bending time required enormous energy, and the burst that it took to tear through time and space could be deadly at very close range.

"Wharton Command, you are clear to bend. Good luck," a voice said.

Everly switched her frequency back and told the group, "We are clear to bend."

"Well, what are we waiting for?" howled Valerie.

Everly drew in her breath and pulled a silver lever to the left, which activated a large, glowing button. She slammed her hand down on it and the machine came alive; the massive mess of interconnected gears above them thrust into motion, turning with a steadily increasing speed. They clacked against one another, creating a thunderous roar. In front of her, Edison clapped his hands over his ears, furiously writhing in his leather restraints beside Finn.

Above their heads, the turning gears spun ruthlessly, showering the young time travelers with pandemonium. However, after a moment, the noise dissipated. Everly raised her eyes; the gears were spinning so impossibly fast that they blurred together as one. If not for the turbulent wind that the spinning generated, it would look like a solid, blurry ceiling. The noise had vanished and was replaced by a deep, vibrating hum. The entire machine began to rattle, lightly at first and then violently. Everly could see the empty warehouse through the small porthole, but the shaking was making it increasingly difficult to make sense of anything.

When the shaking subsided, the glass flooded with intense, blue light and the world went completely silent. Everly felt gravity lurch out of the machine, leaving the team weightless. For a moment they floated in their restraints like astronauts in space. The window went black and the vibration and clatter of the gears smashed back into existence. Gravity poured into the machine, securing them to the world once more.

The Bender hissed and powered down in a mechanical diminuendo as the gears overhead decelerated in the darkness, until the only sound in the tired machine was the frantic breathing of the four teammates.

CHAPTER 20
INSTINCTS

Everly opened her eyes and tried to shake away the pounding in her head. There was a sharp ringing in her ears, and the only visible lights were the blinking buttons to her right and the circular ones which framed the entry door to the Time Bender. In the darkness, she felt for the alternate power generator with trembling fingers, knowing that every moment was important. Her fingers found and flipped the familiar switch, and the porthole lights inside the machine powered on, dimly at first, before growing in intensity. As her eyes adjusted to the light, she unfastened her leather harnessing.

"Is everyone okay?" Her voice shook.

To her right, Valerie rubbed her head with one hand and gave Everly a silent thumbs up with the other. Everly turned her eyes to the seat directly in front of her, where Finn struggled with his harness as he attempted to wriggle out of it.

There was movement and noise coming from Edison's seat. Lots of it. Their teammate was rocking back and forth, wildly jerking against his leather restraints. His breath came in rapid gasps, as if he had just been held underwater and was only now being allowed to breathe.

In a flash, Finn and Valerie were both kneeling in front of him.

Finn looked to Valerie, one hand dragging itself helplessly through his hair. "Do we undo the restraints?"

Valerie's voice was calm and low, barely audible over Edison's manic breathing. "We have to ground him." By now SCRAP had popped out of his spot in the wall and was watching Edison convulse. He scuttled up to Edison's chair and began to click and beep with urgency as Edison continued his rocking.

"Ground him?" Finn looked to Valerie with a raised eyebrow. "I don't think taking away his TV privileges is going to help."

Everly watched Valerie unfasten Edison's buckles and straps, guide him out of his seat and lower him to the floor. She took both of his hands in hers and helped him press his palms to the floor of the Time Bender. Edison's violent convulsions diminished to a mild rocking.

Everly sank to her knees beside them. "What happened?"

"I think...I think it was the noise," Finn whispered. "He always uses earplugs when I play guitar in our dorm." He glanced at Everly and then down at his hands. "I can't believe I didn't see this coming."

"No." Valerie's reply was quick. She didn't take her eyes off Edison. "It was me who should've seen it coming. Edison," she ventured, "look around you. Tell me five things you can see."

Edison drew in a shuddering breath. "The porthole." His eyes flitted around erratically. "SCRAP. Finn's shoe..." his breathing became smoother and slower as he raised his gaze to the ceiling, "...a bunch of gears..." he dropped his stare back to Valerie, "...and you."

A smile spread over Valerie's face. "Good."

As Valerie asked Edison to identify four things he could feel, a sinking feeling sluiced through Everly as she looked at her pocket watch, which was set to count down the time they had before the *Titanic* would collide with an iceberg and seal their fates. They had already spent two minutes and thirty seconds on the ship, and they hadn't even left the Bender. She drew in a deep breath and expelled it slowly, feeling her heart begin to race. "We need to get moving."

Valerie's smile disappeared as she threw a look at Edison. "He...he can't go. At least not right away." She removed Edison's earpiece with a light touch and handed it to Everly. "We need to decrease the stimuli. Keep him calm." She rose to her feet and looked to Finn. "It's up to you and me now, Mallory."

Everly glanced at her pocket watch. "We have twenty-six minutes to get this done." She reached deep within herself for the calm she knew everyone expected. "We need to create a panic below so that people start to fill the lifeboats. Then get to your places—Valerie, your post is at the bow of the ship. Finn, yours is in the stern." Her eyes dropped to the floor, where Edison was listing three things he could hear to SCRAP at Valerie's behest.

Valerie threw a final look at Edison, nodded to Everly, and rose to her feet. She activated her pocket watch, and from her black wetsuit, a clean, white apron unfurled from nowhere and a starched, white collar materialized around her neck. Her sleeves formed into carefully pleated, black wool, cuffed in white linen. Beneath the apron, the modest black dress of a servant rippled out and floated down stiffly around her pointed, black boots.

Valerie took a look at her stewardess's outfit and rolled her eyes; no matter how many times she'd seen the costume during practice, she couldn't seem to get over how matronly it made her look. It was like putting a NASCAR driver into a mini-van.

Everly pressed a series of buttons on the panel to her left and the curved, glass door at the front of the Time Bender began to lift. With a few more button pushes the brass inner-door unfolded and a blast of cold air rushed into the machine.

Valerie activated the lamp function on her pocket watch, causing the screen of the device to emit a brilliant glow, filling the

Time Bender with soft, white light. She ducked out of the porthole and began to search for a way out of the cargo hold.

Finn glanced at Edison, who was still rocking mechanically but had at least gained control of his breathing. He turned to follow Valerie out of the cargo hold, but stopped at the sound of his name behind him.

He swiveled to face Everly, eyebrows raised.

"You're still in your wetsuit," she whispered. Finn's eyes dropped down to his body, still clad in black, practically painted-on holo-cloth, and fumbled for his pocket watch. He winced when it clattered to the floor and he bent down to retrieve it, floundering through the different functions until he found his presets for this challenge.

Hot with embarrassment, he rose to his feet and pressed the top screen of the pocket watch. A dark navy, wool suit enveloped him, covering a crisp, white shirt and a vest, studded with shiny brass buttons. A black bow tie spun around his neck as a peaked cap with a leather visor materialized on his head, the center of which featured a white embroidered star.

Everly nodded in approval and Finn scurried out of the porthole to join Valerie, his face still warm. The light from Valerie's illuminated pocket watch made the room look eerily similar to the videos of the sunken *Titanic*, which the team had watched in Professor Moskowitz's office during one of many research sessions. The smell of freshly cut pine permeated the dark room, which was filled with stacks of wooden crates, bundled together by thick rope netting. The names of the owners of this cargo were stamped diagonally on the crates in black ink. It was both bizarre and chilling to know that this cargo, along with so many of its owners, would never make it to their destinations.

By now, Valerie had located a white, metal door that led to the steerage decks. She beckoned to Finn behind her, and when she spoke, Finn heard her voice inside his earpiece in addition to hearing her in person.

"Command," she said, her voice quick and controlled, "I've located a way out and we are proceeding outside."

"Copy that," Everly's voice answered through their earpieces.

Valerie turned a long lever and pushed the door open cautiously, peering around the riveted frame into a corridor.

"We are at twenty-four minutes and thirty seconds." Everly's voice was even through their earpieces, but Finn thought he could detect a thread of fear in it. He and Valerie leapt through the open door and looked around wildly to establish where they might be. They were standing in a long, sterile hallway.

Finn braced a hand on the cold, white metal of the wall. "You seemed to know what you were doing. With Edison, I mean."

Valerie shrugged but wouldn't meet his eyes. "Practice." Before Finn could ask what she meant, she cuffed him in the shoulder. "Let's fill some lifeboats. Good luck, Jimi Hendrix." Then she was gone, disappearing around the corner, leaving Finn alone in the silent, white hallway.

But it wasn't *completely* silent; standing still, Finn could detect the distant sound of music. A fiddle—quick and lively. Where there was music, there would be people—people to warn. People to save.

He jogged down the hallway, tracing the sound to a set of white double doors. He peered through one of the circular windows, finding a sea of derby hats, berets, and newsboy caps. Men in suspenders, their clothing worn and threadbare, many with sleeves and pant legs rolled up and shirts slightly open. They sloshed beer into cups from a half-full pitcher. Cards were spread over a table, and in the corner a man sawed away at a fiddle while stomping his foot to the beat. Finn opened the door and stuck his head inside, but none of the men seemed to notice him over the music and the sound of their own drunken chatter.

The room was full of raucous laughter, cigarette smoke and merriment, and as the fiddler's bow flew over the strings, Finn's ears were assailed by more accents and languages than he could count. His articulator translated snippets of their conversations, but their words flowed so rapidly and with such excitement that the device skipped and garbled at times as it tried to keep up. Finn listened raptly as the men—an assortment of Swedes, Norwegians, Irishmen, and Italians—bantered about work, women, and what they hoped to do—the dreams they hoped to chase—when they reached America.

A smile blossomed on Finn's lips as he listened; an Italian, hands flying as he spoke, vowed to start his own bakery in New York City to sell handmade cannoli. An Irishman pined away for a daughter named Siobhan who would join him from County Cork next year. A Norwegian who had sold everything but the shirt on his back for a ticket aboard the "Unsinkable" *Titanic* had no real plan to speak of, but was thrilled at the prospect of new starts and bold adventures in the land of opportunity.

But Finn's smile wilted as a horrible realization beset him; even if he and his team managed to save the whole ship tonight, this room full of dreamers had undoubtedly been counted among the dead during the ship's real sinking in 1912, their bodies lost to the bottom of the ocean. There was no question about it—the highest number of casualties had been third class men.

Standing in the doorway, Finn watched their tipsy smiles, their tapping feet. They had no idea. No idea what was coming, and even less of an idea how expendable they were perceived to be.

One of Finn's hands held the door. The other curled into a fist at his side.

You're here to warn them.

So, do it.

He opened his mouth to shout—to tell these men to run for A deck like their hair was on fire—but he stopped when he heard a subtle but intensifying sound. Something rolling. His eyes fell to his feet as something lightly tapped the side of his shoe.

Finn crouched and picked up a marble with two fingers. He narrowed his eyes at it, then looked past it to see a small figure sitting on the ground at the end of the corridor outside one of the cabin doors. A child.

He let the door fall shut as he strode toward the child, a girl who couldn't have been more than six. Her hair was long and so blonde it was nearly white, and she wore a light blue pinafore and shoes that looked like they'd been handed down several times before they reached her. An assortment of marbles covered the ground in front of her.

"*Hej, herr,*" she murmured, not looking up from her playthings.

In his earpiece, Finn heard the translation: "Hello, sir."

He dropped to a knee in front of her. "Lose this?" He tried to disguise the shock and thrill he felt as he heard Swedish spill out of his mouth, setting the stray marble—a blue and green cat's eye—in front of the child with the others.

"*Tack,*" the child said.

Thank you.

She looked up at Finn with a pair of huge, innocent eyes. They were a startling green—the same shade in the cat's eye marble—and Finn felt his own eyes widen as he sucked in his breath.

"What are you doing out here so late?" He threw a look at the closed cabin door.

The girl's slim shoulders rose and fell in a shrug. When she spoke, Finn heard her twice—once out loud in Swedish: "*Jag kunde inte sova, så min mor skickade ut mig hit så jag skulle inte väcka barnet*"—and simultaneously in his earpiece: "I couldn't sleep, so my mother sent me out here so as not to wake the baby."

Finn smiled, but inside his stomach was churning, his heart hammering against his ribcage. "Hey, listen. I need you to do something important."

The child cocked her head. Blinked her pale eyelashes.

"Go inside. Get your mother and tell her to take you to A deck."

The girl furrowed her brow. Finn stood up and tried his best to adopt a stern expression, which wasn't easy. "Go on. Don't be slow about it."

The child warily stuffed her pockets full of marbles and smoothed her pinafore across her knees as she stood.

Finn wasn't sure why he asked the next question, but he did: "What's your name?"

"Ebba." The girl blinked her emerald eyes again, her pale lashes fanning against her porcelain skin. "Ebba Andersson." She pushed open the door to her cabin and closed it behind her, but not before producing a single marble—the green and blue cat's eye—from her pocket. She pried Finn's fingers open and placed it in his palm. *"Behåll det."*

Keep it.

As soon as the child was out of eyeshot, Finn's mind began to race, his breath coming quicker as he stared at the marble in his hand.

He had to save this ship and everyone on it—there was no question about that now.

That child had a family. She had a name.

Ebba.

Finn stowed the marble in his pocket beside his pocket watch. Mind spinning, his legs carried him down the hallway, a lump in his throat nearly blocking his breath as another thought gripped him—an awful one that he'd pushed away time and time again in the weeks prior as his team had prepared for this challenge: if the team had been passengers on the real *Titanic*, he himself would have died with certainty. Everly and Valerie would have been among the first to board a lifeboat—they were women, and affluent ones at that. Edison's fate would have been debatable—simply being a guy was a near death sentence that night, but at least Edison would have held the advantage of a first-class ticket. But

Finn? Finn would have been one of those third-class men, laughing, joking, dreaming to the fiddler's song, oblivious to what was to come, stuck in the bowels of the ship as it was claimed by the ocean. He wouldn't have stood a chance.

He rested his forehead against the metal wall, struggling to summon a sense of calm, only now realizing that as he'd been thinking these horrible thoughts, he'd been *walking*.

He'd gone up at least one flight of steps and now he had no idea where he was standing.

How much time had he wasted?

Where *was* he?

He barreled up the steps of a narrow staircase and emerged in another identical corridor. Panic began to set in. Everything looked the same. This wasn't how this was supposed to go; they had come up with a careful plan, but it was already falling apart.

He closed his eyes and tried to remember the path that had seemed so simple on the map during practice. Maybe he'd gone a level too high? Made a left when he was supposed to make a right? He pictured Everly on the other end of his communications channel, cool and composed in the Time Bender. He didn't want to tell her that he had managed to get lost so quickly, but when he glanced at his pocket watch, he sucked in his breath through his teeth: seventeen minutes left.

Dismally, he activated his communication channel.

"I'm lost."

"What?" Valerie shrieked through the earpiece.

"Relax, Finn." Everly's voice was calm. "We have time. Remember—the ship doesn't sink for a few hours. We can still do this."

Finn felt his nervous system begin to relax just a bit at her words, or perhaps it was only the sound of her—tranquil and unruffled, the antithesis of his inner voice.

"Look around you," she said. "What do you see?"

Finn spun around, eyes flitting about in search of something, anything, familiar.

"Slow down, Finn. Take a breath. We studied this. *You* studied this."

Finn forced the machinery of his mind to slow, trying to quiet the bubbling anger that he felt resurfacing within himself. He cursed under his breath; he'd gotten lost in the maze of white, steel hallways, so confusing and unforgiving in their similarities. And hadn't this been done by design? When the wealthy had designed this ship, they purposely stowed the third class away, making the route down to their quarters a complicated maze. Third-class children—children like Ebba—had drowned because they were patiently waiting for their turn to be saved by the lifeboats, which the wealthy had filled to half capacity during their early departure. Now he was here, trying to save them, and he couldn't even figure out where he was. Finn was just another third-class passenger, hopelessly lost.

Reduce the stimuli.

Finn shut his eyes, dropped to one knee and pressed his palms against the carpeted floor. He tried to envision the old photographs of the *Titanic* that he had spent so much time studying. When he had pored over those photographs late at night he had even seemed to smell them. Hear them. See them in color.

His eyes flew open.

He *could* smell something.

Food.

He closed his eyes again. There were sounds, too: the tink of silverware. Muffled voices. He shot to his feet, spun around and raced toward a set of open doors.

Warm, oak columns. Patterned, white ceilings. Acorn shaped lights. Finn recognized it all. He had imagined the sounds of families laughing while they enjoyed a meal in this long, open hall. Those families had gone to sleep hours ago, but the staff was still working at clearing away the china, preparing the room to serve the next round of hungry passengers in the morning.

"Everly, I know where I am," he panted. "I'm at the second-class dining room!"

"That's great, Finn." There was a smile in Everly's voice. "There's a staircase at the other end of the second-class dining hall. Take it down."

Finn sprinted through the dining hall, weaving his way past a sea of ornately carved swivel chairs and working his way around the piano at the center of the room. He shot through the double doors at the other end, throwing a nervous look at his pocket watch.

Fifteen minutes left.

He ran to the staircase but came to an abrupt halt. The feeling of diving deeper into this damn ship aggravated him. He glanced at the doors in front of him, which would lead to the deck outside.

He came to a dead halt as he remembered how the third-class passengers, mostly immigrants, were discouraged from joining the more affluent passengers on the upper decks for fear that they would spread disease. He remembered his horror when he had read about the *CS McKay-Bennet*, overwhelmed in their effort to recover bodies after the sinking, tossing the corpses of the lower-class passengers back into the freezing water to make room for those of the first- and second-class dead. They had determined which bodies were worthy enough to save by the clothing they wore and what they had in their pockets. Even in death, the poor were expendable.

Money made you different.

Suddenly, Finn was shaken by a thought. "Yeah," he murmured. "Money makes you different." He couldn't believe this hadn't occurred to him before. "Everly...I have a plan."

"We already *have* a plan," cut in Valerie sharply.

"Valerie, this is my call," said Everly. "Finn, we have thirteen minutes before this ship hits the iceberg and starts sinking. If we deviate now, it's dangerous."

"I can save them all, Everly." Breathless, Finn sprinted towards the deck at the back of the ship. "Just like we said."

"Finn," Everly's voice was soft in his earpiece, "remember what my grandfather said: these people are already gone. They died almost a century ago."

As he burst through the double doors, the colossal loading cranes, tucked away at the stern like sleeping giants, came into view.

"The professor also told us to trust our instincts," he said as he elbowed through a pair of passengers who were taking a late stroll. "I can save them all, Everly."

"They won't stop the ship just because you tell them to," Valerie fumed.

"No," Finn agreed as he shot up a set of stairs and the stern of the ship emerged into view. "But they *will* stop if someone goes overboard."

CHAPTER 21
OVERBOARD

The title of Command certainly felt ironic.

Everly was helpless from her position in the Time Bender as their carefully crafted plan spun out of control. She had worked to calm Edison, who seemed to be nearly back to normal, quietly communicating with SCRAP using his pocket watch, but now they had a new problem. A big one.

Everly didn't need Finn to elaborate—she knew what he was thinking: if he jumped overboard, the crew would stop the ship immediately, which would in turn change the ship's course.

She glanced down at her pocket watch. More than eleven minutes left. Any change in course at this point could theoretically save the ship, and there was enough time left that it might actually work.

Everly bit her lower lip. That conversation last night in the Wharton Gardens. The determined look in Finn's eyes as he talked about saving them all. How had she not seen this coming? Finn was so obsessed with saving the entire ship and everyone on it that he wasn't thinking about the water he was jumping into.

How cold was it again? Twenty-eight degrees Fahrenheit—below freezing. The water around the iceberg was actually colder than the iceberg itself. Everly's skin prickled at her next thought: even if Finn made it past the massive, churning propellers, the ship would never be able to get to him in time. Not in water that cold.

"Finn, stop!" She barely recognized her own voice for all the panic in it. "You're going to kill yourself!"

"Finn, don't do anything!" Valerie broke in. "I'm headed your way. Stop now!"

Would he listen?

Was it already too late?

A terrible moment ensued that seemed to stretch for hours as Everly held her breath, hearing nothing but soft static in her earpiece. It was only when Finn's voice broke the silence that she exhaled.

"I'm not jumping in. They would never stop the ship for me. Besides, I'm not suicidal."

Relief washed over Everly, but it was quickly replaced by confusion.

If Finn wasn't jumping, who *was* going overboard?

"Man overboard!" Finn was nearly out of breath, waving his arms above his head as he tried to get the attention of the deck stewards who were trying to keep warm from their lookout post on the *Titanic's* docking bridge. "Man overboard!"

As the deck stewards flashed each other looks of concern, Finn cupped his hands around his mouth and drew all the strength he could into his voice. "It's Madeleine Astor!"

At the sound of the name, the deck stewards' eyes flared. They leapt into action, nearly tripping over their own feet as they clambered down the stairs. The quartermaster seized the phone and screamed into it as the other deck steward sprinted to the back of the aft deck to search the black water for a sign of life.

Finn knew the names of many of the *Titanic's* passengers—particularly the most prominent—thanks to Valerie's flashcards. Colonel John Jacob "Jack" Astor was perhaps the most prominent. Finn could even see his face—a black and white picture tacked with Elmer's glue to one side of an index card. Astor was a businessman, real estate developer, investor, inventor, writer, and a lieutenant colonel in the Spanish-American War. In addition to all of these titles, he also happened to be the wealthiest man aboard the ship, and his eighteen-year-old wife, Madeleine, just happened to be five months pregnant. If there was one name that had the power to stop the greatest ship in the world, it was hers.

Standing aboard a vessel as massive as the *Titanic*, it was difficult to discern the ship's movement. In fact, Finn had read that when the ship fatally collided with the iceberg, many of the passengers had slept through it. Maybe he couldn't feel the *Titanic* stopping and changing course, but he knew it was happening. A ship this size took half a mile to come to a stop, but he knew it would be done anyway; even if a rescue was impossible, the consequences of *not* going through the motions of a rescue to save Madeleine Astor would be severe.

Finn looked at his pocket watch.

Ten minutes left.

Valerie had mentioned that the ship was going almost twenty-six miles an hour on the night she hit; that meant the iceberg was still about four and a half miles away, give or take a bit. Finn fought to keep from smiling. This would work. The ship would undoubtedly slow and change course. There would be no collision tonight, and every person aboard this ship—first, second, and third-class passengers, captain, and crew—would survive in this version of history.

Finn's eyes cut from side to side. If there was ever a time to slip away, this would be it. The deck stewards were gathered in a frantic cluster on the port side, and the rest of the crew was similarly preoccupied with the horrifying news of Madeleine Astor's tragic mishap.

He began a slow backward walk, but ran into something solid. He spun and stared into the wary eyes of a stocky deck officer.

"Are you the one who saw Mrs. Astor go over?" He spoke in a thick, Irish brogue, his breath a white cloud in front of him.

"Yes," said Finn stiffly. "She was walking her dog on the port side of the aft deck. She stopped to look at something in the water and slipped."

"Where did the dog go, lad?" The officer searched Finn's face.

Finn forced himself to make eye contact. "It ran off."

"Is this the one who saw her?" Another officer approached with a small crew of wild-eyed men.

"He's the one," the first officer confirmed. "Says she went over on the port side."

Three of the men peeled off and ran for the port side of the deck.

"What was she wearing?" asked the new officer through tight lips, his eyes as doubtful as the first's.

"She had a...coat. One with a fur shawl." Finn stood up a bit straighter as he remembered the pictures of her that he'd pored over during late study sessions.

He smiled inwardly. *Practice.*

The Irish officer issued a grim shake of the head. "A heavy coat would have taken in water. Even if she survived the fall and the cold, she'd be dragged to the depths." A pained expression crossed his face. "Has Mr. Astor been alerted yet?"

"He's in the first-class smoking room," answered the other officer. "We're getting him now, but it doesn't look good. No, very bad. Very bad indeed." He began to pace the deck, hands clasped behind his back.

A pit formed in Finn's stomach. He needed to get out of this area now, before any more questions were asked, but these officers weren't going anywhere, and a crowd of men in White Star uniforms were steadily trickling to the scene, followed by a growing number of passengers who were attracted by the activity.

It was then that Finn realized he was freezing. It looked like he was wearing a wool uniform, but in reality, he was still only in his wetsuit, and his body, which had been warmed at first by his sprint to save this ship, had now begun to shake in the cold night air, which only made him look more guilty. He again tried to back away into the crowd, but the Irish officer set his mouth and stepped toward him, his face a mask of suspicion.

"Finn," Everly said, "you have to get out of there."

I'm trying.

Out of the corner of his eye, he found Valerie in the crowd, barely recognizable in her stewardess' uniform, rubbing her own arms vigorously. She was pushed out of the way by a stern-looking man in a dark uniform. His hat bore the insignia of the master at arms of the ship.

Oh...shit.

"Where is this boy?" His eyes found Finn without assistance. "You say you saw Madeleine Astor go overboard?" His eyes were dubious, his moustache quivering. "Are you sure it was her?"

"It was her." Finn tried to keep a tremor of fear out of his voice. "I recognized her dog—an Airedale."

"Madeleine Astor is in her room," the master at arms growled, hands flying to his hips. "She was asleep until I pounded on the door and woke her up." He redirected his wrath towards the two deck officers. "You let this kid make fools of you? What is Madeleine *Astor* going to be doing up at this hour? In her delicate condition?"

The men looked to the ground in embarrassment, unwilling to challenge the livid master at arms.

"Well," the officer seized Finn's wrist, "if it was a ruckus you wanted, boy, you got your wish. Let's have a chat in my office."

Finn felt the bite of cold metal as a pair of handcuffs closed around his wrists.

CHAPTER 22
JAILBREAK

"What's happening?" Everly's knuckles were white as she gripped the hand rests of her seat in the Time Bender.

"Finn just got arrested," Valerie answered. "I'm following them now. We'd better start thinking up a plan."

"Just don't lose him. If we do, we'll have to search the entire ship and we don't have that kind of time." Fear's sharp teeth were beginning to nip at Everly, but she refused to let it be heard in her voice.

"Copy that."

Everly took a deep breath. The good news was that the ship should have hit the iceberg ten minutes ago, but it hadn't, meaning that Finn's risky, last-second move had worked.

For a moment, Everly had truly thought Finn was going to jump into the water to attempt to stop the ship, risking his life, and while she now knew Finn was safe from the icy waters of the Atlantic, they had yet another mess to clean up: getting him out of trouble and back to the Bender before their time was up.

Everly felt a bit sick as she imagined Finn being left behind in 1912 as she, Edison, and Valerie returned to the present. She would feel awful leaving Valerie or Edison behind, of course, but somehow the idea of leaving without Finn was different. She couldn't place why, but the image of his lopsided smile forced its way into her mind, and she imagined the feel of his rough fingertips on hers as he'd taken her hands in his in the garden last night.

Oh my God.

You're doing it again.

She pinched the bridge of her nose. She would have time to sort all of this out later. Right now, she needed a plan.

The master at arms had an office on the lowest deck towards the front of the ship. She knew from the schematics they had studied that the *Titanic* didn't have a brig, and therefore the master at arms' office would be the most likely place they would take a prisoner. But if they took Finn somewhere else, finding him would be like finding a needle in a haystack.

Breaking Finn out would be tricky as well; they would run the risk of being caught themselves, which would further compound the problem. Rescuing two—or three—would be much more difficult than one.

Valerie's voice came through her earpiece, disrupting her thoughts. "He's on E deck. They took him into the master at arms office."

"I figured they would." Okay. At least Finn was accounted for. Now what?

"I assume we're going to get him before we leave?" Valerie joked. "Do you want me to head back so we can form a plan?"

"Negative. Don't lose sight of that door. We can't risk losing track of where he is."

"Understood." Valerie sighed. "I'll just be here dusting things, I guess. Hurry up—passengers keep asking me for stuff and I'm running out of ways to blow them off."

Everly turned to Edison. "Edison, we need you. *Finn* needs you."

Edison looked back at her, expressionless, still crouching beside SCRAP on the floor of the Time Bender.

"We need to figure something out quickly and we don't have a lot of time." Everly felt a touch of anger flare up within her. Was he even listening? Or maybe he didn't understand the gravity of the situation. It was difficult to tell with Edison sometimes. Her frustration intensified as SCRAP rattled off a series of clicks and beeps and Edison redirected his attention to his pocket watch.

Everly was about to lose her temper when Edison stated, "SCRAP says he can burn through metal."

As the little robot lifted a finger in the air, the tip of the metal appendage popped back and a narrow, blue flame hissed out of it. The finger snapped back into place, and SCRAP beeped some more, faceplate glowing.

"That's useful." Everly felt the frustration drain out of her. This could work. "Edison, let's get you in costume. I need you to go out and find a service cart. There should be plenty of them around."

Edison nodded. Tapping his pocket watch screen, his wetsuit instantly turned into the uniform of a White Star Line steward. He darted out of the Time Bender toward the metal door out of the cargo hold.

"We have a plan," Everly said into her earpiece. "Finn, just hold on. Edison is bringing SCRAP. He can get us into the room and cut you free. We just need to get the master at arms out of there. Valerie, I'm sure you can think something up."

"I'll send him on a goose chase. Just hurry up."

Edison returned, pushing a service cart with a white table linen draped over it. SCRAP hopped out of the Time Bender and folded himself into the space below so that the table linen concealed him completely.

"The master at arms' office is on this same floor, thankfully," shouted Everly to Edison from the Time Bender. "Do you want to see the map one more time?"

"I have a photographic memory," said Edison matter-of-factly.

"Oh." Everly felt her eyes widen. "Well...good. Let's get going then."

"Excuse me, lass? My room could use a set of fresh sheets." Valerie turned to see a red-haired woman in a fawn-colored hobble skirt looking at her with expectation. She seemed frazzled, with the sleeves of her white, Edwardian blouse rolled to the elbows and a few wisps of red snaking out of her softly swirled pompadour.

"Do I look like a maid to you?" Valerie snapped, before dropping her gaze to her own cringey, black dress. She winced.

Oh. Yeah.

But the woman seemed scarcely to have heard Valerie. "I beg your pardon, but my Seamus is just a touch seasick." She offered an apologetic shrug as she continued in a thick, Irish accent. "Still getting used to all the water, I suppose. He's delicately made, I fear, with the weakest stomach of my four babes. I think perhaps the Good Lord—"

"Cool." Valerie cut her off mid-sentence, staring beyond her down the corridor in search of Edison. Where the hell was he? "We'll be right on that, ma'am. You, uh, have a White Star Line day, now." She froze, registering the look of wariness on the woman's face before forcing a smile to her own.

The accent. She'd forgotten to use her articulator.

Seamus' mother gave Valerie another weird look before she disappeared down the hall to await fresh sheets and tend to her "delicately made" son.

Valerie passed a hand over her face. She looked the part, but needed to sound like it, too.

"Hurry the hell up, Edison, I'm not exactly maid-material, here."

It was true; back home, she *had* a maid. Two of them, actually...

She watched the iron door to the master at arms' office, leg jiggling nervously within the confines of her ugly-as-hell servant's dress. Through her earpiece, she could hear Finn being interrogated inside. He was saying precious little—it was his captors who were doing most of the talking—and that was probably a good thing. But it was only a matter of time before he accidentally referenced some stupid song lyric from an obscure 90s band.

Still, Valerie was impressed by his ability to think under pressure. He'd thrown up a Hail Mary with this whole "Madeleine Astor overboard" thing. It was risky, impulsive, and maybe a little stupid, but a score was a score.

Someone rounded the corner. Peaked cap. Navy slacks. Crisp, white shirt. Service cart draped with a tablecloth.

Another White Star Line crew member.

Greeeat.

Hopefully they'd pass quickly and move on to serve some snob their tea and crumpets or whatever was hiding under that tablecloth.

But what if they stopped, tried to make small-talk, and recognized her as not being one of their own? Or what if they didn't, and instead decided she was being a bad maid and had her written up for slacking?

She began to turn to face the wall—the less they saw of her the better—but stopped as the deck steward drew closer. This crew member looked oddly familiar: in addition to his service cart, he had thick, square glasses and a blank stare.

Valerie exhaled.

Finally.

As Edison approached, a series of clicks and beeps sounded from beneath the tablecloth, and a few spots of light pulsed beneath the white linen.

Edison's lips lifted into something close to a smile. "SCRAP says—"

"Shut up!" Valerie hissed. "Here's the plan. I'm going to tell the master at arms that there's a fight down the hall. You push the cart to his office and that little piece of junk can use his magic finger to free Finn."

Edison looked at Valerie blankly.

"Do you understand, Edison? We don't have time to play around!"

"If by 'piece of junk' you mean my best friend, SCRAP, then yes, I understand." Edison pushed his glasses up further on the bridge of his nose and crossed his arms.

Valerie rolled her eyes and marched to the door of the office, issuing a series of quick raps to it with her knuckles. The master at arms threw the door open, eyebrow raised.

Valerie froze again; she'd forgotten to use her articulator a second time, and now it was too late. She'd have to improvise.

"There's a fight in the third-class dining room!" she blurted in a horrific imitation of an English accent. It had sounded so much better in her head.

The man narrowed his eyes. "Why wasn't I called?"

"Blimey!" Valerie threw up her hands. "The phones are down and things are getting rowdy over there, you...wanker!"

The master at arms opened his mouth to say something, but thought better of it and stepped out of the room, locking the door behind him. He cast Valerie another wary glance over his shoulder, moustache drooping as he scowled past Edison, who was pushing his dining cart in the opposite direction.

"You called him a...*wanker*?" Everly's smile could be heard in her voice over the earpiece. "Why didn't you just use the articulator?"

"I forgot!" whispered Valerie. "It worked, didn't it?"

SCRAP popped out from the dining cloth below and scolded Valerie in his robotic language.

"Hurry up before I toss your bollocks overboard!" Valerie said in her horrible accent.

SCRAP shook his head and lifted his finger, bringing a blue flame to the door handle. Sparks began to shower onto the carpet, and within a minute the door swung open.

"Not bad," Valerie muttered under her breath as she entered the office.

Finn was stationed in a chair, his arms handcuffed behind him. He half-smiled under the visor of his White Star Line cap. "About time."

"Finn, I *will* leave you here."

SCRAP cut through the handcuff chain in another shower of sparks as Valerie cracked the door open and peered around the frame to ensure they were in the clear. She nodded to Finn, who followed her out of the office into the hallway. They walked briskly, yet attempted to feign nonchalance as Edison began pushing his service tray out the door. He was halfway into the hall when Valerie came to an abrupt stop and Finn crashed into her back. The master at arms stood in front of them, face contorted with anger.

"You there!" He charged forward.

Edison pulled the door to the office closed, hiding himself and SCRAP inside as Valerie and Finn cut around the master at arms, who fruitlessly tried to grasp Valerie's dress as she darted down the white, steel hallway. The man's face registered an expression of confusion as the holo-cloth's projection passed through his fingertips, giving Finn and Valerie a few extra seconds of lead time.

They barreled to the left, finding themselves in a gymnasium-like room with high, white walls and a railing above that was, thankfully, deserted at this late hour. Finn and Valerie skittered across the squeaky, wooden floor, frantic footsteps sounding behind them. As the footsteps grew louder and closer, Valerie grabbed a racquet that lay discarded on the floor and hurled it in the direction of their pursuer. Not waiting to see the master at arms' reaction or if she had even hit her target, she high-tailed it out of the room.

She followed Finn past a swimming pool and careened into another hallway, which spit them out into an open room, tiled in a black and white, quilt-like pattern. Valerie breathlessly pointed upward at a staircase, flanked with oak newel posts and adorned with wrought iron. The two of them hurled themselves up the stairs, taking two at a time and nearly knocking each other over.

The staircase deposited Finn and Valerie in an open room with white pillars and plush, red carpeting. They dashed to the left, nearly toppling one of the many potted palms that dotted the room.

Finn pointed upward in excited silence to a sign that dangled above their heads: "D Deck Elevators." She could hear the soft thudding of footsteps catching up to them.

Think fast.

Valerie pulled Finn into one of the elevators, which was enclosed in a cage-like gate, watched over by a young man in a blue jacket and cap, not much older than Finn. A lift attendant. He fixed them with a curious look.

"E deck, please," Valerie panted. "*Now.*" The young lift attendant gave her a once over, scoffing as he took in her clothing.

"What're you doing? Use the service hoist—this one is for passengers only." He sneered at Finn. "And what kind of man takes a lift, anyhow? Lifts are for ladies."

Valerie fiddled with her pocket watch with impatient fingers. Her stewardess' uniform transformed, leaving her in a simple, white Edwardian dress, her hair still arranged in an up-do, but without the servant's cap. The lift attendant's jaw went slack as he backed away in shock.

"Okay, I'm a passenger now. Happy?" Wasting no time, Valerie seized Finn's pocket watch and scrolled through the presets. In a flash, Finn was wearing a dark, A-line skirt, a white blouse, and a wide-brimmed hat.

He threw Valerie a look of pure indignance. "Come on. Seriously?"

"What? You're not the only one who can pull off a last-second audible, Mallory." She smirked. "Besides, it kind of works for you. The color of your skirt makes your eyes pop."

The stunned attendant cowered against the wall of the lift, and when the elevator stopped, Valerie and Finn filed out, walking casually down the hall, as quickly as they could without arousing suspicion. Valerie cast a quick look at Finn. The wide brim of his hat obscured his face, and he clasped his hands demurely in front of him as he walked.

Someone was waiting in the hall, eyes darting around: the master at arms. His gaze landed on Finn and Valerie for a moment, but it didn't rest there long, having seen nothing other than two second-class female passengers out for a late-night stroll.

As soon as they were out of eyeshot, Valerie and Finn broke back into a run, sprinting through a hallway of engineer's quarters until they finally reached the staircase down to the cargo hold.

CHAPTER 23
WEAKNESS

Now that his granddaughter and her team had successfully made it back to the present, Professor Moskowitz could finally breathe. He had watched their success on a projector screen from the safety of the observation room at the Historians' Society Headquarters, white-knuckling the armrests of his chair in rapt silence. He'd even waved away the refreshments offered to him by Historians' Society butlers, ignoring his complaining stomach, unable to look away.

Being given the *Titanic* as their first challenge was an honor that was not lost on him, but the professor knew that the timekeepers would not be happy with the results. They would never show it, of course, but Finn's uncomplicated and obvious solution would seem so simple in retrospect that the timekeepers might even feel embarrassed by how easy the challenge had proven to be for the team. Their only saving grace was that Finn had come up with the solution on the fly which had allowed for some enjoyable drama for the crowd.

The team had been smart enough to avoid going for Captain Smith. They must have assumed that the solution could not be that easy. The irony, of course, is that they managed to find one that was even easier. Whatever the next challenge would be, Professor Moskowitz was sure that it would not be this easy twice.

At the close of each challenge, teams were taken to the medical bay, where they were observed and scanned to ensure that they were in good health and not reintroducing some long extinct disease before they were ushered into the customary post-challenge interview. In a competition like Marbles, where numbers would determine the winner, this interview was more of a formality; there were some challenges, however, where the winners were more subjective, and in these cases, the interview was everything.

Now, the crowd eagerly awaited the announcement of which timekeepers would be tasked with interviewing which teams this season. The professor looked up as the observation room quieted, and traced the onlookers' gazes to the open double doors, where Timekeeper Garridan stood, hat in hand.

"For Vale Academy: Timekeeper Maverick Doherty."

The room erupted into polite applause as Timekeeper Doherty rose from his seat and took a bow before swiping his top hat off the table and disappearing out the double doors.

"For Wilmington Prep: myself!"

The crowd applauded again, some of the onlookers punctuating their clapping with laughter, and Professor Moskowitz smiled, hands in his lap, awaiting his team's name.

"For Halls of Ivy Prep: Timekeeper Keenan Wakefield!" Timekeeper Wakefield's abundant cheeks bunched up beneath his brass goggles as he smiled. He strode through the crowd and out the door, ushered out by more light applause.

"And finally, for this season's first winners, Wharton Academy: Timekeeper Philomena Vandecraft!"

A hush fell over the crowd, followed by a swell of whispers. It wasn't until Timekeeper Vandecraft stood that the room erupted, producing the amount of ear-splitting noise that one would expect from a football stadium.

As Vandecraft glided across the room and past the Grand Timekeeper, Professor Moskowitz felt his stomach drop, though he couldn't quite place why. He brought his hands together in polite applause, the smile still frozen on his face.

Finn, Everly, Valerie and Edison found themselves ushered into a clean, white room. The room had four hospital beds with dividers on three sides of each. There was an assortment of strange machines on stainless steel carts at each station, which were crammed with pulsing dials and flashing indicator lights. Some of the machines were connected to small, vintage television screens, which teemed with bewildering data.

As Finn sat down on the edge of a bed, a gaggle of strangely dressed doctors flooded into the room, three of which approached him. Without speaking a word, they began their frantic work. One doctor pulled Finn's arm out and attached a strap around it. Another waved a strange metal rod in front of him, listening intently to a pair of headphones as he did so. The last doctor shined a light into Finn's eyes with an unusual device which omitted a soft blue glow. The doctor wore a pair of glasses with multiple lenses, which he switched between carefully as he shined the light from one eye to the next.

All at once, the doctors left as quickly and quietly as they had arrived. Finn looked across the room and raised his eyebrows at Valerie, who looked just as unsettled by the exchange as he was. He wasn't sure if he was supposed to keep sitting on the edge of the hospital bed or not. His head pounded from the stress of the day, and he rubbed his temples, hoping to quiet it.

The door opened once more and a woman strode in, the sound of her boots clipping against the floor announcing her arrival before she even stood in the doorframe. Finn recognized her as the Historians' Society's only female timekeeper—the one who had looked at the teams with the most scrutiny during the Summit of Selection. She breezed past the medical stations without a word, and Finn looked across the room to Valerie again, who shrugged. Together, they edged off their beds and peeked in the direction that the timekeeper had gone.

A long, metal table was situated at the end of the room with four chairs on one side, opposite a single chair on the other. The timekeeper took that seat and waited.

Her black dress sported a high collar and considerable pads in the shoulders. It featured a row of polished, brass buttons, which ran from the bottom of the dress in a sweeping arc all the way to the opposite shoulder, making it look almost as if she was wearing a diagonal sash or a bandolier. The dress had a military quality to it, which was amplified by her disciplined posture. Her hair was pulled up into a tight bun and disappeared under a cloche hat, which supported a dark pair of brass goggles. Even from here, Finn could see that the timekeeper had the same flawless skin that Garridan had, smooth to the point of impossibility, and the same, bizarre, white hair.

Everly and Edison joined Finn and Valerie and the four of them took their seats across the table from the white-haired woman in the cloche hat. She threw them a smile, but something about it was off-putting; it seemed forced—condescending—the kind of smile that adults offer children out of obligation rather than authenticity.

"So, let's begin." She folded a pair of lineless hands in front of her on the table. "My name is Timekeeper Philomena Vandecraft. A short inquiry is customary following a competition of the Trials. I ask only that you be honest and thorough with your answers." She angled her head to the side. "I...*we* were all very impressed with your handling of this challenge. Your solution to the problem was elegant in its simplicity. I don't believe I can recall such a creative approach in recent memory." Vandecraft's grey eyes darted between each of their faces. "Whose idea was it?"

The teammates stared at Finn, as if waiting for him to take credit for his plan, but he avoided their eyes. He resisted the urge to scoot his chair backward, knowing it would only call more attention to him.

"It was Finn's idea." Everly said it readily. "He saved the ship."

Finn looked at her for a moment and then back at the tabletop. He was uncomfortable with the attention, but he would have been lying if he said he didn't like the admiration he heard in Everly's voice.

"Is that so?" Timekeeper Vandecraft's voice softened as one eyebrow crept upwards. "Finn Mallory doesn't seem to want to take credit for such an exquisite plan."

Finn looked up at her, feeling the heat of her gaze as she bore into him with intense, gray eyes. He was going to have to say *some*thing.

"It was a team effort," he muttered, wiping his palms on the thighs of his skin-tight wetsuit, which was by now long deactivated.

"Oh, come now." The timekeeper's lips lifted in a slight smile. "There is no need to be coy. Claiming that the wealthiest woman aboard the ship had gone overboard was clearly not the original plan. You looked very confused at one point." She tilted her head to one side. "I'm curious, Finn Mallory; your team seems willing to give you the credit. I wonder why you refuse to let them."

Finn's cheeks caught fire.

"He's humble," Valerie interjected on his behalf, giving him the barest of jabs to the ribs with her elbow. "We try not to 'take credit' on this team."

Everly nodded her assent while Edison tracked the exchange in silence.

The timekeeper didn't acknowledge that Valerie had even spoken. "You felt a need to save them." She kept her unblinking eyes locked on Finn. "Didn't you, Finn Mallory." It was a statement, not a question.

Finn dropped his gaze back to the steel tabletop, but the timekeeper seemed to be able to read his eyes without seeing them. "That is very interesting." Out of the corners of his eyes, Finn could see Edison begin to rock in his chair, almost imperceptibly.

"He trusted his instincts," Everly chimed in, seeming to sense Finn's discomfort.

"He did." Finn looked up to find the Timekeeper's eyes settled on Everly, who seemed determined not to look away. It looked as if the two were in a staring contest of sorts. "I wonder, Everly Caldwell—do you consider compassion to be a strength or a weakness in a game like this?"

A bit of hesitation read on Everly's face before she lifted her chin and replied, "A strength."

"Truly?" The timekeeper issued a soft laugh—it was girlish. Coquettish, even. "So, you believe that Finn's call was the right one?"

"He saved the entire ship." Everly set her mouth.

"The ends justify the means in your eyes, then."

"Not always," admitted Everly, with a hint of contention, "but you asked if his compassion is a strength or a weakness. My answer is that it's a strength." She straightened her posture and looked directly at Finn. "Finn was the best of us today. He did something amazing and he did it *because* of his compassion. He cared about the people on that ship; whether it changes their story in the end or not, at least they got a happy ending today. They got that because of him."

Despite the bewildering awkwardness of this interview, Finn straightened in his chair, Everly's words filling him up with a warm sense of hubris.

Timekeeper Vandecraft tapped a finger against her forehead as she listened. "You obviously think quite highly of Finn Mallory, Everly Caldwell. The results certainly speak for themselves." She sat forward in her chair as Everly's face took on a slight flush.

The timekeeper's lead-gray eyes intensified under the lights overhead. "I wonder, do you think that he saved those people on the ship for the team—or for himself?"

Everly bit her lower lip and looked at her hands in her lap and the timekeeper took her silence as an opportunity to elaborate. "You see, Valerie Konrad said that you don't 'take credit' on this team, which I find admirable. And Everly Caldwell, you seem to believe that the ends justify the means, which is certainly the way that *this* game works. Nobody can deny that Finn's quick thinking has won the day for Wharton Academy. But if we are to be honest, I have always been more interested in the motivations above the results. Thus, Everly Caldwell, it is a simple question: Do you think that Finn Mallory was motivated by what was best for the team, or was he motivated to these heroics by his own sense of morality?" She blinked. "Was he selfish and lucky?"

That cozy sense of pride that had begun to bloom in Finn's chest dissipated as quickly as it had come. Was Finn lucky? Yes. But selfish?

Finn averted his eyes to the wall beyond Vandecraft's head.

Was he? Why *had* he taken those risks?

For the first time, Timekeeper Vandecraft settled her sights upon Edison, who had been silent throughout the entire exchange, but her eyes didn't rest upon him for long. She cast them back to Everly, seemingly disconcerted by Edison's blank, unwavering stare.

As Everly stared at the tabletop in silence, the Timekeeper smiled and rose slowly from her seat. "Thank you for a most amusing evening." She reached up and readjusted her cloche hat. "I truly look forward to watching Wharton in the future."

After issuing a deep bow, she left the way she had come, high boots echoing softly as she strode away.

CHAPTER 24
STRENGTH

Finn and Edison climbed the steps to Raine Manor, the most extravagant of Wharton's female dormitories. Like most of the buildings at Wharton Academy, the exterior had a medieval magnificence to it. Ivy worked its way up the stone walls, giving the building a seasoned appeal, and the large, bay windows cast a warm light into the quickly darkening evening.

Raine Manor was almost as exclusive as Wharton itself. The only reason that Finn and Edison found themselves there was because Everly and Valerie had invited them to celebrate their victory in the last challenge. Everly had passed Finn a note in history class that read, "*Victory party at our place, 8:00. Bring your wetsuits and pocket watches. DON'T BRING SCRAP.*" It had taken Finn a full hour to convince Edison to go after reading that last part.

The heavy front door creaked open and a stern face peered out. A full head taller than the boys, a large woman stared at Finn and

Edison with cold, unblinking eyes. Her blonde hair was tied back into a severe bun. She wore a black dress and a flinty expression.

"It's late." Her voice was gruff and heavily accented. German, Finn guessed.

"We are not 'late,'" corrected Edison, staring up into her eyes through his glasses. "We are on time. The note said 8:00. It's 8:00."

"Sorry," murmured Finn, his hand running itself over his face. "We're here for Everly Caldwell and Valerie Konrad. They invited us."

The woman stared at the two of them, expressionless, for what felt like a long time before erupting into a fit of deep, rumbling laughter and slamming the door in their faces.

"That was rude," Edison said without inflection.

Finn heaved a sigh and stared down at the white toe cups of his shoes. "That was *predictable*."

The door swung open again. Begrudgingly, the giant woman waved them in.

Valerie stood behind her, arms crossed, eyes narrowed. "You'll have to excuse our house-mother, Greta." She spoke loudly, pronouncing the large woman's name with deliberate emphasis. "She's not the most gracious of hosts."

The massive woman shrugged and lumbered into the room nearest to the front door.

Finn waited for her to disappear. "You said she's your...house-mother?"

"Yep." Valerie watched the door to Greta's room close. "Not all the perks of living in Raine Manor are good, Finn."

"Is she, like, a housekeeper or something?"

Valerie scoffed. "No, although we have plenty of those, too. Greta's primary job is to protect our virtue. Let's just say she likes you guys. She would have been much more aggressive if you were, say, Liam Fillery."

Finn arched an eyebrow.

178

"Greta dragged him back to Kingsley Tower by the scruff of the neck the last time he tried to sneak in here."

"I think I like Greta now," mumbled Finn, still staring at her door, the pleasant image of the huge woman punting Liam Fillery out the open door lingering in his mind.

"Well, this is home." Valerie made a sweeping gesture with her arm. Everything about Raine Manor was extravagant. The foyer housed a grand piano, which sat to the left of a dramatic, curved staircase. The polished, white marble floor was inlaid with a beautiful, quartz compass rose.

Valerie led them up a grand staircase, which curved to either side and bent around as it climbed to the second level of Raine Manor. When they reached the top, Valerie jerked her thumb at the nearest ornately carved door. "This is us."

The door opened into a colossal main room. While Finn and Edison shared their modestly-sized quarters, Everly and Valerie had their own master suites, which were joined by a spacious living room. The room was warmed by a stone fireplace, framed by a pair of tall, sandalwood bookshelves. These were crowned by a pair of domed windows, both blue as they absorbed the last light of the dying twilight outside. A crystal chandelier hung from one of the thick rafters, twinkling magically above two velvet fainting couches and a plush, Oriental rug.

Valerie pointed left. "That's Everly," then right, "and this is me."

"Did Valerie give you the tour?" Everly emerged from her room, and Finn felt like he'd had the wind knocked out of him, the way he always did in her presence.

Valerie threw her a knowing look. "We had a Greta incident."

"Yeah," Everly laughed softly into her hand. "Greta is...formidable. You'd think this was a nunnery."

As Finn and Edison followed her through the arched doorway to her room, Finn realized that all of Raine Manor smelled like a mix of vanilla and something floral; this room was that combined with Everly's signature smell—apple and Ivory.

Everly's room was surprisingly simple. Her canopy bed had a dark green chenille throw casually draped at the end, and a few pictures were displayed on shelves. Finn recognized the faces in the photographs as the same people who were prominently displayed around Wharton in various showcases. One picture featured a man laughing, his glossy, blonde hair combed back, while a woman with dark, cascading ringlets stared at him, raising a fierce, sarcastic eyebrow.

These, Finn decided, must be Everly's parents. Everly had inherited her father's looks, but her expressions were distinctly those of her mother. Another photo featured the same couple, slightly older, with a petite, blonde girl seated primly between them, staring at the camera with large green eyes.

Everly's room wasn't quite what Finn had expected, much like Everly herself. Most of the furniture in the room was unexpectedly plain. The entire room, in fact, was a pleasant disappointment, the one exception being the absolute royalty of her walk-in closet. Through its open door, Finn could see that it was packed with lines of designer dresses and rows of neatly-stacked shoe boxes.

Cork boards were mounted above a desk on one side of the room, loaded with images of the *Titanic* and an array of yellow Post-It notes scribbled with words and ideas.

To the left of the desk was a framed photograph of a weathered woman staring off camera.

"It's Dorothea Lange's *Migrant Mother*." Everly joined Finn in front of the image, her shoulder brushing his as she sidled up next to him. "Haunting, isn't it? It was taken during the Great Depression in Nipomo—a little town in California. The woman and her kids were living off frozen peas and some birds that the boys had killed with rocks."

"I wonder where the father is," Finn wondered aloud, before he realized he'd spoken.

"I guess he left when times got hard."

Finn searched for inspired words but came up short. "Well that...sucks."

Everly smiled. "It does." She directed her sharp, green eyes back to the photo. "Do you know what I see, though?"

"What?" asked Edison loudly, seeming to appear out of nowhere.

"I see strength." Everly's eyes were still fixed on the photo, her voice quiet. "Everyone loves this photograph because it captures the destitution of the Great Depression. It's powerful because she seems so powerless." She angled her head a degree. "But I never saw it like that. I always thought she looked sad, but strong. Resolute, somehow."

Finn stared at her thoughtful profile. He hadn't really had much time to think about what he'd told her in Wharton Gardens before their challenge until last night, when he'd lay awake in his bed, reaching for sleep. Spilling that secret had been like eating a rich meal—it felt good in the moment, but left you wishing you hadn't. Part of him felt like he'd overshared. Everly had a part of him now that no one else did. He wasn't sure why he'd chosen to make himself vulnerable that way—he never had before, even to the battery of counselors he'd been sent to during his stint in foster care. But in the moment, under Everly's green gaze and the light of the streetlamp, it had felt like it was safe to. In any case, Everly hadn't brought it up once, just as she'd mercifully refrained from talking about the incident on the lacrosse field.

Valerie popped her head around the doorframe. "So, are we going to celebrate this amazing victory, or what?"

The three teammates came out of Everly's room and settled in by the fireplace. Valerie had arranged some snacks on the coffee table, which Edison regarded with undisguised disdain. He opened his fanny pack, withdrawing a plastic bag stuffed with bananas chips.

Valerie aggressively bit into a carrot stick. "What was up with that timekeeper?"

"It was weird," Everly agreed, the firelight dancing over her hair. "It was more like an interrogation than an interview."

"She was probing us for weakness," stated Edison.

Finn watched him stuff another banana chip into his mouth. Was he right?

Timekeeper Vandecraft had spoken almost exclusively to Finn. Did that make *him* a weakness?

The image of the timekeeper's cold, grey eyes stuck on his mind like a leech on bare skin. "Maybe we should just forget about the Time Trials for tonight."

"Agreed." Valerie cast a mischievous look in Everly's direction. "We have an idea, but you have to change into your wetsuits."

"Just us?" Finn raised a defensive eyebrow.

Valerie grabbed a handful of her sweater, allowing it to distort as the hologram tried to account for her fingers. "We're already wearing ours."

When Finn and Edison returned from changing they were wearing the awkward wetsuits.

Everly fiddled with her pocket watch. "I'm not sure if you've seen what types of apps these things have, but there are some very cool features." She swiped around and located a musical note icon. "Valerie discovered this one." She gave Finn a playful nudge. "It plays period-appropriate music when you enter a time and place. You use your earpiece to activate it."

She activated her own earpiece, commanding, "Play 1940s." Finn's jaw went slack as big band orchestra began reverberating out of the coffee table. The sound quality was amazing, deep and rich. It felt like the band was right in front of them.

Valerie's shoulders rose and fell in a laid-back shrug. "We're calling it 'Time Tunes.'"

"Where do you think all this technology comes from?" Finn let the chain of Valerie's pocket watch pool in his palm as she offered it to him.

"It's been bothering me," admitted Everly, looking at each of her teammates' faces. "Why would the timekeepers make this contest so secret? Wouldn't a normal person want to broadcast it nationally? It seems like there would be a lot of money to be made off something like this."

"And have you noticed that we never have to charge these?" Finn spoke without looking up from Valerie's pocket watch as he scrolled through the musical choices, feeling a thrill course through him as he noticed it even included Nirvana.

"Let's not even mention SCRAP," added Valerie. "He's amazing, and he's one of the *old* models?" Seeing Edison perk up, she rolled her eyes at him.

Everly smiled and plucked her pocket watch from the top of the glass coffee table. "Anyway—we're supposed to be celebrating our big win."

"The official results haven't been released yet," reminded Finn, handing Valerie's pocket watch back to her.

"Oh, please," Valerie laughed. "We won and everyone knows it." She picked up a carrot stick and held it up with a triumphant hand. "To Finn, savior of the *RMS Titanic!*"

"Don't do that," murmured Finn, although he warmed slightly at the memory of Everly's glowing comments about him to Timekeeper Vandecraft.

Edison lifted a banana chip and Everly raised a brownie.

Finn offered a sarcastic smile. "Okay. We've celebrated. Now someone please explain why I'm wearing this wetsuit."

"Oh, yeah!" Valerie laughed, looking him and Edison over, both of whom had drawn their knees up to their chests. "Everly and I were playing around last night and we invented a game. We'll call it 'the wetsuit challenge.' We all sit around in our wetsuits and take turns pressing the 'random' button. Then we vote on who looks the best and do it again."

"What's the point of that?" asked Edison. "We don't actually win anything."

"You win *respect*, Edison. And respect can't be bought, it must be earned."

Everly giggled.

Edison considered this for a second and put his bag of banana chips down. "I would like respect."

"Alright, we're all playing then!" Valerie clapped her hands. The firelight danced over the silver shells of their pocket watches while 1940s big band music picked up the tempo in the background.

"Okay." Valerie was barely able to contain herself. "On three."

The teammates positioned their thumbs over their random buttons and looked at her with expectation.

"One...two...*three!*"

They pressed their thumbs down simultaneously and howled with laughter at the results.

CHAPTER 25
100 YEARS AWAY

Everly's designer pumps clicked sharply on the banquet hall floor as she entered, signaling her arrival. Janelle Burr, Amanda Ayers, and Lacy Locatelli looked up with attention as she approached and took her rightful place as queen at the head of their table.

"Almond milk latte. That's what you usually get—right, Everly?" Janelle's lips curled into an ingratiating smile as she slid a hot beverage across the table. Everly forced a restrained smile in return. "Thanks." She set her Coach handbag next to Janelle's identical one, which Janelle had purchased the very day after she had first seen Everly carrying hers.

Imitation: the sincerest form of flattery.

Right?

Not at all obnoxious...

It had been weeks since Everly had been present at a meeting of the Social Committee of which she was the chair, and she was soon to find that her absence had not gone unnoticed.

"Where are you these days?" an ever-vocal Amanda challenged around a mouthful of chewing gum. It was strawberry-flavored this time. Everly could smell it. "We've had to plan, like, half of the Fall Fling menu without you."

"I've been busy." Everly avoided Amanda's gaze by turning the cardboard coffee cup sleeve around in her hands, absently ripping small tears in the edge of it. "With other stuff. The soup kitchen, homework...Young Historians..." she shrugged.

"Even when you *are* here, Everly, you're different. It's like you're a hundred miles away."

Try a hundred years away.

Everly cast a look of resentment at the color swatches and vendor catalogues that were splayed across the table. How could she focus on something so trivial? The last few weeks had been a blur of excitement. She'd been through so much that she barely felt like the same person. Her mind was awash with *Titanic* schematics, pocket watch sequences, and Time Bender protocols.

The unexpected image of Finn' lopsided smile, the laugh in his eyes as he looked at her over his shoulder before the launch, flashed into her mind. She flushed, nearly dropping her latte.

Amanda was still talking, her tongue rolling her wad of strawberry gum around in her heavily-lip glossed mouth.

"Everly. Can you even hear me?" She waved a hand in front of Everly's face.

Everly blinked. "Of course," she snapped. "You said something about wanting live music instead of a DJ. Right?" Janelle and Amanda exchanged a look of concern, and Lacy's face went into a full-on grimace as her eyes fell upon Everly's chipped nail polish.

Nick's entrance interrupted both Amanda's interrogation and Everly's flustered thoughts. He and Liam strutted into the banquet hall, taking long strides, carrying their lacrosse sticks over their shoulders. As the girls talked, Nick stared shamelessly toward their table. His eyes settled on Everly. When he winked, she purposely looked away, pretending not to have seen it.

Lacy released a long exhale and lowered her voice. "He's a total snack. Everly, if you don't go out with him already, I'm going to."

Everly rolled her eyes and drank deeply of her latte.

What Nick lacked in brains he made up for in boldness; he had been patiently waiting for Everly to go out with him for three years, with his most recent attempt at asking her out having been yesterday. The answer had always been no.

"It isn't like that between us." Everly's voice was cool, with a note of that patient impatience that teachers often use on students. "And anyway, I'm just too busy right now. Lacy, if you want him, he's yours."

"Everly..." Janelle leaned forward, glancing furtively from side to side, her voice a whisper. "...is this because of someone...else?"

She threw Everly a meaningful look, and Everly froze, feeling suddenly naked. "What do you mean, someone else?"

"You know, that *guy*. The *Unfortunate*." She paused. "Do you...like him?"

"Gross," Lacy breathed, only half-listening as she splayed her fingers out in front of herself to examine a glittery, hot-pink manicure.

Everly's face hardened, and when she spoke, each word was stamped out of cold steel. "You said it yourself: I've missed a few meetings and I have a lot to catch up on." She lifted her chin. "Do you think we could maybe skip the idle gossip and just get to it?" She seized one of the vendor catalogues and began to manically thumb through it.

The three girls were silent for a moment and then, flustered at having provoked the ire of their queen, returned their attention to table linens and seating arrangements.

CHAPTER 26
CHAMPAGNE IN A SOLO CUP

As Finn, Edison, and Valerie faced each other on the blue plastic seats of the subway, Finn and Valerie exchanged a smile, both of them glazing over as Edison provided a rather thorough history of the New York Subway system, along with data on average wait times and approximate number of riders per day, month, and year.

It was Saturday, and they were headed to meet Everly at the Sanctuary, a homeless shelter where she volunteered every other weekend. Besides that, today's jaunt to the city had a couple other purposes: to pick up Valerie's Fall Fling dress—specially ordered and tailored, and for Everly to discuss some "important details" about the dance with them. Getting away from Wharton for a day was a welcome reprieve from the extraordinary events of the recent weeks. Today they were not time travelers—they were simply four friends exploring the city on a weekend.

When Everly appeared on the sidewalk outside the soup kitchen, Finn did a double-take; he almost didn't recognize her. Usually dressed impeccably, like some sort of teenage first lady,

Everly never quite looked casual, but today was different. She looked almost like a regular person, wearing a simple pair of jeans rolled at the ankles, a white t-shirt, and black canvas flats.

Finn tilted his head as he looked at her; her simple attire combined with her exceptional beauty—especially here, in this slightly seedy area of town—had a certain dissonance to it, like serving an expensive champagne in a red Solo cup, or caviar on a paper plate.

"Earth to Finn!" Valerie's assertive voice shook him back to reality. "You're hungry, right? Edison said he wants pancakes. Let's get some."

Finn shifted the strap of his messenger bag higher up on his shoulder, pried his eyes from Everly's denim-clad legs, and grunted his assent, joining this ragtag team of Wharton students as they continued down the block.

"This'll work, right?" Valerie didn't wait for a reply as she pushed open the door of a diner. A flickering neon sign over the door announced that the place was called Roscoe's. Her three friends followed submissively.

The place was redolent of grease and coffee beans, and as Finn looked around at the jukebox and checkered linoleum, he suddenly felt ten years old. One of his mother's three jobs had been waitressing at the Coffee Pot, a diner quite like this one. On the weekdays she worked, Finn had come to the Coffee Pot after school to wait for her until the end of her shift. Her manager had been cool, letting Finn choose a couple free jukebox songs each time and allowing him do his homework in the booth that came to be known as his. Finn's mom had always brought him a complimentary bottomless hot chocolate and a basket of onion rings.

He smiled at the memory.

The team slid into a booth, upholstered in worn, red vinyl— Edison and Valerie on one side, and Finn and Everly on the other. A middle-aged waitress sashayed up to them to take their drink order.

"Hot chocolate, please," Finn requested, before adding a meaningful, "Thank you," taking care to make eye contact with the waitress. He remembered watching his mother deal with the rude customers, some of whom seemed to purposely complicate their orders with too many substitutions, others who seemed to delight in sending things back, and the gross old men who had tried to flirt with her, calling her honey, baby, or other disgusting variations. This waitress smiled, scribbled on her notepad and disappeared.

"So. About Fall Fling." Everly's voice was tentative as she looked at her friends from under lowered lashes. "I know." She sighed and bit her lower lip. "After everything we've been doing, talking about a dance seems sort of...pedestrian. But there are some particulars."

"What kind of particulars?" Valerie didn't look up from the plastic, ketchup-stained menu, which she looked down at with a curled upper lip. The waitress returned, plunked down their drinks on the tacky formica tabletop, and took the rest of their order.

"Well," Everly continued, "the Fall Fling isn't just a dance." She paused to take a careful sip of her latte. "I mean, there's definitely dancing, but that's not the whole point of it. It's supposed to be kind of a kick-off for the new school year—welcoming the new class, introducing clubs...stuff like that."

"You're taking your time, like your grandfather does," laughed Valerie. "Apple doesn't fall far from the tree, I guess."

Everly smiled nervously. "Well, first of all, we can't really formally introduce the Young Historians, like the rest of the clubs. I mean, it would be weird, right? What would we say we *do*?"

Edison nodded slowly. He'd dumped all the little multi-hued packets out of the melamine container on the table and was now reorganizing them by color—white cane sugar, pink Sweet 'n' Low, tan Sugar in the Raw, and green Stevia.

"Believe me, I'm fine with not having to go onstage," responded Finn. "But what if Headmaster Bruce says something? He definitely knows about the Young Historians. He was the first one to mention it to me when I started at Wharton. He just...doesn't know what it really is." He smiled wryly before taking a sip of his hot chocolate. "Obviously."

Edison looked up from his sugar packets and stared at him until Finn realized he had whipped cream on the tip of his nose and wiped it away.

Everly shrugged. "I guess if he says something, we can just claim it was an oversight. And since it isn't a sport, he probably won't even notice anyway."

The waitress returned yet again to their table to serve their food, and Edison immediately dove into his pancakes.

"But you're not exactly off the hook, Finn." Everly's green eyes settled on him. "I know you don't really love being the center of attention, but..."

Finn lowered the onion ring that had been halfway to his open mouth. "But what?"

"I sort of have to introduce you. It's my duty as Social Chair to introduce the annual recipient of the Good Fortunes scholarship. And this year, that's you."

Finn raised an eyebrow. "Fantastic."

Everly offered him a reassuring smile. "Don't worry. You don't have to say anything, and I'll be up there with you."

Finn sipped at his hot chocolate again. "Okay. Whatever. I'll do it." He said it casually, pretending that the idea of standing onstage in front of the entire Wharton student body didn't make him feel like throwing up or passing out. Everly smiled at him again, and Finn thought he saw just the hint of pink rise to her cheeks. But maybe that was just his imagination.

Meanwhile, Valerie shook with laughter into her cupped hands at Edison, who had completely wiped out his pancakes in the time it took them to have this short conversation and was now scraping syrup off the empty plate with the side of his fork.

"What?" Edison asked flatly, looking up.

"I think the only way Edison could have liked his pancakes more is if they'd been shaped like stegosauruses," Valerie managed through her laughter.

The check came and Finn reached for it, but so did Everly. "I'll get it," she said.

"No." Finn winced at the sound of his voice, which had come out much more sharply than he had intended, and Everly looked slightly stunned. "I mean, thanks, but no." He smiled. "I've got it."

Valerie, the architect of this little outing, had purposely planned the day so that she could pick up her designer dress last, not wanting to have to lug the garment bag through any other stops. Finn looked at his sporty friend, hair slicked back in a ponytail and wearing a pricey pair of athletic shoes, and tried to imagine her in a formal dress. It wasn't easy to picture.

Then he visualized his own closet, full of flannel, denim, and vintage t-shirts so thin you could almost poke a hole in the cotton by looking at it. What was *he* going to wear to this stupid dance? He forced the matter out of his head. No use worrying about it now. After paying for lunch, he had exactly $43.65 to his name.

"We'll be right back." Valerie and Edison made a strange pair as they disappeared into a designer boutique, the large windows of which boasted intimidatingly beautiful gowns that would have cost Finn's parents several months' rent.

Finn, made uneasy by the stream of obviously wealthy customers coming and going from the shop, opted to wait outside. He eased himself down to the ground to the right of the door, back pressed against the storefront, and pulled his Walkman out of his messenger bag. He waited for Everly to go inside, but instead she lowered herself next to him.

Finn froze. She was so *close* to him.

Onion rings. Great choice, genius.

But they'd been close before, sitting just like this in front of the gazebo. Closer, even, when he'd accidentally taken her hands in his during his earnest appeal to save everyone on the *Titanic*.

But today was somehow different; Everly seemed more human, more accessible. Maybe it was the jeans, or the change in setting. Or maybe it was the way she was looking at him. She looked almost...nervous.

Everly tucked a lock of her white-gold hair behind an ear. "Thanks."

Finn cocked his head. "For?"

Everly's shoulders rolled in a shrug. "For being willing to go onstage. I know it's not your thing."

Finn gave her shrug right back to her. "Not a big deal. You said it would be quick."

Everly issued a small nod as she nudged his foot with hers. "You found one." Her smile was knowing. Finn tracked her gaze to the outsole of his shoe.

~~Oysters, no~~ *pearls.*

He'd forgotten he'd done that—crossed out the first two words. But he hadn't forgotten when and why: he'd done it after the post-challenge interview, Everly's glowing comments filling him up and drowning out those of the lacrosse players who slung derisive remarks his way.

Finn was the best of us today.

He felt himself redden and he wanted to look away, but Everly's eyes caught his and seemed to snag on them.

Finn's throat jammed, and he swallowed hard to clear it. As he clamored for what else to say, a breeze kicked up, sending a bundle of dried leaves skittering down the sidewalk and the smell of Everly's hair into Finn's face. Everly visibly shivered, and Finn seized the opportunity.

"You're cold." Before Everly could answer, he whipped off his red flannel shirt, which he had been wearing open over a Sub Pop Records tee, and draped it around her shoulders. It was a surreal picture: Wharton Academy's queen enveloped in the shirt of the Unfortunate, sitting on a crowded city street. His arm lingered around her for an instant longer than it should have...and then he left it there. Finn was shocked at his own boldness, but Everly didn't object.

Now what?

"Do you, uh, like Soundgarden?"

Everly wrinkled her nose and cast him a mischievous look. "You mean, like, those windchimes in parks? Sure, I guess."

Finn could see all the gradients of color in her irises now—mostly jade green with a bit of sage mixed in, and a corona of amber right around the pupil that one could only see up this close.

He drew her closer to himself without thinking about it. "You need a music education, Caldwell."

With his free hand he produced his Walkman from his messenger bag, put on the headphones, and positioned one of the speakers toward her, the way he'd done in the Wharton gardens. He pressed play, and Chris Cornell began shrieking into their ears about a black hole sun.

Everly raised an eyebrow, unimpressed, her face about an inch from Finn's.

He threw her a lopsided smile. "I get it: not digging the Soundgarden. Alright, fine." He pressed stop and then fast forward. "I know you'll like this one." His finger came down on the play button, and the first notes of "Wonderwall" started.

A strange, dizzying moment ensued. Neither of them seemed to notice the distance between their faces growing smaller, but Finn instinctively closed his eyes. Their noses were all but touching and their mouths not much further when...

"The next train will arrive at 77th Street station in approximately ten minutes." Edison's monotone voice smashed through the moment like a runaway subway car.

When Finn opened his eyes, Everly had already pulled back, the hue of her face now matching the red flannel that was still draped around her shoulders.

Seriously?

Edison stood over them, completely oblivious, removing his glasses to shine the lenses on the hem of his shirt before restoring them to his face and squinting down at him. "If we leave now we'll have five minutes of walking time."

Edison's eyes darted from Finn to Everly and then back to Finn, giving him only that blank stare as he pushed his glasses up further on the bridge of his nose. "What?"

Valerie came out of the store then, a garment bag slung over her shoulder. "I swear, when I die, I'm going to be buried in this dress. They said it'll take a few more days for the matching wrap to come in, but—" Valerie's voice cut to a gasp at the sight of Finn's arm, still folded around Everly, and slowly panned to Edison.

"*God*, Edison—read the room."

Edison squinted in indignation. "This *isn't* a room, Valerie—it's a sidewalk."

CHAPTER 27
A GOOD LOOK

On Monday evening, Finn lay on top of the covers in his loft bed, listening to the last few chords of a Collective Soul song before the cassette switched to the next track. He'd spent most of Sunday in a bit of a fog—tripping over things and spacing out during conversations with Edison.

One of four things had happened on Saturday, and he couldn't figure out which:

1) He had nearly kissed Everly Caldwell. *Good.*

2) Everly Caldwell had nearly kissed him. *Better.*

3) He and Everly Caldwell hhad nearly kissed each other. *Best.*

4) Finn had somehow misinterpreted the entire situation, and nothing significant had happened on that crowded city sidewalk at all. *That would...suck.*

Finn preferred one of the first three scenarios.

The trip back to Wharton from the city had been...awkward. Only Edison prattled on about random trivia, completely unaware that anything of importance had unfolded, and that he himself had interrupted it. Finn had spent the trip trying to gauge Everly's feelings. Everly had stared out the window, giving him absolutely no indication of how she felt.

Nothing.

Finn's only assurance that anything had happened at all had been Valerie's knowing smirk.

This morning, Finn had walked to history class full of trepidation. He hadn't seen Everly on Sunday, and their last interaction had been an awkward bye, as they returned to campus before Valerie had rushed Everly back to Raine Manor. As Finn entered class, he tried to forget the way Everly's face had looked as it drew close to his. The way her green eyes had settled on his mouth, almost in invitation. The way his flannel had looked around her shoulders—unsuited to the polished girl wearing it, and yet somehow completely right. He drew himself to his full height, forcing himself to believe that he had imagined the entire near-kiss.

Just...act normal.

Everly was already in her seat, looking as composed and unflappable as ever. As Finn passed her, she studied him, as if assessing the status of things. Finn mustered a casual smile and she returned it. Whether anything had happened on that city street or not, both of them had clearly decided to proceed as if it hadn't—for now, at least.

Friday was the highly-anticipated Fall Fling, and Finn still hadn't decided what to wear.

"Maybe I should just show up in a flannel," he muttered, staring at his ceiling from his loft bed. He flicked a guitar pick upward with his thumb. It bounced off the ceiling and came down on his face. He swatted it irritably away.

Edison leaned against his chest of drawers below and stared impassively up at him, offering no reply.

"Imagine what Nick Dain and his goons are going to be wearing," Finn continued, his voice rife with cynicism. "Nick's clothes for this thing will probably cost as much as my entire wardrobe."

Edison adjusted his glasses, casting a glance at the open closet. "I'd guess more."

Finn sighed. He didn't own anything that came even close to acceptable for something of this magnitude. He'd have to use a school-issued voucher to buy something new, a thing which would deal a considerable blow to his sense of pride.

"Seriously," he muttered. "I wonder what would happen if I just don't show up." But even as he said it, he knew that wasn't an option. He could see Everly sitting next to him in the diner, her voice honeyed and reassuring. *"Don't worry...I'll be up there with you."*

Edison tilted his head, the light from the window reflecting off the lenses of his glasses. "You keep saying you have nothing to wear, but you have *everything*."

Finn scoffed. "Uh, yeah, everything off the discount racks."

Edison pointed. "No. I mean right there, next to you. You have an entire wardrobe at your fingertips."

Finn's eyes fell upon his pocket watch, sitting next to him on the bed, its silver chain pooled against the fabric of his bedspread. How had he not thought of this before?

"Edison," he murmured. "You're a genius."

His roommate looked at him blankly. "I know." He eased himself into his desk chair and began to leaf through a book about the early Cretaceous period.

Finn stared down at the pocket watch in his hand, its shiny shell, its elaborate moldings hiding the staggering technology that it contained inside. He vividly remembered the day he and his team had first received these; they had been overcome by the novelty of it all, caught up in the fun of playing such a high-tech game of dress-up. He pictured the 1930s suit—grey wool vest and overcoat, crisp white shirt, green tie. He remembered Everly's words as she had looked at him, as she had swirled around in a Victorian ball gown: *"Not bad, Finn. It's a good look on you."*

Finn smiled: problem solved.

Chapter 28
Tonight, Tonight

Finn knew that the Wharton Academy Fall Fling would be far more than a DJ and some crepe paper strung up in a gym. This highly anticipated dance was going to be, he gathered, more like a red-carpet event or the reception of a royal wedding.

He wasn't wrong.

The Wharton Academy ballroom looked like a cross between an opera house and Jay Gatsby's mansion, boasting a spiral staircase, a marble dance floor, and a large stage surrounded by an ornate, lit facade. Heavy, velvet curtains cloaked the stage. Art deco murals graced the walls and the ceiling had been painted to look like an iridescent night sky. The stars, painted in metallic silver and gold in the style of the silent-film era, immediately made Finn think of the music video for the Smashing Pumpkins' "Tonight, Tonight." Four wrought iron chandeliers hung moodily from the heavy wood beams in the ceiling.

This overwhelmingly beautiful venue had been carefully decorated from floor to ceiling. Metallic Chiavari chairs surrounded elegantly styled tables draped in silver table linens. Tall vases of amber roses and dark purple calla lilies rose from the center of each table, encircled by flickering votive candles. Place cards written with flawless calligraphy marked each student's spot atop fine china. Glittery fall leaves had been strung onto transparent wire and suspended from the ceiling, and garlands of leaves and flowers in autumnal colors adorned the chandeliers.

As Finn and Edison found the table at which they'd been placed with five other students, Finn noted the fluted glasses at each place setting and a startling number of forks. He smiled to himself, remembering the Feast of Yesterday and its excessive silverware. He hoped the food at this dance would be something more palatable than braised flamingo tongue. He walked the perimeter of the table before he sat, scanning the place cards for familiar names. None of them were recognizable except for the one that rested on the fancy china plate directly to his right: Everly Caldwell.

The corner of Finn's mouth lifted into a smile. As social chair, she'd made the seating chart. Maybe this night *wouldn't* be a total trash fire.

Most students had been seated with the other members of clubs they were in. Where was Valerie? Well, the sheer number of clubs, teams, and activities that she presided over as either captain or president meant she could be anywhere, sitting with anyone. Everly, he knew, was behind the scenes, making sure the Fall Fling went seamlessly.

His eyes roved around. Nick Dain and the rest of the lacrosse team stood near the hors d'oeuvres, seeming to keep watch over the room, showing particular interest in Finn's table. Nick looked like a poster boy for Armani as he quietly brooded, glancing at Everly's empty seat and place card, then at Finn, who met and held his gaze for a tense moment before they both averted their eyes. The lacrosse captain turned to his teammates and snickered with a derisive shake of the head.

Edison dragged his bespectacled, expressionless gaze between Finn and Nick. "Male peacocks have more vibrant feather displays than females in order to attract potential mates. They compete for a female's attention by vibrating their feathers and chasing away potential competitors."

Finn scoffed. "Yeah, well, *that* peacock's feathers are really expensive, so..."

Edison shrugged. "Yes, but your feathers are incomparably high-tech."

Finn threw Edison a wry smile. "Fair enough."

As the room began to fill with Wharton students, the chamber orchestra that had anchored itself to the right of the stage began to play. Some of the braver students began to filter over to the dance floor. It took Finn a moment to realize that they were playing a song he knew, because this version was slowed down and purely instrumental.

Wonderwall.

He smiled down at his hands. Everly must've been in charge of music, too.

As if on cue, Finn heard a soft voice behind his chair. "Finn."

Everly's hair was arranged in an elegant chignon. She wore a hunter green ball gown with subtle beading on the bodice. Its verdant hue played up her eyes and, in a moment of true serendipity, matched the tie that was part of his 1930s suit. As Finn stood to meet her, Everly gasped as she took in his wardrobe choice.

"Is that your...." she dropped her voice to a whisper, "...*wetsuit*?" Finn half-smiled and bowed his head. "Well, you'd said you liked it."

"You clean up pretty nicely, Finn Mallory."

Finn dragged his eyes up from the hem of her dress, which grazed a pair of silver heels. "You're not exactly ugly yourself, Everly Caldwell." He died a little on the inside at his awful attempt to be quippy.

Just tell her she's beautiful, moron.

But Everly's eyebrows lifted playfully and her smile persisted. For once, Finn started to forget that he was an Unfortunate; he was actually beginning to feel something that resembled comfortable. He'd been approaching this night with equal parts dread and cynicism, but maybe his worries had been unwarranted.

He surprised himself then, blurting in a sudden burst of confidence, "Do you want to dance?" Everly nodded, that smile that bordered on nervousness returning to her face—the same one Finn had seen on the city sidewalk.

Finn now realized that he had to actually touch Everly—on purpose and for a sustained period of time. This was suddenly terrifying. He had no idea where he was supposed to put his hands, and he didn't want to get too close to her for a host of reasons; the holo-cloth was thin and there was less separating them than it appeared. Yet he also didn't want to distance himself too much and appear aloof. He looked around him at the other dancing couples. All the guys in the room were gripping the hips or waist of their dance partner, while their female counterparts rested their hands around the back of their neck. Finn placed his hands around Everly's waist in imitation but maintained a distance between them.

As Everly moved, one of her expensive, silver high heels came down on Finn's foot. She stumbled and Finn caught her, his hands involuntarily finding her waist. The change in position put the two of them closer together. His arms were locked around her back now. He left them there.

Everly reddened. "Sorry."

Finn smiled, heart quickening. "Klutz."

It was then that he noticed Everly's necklace: a delicate silver chair adorned with a single pearl. She smiled as she watched him notice it, and he held her gaze, allowing his hands to encircle the small of her back and draw her closer.

The gap between them grew thinner until Everly was pressed against him, and with her face so close, Finn could feel her exhale softly onto his neck, her cheek resting against his shoulder. Her heartbeat pulsed through the satin of her dress and the scant fiber of his holo-cloth suit.

Everly and Finn never noticed when "Wonderwall" ended and the next song began, but Finn became very aware of the paparazzi-like cluster of students watching them from a distance. Nick lurked among them, clearly trying his best to pretend he wasn't watching.

Finn drew back from Everly. The eyes on him were accusing, as if Finn were shoplifting or trespassing. It pissed him off, but what made him even more angry was the sudden wave of shame that crashed over him, as if he were truly guilty—of having something he shouldn't have. Of being in a place he ought not be.

"What?" Everly searched his eyes.

"Sort of seems like you have an audience." Finn let his hands go limp and drop from her waist, and Everly tracked his gaze to Nick's scowl. "Pretty sure he likes you."

She wrinkled her nose, as if having smelled something repugnant. "Don't be gross, Finn. He has all the depth of a frisbee."

Finn suppressed a smile, relief replacing the shame and anger that had begun to creep up on him minutes before. His hands found her waist again and he pulled her back in.

"Hey." He spoke against her ear. "About last Saturday…"

Green eyes fixed on his, Everly nodded in expectation with the hint of a smile. Finn opened his mouth to speak, to finally acknowledge all the unsaid things that had hung between them for days, but Lacy Locatelli came in like a wrecking ball in a magenta ball gown. She seized Everly's arm with a bejeweled hand and tugged, as if to pull her out of the way of a speeding train. "Everly, come on."

Everly shook Lacy off, casting her an admonitory look out of the corner of her eyes. "Just a *minute*, Lacy."

"No." The captain of the dance team set her mouth and eyed Finn with unfiltered disgust. "Now. We need you backstage."

Everly heaved a begrudging sigh and released her arms from around Finn's neck. "Guess it's almost time for introductions."

Apprehension gnawed at Finn's stomach.

Introductions.

The warmth of Everly's arms around his neck had almost allowed him to forget all about those.

"Don't worry," Everly said. "It'll be quick, like I said, and you won't be up there alone." She squeezed his hand before she made her way through the crowd in a swish of green, casting a small smile over her shoulder at Finn as she went.

The music stopped as she approached the microphone. She took to the stage like an award-winning actress about to accept an Oscar, and the audience reacted accordingly. Like a queen addressing her adoring subjects, Everly greeted the students of Wharton Academy.

"We're so thrilled to welcome you to this year's Fall Fling. It's been a promising start to the new school year, and we're looking forward to introducing you to some of Wharton's finest. We hope you're as excited to hear about our clubs and programs as we are to tell you about them."

As the crowd of students erupted into applause, Everly was joined onstage by Janelle, Lacy, and Amanda. The worker bees surrounded their queen, attempting to absorb some of her star power.

Everly introduced the Drama Society, Debate Club, Young Astronomer's Guild, the sailing and rowing teams and the Dance Team. Each club president spoke about the group's purpose and criteria for joining. Valerie graced the stage with both the polo and tennis teams, clearly reveling in the attention in her designer dress—a classic, black ensemble that was as no-nonsense as the person wearing it.

The last and most highly anticipated sports team to be introduced was, of course, the lacrosse team. Nick strode onto the stage with the same cool indifference that Finn had seen him demonstrate on the practice field. His blue eyes sparkled under the stage lights, and the crowd went wild as he casually draped his arm around Everly's shoulders, as if to claim her.

Finn felt a knot forming in his stomach as all the confidence of earlier began to dissolve and the roar of Wharton Academy's student body filled his ears. Everly Caldwell and Nick Dain sharing the stage made sense. They fit. The two of them together assured order in the universe. It was the world as it should be.

Depth of a frisbee, Finn told himself, drawing his eyes away from the stage and toying with one of the small, silver forks to distract himself. But he still couldn't shake his insecurity as Nick and the lacrosse team received their final accolades and exited the stage.

The last group to be introduced was the Young Philanthropist's Club, another of Everly's extracurriculars. Everly was joined by the rest of the club onstage. Under the stage lights, she was radiant.

"The purpose of the Young Philanthropist's Club is to give back to the community in hands-on, concrete ways," Everly explained, her hand absently raising to touch the single pearl around her neck mid-speech. "As Young Philanthropists, we operate by the motto, 'Do what you can, with what you have, where you are.'"

Everly explained some of the activities the club had engaged in this year and how they hoped to proceed—the causes they would take up and the benefits they would host. A host of bake sales to raise money for youth development services. A dance-off, with the proceeds slated to be donated for cancer research. An auction to fund a second dining room at the Sanctuary.

The ballroom again burst into applause, and the other Young Philanthropists filed offstage. After the noise subsided, Finn could see Everly's eyes, sparkling like a pair of emeralds under the spotlights, searching the crowd.

"We have one final introduction tonight that I'm so honored to make," she began. "Will Finn Mallory, please join me onstage?"

Finn hesitated, fingers gripping the sides of his seat as her question—and his name—hung in the air as heavily as Lacy's perfume.

His introduction directly followed the Young Philanthropist's Club and it wasn't lost on him. How fitting, he thought bitterly, to introduce the school's charity case right on the heels of the club which specialized in good deeds.

I'm a cause.

He remembered that first train wreck of a conversation that he'd had with Everly in the banquet hall, and felt that familiar resentment building within him, but this time it was mingled with another feeling that he struggled to identify. Something like pain.

"Finn?" Everly spoke his name again, pulling him out of his thoughts. Reluctantly, he rose to his feet and trudged through the sea of gorgeously-decorated tables and appraising eyes. He forced his begrudging legs to climb the stage steps to join Everly beside the microphone, stomach lurching as he stared out at the crowd in front of him—a crowd which already felt they knew exactly who he was. A crowd which had no intention of accepting him.

"Joining us from nearby Tellerville, Finn Mallory is this year's recipient of our school's Good Fortunes Scholarship." Finn could barely register Everly's hand on his arm. "*We* are the fortunate ones to have Finn join our ranks. We know he has so much to offer our school and our community."

Finn felt the heat of the stage lights on his face and wished he could loosen his collar, but remembered he was wearing holo-cloth that would distort if he tried. He forced a weak smile, but inside he boiled. It was as if Everly was trying to sell the idea of him—to convince the room to accept him by endorsing him herself. A celebrity hawking a product.

"If you don't already know Finn, please give him a warm welcome," Everly finished, seemingly oblivious to his discomfort.

A warm welcome.

Finn's mind returned to his first day—the stares, the whispers, the way the other students had recoiled in their chairs as he passed them. His mind revisited the lacrosse field—the predatory faces peering down at him as he sat on his hands in the grass.

Too late.

A few weak claps sounded from the crowd as Finn left the stage. It was then that the snickering and whispers started. They began like a breeze and then intensified into a full-on gale.

"Unfortunate."

"Tellerville Trash."

Liam Fillery, leaning forward on his elbows at his table, cupped his hands around his mouth and shouted. "Nice suit, Welfare!" The throng of cretins surrounding him erupted into raucous laughter and slapped him on the back.

As Finn retreated down the stage steps leading down to the dance floor, he passed a well-dressed figure leaning against the muraled wall, half-obscured by the stage curtain.

"Everly always did have a soft spot for strays." Nick smirked and winked a blue eye. He brought a flask to his lips and then restored it to his inner vest pocket before Headmaster Bruce could see him.

Finn turned on his heel and went the opposite direction of the ballroom and the magnificent meal that was being served. As he passed through the curtains to the backstage area, he heard the buzz of student voices, and the chamber orchestra striking up a new song. He made for the backstage exit and threw open the door, the cold night air rushing into his face.

"Finn." Everly's voice was soft behind him. Finn stopped at the top of the back stairs and turned slowly.

He released a deep sigh and looked at the toes of his shoes. He'd hoped to slip away without incident. He couldn't talk to her right now. He didn't want to look at her, even; he was afraid of what he might say.

Yet Everly drew closer, studying his face in the dark.

"What is it?" Her hand moved toward his face as if to touch it, a gesture that would have been welcomed, even wanted, just an hour ago. But now he recoiled.

"What *is* it? Are you serious?" He raised his eyes, fighting in vain to keep the anger out of his voice. "Were you not on that stage just now?"

"I heard them." Everly looked down at the toes of her silver high-heels that poked out from under the hem of her dress. It felt like a lifetime ago that they had been dancing. That his arms had been around her waist, that he'd felt her heartbeat. He felt miles away from her now. "And I know it's—"

"I'm not *like* you, okay?"

Everly's eyes snapped up from her shoes.

"This doesn't...work."

"Finn, don't...do that." Everly blinked her green eyes in bafflement. "You're not making sense. Why do you always—"

"Why do I always *what*?" Finn registered that he was being cruel, that his anger was at least partially misplaced, but the pent-up steam of his anger propelled his words. "*I* don't make sense?" He heard himself scoff. "*This* doesn't make sense, Everly. You and me. I'm from Tellerville, okay?" He dragged out the word as if speaking to a small child. "Tellerville." His voice softened then. "*We* don't make sense."

He waited for her eyes to show that she knew he was right—for her chin to lift, for her mouth to set. He waited for her to turn to stone, like she'd done in the banquet hall the day they'd met—for her to throw him that searing look that she'd given to Liam, to Nick.

But he didn't find ire in Everly's eyes—instead he found rapidly pooling tears.

Goddammit.

Resisting the overwhelming urge to reach out to her, Finn turned and disappeared down the backstage steps toward Aion Hall.

It was better this way.

CHAPTER 29
I KNOW

Finn stormed into Aion Hall and shut the door with such force the frame rattled. His behavior, he knew, was the very definition of self-sabotage, and yet there was nothing he could do to fix it. Not this time. And what he'd said to Everly—about the two of them not making sense together—as much as it pained him, had been true.

He climbed into his loft and pulled his headphones over his ears, hoping the music would drown out his own bitter thoughts. He closed his eyes and pressed his palms over them.

When he opened them, he startled; Edison was there, sitting below his loft bed, quiet and still as he watched him. Finn took off his headphones and killed the music. He sat up, swung his legs over the edge of his bed, and faced his roommate.

He looked down at himself. He was still wearing his 1930s suit hologram. Would it be more awkward to leave it on, or deactivate it and talk to Edison in a black bodysuit? He opted to leave it on.

He looked at the window, too embarrassed to make eye contact. "Didn't hear you come in."

"I know," Edison said. "You were listening to your illegal contraband."

In the brief silence that followed, Edison continued to stare, and Finn ran his fingers through his hair, eyes on the ground. "How was the rest of the dance?"

"The music was unnecessarily loud. I did bring ear plugs, however. That made it tolerable." Edison cocked his head. "The food was passable."

Finn nodded and fell silent again, but when Edison didn't speak either, he found himself confessing. It was as if Edison's silence drew it out of him. "I ruined it. With Everly, I mean."

Edison's eyes fluttered in a rapid succession of blinks. "Yes. I think you probably did."

Finn felt himself become defensive. "What would *you* know about it?" He knew his anger was misplaced and unjustified but he kept at it anyway. "You don't know how lucky you are." He looked up from the floor. "You can just shut things out. We can't all be that lucky, Edison. Most of us know when we're being laughed at."

Edison looked up at Finn with the same vacant expression that he always had, and for some reason, this threw another log on the fire of Finn's frustration. Edison was Finn's roommate, and possibly the only friend he had left at this stuck-up school, and he couldn't even have a real conversation with him. All he would get was that stupid, blank look.

"Forget it." He rolled himself back into bed and faced the wall. As with every impulsive move that he made, he felt an instant regret well up inside of him. He was about to restore his headphones to his ears when the monotone of Edison's voice sounded from below.

"You think I don't know when people laugh at me." It was a statement, not a question. Finn continued to stare at the wall.

"I know," continued Edison. "I *always* know."

Finn rolled over to face him.

"I know when people laugh at me," Edison kept on, his body beginning to sway in place as he rubbed at his forearms. "I know that Nick Dain and his friends were laughing at me at the dance tonight, and I know that they laugh at me whenever we pass them on the lacrosse fields. People are always laughing at me. They do it because I have autism and they think I'm weird."

As Edison's swaying reduced and finally ceased altogether, Finn's anger melted away into shame. He opened his mouth to apologize, but Edison continued before he could get a word out.

"They call you 'Tellerville Trash' because you are from Tellerville and they think you are poor."

Finn managed a half-smile. "I *am* poor, Edison."

"You probably are," Edison nodded. "But Everly Caldwell likes you."

An avalanche of guilt and embarrassment covered Finn as the memory of Everly's rapidly filling eyes rushed to his memory. "I'm not sure if she likes me anymore, Edison, but thanks."

"She does."

Edison turned and began to order his things on his bedside table, ensuring that his comb was the same distance away from his hairbrush than from his glasses case, and Finn let out a deep exhale through his nose.

"Edison," he ran both hands over his face, "I'm sorry for what I said earlier."

"Don't worry, Finn Mallory." The corner of Edison's mouth lifted in the suggestion of a smile. "We are still friends."

CHAPTER 30
RED ROVER

Professor Moskowitz held the game assignment record from the Historians' Society in his hands, waiting for his team to arrive. Any challenge was fair game, with the exception of Marbles, which had already been selected.

The professor had tried not to enjoy their most recent victory too much, but it was difficult not to be proud of the way the students had performed. His granddaughter, unsurprisingly, had risen to the occasion and kept a cool head as Command. Edison, even after a rough start, had rallied and thought quickly on his feet. Valerie had not only been indispensable in helping Edison overcome his episode in the Time Bender, but had also been able to put her need for control aside long enough to allow for a change of plans that ultimately brought the team to victory. And Finn, who had perhaps been the biggest question mark of them all, had shown more confidence, leadership and pluck than the professor had thought possible. If the team continued to work together like this, there wasn't much they couldn't do.

Professor Moskowitz looked up at the sound of the door. Finn arrived to their meeting first. He was alone, looking sleep-deprived and agitated. The old teacher studied him in silence, immediately beset by curiosity and apprehension. Typically, the team arrived to meetings together, a lively unit full of chemistry and eagerness, and the last he'd seen them, they'd been high on their victory, all but bursting at the seams at having saved the *Titanic*. Professor Moskowitz had always been a bit surprised—touched, even—by how quickly this motley crew of students had bonded. Some of them perhaps would never have even spoken if not for the extraordinary experiences that this club allowed them to share. But, if the look on Finn's face was any indication, something was amiss today.

A few moments later, Valerie and Edison arrived together and took their seats. Edison, as usual, was more difficult to read than Egyptian hieroglyphics, but Valerie looked unusually subdued. Not tortured, like Finn, who had by now nearly curled in on himself in his chair, but preoccupied, her typical take-charge energy seeming to have been sapped.

Everly was last to arrive, deposited at the door by a smug-looking Nick Dain. The professor raised his eyebrows and looked away.

Really?

Him?

He didn't make a habit of judging his own students, but Nick Dain was truly a moron by any standard, albeit a well-dressed one. He'd wanted his granddaughter to let her hair down a bit and enjoy her youth, but he hadn't counted on this. There must be a reason for it; he didn't know Everly's type—old men are seldom privy to the romantic inclinations of their granddaughters—but he was willing to bet she wasn't attracted to absolute imbeciles, no matter how good-looking.

As Professor Moskowitz faced the chalkboard, Nick lingered in the doorway in a clear attempt to allow the occupants of the room to see him possessively enveloping Everly's shoulders with a muscular arm. The professor turned in time to see Everly make brief eye contact with Finn, who looked like he would disappear into the seat of his chair if he could, before looking away in a decidedly nonchalant fashion. As she breezed into the room and sat beside Edison, Finn dropped his chin to his chest and pressed his lips together. Valerie cast an almost pitying look at him before focusing her attention to the front of the room, and although Edison appeared oblivious to everything, the professor noticed that he didn't announce that Everly had been a minute late.

"Thank you for being so gallant as to escort my granddaughter to this meeting, Mr. Dain. But as this is a closed meeting it will require your departure to begin." The lacrosse captain flashed a final triumphant smile before retreating down the corridor, and the professor winced inwardly.

Finn and Everly were ground zero for whatever had gone awry on the team—he was sure of it. As a teacher of high school for close to forty years, he'd watched dozens of teenage romances catch fire and burn to a crisp before his very eyes, pretending not to notice as the drama played out in wordless suspense—the covert glances, the passed notes, the lingering gazes that indicated a blooming relationship, and the hard stares, awkward pauses, and sullen avoidance that betrayed a wilting one. So how had he missed this?

He lowered his gaze to the envelope that he clasped before him. Whatever teenage angst was unfolding behind the scenes, there was a challenge to reckon with. He pushed past the awkward vibe in the room and issued his usual, warm smile.

"The first game is always the hardest." He set the envelope on his desk, raised his hands, and brought them together in front of him. "Now you know what to expect. It's not uncommon for teams to freeze completely in the first mission and pull their chain before they even make the bend." He rose from his chair and stood directly before his team. "You handled yourselves wonderfully, and I want you to know that I am proud of what you were able to accomplish together."

The professor had put particular emphasis on that last word, and he hoped his positivity would coax some life out of the team, but it seemed to only work for one member.

"Did we win?" Valerie leaned forward in her seat.

"We did," the professor nodded. "It's always nice to win the first game. Takes some of the pressure off."

Valerie held a hand up to high five Edison, who stared at it until she shrugged and put it down.

"How did the other teams do?" Everly's voice was cool, and the professor noticed she took extra care to keep her eyes from drifting to her right, where Finn slouched, eyes fixed to the top of his desk.

"I thought all the teams performed quite well," answered the professor, pretending not to notice the telltale sign of a lover's quarrel. But when had these two even been...? He shook the thought away. "This game will not be handed to us, that's for sure." He rocked on his heels. "It seems the theme of this round of Marbles was historic ships. Vale Academy received the sister ship of our *Titanic*—the *Britannic*, which sunk in 1916."

"Remind me to never buy a steamer ticket from White Star Line," joked Valerie. She looked beside her to Finn, but her smile faded when he offered no response, instead to fiddling listlessly with a loose thread on his sweater vest.

"Well my dear, the *Britannic* was a cruise liner, but she was repurposed as a hospital ship to transport wounded soldiers during World War I." The professor moved to the turntable and began to pry open the seal to the envelope. "Thirty people lost their lives when she sank after hitting an underwater mine. Most of them actually died from releasing the lifeboats too early, which were sucked into the propellers. Vale Academy attempted to redirect the ship by reaching the captain, but they didn't make it in time."

Valerie nodded at Everly, clearly feeling validated about their tactical maneuver to avoid going after the captain at all costs, and Everly gave her a quick, distracted smile.

"The Halls of Ivy Prep was given the *RMS Republic*, and Wilmington was assigned the *Lusitania*. None of them had near your success rate, of course." The professor looked at the team intently. "You have won the first game, but that comes at a cost. You will be under closer scrutiny now and winners tend to be given more difficult assignments."

Edison pointed to the record in the professor's hand. "Is that our next challenge?"

"It is." The professor had been delaying this moment for as long as possible, afraid of what news that record might bring, but now he found himself eager for something to fill the awkward silence in the room beyond his own voice. Gratefully, he placed the record on the turntable.

"*Greetings, Wharton Academy, and welcome to the second game of the Time Trials! We are thankful that you were all returned safely to the present after the last game of Marbles, in which you impressed us greatly with your ability to improvise. As the winner of the first challenge, you are already making waves with the Historians' Society!*"

The professor smiled at his feet at the Grand Timekeeper's attempt at a joke; Dashiel always did enjoy being quippy.

"*Red Rover is a game of strategy on the playground, and it will be a game of strategy here in the Trials. On the playground, you must select your runners carefully, and if you are the one 'called over,' you must choose where you can best break through the enemy line.*

"*In the Time Trials, Red Rover is equally strategic. You have had a chance to meet the other teams during both the Summit of Selection and the Feast of Yesterday, and I hope you were paying attention; during a special ceremony, you will select one member of another team to participate in a four-person trial. The criteria by which you make the selection is up to you. The members of all teams who are not selected will join our society in the viewing room to watch the trial in good company."*

At this, the tense vibe in the room seemed momentarily forgotten. Finn raised his head to glance at Everly. They held each other's gaze for the fraction of a second before averting their eyes.

"I am pleased to announce that Wharton Academy will be selecting who will participate from the eminent Vale Academy. Choose wisely, as they will be, in turn, selecting one of you. After the selection ceremony is complete, the official game that our new team of four will engage in will be announced, and your team will have one hour to prepare before the game of Red Rover officially begins.

"As always, your safety should be of the utmost concern, and we wish you the very best of luck!"

Valerie's brow furrowed as the record crackled to a stop. "Let me get this straight: those snakes at Vale Academy get to pick one of us, we get to pick one of them, and the rest of us just have to *watch?*"

"That is correct." The professor nodded over his shoulder as he removed the record from the turntable. "It will be up to you to decide which team member you select from Vale, and to try to anticipate which of you will be chosen. This is no easy task."

When he turned, he found Finn staring across the room at his chalkboard, looking equal parts sad and irritated. Everly wore a cool expression as she coiled a lock of hair around her finger. Edison had begun to rock back and forth ever so slightly in his chair.

Yes, something was definitely amiss today.

"If I may..." The professor pulled his chrome spectacles lower on the bridge of his nose and regarded the team over their rim. "Red Rover will test an individual as never before. Trusting in oneself is just important as trusting the team." His eyes swept each of their faces. "I am proud of the way you have come together. You are family. Don't ever forget that."

Everly's chin dipped in a begrudging nod before she stood, her shoes against the floor sounding as annoyed as she looked when took her leave. Valerie followed, with Edison on her heels. As Finn peeled himself out of his chair, the professor halted him.

"Mr. Mallory, stay back a minute, if you will." The old man had no plan for what he would say, but looking at the way the boy's shoulders sagged, he simply knew he must say *something*.

Finn made a slow turn, looking as if it pained him. "Yeah?"

The professor crossed his arms and leaned back against his desk. "How was the dance?"

Finn shut his eyes for a second and then opened them. "Honestly? It sucked. *I* suck. I shoved my foot directly in my mouth. Just like I always do."

The professor said nothing, sensing that if he was quiet, Finn would keep talking. He wasn't wrong.

"I don't deserve her. I never did. And now she knows it too. So, it's all for the best, really. Right?"

Professor Moskowitz pressed his lips together. "My granddaughter is of strong mind and will..."

Finn ran a hand over his face and raised a pair of exhausted brown eyes to meet the professor's. "Uh, yeah, I gathered that."

"...but she is not immovable." The professor watched Finn's face.

"Not sure I follow."

"Look. Mr. Mallory." The professor moved behind his desk. "I've known Everly all her life, and she isn't easily given over to emotion. She is clear-headed. Pragmatic. Sometimes unnervingly so. Even as a young girl she behaved with the grace and composure of someone twice her age."

Finn cocked his head as the professor began to absently wipe his chalkboard with a cloth. "But we all have our moments, don't we? Even the strongest of minds are susceptible to making questionable decisions under the sway of very strong feelings." He dusted his hands and moved back to the front of his desk. "Under the weight of strong feelings, one might say things they regret in the heat of the moment. Others may even be compelled to do things as stupid as dating the biggest idiot in school just to spite someone else." He lifted his palms in a show of innocent ignorance.

Finn snorted and cracked a smile. "Yeah, I'm pretty sure he's not the 'biggest' idiot. I take that prize. Trust me." He moved for the door, hitching his messenger bag up further on his shoulder. "Anyway, I think...I think I get it."

"Good." The professor waved a dismissive hand at the door. "Go on, then—catch up with your team." He leaned forward and narrowed his eyes. "Strategize. This one may be tricky, but it's not impossible."

Finn lifted his eyebrows, and the professor smiled. "I mean the challenge, of course."

"Yeah." Finn nodded slowly before he stumbled out of the room, leaving the professor smiling down at his hands.

CHAPTER 31
KRYPTONITE

Valerie leaned forward, like a runner braced to sprint. "So, we have to do two things: decide who to pick from Vale Academy and try to anticipate who might get selected from our team." She shrugged and looked to Everly. "Let's start with Vale."

As Everly opened her mouth to speak, Finn careened into the library, messenger bag thudding against his hip as he wove through the study tables. Everly pretended she didn't notice him, even as he stood at her elbow, staring at the chair beside her. It was the last available one at the table, and it was occupied with Everly's gigantic Coach purse. On purpose.

Valerie threw Everly a meaningful look across the table, which Everly knew was intended to let her know that Finn was waiting to sit, but she ignored her, pursing her lips as she ripped a clean sheet of paper out of a notebook with more force than was necessary.

Finn finally cleared his throat. "Uh, Everly? Do you think maybe I could...?" As his voice trailed off, Everly glanced up at him, as if only now noticing he was there. She rolled her eyes, grabbed the handle of her bag, and swung it from the seat to the floor.

"Vale's a strong team," she said, returning to business as Finn awkwardly lowered himself into the chair beside her. "The smartest move would be to select their weakest member. The thing is, they're all seasoned veterans, and my grandfather said they've all proven themselves capable in various challenges. There are no great options to choose from, in all honesty."

She leaned over to grab a pen out of her purse, and could have sworn she saw Finn's whole body tense up as she moved in his direction. She felt a small thrill at having made him nervous, and then a dart of sorrow as she caught a whiff of him—he always smelled kind of warm and piney, in the best way—like a forest or something.

Stop, she scolded herself. *Stupid.*

Before she raised her head, her eyes rested on the outsole of his shoe, which stared her in the face almost in mocking.

"~~Oysters, no~~ pearls."

You don't even know what to do with pearls.

"We should avoid the twins." Finn's voice sounded tentative, as if he'd had to will himself to participate. "They're small, but scary. You remember what they were like at the Summit of Selection."

Everly refused to acknowledge Finn's words, but she did remember; the Neil twins had fixated their unflinching, disconcerting stares on him and subtly manipulated Kade Davis into going silent for the rest of the evening. There was a sense of humanity that was missing from them, making them unpredictable in the most dangerous way.

"Doyle Cohen looked like the weakest to me," Valerie agreed. "He wouldn't look me in the eye. You can tell he gets picked on by the others."

"Doyle is the obvious answer," Everly conceded, scrawling "Vale" across her sheet of notebook paper. Underneath it, she wrote "Doyle—weak link. But they'll expect us to pick Doyle and they'll prepare him. Maybe we should go with something they don't see coming."

"What do you mean?" asked Finn.

Everly didn't try to conceal the condescension in her voice as she looked at him. "I *mean* that sometimes the best place to hit an enemy is where they're strongest." Finn wilted under her gaze and she felt a pang of regret, but she shook it off and redirected her focus to Valerie. "With only an hour to prepare, one of the twins might panic."

Valerie's face was incredulous yet intrigued, her voice raising an octave. "You want to go with one of the *twins*?"

Everly nodded and crossed her arms. "Those twins need each other: they finish each other's sentences, they scheme together...they're inseparable." She shrugged. "So, let's separate them. Let's see how strong they are without each other."

Valerie rubbed her chin in thought. "The twins have always been a terrible force together, but they're *always* together—no one knows how they behave when they're apart. It's a risk, of course, because there's a good chance they're just as vile on their own, or maybe even worse..." Her voice trailed off.

"Like my grandfather said," Everly continued, "Vale's entire team is strong and there aren't really any good options here. Breaking up the twins seems like the best play we can make. At least it's unpredictable."

Valerie rubbed her hands together. "Let's make it Emily."

Everly looked to Edison. "Are you okay with this?"

Edison issued a curt nod. Everly could see Finn watching her out of the corner of his eye, clearly waiting for her to ask him his take. She didn't.

"Let's not forget that whoever Vale picks is going to have to *deal* with Emily Neil," Finn finally said, having accepted that his opinion wasn't going to be asked.

"They're going to pick Edison." Valerie looked at the floor as she said it.

"Well...not...not necessarily!" Everly scoffed, surprised by the fact that someone had come out and said what they were all thinking. She instinctively turned to Finn, forgetting she was supposed to be avoiding eye contact with him. His eyebrows were also raised. Everly's eyes caught on his before she blinked and looked away.

"It's going to be you." Valerie addressed Edison directly. He didn't look up as he arranged a fistful of highlights in order by color on the tabletop.

"It could be any one of us," Everly said, though her voice wavered.

"Vale's mentor has been watching the Trials." Valerie continued talking to Edison as if Everly hadn't spoken, voice gentle. "He saw what happened on the *Titanic*, and how you reacted. They'll see it as weakness and try to use it."

Everly and Finn watched the exchange in uncomfortable silence, shocked that Valerie had brought it up with such openness but also relieved that one of the elephants in the room had now been acknowledged and could be discussed. It *did* seem inevitable that Edison would be deemed weakest and picked by Vale Academy. Maybe Valerie was onto something. Maybe hiding from this fact only put him at a further disadvantage.

Edison dragged his focus from the highlighters and stared up into Valerie's eyes. "I know."

"Look." Valerie redirected her attention to Finn and Everly. "I know it sounds like a mismatch—Emily Neil facing off with Edison—but they won't see it coming. And I think we're seeing this all wrong. Nobody matches up *better* with Emily than Edison."

"How do you figure that?" Everly crossed her arms, eyes trained on Edison as she imagined Emily Neil's predatory glare.

"Emily doesn't beat you with brawn, she beats you with brains. She probes you for where you're weak and gets under your skin, cracking into your head and forcing you to make mistakes. It's the only trick in her book."

Everly smiled, beginning to see where this was going. "She's going to have a hard time cracking into Edison. He's unflappable." As she spoke the words, she could have sworn she saw Edison and Finn meet eyes for a flicker of a second.

"Exactly." Valerie patted Edison on the back. "Edison is Emily Neil's kryptonite, and they won't see it coming."

The group lapsed into an awkward silence then—thick, deep and funereal, and Everly was beset by another sudden surge of sadness. How different this was from the study sessions before the *Titanic*, and the time they'd spent sitting around the fireplace in Raine Manor playing the wetsuit challenge. The team had managed to drag themselves through the tension of today's strategy session out of necessity, but now that they'd put their plans together, it felt as if they had nothing left to say.

She didn't look directly at Finn; instead, she looked at him out of the corners of her eyes, secretly hoping he would look in her direction. When he didn't, she cast her eyes to the ground.

He looked so *sad*.

Inwardly, Everly scolded herself for caring. Why should she?

Valerie watched the two of them stare at the floor in silence for a moment before she cringed and rose from her chair. "I better...go. I have polo." She grabbed a handful of Edison's sweater and he stumbled out of the library with her.

Left alone, Everly and Finn lingered for a painful moment until Everly, too, rose from her chair. But she couldn't bring herself to leave outright; she took a long time putting her things back in her handbag, and though she didn't want to admit it to herself, she knew why. She wanted to see if he'd speak. If he'd try to explain himself. She didn't know why she wanted him to—nothing he said would matter, but even so, she took her sweet time reorganizing her pens in the bottom of her purse, and straightening a makeup bag that didn't need straightening.

226

Finn cleared his throat and drew himself to his feet, hands in his pockets. "Everly..." He stared down at his feet.

Everly looked up from her handbag, expressionless. She crossed her arms and gave him a once over, letting him simmer in silence for a full thirty seconds before she spoke. "You look awful."

And he did. His eyes looked sort of hollow, like he'd been up all night, or several.

"Yeah, I mean, I probably do." He looked up from his feet and threw her the faintest of smiles—one of those lopsided ones that made her stomach flip over. "But *you* don't."

Everly narrowed her eyes.

How dare he.

That stupid half-smile.

Those eyes, his smile—they were *her* kryptonite. Did he realize it? He didn't seem to—he wasn't working her—this was just Finn Mallory. Finn didn't realize a *lot* of things—like the fact that she would've kissed him readily in front of the entire school during the dance if she'd had the chance. Like the fact that the only real thing that was in their way was him.

Why does he have to be so...stupid?

She reached for anger and panicked when she couldn't find it, but Finn's next question supplied it.

"What happened to 'depth of a frisbee?'" His voice was soft. Unnervingly gentle. "What's that really about?" Then he winced at himself. Shook his head. "Never mind. I shouldn't have said anything. I should just..." He ran his fingers through his hair.

Everly scoffed in exasperation. "What—it doesn't make enough sense for you?" She leaned against the library table as Finn looked away with a pained expression. "Nick may not be the smartest, but at least he's consistent. That counts for something, you know."

"Fair enough." As Finn returned his eyes to the library floor and set his mouth, Everly felt an eager hope well up inside her.

Say something else.

Do *something*.

Finn finally did; he raised his gaze and took a tentative step forward, gently cupping his hand over hers on the table's edge. "I screwed up. I know that. Nothing I said was even about you. None of it."

Everly felt her heart quicken at the feel of the calluses on his fingers and shook her hand free, knowing the feel of him would only muddy her resolve.

"It's okay." Finn turned and faced the European history collection. "I get it; you probably hate me now."

"I don't." The words came more quickly than Everly had meant them to. She softened her voice. "But I want to. It would be easier."

Finn didn't speak.

"I couldn't wait for you. I've done a lot of waiting in my life."

Finn turned then, and Everly watched a flicker of confusion pass over his face. She knew that wouldn't make sense to him; it was a piece of her he'd never have now. If things had gone differently, maybe she would have told him, but that didn't matter anymore. In the eye of her mind, she could see her grandparent's bay window. The walkway, scattered with leaves in the fall, covered in snow in winter, lined with flowers in spring and summer. She could feel the plush velvet of the window seat cushion where she sat every day, watching. Waiting...

"I'm sorry, Everly." Finn's eyes were sincere. Imploring. He meant it—she could see it. But he was also broken, and his jagged edges had proven to be sharper than she'd counted on.

Every minute she stood here, she stood the risk of caving in as he chipped away at her carefully constructed walls without even trying to.

"Believe me, I'm sorry, too." Everly pulled the handle of her purse over her shoulder and wove through the library shelves as if fleeing rapidly approaching fire. Because if she looked at him any longer, she might change her mind.

CHAPTER 32
THE WEAK ONES

To Edison, it looked like Finn was reading a copy of *Guitar World* magazine, but hidden inside it, he was actually poring over *The Spectrum: A Book About Autism*. He'd checked it out from the library after the team's last strategy session in an attempt to understand Edison's unique perspective on the world in order to better help him through the upcoming Red Rover challenge, and now he was kicking himself for not having done it earlier.

Finn's mind was blown by what he'd read—according to this book, people on the autism spectrum experienced external stimuli all at once: sounds, sights, and smells rushed at them like an oncoming train, and it was overwhelming, sometimes causing them to curl in on themselves or have strong reactions. Suddenly, all Edison's rocking and ear-covering made a lot of sense, and Finn felt like an asshole for ever playing his guitar in their dorm at all. He felt even worse that he'd caught himself secretly feeling glad that it would be Edison picked for Red Rover; if Edison was the perceived "weakest link," it meant that Finn wasn't.

He thought of Everly's green eyes and the disappointment swimming in them.

"Believe me, I'm sorry too."

He'd screwed that up bad; the least Finn could do was be a good teammate. A good friend.

He threw Edison a smile over the top of his magazine and continued to pretend to read about pentatonic scales and distortion pedals.

It was difficult to prepare Edison for the upcoming trial, as the exact nature of the challenge was yet to be officially revealed. Wharton's Time Team did what they could, but the mystery of it all was both frustrating and frightening. Because they had no idea what time period Edison would be sent to, Valerie and Everly focused on the other players he was likely to compete against in the game, only one of whom they knew for sure. The professor was of great help in this area, as he had watched all the challenges and had picked up on the tendencies and personalities of the various players on the other teams. Valerie and Everly peppered the old man with questions, determined to give their friend every possible advantage.

Emily Neil. This one was a given, as Wharton would select her themselves. They were sure that Emily would not anticipate being chosen and would enact some sort of vengeance on Wharton for her surprise selection. Vale's mentor, Gabriel Lochan, who was sure to have watched the last mission closely, and would be well aware of the fact that Edison had an aversion to loud, sustained noise. The professor had helped them to modify an earpiece to drastically eliminate the noise that Edison would hear, but Everly still felt that it was best not to rely on the devices, as Emily would surely find some way to target them. Instead, she helped to train Edison by blasting loud music in his dorm, encouraging him to calm himself with mindfulness techniques and slow counting. Edison protested a great deal at first, but eventually grew to truly enjoy the art of meditation.

Aside from that weakness, Valerie was right: Edison matched up well against Emily. Her insults would bounce off of him like ping pong balls against a concrete wall, and Edison was too smart to ever trust her.

Wharton's Time Team assumed that Oscar Clement would probably be selected for Halls of Ivy Prep. A heavy-set boy who was clearly the brains of his group, his ability to retain and recall facts had kept his team afloat in many challenges. But he was a bit delicate and lacked common sense. The professor also recalled that he had a strong tendency to get down on himself, and this lack of confidence would make him an obvious target on an otherwise capable team.

The person who would be chosen from Wilmington was a bit less obvious, but whoever was selected would probably not be a serious threat to Edison. Leah Stevens was awkward, tended to trip over her own feet. Any physical challenge would be difficult for her, and this might make her a tempting target to select. Much like Oscar, Gage Alvis was purely book smart and lacked common sense; however, he was more physically capable than Oscar, and that might keep him off the chopping block. Valerie and Everly assumed that Wilmington's leader, Prana Kapoor, would be safe from selection, but they had reviewed her weaknesses with Edison anyway: Prana was notoriously bossy, and her attitude could be used to turn others against her if necessary.

Even as Wharton's Time Team boarded the private jet that would take them to the Time Society's headquarters for the second challenge, Valerie and Everly were busy quizzing Edison and stuffing his head with advice, like helicopter parents hovering over their child on the eve of a spelling bee. When they continued to ply him with suggestions as the flight continued, Edison began to slowly count, taking measured breaths until they stopped.

Finn waited for a lull before he dipped his hand into his pocket.

"Hey. Edison. I...I made you something." He extended the gift—nine hole-punched guitar picks threaded onto a piece of twine—to his roommate. "It's a fidget cuff. You know, for when things get intense. You can spin them, chunk 'em by color...you know, whatever."

Edison took the homemade fidget and flicked at one of the guitar picks, a maroon and black swirled Fender one, which spun around the twine and quivered to a stop.

"I have like a million guitar picks, so..."

He'd read that having something to worry with your hands helped to decrease anxiety and self-regulate, and it seemed like one small way he could help. Finn himself actually had his own accidental fidget of sorts—his 1912 marble from Ebba.

...Or maybe this was dumb.

Finn waited for Edison to balk or hand it back, but he didn't; instead, he closed his palm around the gift and issued him a curt nod. "Thank you."

"You've got this." Finn met Edison's stare. "Remember—Emily's comments? Let them roll off you. Like water off a duck's back."

Across from him, Valerie smiled, and Finn couldn't stop himself from glancing at Everly. He felt like he could detect the slimmest of smiles on her lips, too, before he turned to face the window.

There had been palpable awkwardness between Finn and Everly for weeks. When forced into trainings and study sessions together, they barely exchanged a word, and every time Finn saw her he felt like he had been kneed in the groin. The vibe among the team was tragically discordant, reminding him of the way his music sounded when one of his guitar strings were out of tune. He bore Everly's monosyllabic replies and subtly scornful comments with grace, ever the humble penitent atoning for his sins, figuring if he did his time, she might eventually look at him the way she used to.

But then he'd think of Nick Dain's arm draped around her as if it belonged there and come to his senses.

Wishful thinking.

But lately the ice had begun to thaw a bit. Finn attributed it to Edison—neither of them wanted to argue in front of him; they were cordial but distant, like divorced parents getting along for the sake of a child.

When the jet landed, the team emerged into the dusty, desolate exterior of the Historians' Society's headquarters. Last time, it had been Grand Timekeeper Garridan who had greeted them and escorted them into the massive, rusted warehouse that acted as the arena for the Time Trials, but today they found themselves met by someone else: Timekeeper Philomena Vandecraft.

Hands clasped before her, she smiled at the group in her customary black dress, its large shoulder pads vaulted up by her impeccable posture. Instead of a cloche hat, she sported a low-rise top hat which was encrusted with gears on one side and housed the odd goggles which seemed standard apparel for the Historians.

"Wharton Academy." She smiled, her eyes flaring in such a way that Finn took a step backward. The professor issued a respectful bow.

"Red Rover is such an exciting game, don't you think?" Timekeeper Vandecraft didn't seem to expect an answer as she led the team inside. "I do enjoy letting the weaker ones get their time to shine."

Valerie's fist balled up at her side as she shot a protective glance at Edison, who was quietly chatting with SCRAP, seemingly oblivious to the comment. Finn was fairly sure Edison had heard the timekeeper, but had chosen to ignore it. He smiled; if he could ignore Philomena Vandecraft, then Emily Neil didn't stand a chance.

They rounded the corner and the room opened up to the arena, where the school banners were hung above four rustic tables. The setup was almost identical to when they had first arrived for the Summit of Selection, except there was only a single Time Bender beneath the banners rather than four.

Wharton's Time Team took their seats and waited. They, along with Wilmington and Halls of Ivy Prep, were all clad in their wetsuits as had been instructed; each competitor had been told to act as if they themselves might be selected. There were four empty seats; Vale Academy's jet had yet to arrive.

Finn cast a sidelong glance at Edison, who was seated next to him, absently spinning a guitar pick on his fidget cuff. He wanted to reassure him, but couldn't think of what to say. Edison would be selected today, and there was nothing Finn could do about it. All he could hope was that his roommate was well-galvanized enough to withstand Emily. As Finn raised his eyes from Edison's hands, he met Everly's stare, who was seated on the opposite side of Edison, no doubt having the same thoughts.

Vale Academy rounded the corner and filed past the spectators, three out of four of them already appearing convinced that they would take this challenge. The androgynous Neil twins led the way with their noses in the air, their straight, black hair near identical, and Maira Nicholson strutted behind them, her mouth a smug twist. Doyle Cohen brought up the rear of the group, the only one looking at his feet. He seemed to believe that he would be selected today, if body language was any indication.

Vale took their seats as Timekeeper Garridan stood, lulling the crowd to silence with his hands. "Greetings to the honored members of the Historians' Society, to our esteemed guests, and to our brave competitors." The audience issued a round of light applause, eager to get to the selections.

"According to the rules of the Trials, each team will have the chance to select a name from another school in order to determine who will compete in our next game. Wharton Academy has won our game of Marbles." The Grand Timekeeper paused for a moment, gesturing to Wharton and allowing the soft applause to swell and subside. "Once the team is selected, the game to be played will finally be revealed, and we shall take a brief recess of one hour, during which teams may prepare in any fashion they see fit." The corners of his mouth curled into a mischievous smile. "Without further ado, Wilmington is on the call first!"

As the Grand Timekeeper took his seat, a nervous murmuring permeated the crowd. Prana Kapoor of Wilmington School strode to the designated podium and spoke into the microphone with confidence. "Red rover, red rover, send Oscar right over!"

Oscar Clement bowed his head for a moment before he stood. Reluctantly, he made his way to the front and stood before the timekeeper's table, hands clasped in front of him, making a study of his feet.

Kade Davis rose and made his way to the podium for Halls of Ivy Prep. His voice was clear and deep. "Red rover, red rover, send Leah right over."

Leah Stevens' chin dipped in a resigned nod before she stood. Prana rose with her and pulled her into a quick hug before Leah awkwardly ambled to join Oscar before the timekeepers, nearly tripping over her own feet as she went.

Valerie threw her team a wicked smile and stood, walking with a spring in her step to the podium for Wharton. She paused for dramatic effect before nearly shouting, "Red rover, red rover, send *Emily* right over!"

She spun around to bask in the shock of Wharton's surprise decision and the crowd certainly reacted, whispering wildly amongst each other as they tried to make sense of this unexpected choice. An array of bright flashbulbs went off from the press box and Finn caught Felix Winkler scribbling furiously onto the pad of paper in his fat palm. Beside Finn, Edison had begun to rock in his seat, but stopped to chunk the guitar picks on his cuff by color— maroon on one side, brown in the middle, blue on the other end.

At the podium, Valerie sent a triumphant glance toward Vale's table, but as Finn tracked her gaze, his heart sank. Emily's face was painted with a serene smile. Valerie's face fell, her hands clenching at her sides. Emily had anticipated this. She shared a victorious moment with her twin brother before rising coolly, gliding to her spot with the others in front of the timekeepers' table. She certainly didn't fit in with the others; she looked like she could eat them alive.

Valerie returned to Wharton's table and threw herself next to Everly, who looked as stunned as she was.

"That *bitch*," she seethed through clenched teeth.

As Elden Neil of Vale Academy rose to make the final selection, Finn draped a supportive arm around the back of Edison's chair in anticipation.

Elden took his time walking to the podium, looking over Wharton's table with an air of superiority. His pallid face stretched into a condescending smile as his lips hovered over the microphone. "Red rover, red rover, send Finn right over."

CHAPTER 33
TRUTH OR DARE

Finn leaned forward in his seat, his eyes darting between the shocked faces of his teammates, second-guessing his hearing. Before he could even begin to process what he believed he had just heard, a voice rang out sharply. *"WHAT?"*

Heads swiveled in Everly's direction, who sat slack-jawed between Edison and Valerie. There was an awkward silence before the room came alive with excited whispers. Finn, realizing everyone was staring at him with expectation, accepted that he had, in fact, heard his name.

It's me.

He forced himself to his feet, blinded by a fresh round of flashes as the antique cameras captured his candid reaction.

They picked me.

Felix Winkler shook his head with a smile that seemed to shout this is too good to be true, and directed his cameraman to get a shot of Everly, whose mouth was still slightly ajar.

As if in a dream, Finn found his way to the three other competitors, asking himself which walk was longer and more uncomfortable—this one, or the one to his seat on his first day of history class. He decided this one took the cake.

Emily Neil smirked as he approached, just as she had the first time she had seen him, making it clear that she saw him as anything but a threat. She simpered and shook her head as he passed. "Don't look so shocked," she whispered. "It wasn't exactly a difficult decision."

Grand Timekeeper Garridan's whole face was a smile, clearly pleased at the excitement that the last two selections had stirred in the audience. "Ah." He rose to his feet. "What a terrific group! I am delighted to announce the official second game of the Time Trials! The four of you will have the honor of playing...Truth or Dare!"

The audience applauded their approval, something that Finn figured was probably a bad sign.

"You have chosen your competition wisely," continued the Grand Timekeeper over the noise of the crowd, "and you must choose even more wisely while playing this most dangerous game! You will have one hour to confer with your mentor and teammates. As always, your safety should be of the utmost concern. We wish the very best of luck to you all!"

With that, the timekeepers rose from their seats and began to make their exit, Philomena Vandecraft lingering for a moment to take in Finn and Emily with excited eyes.

Wharton's Time Team dazedly filed toward their prep room, Valerie taking the lead and Professor Moskowitz at the rear. As Valerie, Edison, and Finn went inside, Everly pulled the door closed behind them and stalled her grandfather outside the room.

"Wait." She fixed her eyes on her grandfather's face, her whisper rushed and urgent. "I need to switch with him. I need to switch with Finn."

The old professor raised eyebrows. "Now, my dear, you know that isn't possible." His voice was patient. "I know you are concerned about your...friend..." At that last word he rose his head and looked at Everly cautiously through his chrome spectacles.

Everly grabbed her grandfather's hands. "You don't understand. Emily Neil's specialty is mental warfare. There are things about Finn...things he's told me. Things that make him vulnerable. The Neil twins have done their homework—there's a reason they picked him." Her eyes darted from her grandfather's face to the door of the prep room and back again. "She'll eviscerate him."

"My dear, tell me." The professor pursed his lips. "Do you think Finn to be...weak?"

Everly opened her mouth and then closed it. "I didn't say that. I'm just saying that he...he gets in his own way. He gets lost in his own head. He overthinks and he always assumes the worst. I've seen it firsthand." Her voice softened and she looked away, remembering him disappearing down the backstage steps of the ballroom. "All I'm saying is that Emily will use that."

She heaved a regretful sigh and withdrew her hands from the professor's. "Emily wouldn't even be competing if it weren't for me. I was the one who pushed for choosing one of the twins."

"Everly." The professor narrowed his gaze. "Mr. Mallory has surprised you before." He searched Everly's face. She nodded, recalling Finn's quick thinking on the *Titanic*, the decisiveness in his voice over her earpiece as he'd commandeered the entire challenge and brought the team to victory, and above all, the way he'd hijacked her emotions with a single glance without even trying to.

Her grandfather's smile was gentle and knowing. "Perhaps you should allow him the opportunity to surprise you again."

* * *

As Everly and Professor Moskowitz stepped into the prep room, Edison straightened his glasses. "It wasn't me." When no one answered, he spoke again. "They picked Finn—not me."

Valerie rolled her eyes. "Yeah, Edison, we caught that."

"I learned to meditate and listen to loud music and I didn't have to." As Edison flicked one of the guitar picks on his fidget cuff, Finn watched it spin so quickly around its twine axis that it blurred. He could use his own fidget cuff right about now.

"Sue me," Valerie muttered, fanning Edison's comment away.

Edison stared blankly back at her. "A judge would never—"

Valerie threw up her hands. "Edison, be quiet!" She turned to Finn, who was now staring at the ceiling, silent as his stomach churned within him.

They picked me.

I'm *the weakest link.*

"Finn." He could hear Valerie saying his name, but she sounded far away. When he didn't respond, Valerie grabbed him by the shoulders. "*Finn!*"

He lowered his eyes to meet hers.

"It's going to be fine," Valerie assured him. "You were in the room when we were preparing Edison. You heard everything. You know what to look out for—what Emily's like. You can do this."

Finn's gaze instinctively made its way to Everly. She stared down at her knotted fingers, brow furrowed, looking as shocked as he felt. He remembered her reaction as Elden had called his name. On one hand, her shock revealed that she hadn't expected him to be deemed "weakest." But the look on her face was more than surprise: it was worry.

She *doesn't think I can do this.*

He straightened in his chair as the professor threw an apprehensive look at his pocket watch. They didn't have much time.

"So." Finn cleared his throat, still looking at Everly out of the corner of his eyes. "Truth or Dare. Do you think we'll braid each other's hair after we play? Maybe make some prank calls?" He hoped the sarcasm in his voice would mask the shame, fear and uncertainty that coursed through him.

"Truth or Dare is a simple concept." The professor's voice was tranquil. Even. The sort of tone you'd use if you were trying to reassure someone before a big surgery with a low success rate.

"You will be sent to a location in time," the professor continued placidly, "that could be anywhere and in any time period." The old man clasped his hands behind his back as he began to pace the prep room. "The game is played with four key stations. Sometimes there is a map provided to lead you to these stations and sometimes there is no guidance at all. In many cases, getting to the stations can be the most difficult and dangerous part. At each station, there will be two options: truth or dare. You choose one of the two and you either tell the truth or complete a task."

"Yeah, I would go with truth if I were you," said Valerie, hands on hips.

"You could," the professor's chin rose and fell in a slow nod as he paced the modest space, "but be warned: the questions are typically...difficult to answer. They are often subjective and thus confusing, and many of them are intensely personal."

"Can't I just lie?" Finn muttered, leaning forward on his knees and speaking through his hands.

"You can always lie, Mr. Mallory, but in this game, as in life, there are consequences for doing so. Your wetsuit takes vital signs, which are processed by an algorithm, which very accurately determines whether you are telling the truth. If your suit detects a lie, you lose the game and must return to the present."

"Well..." Finn heaved a gusty sigh and ran both hands through his hair, slumping back in his chair again, "...*that* sucks."

"It sucks indeed, Mr. Mallory." The professor threw him a wry smile.

"Well, I'm guessing that the dares are no picnic, either," said Everly, finally joining the conversation. Her voice was quiet, and she sat away from the group, fist to mouth.

"No," admitted the professor. "They also 'suck'."

"Is there a Command?" asked Valerie.

"There are four; each player in the game is his or her own Command, and each player is in charge of pulling their own chain should they require it. Pulling another player's chain, however, results in disqualification. Otherwise, you could just pull the chains of your competition, and this becomes much less exciting for the Historians' Society to watch."

There was a thick silence in which the only sound was that of the *tink tink* of the guitar picks knocking against each other on Edison's fidget cuff.

"Well, it's their mistake, Finn," Valerie finally said. "They must have missed the last challenge where you saved the day for us. They just picked the best of us and they don't even know it."

The best of us.

Finn remembered when it was Everly who had used that term to describe him.

But that had been a long time ago; or at least it felt that way.

The door opened and an arbitrator entered. "One minute." He was gone as quickly as he'd come.

Professor Moskowitz gave Finn's shoulder a firm squeeze before he ushered Valerie and Edison out.

But Everly didn't leave. She was silent a moment before she spoke, standing a few paces from the door.

"Finn." It was the first time she'd addressed him by name in weeks. She looked down at her hands and bit her lip.

Nervous.

She was *nervous.*

Because she didn't think he was capable of handling the challenge? Because she cared?

Maybe it was some mixture of both, but Finn didn't have the luxury of time to ruminate on it. He had minutes before he would make the Bend to an unknown time and place with a new team, to face undisclosed dangers, both physical and psychological.

He drew himself to his feet and took a step forward, and Everly raised her eyes, brilliant green and replete with uncertainty, but devoid of the ice they'd held all these weeks.

Somehow the fear in her eyes made some of Finn's fear dissipate. "It'll be fine." He stuffed his hands into his pockets. "You told me that if something freaks you out you should just look at it. Right? Face it." He rolled his shoulders in a shrug. "So, I'm looking at it. Dead in the eyes. Okay? Or trying to, at least."

He didn't give her a chance to respond; he withdrew one hand from his pocket and let the tips of his fingers brush hers as he passed, before he left the prep room to make the Bend.

CHAPTER 34
THE ONE-EYED MAN

Finn rubbed his head, trying to soothe the searing pain as the gears above slowed their rapid turning. The pain was crippling, and for a moment he found it difficult to breathe within the confines of the Bender. Oscar Clement of Wilmington sat beside him. Across from him were Leah Stevens of the Halls of Ivy Prep and Emily Neil from Vale Academy. All four time travelers groaned as they tried to massage the agonizing pain away from their heads with little success. The Bend had brought a slight headache last time, but this one was worse.

It was strange to be in a Time Bender with a different team, and Finn felt somehow traitorous, despite the fact that he hadn't chosen to be here. It had only been a few minutes ago that he had said his goodbyes to his own team, but they could now be centuries apart for all he knew.

Emily punched in the code to release the two doors of the Time Bender. As they screeched open, the team covered their ears, wincing at the sound, and humidity flooded into the machine, making the air suddenly heavy and sticky. The new team of four fumbled out of their leather harnesses and ducked out of the brass porthole one at a time.

The sudden brightness forced a squint as Finn made his way down the ramp. As his feet sank into sand, the soft lapping of ocean waves against the shore competed with the buzzing in his ears.

The team found themselves on a white beach with a lush, green mountain behind them. In front of them, steep, green islets shot out of the water, as if the spiked back of some emerald sea monster were exposed as it basked in the tropical sun.

"It's beautiful," said Leah breathlessly. The sun was just starting to make its descent into the horizon and parts of the sky were beginning to catch fire.

Finn looked around, trying to get his bearings. The beach was stunning, curving around a sapphire bay, reminding him of a postcard on one of those spinning racks at a convenience store. He'd never seen a place like this in person. But this picturesque, tropical setting was purely for show. What hidden dangers were lurking behind the curtain?

On one end of the bay, the remnants of an old, wooden ship were carelessly flung onto a cluster of sharp, black rocks. The waves beat against the eerie ship, attempting to reclaim her from the black jaws which embraced her. The white sand of the beach was devoured by the edge of the hungry, tropical forest, which grew thick and rank, opening in only one spot where a path disappeared into shadow.

Finn spotted a neat stack of firewood and a few wooden crates sitting next to a canvas tent in the middle of the beach. The group walked instinctively towards the makeshift camp, and naturally fell into an unspoken chain of command: Emily led the way, followed by Finn, with Leah behind him and Oscar last, panting to keep up. They were a team, and yet not: at the end of this challenge, there would be a single winner. It was everyone for themselves—or at least it was supposed to be.

Finn eyed Emily's back, her long, black hair falling to her waist, trying to galvanize himself for the fresh hell she likely had in store for him and everyone else on this team.

Like water off a duck's back.

The wooden crates needed to be pried open with a crowbar, which had been conveniently stuck in the sand nearby. Oscar and Finn began to unpack the contents of the boxes. There were several jars of water, some burlap sacks of dry rice and beans, a modest assortment of fresh fruit, a small shovel, a hatchet, two survival knives, a basic first aid kit, and some thick, wool blankets.

A map was painted on the side of one of the supply crates. Finn squinted at it; he could see the curved beach and identified the mysterious shipwreck on one side of the cove. Four red Xs marked various parts of the map, which Finn assumed were the sites of the Truth or Dare stations.

He shaded his eyes as he raised his face to the sun, which was setting quickly in the fiery sky. "We should make camp for the night." He was the first to speak, and everyone raised their heads. "We have all of tomorrow to play the game."

Emily's lips curled up into a smile. "I'm good with a little fireside chat." She rolled her shoulders and crossed her arms, her long, black hair blowing lightly in the breeze.

"They gave us some flint," said Oscar, seeming eager to establish himself as part of the group, "but there's no tinder. I'll go see if there's some dry grass along that pathway." He lumbered off, breathing heavily as he trudged through the thick sand.

As Leah wordlessly began to stack the firewood into a pyramid, Emily watched her with a condescending smile. She waited until Leah had finished before saying, "You know that's never going to work, right?"

Leah looked up at her, brushing some of her messy, red hair out of her eyes.

"You need to dig a pit in the sand so the core of the fire is protected from the wind." Emily rolled her eyes. "Obviously."

Leah returned her gaze to the stack of wood, embarrassed, and quickly began to dismantle it with trembling hands.

Finn dropped to a knee beside her. "Easy fix." He threw her a reassuring smile over the pile of wood. "I don't know the first thing about fires, either."

Leah bit her lip in a smile and pushed another tangled strand of hair out of her face before removing more of the wood.

A shrill screech echoed out of the forest and all three of their heads swiveled. Finn and Leah looked at each other before scrambling to their feet. Finn grabbed one of the survival knives, sprinting in the direction of the screaming after taking a moment to help Leah, who had tripped over the lid of an open crate and tumbled, face first, into the sand.

Finn reached the makeshift path and plunged into the dense jungle, holding the survival knife in front of him with an uncertain hand. His eyes roved the jungle for movement, but there was none other than the gentle swaying of plants in the scant breeze. The screaming had to be Oscar. But, where was he?

As Finn reached a thick tree with massive buttress roots anchoring it into place, his ears were assaulted by a fresh round of screams, which faded into a pathetic whimper, accompanied by an unidentifiable creaking. He whirled around, confused by how close Oscar's voice sounded, but unable to locate the large boy.

Finn cupped his hands around his mouth. "Oscar...?" He felt his face scrunch up.

Where the hell is he?

Leah finally caught up with him and pointed a silent finger into the canopy of trees above. Finn's eyes tracked her finger to find Oscar suspended in the air, swinging gently in the wind like a pinata at a child's birthday party. He dangled by one leg, his ankle snared by a thick, frayed rope.

Emily appeared then, snickering as she bit into an apple. "Looks like the island's booby trapped." Her eyes flicked upward. "How's it hanging, fat boy?"

Finn glared at her but didn't let his gaze rest on her for too long. She was a wisp of a girl; it was surprising how much malice could be contained in such a small package.

"Don't worry," he called up to Oscar. "We'll cut you down in a second."

Oscar nodded—or attempted to, hanging upside down—and tried to hide the fact that he had been crying.

"Aww, you're so charitable, coming to the rescue like this!" Emily threw Finn one of those simpering smiles that he hated so much. "But you know a lot about charity, don't you?" She took another bite of her apple and headed back to camp with a bounce in her step.

Leah watched her leave, not having said a word since they had arrived, and Finn tapered his eyes as he returned his attention to Oscar. He rubbed his chin as he studied the rope that held Oscar in place. He figured he could probably climb up the broad branch to which the rope was attached and saw through it, but he was worried about Oscar getting hurt; Oscar was suspended at least fifteen feet in the air, and at his weight, the fall could seriously injure him. Finn took the long survival knife and began to dig into the earth directly below Oscar, breaking it apart to soften it. He worked quickly, tossing any rocks to the side and creating a bed of dirt that he hoped would at least partially soften the blow.

When he was done, he crawled up the tree until he had edged over to where the rope bent around the thick branch.

"Okay," he called to Oscar, wiping some sweat from his brow, "I'm going to cut you loose. Think you can try to bend your neck forward so you land on your back?"

"I think so," Oscar stammered, his face red and beginning to bloat from hanging upside down for so long.

Finn sawed at the rope with the survival knife with vigorous swipes. As the blade cut through the strands, they frayed and curled. When he was partially through the rope, it snapped, sending Oscar plummeting back to earth. The branch, suddenly free of his weight, propelled upwards and nearly shook Finn off it. He waited for it to stop bobbing before he carefully shimmied down the tree to find Oscar panting, his head resting on his drawn-up knees. Leah patted him on the back in silent consolation.

"I'm sorry," Oscar mumbled through a shuddering sigh.

"Don't worry about it." Finn eased himself down next to him. "This trap was going to get one of us; I'm just glad it wasn't me."

As Oscar and Leah smiled, Finn's face became a bit more serious as he looked toward the path back to camp—the one Emily had all but skipped down a minute ago. He looked intently from Leah to Oscar, taking care to make eye contact with both of them. "Don't let her get to you. She searches for where she thinks you're weakest and uses it. She's trying to put you off your game. If you just try to ignore it, she's got nothing." He recalled Valerie's words and echoed them. "It's the only trick in her book."

When they returned to camp the fire was roaring, sending a column of sparks up into the gathering dark. Emily had used the packing material in the crates as kindling. Finn suspected that she had thought to use it long before Oscar had volunteered to find some dry grass in the jungle. He also noticed that she had eaten about half of the supply of fresh fruit—the beach was littered with banana peels and apple cores.

The team sat down to eat, cooking some of the rice and beans in a cast iron pot. When the meal was hot, they threw some more wood on the fire and rested comfortably, almost forgetting the reason why they were there.

"I know we're here to compete," Finn stared into the popping fire, the first to speak for the second time, "but maybe we should work together through these challenges."

This drew a scoff from Emily, but Oscar ignored her. "What do you mean, Finn?"

"Well, this place is obviously rigged." Finn stretched his legs out in front of him. "I mean, can you imagine if any of us were on this island alone and that trap had snared us? We'd be stuck hanging in the past forever."

Oscar nodded, shuddering at the thought.

"Who knows what these Truth or Dare stations are going to have in store for us," Finn continued. "We might get further if we work together."

"It's smart." Leah spoke in a small voice for the first time today. "If one of us reveals what the question is for the Truth or what the task is for the Dare, the others can make a more informed decision about which to choose."

"You can go first, then," Emily spat.

Leah looked back at the ground, hooking her red hair behind her ears.

"It's a great idea, Leah." Finn nodded. "We take turns and help each other." He cast Emily an admonitory look out of the corners of his eyes.

Leah looked at Finn with an appreciative smile. Oscar smiled too, adding, "Yeah, great idea, Leah."

Emily rolled her eyes, annoyed with the camaraderie forming between this new group.

"I wonder what the challenges are going to look like." Leah toyed with a frayed end of her red hair, the firelight dancing over the planes of her freckled face.

"They're going to suck." Finn said it plainly. "But we can get through them if we do it together."

"Such leadership! Such valor!" Emily brought her hands together in slow, sarcastic applause. "Finn, you're so confident now! Who knew?"

Finn cast his eyes down, suddenly self-conscious. Emily seemed to smell blood in the water and continued. "You always seemed like such a loser. You had even less confidence than that weirdo in the glasses, but now..." she crimped an eye and traced a finger in the air from Leah to Oscar, "...you fit in here, don't you? In the land of the blind, the one-eyed man is king, I guess. Isn't that what they say?"

Finn raised his eyes but fixed them on the fire.

Is that *why they picked me?*

An image of Everly's wounded eyes in the backstage area of Wharton's ballroom invaded his mind, followed by one of his mom and dad, singing to the radio for the last time, on their way to Greely...

...a trip they hadn't survived.

A trip they'd made for him.

I do *belong here.*

I wreck things...it's what I do.

I take good things and ruin them.

He shut his eyes but opened them at the sound of Oscar's voice. "You're here too, you know," the heavy-set boy said to Emily in heavy breaths. "*You* were chosen for a reason."

Emily giggled. "Don't get me started on *you*, fat boy. I'm here because Finn's team is a bunch of idiots and old man Moskowitz is getting senile."

Finn drew in a deep breath and didn't give Emily the reaction she was fishing for. He'd had some choice words for her on the tip of his tongue all day, but he'd swallowed them. Valerie had said that to react to Emily would only make her stronger—that his emotions would only be tinder to her fire. Finn knew how Edison would handle the situation: with a pragmatic silence. He had a sudden hankering for some banana chips.

"Have any of you told your parents about any of this?" Leah quietly tried to change the subject.

"It's against the rules," Oscar answered through a mouthful of beans. "My parents would never believe that I was involved in something this cool anyway." He smiled, cheeks bunching up around his eyes.

"I guess I wouldn't want my parents to worry about me anyway." Leah said, tracing a design in the sand with a piece of tinder.

"What about you, Finn?" Emily flashed an innocent smile. "Have you told *your* parents yet?"

Finn looked up at her face, which was distorted by the swirling heat of the fire. He should have been irate about her comment. He *wanted* to be angry, but instead he felt stunned, as if someone had just splashed rubbing alcohol on an open wound. His throat constricted as that tide of grief rushed up his shores and drew back out again, threatening to swell into a wave. He willed it to recede.

Everly was watching from the present, in the Historians' Society observation room. The last thing Finn wanted to show her was him curling in on himself again.

He let that grief tide rush out and disappear, allowing himself to fall into an equanimous, Edison-like silence.

But Emily was on a roll. She turned to Oscar, who was still eating, and issued a disgusted snort. "Slow down, fat boy. You wouldn't want to...choke."

Oscar lowered his forkful of beans, reddened, and got to his feet. Without a word, he lumbered away from the campfire toward the tent, leaving his food in the sand. Leah threw an apologetic look at Finn before scrambling after him, seeming to know she would be Emily's next target.

Emily stared at Finn through the flames, eyes dancing with some kind of sick gratification. Finn held her gaze, doing the opposite of what he was inclined to do. He couldn't look away: she would read it as weakness.

Everly's words echoed in his head like a mantra.

Just look at it.

"You know why you were selected, don't you, Finn Mallory?" Her voice was unsettlingly syrupy. Finn raised an aggravated eyebrow but stayed silent.

Face it.

Emily curled a lock of black hair around her finger. "Want me to tell you?"

Finn's stomach dropped, as did his eyes, and before he could stop himself, he mumbled, "No." He drew himself to his feet. "No, I don't."

As he retreated toward the tent, Emily's voice followed him, barely audible over the crackling fire, almost making Finn wonder if she'd said it at all: "What I really don't get is what *she* sees in you."

CHAPTER 35
EVERYTHING

Everly sat beside her grandfather in moody silence. She and the other contestants had been herded into a large viewing room where the Historians' Society watched the Trials in style. It was a gigantic warehouse with a rectangular screen that covered the entirety of one wall. Red, velvet curtains fringed with gold tassels draped the screen, making the room look like a cross between a theater and an old opera house. The spectators sat in rows—the Historians' Society members in front for the best view, while the contestants were seated in the back with their mentors.

Across the room, she spotted Felix Winkler, his beady eyes fixed on her with that creepy smile painted on his face. She threw him a searing look and redirected her eyes to the projector screen in time to see Finn stalk away from the campfire and retreat to the tent, head bowed, a thin layer of sand stuck to his wetsuit.

Everly remembered his fingers on hers as he'd left the prep room, and that touch of bravado he'd put on. She'd wanted to encourage him, but when she'd opened her mouth to speak, words had failed her. Instead, it had been Finn who had tried to reassure *her* in the moments before he'd made the Bend.

He'd tried to put on a brave face, hiding his fear under an armor of sarcasm as they'd talked about the challenge, but Everly knew better. By now she knew his eyes, and she'd seen the question in them: Why me? She'd spent weeks letting him think she was angry at him, giving him one-word answers and barely sparing him a glance, but the truth was, her anger had given way a long time ago to something else. Something she couldn't define. Or maybe it had never been anger at all.

She hardly noticed when a Historians' Society butler refilled her cup, which she held in a tremulous hand. She and Valerie had been sucking down buckets of coffee in order to stay awake and see as much footage as possible, and now she was over-caffeinated, twitchy, and irritable. Edison had a harder time preventing himself from nodding off and had accidentally drooled on Valerie's shoulder, much to her chagrin, Finn's homemade fidget cuff still wound around his wrist.

There were several reasons why Everly was a nervous wreck tonight. The physical danger inherent to Truth or Dare was worrisome enough in itself; who knew what those dares would entail. But the effects of dealing with Emily Neil were also treacherous. Based on what Everly had seen so far, her fears hadn't been unfounded; Emily was torturing Finn, as they all knew she would, triggering his anxieties and insecurities like she was some kind of psychological puppet master. Finn was doing quite well with it all, at least on the surface. But Everly knew he was in turmoil on the inside.

"What I really don't get is what she sees in you."

Everly had seen Finn freeze as Emily had uttered the words, wondering if he'd heard right, before letting the question sink into his mind and take root, self-doubt overtaking him like a fungus infecting a healthy plant. She was furious with herself that she was the reason that Emily was even on that island in the first place—

she had been the one to suggest they choose a Neil twin—but the idea of being used as a tool against Finn was beyond infuriating.

She released a shuddering sigh. There were many things about Finn that were frustrating—she could admit that. He was insecure. He was prone to self-sabotage and he jumped to conclusions. He could be overly cynical and he had an uncanny way of overthinking everything, but then also finding ways to be incredibly impulsive at the same time. He bemoaned the fact that he was judged and stereotyped, and yet he turned right around and did it to others.

And Finn had baggage. Everyone did, Everly knew, including herself, but Finn's was particularly heavy and difficult to carry. She remembered what he'd confessed to her that night, before the first challenge. He punished himself for what he believed he had done, and he would never be able to release himself from the self-loathing he felt, never be able to convince himself that he deserved anything good, until he felt redeemed. What it would *take* for Finn to feel redeemed, Everly didn't know.

Yes, Everly understood Finn. But it didn't make him any less infuriating at times.

In spite of all this, there were many things about Finn that Everly liked very much. Some of these things were significant: His kindness. His incredibly low tolerance for any sort of injustice. His ability to be quite decisive under the right circumstances—especially when innocent people, past or present, were in danger. But then there were the other things...the less significant things. His habit of running his fingers through his hair when he was nervous. The quirky way he ripped the crusts off his toast in the banquet hall before he would deem it acceptable to eat. The way his fingers couldn't keep still when he listened to music, as if he were plucking phantom guitar strings. His trademark half-smile. The way the corners of his eyes would crinkle up when he laughed.

Yes, there were many things Every Caldwell liked about Finn Mallory. They were stupid things, little things...

...but they were also sort of everything.

CHAPTER 36
SHIPWRECK

Finn woke up sandwiched between Oscar and Leah. It had taken him a while to shake off the effects of Emily's comments the night before, but eventually he had rallied and the three of them had shared the canvas tent together after a night of gazing up at the stars. Finn still wasn't sure where they were—or *when* they were for that matter—but the night sky was unlike anything he had ever seen before, saturated with pinholes of flickering starlight.

Emily never joined them in the tent that night and that suited Finn just fine. He had spent much of the night thinking about what he'd say to her this morning. Eager to start the day, he crawled out of the canvas tent, armed with some scathing comebacks for what Emily might have in store next. Something about the camp struck him as odd, and his tired mind worked to piece together what was wrong.

There were dark spots on the sand, as if someone's drink had been spilled, over and over. But what could've spilled? All they had was...

...the water.

Panic fired through Finn. He dove for the crates and plucked out a jar. The lid was missing.

Empty.

He pulled out another.

Empty.

They were *all* empty.

He swore extravagantly under his breath, took a moment to collect himself, and called to his two new companions, who came stumbling out of the tent, rubbing the sleep from their eyes.

It didn't take long to discover that their water wasn't the only thing that had been compromised: their beans and rice were gone, leaving torn and empty burlap sacks scattered on the ground. The tools and first aid kit were all missing, though Finn still had the survival knife he had taken with him.

"She left the map," pointed out Oscar optimistically. "I wonder if she forgot it when she was stealing the rest of the stuff."

"I don't think Emily forgets things," Finn muttered. But why would Emily leave them such an important tool? He ran his fingers through his hair.

"We won't last long without those supplies." Leah's chin trembled. "If she had left the water we would be fine, but we'll last a day, maybe a day and a half, without it."

"Isn't it three days without water?" asked Finn hopefully.

Leah shook her head. "The humidity...it accelerates dehydration."

It grew quiet, then, and Finn realized that his two teammates were looking at him with expectation, as if waiting for direction. It was odd, being looked at this way, almost like he was some kind of leader.

"Well, we'd better get moving then," he decided, providing his teammates with the direction they seemed to be hoping for. "The first X on the map points to that ship. It looks pretty hard to get to, but at least it's close."

The three new teammates began walking across the beach toward the shipwreck. It was mid-morning, but the sticky heat was already beginning to seep into the air.

"I wonder if Emily got to it already," said Oscar between labored breaths.

Finn took an aggressive step forward. "If we find her, she has some explaining to do."

They got to within one hundred yards of the wrecked ship when they ran out of beach. From where they stood, it looked like they would be able to make their way over the jutting black rocks and reach the ship without having to swim, but the rocks were sharp and both Oscar and Leah were painfully uncoordinated. The sea hissed and thundered below, slamming into the rocks and foaming like the mouth of a rabid animal.

By some miracle, the team made it to where the ship rested, tipped to one side and broken open, her wooden entrails spilling out onto the unforgiving rocks. She wasn't a large ship, but she seemed to be very tall, her mast sticking out of the water like a hand in distress. Finn picked up a splintered piece of wood and squinted down at it. There were words printed on it in faded paint.

"I guess this ship is called the '*Flor de la Mar.*'" He shrugged and handed the battered piece of wood off to Leah.

Oscar's eyes went wide with excitement. "The *Flor de la Mar?*" Noting in disbelief that Finn didn't know what he was talking about, he explained, his chubby hand gesticulating wildly. "This is a Portuguese treasure ship!"

"It *was* a Portuguese treasure ship," corrected Finn with a tired smile.

"Right." Oscar's head dipped in a quick nod before he recovered his momentum and returned to the ship's exhilarating history. "It holds the greatest treasure haul ever recorded by Portugal. Afonso de Albuquerque lost her back in...1511...while sailing back to Portugal from pillaging Malacca. The ship was never recovered, but they believe it went down on the coast of Sumatra!"

"How do you know all of that?" Finn shook his head in wonder. Oscar shrugged. "Obviously, I don't spend my time doing sports."

"This is good," Leah cut in, tapping the piece of wood that bore the ship's namesake in the palm of her hand. "This ship doesn't look like it's been wrecked for too long. It puts us around the early to mid-1500s on an island near Malaysia. That explains the tropical landscape."

"Well, now we know," Finn nodded. "Nice work, both of you." He paused, momentarily warmed by the proud smiles on both Oscar and Leah's faces that his compliment had produced. "Let's figure out where this Truth or Dare station is."

The team edged around the ship carefully. A massive section of it had been ripped open by the rocks, her thick, wooden planking jutting out like exposed ribs. A table which looked like it was slapped together from the remnants of the ship stood inside the giant hole with two sets of jars stacked on either side of it. The jars were of various shapes and sizes, all made of a thick, opaque sea glass. One set was red and the other was blue. The word "truth" was painted in thick, black letters in front of the blue jars, and the word "dare" stood out ominously in front of the red ones.

"So, this is it," muttered Finn. He had almost forgotten about this part, having been wrapped up in the adventure of exploration. He hadn't even really considered which of the two options would be worse: truth or dare.

He let his gaze come to rest on the cluster of blue jars. Any child who plays the game knows that truth is the easier option, but that's because most children have the ability to lie without detection or consequence. But now, without the option of lying available, truth almost seemed like the scarier of the two options.

His stomach lurched as his eyes swerved to the red jars. The dares could cost him his life.

Oscar's voice cut through his thoughts. "We want to go first, Finn."

"What?" Finn's eyebrows jumped in surprise. "You guys...you don't have to do that."

"We do," Leah agreed. "We want to do our part in this thing."

"Pull our weight," Oscar smiled.

"Seriously, you don't have to do this," Finn argued. "We should take turns. That was the deal."

"Oh, I'm not going to go first *every* time," Oscar said. "I just said I'll go first *this* time."

"Fair enough, Oscar." Finn smiled, dragging his gaze to the blue and red jars, which glowed like sapphires and rubies as the ligh passed through them. "Truth or dare."

CHAPTER 37
SHARK BAIT

"I'll go with truth." Oscar picked up a blue bottle and stared down at it, seemingly confused about what to do next.

Finn shrugged. "Break it."

Oscar pressed his lips together in a nervous smile. Breaking something on purpose seemed to be a rarity for him. He waited for Finn and Leah to back away before he threw the bottle against the ground. It shattered on impact, sending blue glass trickling between the jagged cracks of the black rocks. He picked up a small note with two fingers and shook it free of any slivers of glass before unfolding it.

He read the paper slowly, pronouncing each word with careful deliberation:

There once was a team with no blame
They were equal and treated the same
But for you to move by
You must tell us all why
When you rank all your teammates by name.

Oscar handed the paper to Finn and Leah, who both read it a second time, lips moving in silence as they tried to help him find a loophole.

Oscar shook his head. "I should've done the dare."

Finn understood his apprehension; it seemed like such a simple task at first, but it would expose things that were better left hidden. The thought of having to rank his own team was a frightening one, and Finn would rather risk his life than be forced to open that terrible door. On top of the awkwardness of the task, how could you really rank *people*? Best and worst in what capacity? Intelligence? Kindness? Athletic ability?

Oscar shook his head again and looked up at the sky, clearly trying to figure out how to rank his teammates and friends from best to worst. He mumbled to himself, running through his choices to an invisible audience before stopping to heave a tortured sigh. "Do I have to say their last names, too?" He was obviously stalling.

Finn shrugged. Oscar apologized to his team out loud before whispering, "From best to worst: Kade, because he's the strongest and he's, you know, our leader. Next, Ira because he's the best strategist and works the hardest. Then...Araceli. She's...a good teammate. Loyal. But she doesn't always take practice seriously. And...last, me, because," he rolled his eyes, "well, for starters I'm slow, and I also can't—"

He opened his mouth to continue vilifying himself, but went quiet as his pocket watch began to vibrate in his hand. He flung open the silver casing as Finn and Leah watched in eager silence. Both screens were illuminated with a solid green.

"You must've passed." Finn slapped Oscar on the back. The large boy nodded, but looked like he was on the cusp of tears. He had embarrassed some of his teammates and now everyone knew what he thought of himself.

Leah seemed to sense an opportunity to break the tension. "I'm up, I guess." Pushing some messy red hair out of her face, she took a red bottle and smashed it on the ground. She picked up a heavy, iron key and a slip of paper from the fragments of red. She shook the paper out in front of her before she read it aloud:

Take a deep breath and then take your new key
For this ship has lost chests in the deep of the sea
But the sharks are on guard
So, this swim might be hard
Take a look for yourself, you will not disagree.

Sharks.

Finn's eyes roved the ship interior, coming to rest on a large hole in the half-rotted, sun-bleached deck upon which they stood, just beyond the table. The three teammates made their way to the edge, where the black rock dropped down into crystalline, blue water. Although the water was clear, the constant movement of its surface distorted the shapes below—four rectangular objects that sat against white sand about twenty feet beneath. As the group leaned forward, squinting to get a look, a silent, dark outline darted across their view.

Finn and Oscar jumped back involuntarily, but Leah stayed put, watching as another dark shadow glided past. She took out her pocket watch and began scrolling with intent and focus. Finn threw a look at Oscar, who shrugged, and eyed the hole in the deck with growing trepidation.

Now that he had the advantage of knowing the secrets of both truth and dare for this station, he considered which was worse: insulting your teammates or swimming with sharks?

Finding what she was searching for, Leah looked up from her pocket watch. Her wetsuit activated, spinning into a hideous, zebra print unitard. Finn cocked his head to the side; Leah looked like she was about to do jazzercise.

Before either of her teammates could question her reasoning for this curious getup, Leah set her pocket watch on the ground, grabbed a heavy, black rock, and lowered herself into the hole, disappearing into the water. Finn and Oscar sprinted to the edge. It was difficult to make out what was happening below the surface; they could see Leah—nothing but a blurry, striped shape from here—but another ominous shadow prowled past their line of sight.

Finn held his breath, hearing his own pulse in his ears, time seeming to come to a complete stop as he and Oscar waited for Leah to surface. Finn still had his knife. Should he dive in to help her? He wasn't sure how much of a help he would be.

Shark Finn.

His old nickname was suddenly ironic; he had no experience with marine life whatsoever.

The shape under the water grew larger and clearer as Leah pushed toward the surface. Her head finally emerged. She wiped her matted, red hair out of her face with one hand as she took a deep breath. Finn helped Oscar pull her up out of the water, afraid that a shark would burst through that aqua-blue surface and drag Leah back down with it.

Leah wore a triumphant smile as she held up a golden, jewel-encrusted crown. It glittered brilliantly as she handed it off to Finn. He was shocked by how heavy it was, but resisted the temptation to put it on his head. He handed it to Oscar who showed less restraint, a giant grin spreading over his face as he crowned himself king. Finn chuckled and wiped his wet hands on the thighs of his wetsuit.

"Holding your breath is the hardest part," Leah panted, tilting her head to the side to permit some water to trickle out of her ear. "No, actually, it's opening your eyes in the salt water. You have to do a lot of it by touch." She plucked her pocket watch off the ground and switched off her ridiculous attire before both screens turned green.

"Guess I did it." She took a seat on the rocks and wiped away some of the salt water that still coursed down her face.

Finn watched her with a bemused smile. "Why the leotard?"

"Black and white stripes confuse sharks." Leah gathered her hair together over one shoulder and wrung it out. "My brother surfs and he has a striped wetsuit. I guess the sharks avoid it."

Finn arched an eyebrow, impressed. "And the rock?"

"It helped me sink to the bottom. Sharks make this dare scary, but they won't attack you, Finn—not unless they feel threatened. The rock helped me sink without making too many vibrations in the water. You just don't want to excite them. Once you're down there you just have to figure out which chest works with your key, and you only have to try three of them—well, two now." She threw a smile at Oscar, who still looked like a rotund royal.

Oscar lifted the crown off his head and set it on the makeshift table next to the sea glass jars. "Which one are you going to do, Finn? Truth...or dare?"

Finn bit his lip in thought. The idea of swimming with sharks was a terrifying one. Leah seemed pretty sure that they were just misunderstood, but Finn had seen Shark Week and he begged to differ. Yet the idea of ranking his teammates was perhaps equally terrifying, as he wasn't exactly excited to reveal to the whole Historians' Society what he thought about certain blonde-haired, green-eyed members of his team. Not to mention what he thought of him*self*.

He glanced at Leah, still dripping saltwater, but safe from harm, and then at the gaping hole in the ship's deck.

Drawing in a deep breath, he opened up his pocket watch, and began to scroll through the 80's clothing options, searching for something in zebra print.

CHAPTER 38
RANGDA

It took Finn three trips to retrieve an emerald necklace set in silver in order to complete his dare. There were at least three large sharks prowling the waters and he was actually relieved that he didn't have the goggles to see them with. He could certainly feel them as they passed, pushing the water into him with their powerful fins.

According to the map on the side of the crate, the next challenge wasn't far away. Finn led the group out of the ruined *Flor de la Mar* and off the rocks. Oscar was showing signs of fatigue, the lack of water beginning to exact a heavy toll on the large boy. His breathing had become more labored, and he stopped frequently to double over, hands on his thighs. The heat was beginning to get to Finn, as well, who wished he were wearing anything other than this wetsuit, which was soaked in perspiration and practically shrink wrapped to his body. Someone was beginning to stink, but it didn't matter who; it was likely all three of them.

Smells like teen spirit.

There should be a Truth or Dare station somewhere near the cliffs to the west of the broken ship, and three teammates set about looking for it. To pass the time as they walked, the group talked about their past challenge, Oscar peppering Finn with questions about the *Titanic* with excitement in his voice. He seemed to be a big fan of ships in general and explained over and over again what an honor it was to discover the *Flor de la Mar*.

The team edged along a sharp cliff, the sea licking her hungry lips below and beating her fists against the wall of black rock. Finn tried not to look down as he led the team across a particularly narrow ledge, but then stopped.

Just look at it.

He willed courage into himself and anchored his feet to the ground, allowing his eyes to fall to the sea below. The ocean was capable of being so many things; beautiful, powerful, humbling in its mystery. But it could also be temperamental, angry, unforgiving. He watched as another wave assaulted the side of the cliff, sending spray into the air, some of it misting his face even from this far away.

"Hey, Finn, you okay?" Oscar's voice sounded behind him.

"Yeah." Finn turned, raising his eyes from the waves. "I'm good."

Finally, the pathway opened up into a dark cave which bore into the steep rock face.

"This seems about right." Finn activated the lantern mode of his pocket watch, flooding the cavern with light. The cave was wet and fairly narrow inside, the air pleasantly musty.

Finn began to make his way through it, leading the way, but he came to an abrupt stop, recoiling as he noticed what looked like a snake slithering out of a puddle. But the creature was motionless. Finn crept forward, eyes narrowed, and let out a sigh of relief; the "snake" was actually just a thick rope—the same sort of rope that had snared Oscar yesterday. He reminded himself that the island was booby-trapped. In all of the excitement of getting to their first challenge, he had forgotten to keep a close eye out for traps. He wondered what triggering this one would do, but didn't care to risk finding out.

"Don't step in the puddles," he warned over his shoulder, holding his pocket watch in front of him to illuminate the threat. "They're using the water to mask traps."

Behind him, Oscar and Leah nodded, eyes cutting from side to side with suspicion.

After a painstakingly slow and careful walk deeper into the cave, the team found themselves standing at another wooden table with more sets of the same red and blue jars. But there was a curious sight behind the table: four heads were carved into the stone of the rock wall. The faces were hideous, with bulging eyes beneath a mess of ornately carved hair. The noses were large and the nostrils flared, and each face had an open and waiting mouth full of a row of flat teeth bookmarked by enormous, stone tusks. A thick blanket of moss ran out of each mouth, making the creatures appear as if they were belching out slime.

Finn curled his lip and turned to gauge the reactions of his new companions. Leah's face was frozen in a wince, but Oscar looked unperturbed as he regarded the carvings, stroking his chin in thought.

"Oscar," Finn ventured. "Do you...know what we're looking at?"

Oscar nodded but seemed reluctant to tell the group. "I've never heard of this cave before. But...given that we're somewhere in Sumatra, these faces have to be Rangda."

"Rangda?" repeated Leah.

"It's no big deal." Oscar took a step toward the stone heads, leaning forward with interest like an anthropologist. "She's just a demon queen from Balinese myth."

Finn stared into the wicked eyes of the stone heads. "Yeah...uh, that sounds like a pretty big deal, Oscar."

Oscar pointed to the carvings. "See how her mouth has that mess of stone spilling out of it? Those are the entrails of the youth she's devoured. She ate babies." He said the last part so casually that Finn had to stifle a scoff.

He felt his face scrunch up. "Yeah, that's not helping, Oscar."

Oscar began to stammer. "Well, it's just that we're not babies, so—"

"Stop, Oscar," advised Leah quietly.

"Well, whatever this is, it's not good," Finn sighed. "It's my turn to go first."

He weighed the options: take a chance with demon heads, or take perhaps an even bigger gamble on some sort of vague question that would leave his inner workings visible to his team and the whole of the Historians' Society?

Despite the sticky heat, he shuddered. "Guess I'll go with a dare."

He seized a red bottle and hurled it against the ground, all three teammates taking a step back as glass shot out in all directions. Taking a piece of paper carefully out from among the shards, Finn held it to the light of his pocket watch and read it to the group:

"These demons might settle a score
Put your hand in a mouth, one of four
They can sting, crush, or bite
So, choose wisely and right
Or you might lose a finger or more."

Finn let the piece of paper flutter to the ground and looked at Oscar and Leah with exhausted eyes. "Great. So...I guess we just have to push our hands into these infant-devouring demon heads. No big deal."

"What do you think's inside?" Leah threw the stone heads a wary look, hugging her arms.

"It could be anything." Finn tried to project the calm he didn't feel, knowing that Leah and Oscar were looking for him to be the strong one. Somehow, he'd been elected their leader and he didn't want to let them down.

"Scorpions, spiders..." Finn rattled off, "...venomous snakes..."

"It could be spikes or some sort of machine that crushes your hands, maybe," offered Oscar.

Finn stared at him through narrowed eyes until he looked away, then turned to assess the four stone carvings. They were nearly identical with no indication as to what might make one more dangerous than the others. The moss spilling out of the mouths made it impossible to see into them, and Finn was sure that removing it would get him disqualified. To get disqualified after all this would suck.

He drew in a deep breath. "Well, I guess waiting around doesn't help, and Emily might be done with half of the challenges already, wherever she is." He took another deep breath and let it out slowly. "I'm just going to pick one."

He shrugged and approached the third head.

"Not that one, Finn!" Oscar shouted, making Finn jump at least a foot.

"Why not?" he muttered, annoyed that Oscar had ruined his momentum.

"Do the first one." Oscar crossed his arms over his portly middle. "Nobody would *ever* pick the first one. I feel like that's the safe one."

"We don't know if *any* of them are safe," Finn pointed out. But what did it matter? He walked to the first statue, its horrifying eyes watching and its open mouth waiting. His heart began to thud in his chest as he set his pocket watch on the table. He held out both his hands in front of himself and looked at them, feeling a sudden swell of nostalgia. Which one was he willing to sacrifice...fret hand or strumming hand? He sighed; neither, but he had to pick.

He shook himself out a little, bouncing on the balls of his feet and trying to find his courage. Raising his right hand, he pressed his fingertips into the spongy moss of the demon's greedy mouth. He closed his eyes and waited. Behind him, Leah and Oscar winced in anticipation. The silence was so thick you could have cut it with Finn's survival knife.

Nothing.

Finn forced himself to push the hand deeper, feeling along the stone throat and cringing at what might come next. He was deep enough that his elbow was rubbing against the stone fangs. How deep did this thing *go*? With a frustrated effort, Finn shoved his arm all the way into the mouth, up to his shoulder, his armpit pressed painfully against the stone.

It was then that light drained from the cavern. Finn felt his eyes widen as he braced for something terrible.

"You did it, Finn!" Leah's voice sounded behind him. It took a second for Finn to realize that the room had gone dark because his pocket watch, set to lantern mode, had been overridden to produce a green screen. He carefully edged his arm out of the mouth, grinning in relief.

"I guess that means Oscar was right." He laughed, collapsing into a crouch on the rocky floor. As he rubbed his fingers he appreciated them more than he ever had.

Leah approached the table next. "It's my turn." She glanced with trepidation at the stone heads and shuddered. "Guess I'm going with a truth."

She grabbed a blue bottle and flung it to the ground. Picking up the paper from the glass debris, she read it aloud:

*Think of the things you've been through
Have you handled them all straight and true?
For we now will all tell
If you know yourself well
Tell us—how good a person are you?*

"What?" Leah's freckled face wrinkled in indignance. "This question isn't fair!"

"It's asking what you think about yourself?" Finn was secretly thankful that he had dodged this one by choosing a dare.

How good a person are you?

How would Finn answer this question? Did being "good" factor in intentions, or just the outcome of your actions? Because, as far as he was concerned, that made a pretty big difference. He pictured the Bird's Eye View flier. His parents' wounded expressions as he'd complained about their lack of means. Everly's eyes as he'd callously told her they "didn't work."

"I guess, but it's just so vague!" Leah complained. "This...this is a stupid question!"

"You have to answer it, Leah." Finn threw her a sympathetic look. "Oscar and I can leave if you want. You know, if it's awkward."

"No." Leah shook her head and heaved a resigned sigh. "The whole point is that we help each other. I just don't understand the question. How are they quantifying 'good?'"

She took a deep breath. "I'm a good person. I try to be. I do my best." She began to breathe heavily. Chewing her lower lip, she stammered, "No, never mind. I'm not. I mean, I shouldn't call myself a good person. Right? Because, that's like, conceited. And conceited isn't 'good.' Maybe that's what they're testing. I'm not as good as I *could* be I guess. I mean, I don't know—"

Her rambling came to an abrupt stop when the pocket watch in her hand switched to red. "Great." She threw her arms into the air and let them slap back down to her sides.

Finn was doubly grateful that he'd chosen the dare. This was definitely scarier than demon heads. "I guess the question was designed to make you second-guess yourself."

"You're a good person, Leah." Oscar awkwardly patted her shoulder.

Leah rolled her eyes. "So, I guess I'm out. I just hate doing all of this for nothing." She smirked and blew a strand of red hair out of her face. "At least I won't run into Emily Neil now. Will you guys do me a favor?"

Finn and Oscar nodded in unison and looked at her with expectation.

Leah threw them a rueful smile. "Win."

"We will," Finn assured her.

"I guess I have to head back to camp and wait for a Bender," Leah said, "but I think I can wait until you guys finish this challenge."

Oscar nodded. "We'll walk back with you after." He drew in his breath and let it out slowly. "I guess I'm up."

He grabbed a red bottle—a dare.

"Wait a second." Finn raised his eyebrows and glanced at the creepy stone heads. "You sure about that?"

"That question will get me just like it got her." Oscar wound up, red bottle clutched in a chubby hand. "Besides, I think I know a way to cheat the system."

With that, he settled things by smashing the red bottle against the rocks. With a sly smile, he walked over to the first mouth, which Finn had already revealed as safe, and inserted his arm, having to bend over quite a bit to fit. He left his arm in the stone mouth for a cursory moment before pulling it out safely.

But Oscar's pocket watch didn't go green.

The large boy's lip curled as he stared at the blank screens. "Well, *that's* not good."

"Maybe it just takes a while," Leah offered.

Finn ran a hand over his face. "It doesn't count."

"Yeah." Oscar's gaze fell to his feet. "Guess I thought I had a freebee on that one. I should've known." He threw a nervous glance at the three remaining heads with their hideous mouths waiting patiently. "You know, they're probably *all* safe."

"The sharks were more of a show than anything else," Leah agreed. "Maybe this is the same sort of thing."

"And that trap that snared you? It sucked, but it definitely wasn't lethal," Finn added.

Fortified by their confidence, Oscar strode up to the third head, and with only a hint of hesitation, pressed his thick fingers into the moss of the stone mouth. Pushing deeper, he smiled as his arm disappeared, unharmed, into the monster.

The group let out a collective sigh as the pocket watch flashed green, signaling that the dare was completed. But Oscar's smile disappeared as he yelped, frantically withdrawing his arm from the mouth. Howling, he shook his hand violently, beating it against his thigh.

"What happened?" shouted Finn. Leah covered her mouth in terror.

"I don't know!" Oscar shrieked, holding his right hand with his left. "Something...something bit me, I think!"

Finn grabbed Oscar's hand and looked his palm over carefully. He couldn't see anything, but Oscar seemed to be in real pain. Finn frowned, turning the hand over to find two, small puncture holes. He felt his gut turn over.

"Leah. Help me." Finn spoke softly, trying to keep his voice even and composed. Pressing his lips together, he showed Leah the wound. Finn didn't want to panic them by uttering the word "snakebite."

As Finn eased Oscar to the ground, he combed his mind for anything and everything he knew about snakebites, which wasn't much. All he knew was to position the bite lower than the level of Oscar's heart. As he moved Oscar's arm accordingly, Leah screamed.

Finn's head snapped up to see a green snake with a triangular head slithering out of the open mouth of the statue. Finn didn't know much about snakes, but he knew that the head could tell you a lot; a flat, triangular one wasn't good. He picked up a rock and slung it at the snake, causing it to retreat back into the dark safety of the carving.

Finn glanced down at Oscar, who was no longer screaming, but moaning heavily as he cradled his hand. It had grown swollen and scarlet in seconds. Without hesitation, Finn's fingers fumbled to find Oscar's pocket watch and yanked the chain three times.

"We have to get him to the beach," he told Leah. With Oscar in this condition within minutes of being bitten, they needed to act quickly; it might take hours to get back to camp. With difficulty, Finn cut away Oscar's sleeve with his survival knife and tied the holo-cloth around Oscar's upper arm as tightly as he could to help stem the flow of blood and slow the poison. When he looked up at Oscar's face, he was horrified to see that the large boy's eyes had grown rheumy and unfocused.

"We have to go! Now!" Finn shouted, abandoning all composure. Leah issued a shaky nod and the two of them struggled to help Oscar to his feet. Oscar's breathing was becoming increasingly shallow, but he was still conscious enough to joke, "I hope Emily finds this truth or dare station soon, Finn. And I hope she picks dare."

Finn managed a brittle smile as the three of them struggled towards the mouth of the cave.

Oscar's left arm was draped around Finn's shoulder and neck, and Finn could feel the heat emanating from it. The flesh had become so swollen that it had grown firm to the touch. Finn knew that Oscar would probably lose the arm, but getting him to the Time Bender was all that mattered now.

Within a few minutes, Oscar became delirious, and they weren't even yet out of the cave.

"Don't leave me, please...don't leave me." Oscar repeated this over and over again, becoming more anxious and less coherent as the seconds passed.

"I need to rest, please," he pleaded, his glazed eyes desperate. Finn set him against the wall and cast a grave look at Leah over

Oscar's head. Every minute they spent here, poison was coursing through Oscar's blood, coagulating it and rendering it toxic.

Finn sprinted to the opening of the cave to see if help was coming.

I pulled the chain.

Where the hell are they?

But there was no sign of help—all Finn could see over the precipice was the raging sea, smashing mercilessly against the cliff. He ran his fingers through his hair, mind spinning. Oscar seemed to be getting heavier and heavier, and he was in no shape to negotiate the narrow pathways ahead.

When Finn returned to Oscar, he found Leah kneeling beside him, hand clutched in hers, head bowed. She looked up at Finn, tears streaming down her dirty face. They were both desperate for the other to come up with something—some miracle that might save their new friend, but there was nothing either of them could do, and they both knew it.

CHAPTER 39
KENTUCKY DERBY

Everly's knuckles were white as she gripped the handle of her bone-china mug. This was her fifth cup of coffee, but she'd stopped drinking it long ago. She barely breathed, green eyes glued to the screen before her as she watched Finn struggle on a deserted island in the sixteenth century.

Five minutes ago, Oscar Clement had grown still, his delirious rambling having ceased, his breathing almost imperceptible as Leah Stevens wept into her palms beside him. Finn, wild-eyed, was gripping his own head.

"I pulled the chain," he murmured. "I pulled the chain, so, where are they?"

As if on cue, an azure flash could be seen in the distance beyond the palms followed by the echo of hurried footsteps as two, black-clad arbitrators pushed onto the scene. They stood over Finn, Leah, and Oscar, an open book in one of their hands.

The one with the book spoke. "Leah Stevens and Finn Mallory, you have hereby been disqualified from Truth or Dare. Per the

Rules of Trials, you will be immediately dispatched back to Historians' Society Headquarters. Leah Stevens, you are disqualified for failing to answer a truth honestly, and Finn Mallory, you have earned your disqualification for unlawfully pulling Oscar Clement's chain. According to chapter twelve, article seven of the Rules of Trials, pulling a competitor's chain, regardless of reason or motivation, is cause for immediate—"

Finn jumped to his feet, forcing his face inches away from the arbitrator's. "I don't fucking care!" he screamed. He threw a wild gesture toward Oscar's limp body. Oscar's lips were beginning to take on a purplish hue, and his eyes had rolled back. "Aren't you going to do something? Help him!"

Both arbitrators stared back at him, eyes passionless beneath the rims of their bowler hats. Finally, one knelt at Oscar's side, and with no sense of urgency, pressed two fingers into the side of the large boy's neck. The pulse-check was quick and perfunctory— obviously for show more than anything else.

Everly held her breath as she watched the arbitrator rise to his feet. It was then that she noticed the wooden handle of a weapon jutting out of his belt holster.

"He's dead, son." The arbitrator's voice was as flat and impassive as his eyes. "Let's go. You heard the rules: 'immediate dispatch.'"

Leah released an anguished cry from her seat on the ground.

"No," Finn protested. He set his mouth, the corners of which had begun to twitch downward, threatening tears, which he seemed to be biting back. He wiped at his eyes with the backs of his hands. "I won't leave him. I won't." As he drew himself up and took a step forward, the crowd surrounding Everly issued a collective gasp.

The arbitrator crossed his arms and narrowed his gaze, lip curling. "Oh, but you will."

"It's in the rules, Finn Mallory." The arbitrator with the book licked his index finger before beginning to leaf through the heavy tome. He found the page he was looking for and ran his forefinger down it before he spoke. "According to chapter two, article five of the Rules of Trials, the temporal remains of any participant who expires in the past is to be left in the past." He raised his eyes from the page and pursed his lips. "This is non-negotiable."

A primal sound exploded out of Finn's mouth as he lunged at the first arbitrator, fists flying. The book fell from the second arbitrator's hands, but he scrambled to catch it mid-air before it hit the ground, as if it were a sacred item. Finn's fist connected with the first arbitrator's jaw, sending the man's bowler hat sailing to the ground. As he bent to retrieve it, Finn's knuckles smashed into his nose, sending him stumbling backward before he reached up with one hand to attempt to stem the flow of blood, now coursing down his face in rivulets of scarlet.

The Historians' Society members watched the brawl in rapt silence, heads swishing from side to side as if they were watching a tennis match. Many of them carried Oriental fans and whispered behind them as they watched with eager eyes.

The arbitrator with the book stood back, wide-eyed, clutching the *Rules of Trials* to his chest as if to protect it. A tussle ensued, but it was brief; Finn was no match for the black-clad official, who finally managed to dodge Finn's blows long enough to draw his weapon from his belt holster.

Everly felt a scream rise in her throat. Her hand flew to her mouth as if to seal it in, and she didn't even notice when her mug of cold coffee fell from her hands and shattered at her feet.

"Don't worry, honey," a deep voice sounded beside her. She felt herself bristle. It was Gabriel Lochan, Vale's mentor. His mouth turned up into a smug smile. "It's only a stun-gun. It'll put him out for a while, but he'll be alright." His smile grew wider. "Physically, that is; his pride might be another matter."

Sure enough, the arbitrator aimed his weapon and squeezed the trigger, sending a firework-like projectile speeding toward its target. It connected with Finn's side with a small pop, and Finn shuddered before crumpling into a heap on the cave floor. The arbitrator calmly restored his weapon to his holster, restored his bowler hat to his head, and withdrew a white handkerchief from his vest pocket to dab at his bloodied nose.

"Let's go," he said coolly to his companion, throwing Finn over his shoulder as if he were a rag doll. To Leah, he issued a command, his voice as cold as the stone walls of the cave: "Come on. Pick up your feet, and try not to fall, will you? Time is of the essence."

Everly cast her eyes around the room. Kade Davis pressed a closed fist to his mouth, eyes shut before he lowered his head into his hands. This ordeal had likely spurred traumatic memories of losing a teammate, and now he'd lost another. Beside him, Ira and Araceli, the other members of Halls of Ivy Prep, wept softly. All the contestants from the other teams had their eyes fixed to the screen in front of them, their faces either blank or twisted from shock...with the exception of Elden Neil.

"Why so sad, Kade?" he piped up from Vale Academy's row. "Your team just got stronger."

"Are you kidding me?" Valerie jumped to her feet, but Edison placed a placating hand on her shoulder. She looked into his eyes, past the thick, black frames of his glasses and reluctantly sat, contenting herself with raising her middle finger in the direction of Vale Academy's section.

Gabriel Lochan lifted a gloved hand. "Now children, please; there's no need to be uncivilized." His smug smile returned. "Besides—you're missing the rest of the show."

He gestured back to the screen, whispering something to Elden, who snickered as Finn was hauled down the cliff and through the foliage, slung over the arbitrator's shoulder, unconscious. Leah sobbed as she tripped through the vines. As they grew closer to the Time Bender, the foliage became sparser, much of it charred or burnt away by the heat of the machine as it had materialized. They reached the brass porthole and Finn's limp body was thrown inside before the screen went dark.

The members of the Historians' Society, a sea of ridiculous hats who were served refreshments and bubbly in fluted glasses as they had watched Oscar die in charmed fascination, looked like spectators at the Kentucky Derby. The sounds coming from their section were of wonder and awe, not shock or horror; they were not at all dismayed by what they had witnessed but instead tickled, and it made Everly's stomach roil as she watched money pass from hand to hand under tables. A butler drifted among them with a silver platter, offering hors d'oeuvres, which were accepted onto tiny appetizer plates with delight.

Her heart hammering within her, her eye caught a feather bobbing through the crowd as Felix Winkler wove his way through the seats, thrusting his microphone into the faces of the spectators.

"Whadja think?" he demanded of a Society member in a top hat and monocle. But before his interviewee could reply, Felix caught sight of Everly's green eyed stare. His face twisted into his pointy smile and he made a bee-line for her.

He snaked through the crowd and pushed his microphone into her face, black eyes glittering. "Tell me, Miss Caldwell—how do'ya feel? Inquirin' minds wanta know: what wuzzit like, watchin' as—"

"Piss off," Valerie's hand flew out and closed over one end of his microphone, "before I rip off your stupid hat and feed it to you." The pointed smile vanished from Winkler's face. He swallowed hard before backing away into the crowd.

As Everly watched Winkler's feather disappear into the room, her eyes met her grandfather's. The old man's face was a mask of regret, his eyes replete with sorrow and apology. Everly felt a surge of emotion move through her like fire through dry brush as she looked at him—equal parts anger and disgust. She set her mouth and looked away.

By now, a butler had begun to clean up the shards of ceramic at Everly's feet and mop up her spilled drink, wiping furiously at her shoes. He looked up from the ground. "More coffee, Miss?"

She ignored the question, dragging her eyes from the jagged pieces of bone china at her feet. When she returned her gaze to the back of the room, her grandfather was gone.

CHAPTER 40
OPTICS

"Dashiel, I daresay you're losing your nerve." Philomena Vandecraft flashed a grin at the other timekeepers. "By and large, the crowd loved the challenge. It had all of the drama that a game like Truth or Dare demands."

The Grand Timekeeper looked to the others for support, only to find nothing but bowed heads and averted eyes. They sat back in their leather chairs, busying their hands by straightening stacks of papers that didn't need straightening.

Timekeeper Keenan Wakefield cleared his throat. "The numbers speak for themselves, Dashiel. As Philomena said, this was a very dramatic challenge; I'd venture to say the most compelling one in recent memory. That includes the loss of the girl last year during Hide and Seek, mind you."

Garridan shook his head and covered one of his hands with the other to prevent his peers from seeing it shake. "Mordecai Moskowitz has asked to speak to us. Well, he's demanded it, really."

He removed his top hat and ran a hand through his white hair. "I think it would be a mistake to refuse him an audience."

"Why does he have a grievance?" Philomena Vandecraft rolled her grey eyes. "It wasn't even his team who saw a casualty. Sure, the Mallory boy got a bit of a roughing up in the end, but he asked for it." She released a short laugh that sounded almost playful. "I mean, for goodness' sake, Dashiel, one does not just assault an arbitrator and get away with it." She reached up and adjusted her cloche hat with a lineless hand. When she spoke, her voice was laced with a hint of scorn. "Anyway, Halls of Ivy Prep isn't complaining; if the dead boy's own mentor has nothing to say, this is a non-issue. The boy signed the contract. He was fully aware of the risks."

Garridan frowned and mopped some sweat from his brow with a handkerchief. "It would seem insensitive to not listen, at least." When he was met with blank stares from his fellow timekeepers, he added, "Bad optics."

After a weighty silence, Timekeeper Doherty issued a curt nod. "Yes." He adjusted a pair of brass goggles. "Bad optics."

Grand Timekeeper Garridan restored his top hat to his head. "Let's hear Mordecai out and just get it over with." With the flick of two fingers, he motioned to a pair of arbitrators waiting at a pair of double doors at the far end of the chamber. "Show him in."

The doors swung open, and Moskowitz was ushered to a podium in the center of the room. The small man's eyes held unusual fire behind the lenses of his chrome spectacles.

"Mordecai!" A politician's smile painted itself onto Grand Timekeeper Garridan's face, all traces of the stress he'd displayed moments ago wiped away. "How are you, old friend?"

Moskowitz frowned, fumbling with his trembling fingers as he stared the timekeepers down.

The Grand Timekeeper's stomach was troubled, but he refused to show his discomfort. "If this is about your team's disqualification, I assure you, the rules are there for their own protection. And there is still two challenges remaining, providing your team ample opportunity to—"

"Disqualification?" Professor Moskowitz's voice was sharp enough to cut through glass. "You think I am here to protest a *disqualification?*"

The Grand Timekeeper felt his smile falter. "Please, state your business, then." He folded his hands in front of him.

"What has happened to the Time Trials?" The professor's voice was quiet but indignant. He seethed within the folds of his tweed overcoat, exerting visible effort to control a temper that Garridan hadn't known existed. "In a mere twenty years has it really devolved into...this?"

The Grand Timekeeper's smile forsook him completely now. "'De*volved?*'"

"Yes!" Moskowitz slammed a hand down on the podium, making Garridan flinch. "Do not repeat my words, Dashiel! I said them. I used the ones I meant to!"

Timekeeper Doherty nervously twirled the waxed end of a handlebar moustache, eyes darting between the Grand Timekeeper and the diminutive professor.

"Perhaps you should choose your words more carefully, then." Philomena Vandecraft rose coolly to her feet and matched the professor's stare across the room.

"Oscar Clement is dead." Professor Moskowitz's words settled into the air like black smoke. "His body was left in the past like a piece of garbage."

"The abandonment of temporal remains is in the rules of Trials to ensure the continued secrecy of the Historians' Society. A disappearance is much cleaner than a funeral." Philomena Vandecraft spoke for the Grand Timekeeper, hands braced on the edge of the table. "You know this. Or perhaps you've forgotten?" A vicious smile spread over her face. "You've been absent twenty years, if I remember correctly?" She turned to her fellow timekeepers, a shine in her slate-grey eyes. "Besides, it's not as if the Clement boy would have been easy to move."

Keenan Wakefield stifled a laugh, despite his own plentiful girth.

Grand Timekeeper Garridan sat silently, speechless as he was upstaged by one of his own lesser timekeepers.

"Twenty years," Moskowitz confirmed, shaking in place, gripping the sides of the podium for support. "You are correct. It seems much has changed since then. If I had known..." His voice trailed off, and when he spoke again, it had grown louder and taken on a pleading tone. "The Time Trials used to be about *history*. This last trial? It was only vaguely historical. Traps? Where is the respect of the past that we claim to honor with this society?"

"The boy identified the historical ship himself," Vandecraft said. "As I remember, he was quite excited about it." She narrowed her eyes. "And as for the trap? Well, the snake was my contribution. A little added risk makes the challenges so much more...exciting." She trilled her fingers in the air.

Moskowitz's wizened face went red. "The risks involved in the Time Trials have always been inherent to the time period and situation to which we send the children...they are not supposed to be engineered by *us*!"

Professor Moskowitz spoke directly to the Grand Timekeeper now, who would not meet his gaze. "Putting an old ship into the challenge seemed cursory. As if you were checking off a box. This whole thing was tawdry! Like a tasteless game show fit for daytime television. Where is the respect for history in a spectacle like this? Not to mention for the children? A boy *died* today, Dashiel!"

The Grand Timekeeper felt a flicker of remorse pass over his face and he worked to smother it.

"So, it's reality you want?" Philomena Vandecraft's voice prickled Garridan's skin. He looked at her, but cast his gaze away when he saw her grey eyes flare with their trademark excitement.

She leaned forward with a wolfish smile. "Let's make it real, then." She smoothed the folds of her dress and strode to the door, the smile never leaving her face. "Now, if you'll excuse me, I have an interview to conduct."

CHAPTER 41
PIECES

Philomena Vandecraft smiled at the three competitors before her, eyes still electric with excitement. As this was Red Rover and all four teams had participants to be interviewed, there was no timekeeper officially assigned, but she had volunteered, naturally.

"What happened to the boy was tragic, of course," she began, "but rules are rules—the interview is non-negotiable."

She turned to Finn, whose head was still buzzing and his ears still ringing from the effects of the arbitrator's stun-gun, which had been like nothing he had ever seen before. It had looked like an old-school revolver, but it had worked like a cross between a tranquilizer and a stun gun. He'd been helped over to the interview, his legs still shaky, his side smarting from where he'd been hit. He'd woken up alone in the medical bay, the harsh fluorescent lights bearing down on him. Finn had woken up like this once before: almost four years ago, after the car accident that left him with a broken clavicle and no parents. Waking up now was a lot like that— regaining consciousness in a hospital bed with no recollection of what had happened, before it all rushed back at him at once in a tsunami of white-hot pain, forcing him to relive it all over again.

Oscar was dead.

He had watched him die.

He had *let* him die.

"Speaking of rules, my dear boy," Vandecraft wagged her finger in mock admonishment, "you must not have been listening when your mentor explained them to you."

When playing Red Rover, participants were forbidden to pull another player's chain, but Finn had pulled Oscar's when he had been bitten by a venomous snake, and had therefore been disqualified. Leah had already been eliminated by failing to answer one of the ambiguous truths "correctly." When Oscar succumbed to the snakebite, Emily had been deemed victor by default, granting Vale Academy a win.

Finn dug within himself for anger at Vandecraft; through his post-tranq haze, he registered that she was attempting to provoke him, but he simply had nothing left to fight her with. The only anger he felt was folded in on himself. He stared down at the table's surface, looking at the fuzzy outline of his own reflection in the stainless steel, replaying Oscar's last words vividly in his mind: *"Please don't leave me."* Nausea welled up in him at the memory of Oscar's limp body, left alone in the cave.

He pressed his eyes shut.

If I hadn't chosen the dare, maybe he wouldn't have either.

If I had been more prepared...

If I hadn't let them look at me like a leader...

If...

Timekeeper Vandecraft, pouted, seemingly disappointed with Finn's silence.

"Emily Neil." She turned to the victor from Vale. "Congratulations, my dear. Your strategy was most admirable."

Finn opened his eyes. Emily's face was blankly inscrutable as she looked at the timekeeper across the table. She should have been bragging. She should have been teasing. She should have been helping Philomena Vandecraft twist her murderous knife deep into Finn's back. That was Emily's way. Wasn't it?

"It was a brilliant plan," Vandecraft continued, attempting to induce a response. "You sabotage the food supply, thus forcing them to rush...to make mistakes. You knew the dares were dangerous and the truths were troublesome. You knew that they would be trying to catch up to you, thinking you had a head start."

It suddenly became clear to Finn: Emily hadn't even attempted the challenge. It was why she had left them the map. Finn, Oscar, and Leah had rushed because they assumed she wanted to be the first one done, but all Emily had really wanted was to be the last one standing.

"To think," Vandecraft laughed, "while they were diving with sharks and playing with snakes, you were enjoying the last of the fruit on a beach with white sand! Brilliant!"

Finn felt another wave of self-directed anger crest within himself; he had lectured Oscar and Leah about traps, but he had led them into the biggest one. The thought of Emily dropping grapes into her mouth while poison burned its way through Oscar's veins infuriated him. He shot a dark look in her direction, but he felt his eyes soften as he watched her wither under his gaze; all traces of the monster Emily had been were washed away. She looked tortured, wincing at Vandecraft's congratulatory words, her lip seeming even to tremble at times.

"I just wanted to win." Her voice was paper thin as she looked at Finn out of the corners of her eyes.

"Good for you, dear." Timekeeper Vandecraft beamed. "At least *someone* gets it."

* * *

Everly milled at to the door to the prep room, twisting the hem of her dark blue cardigan in a nervous fist. She watched as a somber Leah exited, followed by an unusually emotional Emily.

Everly had been waiting to see Finn since his arrival back to the present, sick to her stomach as he regained consciousness in the medical bay and endured Vandecraft's interview. But now that she had the chance to see him, she was afraid. She stalled at the door.

She had been afraid of what Emily's tactics would do to Finn and she hadn't been wrong to worry about it. But it hadn't been Emily that broke him—it had been Oscar. He was another loss, one that Finn would take responsibility for. There was no possible way that Finn would see Oscar's death as anything other than his own failing. She'd seen the footage: Finn had stepped up as a leader—someone Everly had always known he'd had it in him to be. In Finn's mind, Oscar had been under his charge and had died on his watch.

Finn had come to Everly pre-shattered, in pieces, like the bone china mug in the observation room. Over these months, she had watched some of these pieces come back together and scatter once more, and today she knew that she would find those pieces tossed everywhere, perhaps without hope of ever being put together again.

She pushed open the door with a tentative hand, all but holding her breath in anticipation of what state she might find Finn in. He sat in a metal chair, head down, his dark hair, now as shaggy as the day she'd first seen him, hanging into his face. He didn't look up at the sound of the door.

Before he'd made the Bend, Everly had wanted to leave him with inspired words, but she'd come up short, and today she knew it would be the same.

Nothing she said could fix this.

Nothing she did could fix *him*.

She approached slowly, part of her wanting to run from the room to spare herself the pain she'd find in his eyes, and another part of her wanting to pull him into her arms and absorb that pain for him.

She knew the second part of her would win. Isn't that all she'd wanted to begin with?

She gently lifted his chin. His face was dirty, eyes defeated, but when she gathered him to her, he didn't pull away.

CHAPTER 42
CRICKETS

Everly and Finn sat shoulder-to-shoulder in the shadow of the snow-dusted gazebo. They sat in utter silence, save the sound of Sonic Youth blaring over Finn's headphones, just as they had nearly every night since Finn had played Truth or Dare...

Since the day Oscar died.

Finn had clung to Everly that day in the medical bay for dear life, as if to a raft in rushing rapids, the warmth of their embrace fully melting the ice that had been between them for weeks.

But things still weren't as they'd been before, and maybe they never would be again; everything that had come to pass had dulled the fire between them to embers, and Everly knew now wasn't the time to try to ignite them again.

Finn couldn't be with anyone right now. Finn may *never* be able to be with anyone—not until he freed himself from the prison of self-loathing that he lived in.

Now, beside him in the darkness of the frozen gardens, Everly exhaled, her breath a cloud in front of her. Snow made everything so quiet. The crickets that had chirped here in the fall were gone now, and all the trees were barren. But come spring, the gardens would be alive again. She glanced at Finn's silent profile beside her.

Maybe other things could come back to life, too.

Inwardly, Everly scolded herself as she thought of Nick—a thing she seldom did these days. Nick being the last thing from her mind wasn't new, really, and deep down, Everly knew she'd have to reckon with what that meant, but today was not that day. Nick was none the wiser to these late-night Walkman sessions, and it was probably for the best. Out of sight, out of mind.

In the weeks since that last, tragic challenge, each member of the team had been especially delicate with Finn, each of them trying to give their friend what they thought he needed in their own ways. Valerie had taken him out for onion rings and hot chocolate at a diner that was beneath her. Edison had shared his banana chips, which was a big deal. And Everly offered him her silent companionship every night in the Wharton Gardens, even enduring Soundgarden for his sake.

These meetings were never planned; they had developed an almost telepathic knowing of when the other would come out to the gazebo steps. And here they would sit, saying nothing. There may not have been actual crickets in the Wharton Gardens anymore, but Finn delivered them in the form of his silence.

Everly didn't want to press him; he would speak when he was ready. And yet his silence frightened her. Her own father had gone quiet in the same way after her mother had died. In the weeks before Sam Caldwell had gone away, he'd barely spoken a word to his daughter, making their house a chamber of thick, eerie silence. She wished Finn would say something—anything—even if he raged, screamed or cried. Anything would be better than the silence.

The cassette track had switched, and it was a song Everly knew, after all these nights next to Finn, the foam of his headphones crushed against her ear. "Letting the Cables Sleep" by

Bush. Everly threw another look at Finn in the darkness. His brown eyes were slightly raised, fixed on the night sky, hands stuffed into the pockets of his flannel. He looked sort of hollow. Tired and gaunt. Like every night, Everly waited for him to speak, but she was met with nothing but crickets.

"Do you...want to talk about it?" Everly's own voice surprised her. In answer, Finn dragged his eyes from the sky. He didn't speak, and he made no move to stop the music. Instead, he issued her a wry smile, fished around in the pocket of his flannel, and pulled out something small and round. He took Everly's hand, pried her fingers open and deposited a blue and green cat's eye marble into her palm.

Everly stared down at the trinket, then back up at Finn's face, waiting for explanation.

"Someone gave it to me." Finn's shoulders rolled in a shrug. He looked into Everly's eyes then, another eerily calm smile dancing on his lips. "Ebba. Ebba Andersson. I don't know what happened to her in reality, but if she lived to seventeen, she probably would've looked a lot like you, actually."

Everly all but stopped breathing as he brushed a lock of blonde hair out of her face. His hand stayed there for a moment before it dropped back to his side, and it was only then that she exhaled. She rolled the marble around in her palm, letting the light from the streetlight catch it, but she stayed quiet. If she was silent, maybe Finn wouldn't be.

Finn's face hardened along with his voice. "But the reality is, she probably drowned, or froze to death while she waited to be rescued." Everly looked up at him and he met her stare. "I didn't save anyone, Everly. The reality is, Ebba's probably at the bottom of the damn Atlantic, I couldn't save Oscar, and I couldn't save my parents." He scoffed. "You know what? Vale was right to pick me."

Everly studied his face in the dark, combing her mind for the right words, but she knew there weren't any. As the track finished,

Finn gently reclaimed his headphones, rose to his feet, and turned to leave.

"Finn," Everly started, palm still open with the marble sitting in it. Finn stopped in his tracks, bent and plucked it out of her hand, stuffing it in his pocket.

Everly drew her peacoat more tightly around herself and found the words she was looking for. All she could do was plant them and hope they'd take root. Even if they didn't bloom now, in the dead of winter, maybe they would come spring.

"The past is stealing your present." She said the words slowly, deliberately, searching for Finn's eyes in the dark. "And if you aren't careful, it'll steal your future, too."

Finn looked at her a long moment before he walked back toward Aion Hall, hands in his pockets, leaving Everly with nothing but silence again.

CHAPTER 43
ANKYLOSAURUS

The average person has between three and five dreams per night, but those dreams are seldom remembered. Edison had read about it in *Medical News Today*. The article hadn't said how many of those dreams are nightmares, but Edison was fairly certain that his roommate was having one right now.

Finn had been having them every night for weeks, actually, and each time Edison heard him fitfully writhing around and mumbling in his sleep, he'd contemplated waking him up, but decided against it, thinking at first that they were *another* type of dream.

That could be awkward.

After the Truth or Dare challenge, Valerie had begged Edison to pay special attention to Finn, claiming he required "special handling." She'd taken him by the shoulders and looked him in the eyes, the way she did when she meant business.

"Edison," she'd said. "Just...try to find a way to be supportive. He's fragile right now."

Fragile.

Ever since then, Edison had been picturing his roommate as one of those huge, cardboard moving boxes, words stamped all over him in red. Handle with care. Do not shake. Do not drop.

Edison tended to see things as they were, with little emotion attached to them. But that didn't mean he didn't *feel* emotion; that was a common misconception about those on the spectrum—that people with autism lack empathy. The truth is, a person with autism feels emotions just as much as a neurotypical does—they just struggle to identify those emotions, and they struggle even more to express them.

Edison had been diagnosed with high-functioning autism at the age of five. Back home, he had an occupational therapist who he met with three times a week: Tina.

Tina was there to teach Edison how to navigate the social world: how to maintain friendships. How to decode facial expressions. What certain smiles indicated. What it meant when someone's tone of voice changed.

Tina's perfume had been too strong, leaving Edison with a slight headache in her wake. She also had a penchant for brightly colored, highly-patterned shirts that made Edison's eyes cross, and he disliked the pitch of her voice. Still, Tina was nice, and she had taught him a lot about social interaction. He didn't have a "Tina" here at Wharton; thus, for the past three years, he'd had to draw from what she'd taught him on his own.

In addition to helping Edison decode the feelings of others, Tina had tried to teach him how to identify his *own* emotions. Tonight, as Edison watched his sleeping roommate whimper in his sleep, he believed he was feeling what Tina would call "sympathy."

He'd felt the same thing as he watched the last challenge, in which Finn had tried in vain to save Oscar from a fatal snake bite. Finn was usually pretty even-keeled, but he had *shouted* during Truth or Dare. He'd punched an arbitrator—not once, but twice. Shouting and punching indicated a high level of emotional distress.

And ever since then, his whole team had been wearing expressions that Tina would've described as "tense."

In his sleep, Finn murmured something about a snake. A pearl.

"My fault," he slurred, his voice thick with sleep.

Yes, it was decided: tonight would be the night Edison woke Finn up. What he'd do after, he wasn't quite sure.

He clumsily climbed the ladder to Finn's loft bed and stared down at his roommate in the darkness, but recoiled as his fingers brushed up against Finn's blanket. His nerves screamed in protest and his face contorted in disgust: this blanket contained fleece. Maybe it was some kind of blend, but it definitely had fleece—Edison could feel it. A painful shudder coursed through him. He hated the way fleece felt, nearly as much as he hated the smell of pine needles that emanated from Finn's sleeping form. To others, the scent of Finn's deodorant was probably subtle, but to Edison it was an all-out assault to the senses. He waited for his nervous system to calm down before he returned to the task at hand.

Edison hadn't had any friends before Finn came to Wharton Academy. In fact, he could count on one hand the number of friends he'd had in the whole of his seventeen years. He'd had one other roommate during freshman year, but the arrangement had only lasted a few days before the roommate told Headmaster Bruce that he was "uncomfortable" and requested a room switch. Maybe it was Edison's list of stipulations that had caused his roommate to flee; Tina had warned him more than once that having conditions for friendships was off-putting, but he maintained that his expectations were quite reasonable. Since then, he'd lived as a single in a double room, and that had suited him just fine.

But this year, the school counselor had called Edison in to prepare him for the reality that he would finally be getting a new roommate. Edison had balked at first, much preferring his own space. But then he'd met Finn Mallory. Finn had accepted Edison's rules without question or protest. He didn't make fun of Edison, but he also didn't condescend to him. Most people talked to Edison slowly, as if he were half deaf or seven years old, or they just avoided him altogether, throwing him a polite smile before getting as far away as possible—but Finn didn't do that. Even with his obnoxious guitar and perpetually unmade bed, Edison liked Finn Mallory.

Edison narrowed his eyes behind his thick glasses and poked Finn with his index finger.

Nothing happened. Finn continued to mumble and twitch. "My fault," he whimpered again, his back arching slightly.

A group of loud students passed beneath the dorm window, which was open a precise two and a half inches, and Edison drew back to clap his hands over his ears. He watched the window with disdain until the noise disappeared, and then returned his focus to his roommate.

He poked Finn again—harder this time, in the shoulder.

Finn startled, eyes flying open, popping up like a jack in the box and smacking his head against the ceiling. "Ow!" He squinted at Edison in the dark, clutching his head. "Jesus, Edison, what are you doing?"

Edison crossed his arms, wondering how Finn could've possibly mistaken him for Jesus of Nazareth. He didn't have a beard or long hair, and Edison was pretty sure the typical representation of Jesus Christ did not include eyewear of any kind. Glasses didn't even exist in biblical times.

Finn must be really tired. Probably from all the nightmares.

"You were in distress. Your thrashing and moaning indicated that you were not only having a dream, but an unpleasant one. Thus, I concluded that you needed to be extracted from the dream immediately." He shoved his glasses up further on the bridge of his nose. "You're welcome. I recommend a sleep specialist."

The corners of Finn's mouth curled upward. A smile.

If a person smiles, it means they aren't upset with you.

"Thanks, Edison." Finn's eyes went sad again as he collapsed backward on the bed with a sigh. "Not sure I can get back to sleep, though."

Edison clambered back down the ladder and flicked on the light. "You said 'my fault.'" He adjusted his glasses and stared up at Finn. "When you were sleeping. That's what you said."

Finn didn't respond.

"*What's* your fault?"

"What *isn't*?" Finn's tone of voice changed. It got harder. And the corners of his mouth turned down. A frown.

Angry? Frustrated? One of those.

Maybe Edison had missed an important social cue and said the wrong thing.

"*Find a way to support him.*" As Valerie's voice echoed in his mind, his eyes roved the room and rested on Finn's guitar.

Edison hated loud noise, and Finn's guitar was one of the biggest offenders. The sound of it made Edison's bones hurt. Whenever Finn played, he used earplugs or left altogether. But he also knew music was his roommate's favorite thing in the world. Finn liked music the way Edison liked prehistory.

"Sometimes friendship requires sacrifice," Tina had told him once. "You have to be willing to give and take. That's how relationships work."

It was decided, then. Edison would make a sacrifice.

"Finn, I would like to learn to play guitar." He kept his arms crossed over his chest.

Finn's voice was muffled, his face buried in his pillow. "Man, you know it's like...three in the morning, right?" He sat up in his bed, hair a mess. "Plus, don't you hate loud noise? Pretty sure you called Nirvana a 'sensory nightmare.'"

Edison gathered Finn's guitar into his lap and looked at his roommate with expectation. "I can endure it for approximately ten minutes. What can you teach me in that time?"

Finn was smiling again now. A tired smile, but a smile. "It might take less time than that for someone to come banging on the door with a noise complaint, but sure." He clambered down his ladder, wearing a pair of plaid pajama pants and no shirt. There was a small, angry, red mark on his side from where he'd been shot.

He rubbed his eyes and positioned Edison's hands on the strings. Edison disliked the rough sensation of the steel—the thinner strings actually felt like they could cut his fingers—but he didn't complain.

Sacrifice.

"So." Finn cleared his throat. "I think I'm gonna teach you three chords: C, D, and G major." He rolled his shoulders in a shrug. "They're kind of a big deal—most songs are built around 'em." He yawned, and Edison couldn't help but notice his eyes were wreathed by dark circles.

"Okay. So. C Major." Finn helped Edison bend his fingers and stagger them, pressed against the strings, across the first three frets.

"Like this?" Edison looked up at Finn through the lenses of his glasses.

"Press harder. And let the tip of your third finger touch the sixth string to mute it. Don't *press* on it—just...*mute* it." Edison complied as Finn threw open his bedside drawer, fished around inside, and came up with a guitar pick. "Here. Now strum."

Edison drew the guitar pick down over the strings, resisting the urge to rock in place as sound poured forth and a jarring vibration coursed through his body. Finn crimped an eye. "One of your fingers is touching the G string. Leave it open."

"G string." Edison felt his face scrunch up. "Isn't that a female undergarment?"

Finn's eyes went wide before he covered up his face with his hands and fell backward on the floor, laughing.

Laughing.

Finn was *laughing.*

"Edison, how do you even know what that is?" The corners of Finn's eyes creased with his smile, and tears leaked out of them, streaking toward his ears.

Edison shrugged, fingers still contorted into a C major. "I found a copy of Maxim in my dad's office once and read it cover to cover." This only made Finn laugh harder. Edison wasn't sure what was so funny—it had been a genuine question, but he was sure Valerie would be pleased with his ability to elicit a laugh from their "fragile" friend. Edison hadn't heard Finn laugh since before Fall Fling.

Finn sat up, hair falling forward into his face, which had straightened now. "Dude, why are you even doing this? You don't want to learn to play guitar." His voice grew softer. "Edison, are you doing this...like, for *me*?"

Edison couldn't decipher the tone of Finn's voice. He wished Tina were here to tell him what to say. What to do.

Finn ran his hands over his face, Edison's silence seeming to have provided the answer. "Forget this. Let's...let's do something *you* want to do." He drew himself up from the floor and collapsed into his desk chair.

Edison set the guitar down, secretly glad to let go of it and free his fingers from the awkward, cramped-up position they'd found themselves in just to form a single chord, which Finn claimed to be the most "basic." It hadn't *felt* basic.

Finn leaned back in his seat and shut his eyes. "Edison, talk to me about dinosaurs or something. Isn't that your jam?" His voice went quiet. It was almost a whisper. "Talk to me about...anything."

Edison felt himself brighten. He stood and plucked a book off his desk—*Wonders of the Cretaceous Period*—and began to leaf through it until he found a page he liked.

He drew his glasses down further on his nose and looked at Finn over the rim as he read. "'Thyreophorans: dinosaurs with defensive armor.'" His eyes roved over the images of the prehistoric beasts covered with osteoderms—armored plates—but slowly drew his gaze back up to Finn.

"*You* have defensive armor." He said it without thinking.

Finn kept his eyes shut as he answered. "Is that why you like me, Edison? Because I remind you of a dinosaur?" His voice was friendly, but it had another sound to it, too—something Tina called "sarcastic."

Edison looked down at his book. "The ankylosaurus, maybe. It was an herbivore, so it was mostly pretty benign, but it protected itself with fused plates of bone, and it had a club tail that could do some serious damage...if it got scared. If it felt threatened."

He watched Finn open his eyes. They looked shiny.

Fragile.

Do not drop.

Do not bend.

But Finn sighed and whispered, "Fair enough, go on."

"Sometimes you're unpleasant—like after the dance. You lose control of your club tail and say things that are damaging. And your armor's so thick that it might keep people from getting close to you."

Finn's expression was now completely unreadable. Edison couldn't keep his own voice from being deadpan, but he could control the volume, so he softened it. "But you're mostly tolerable. Nice, even. You're one of the only people I know who talks to me like a person." He took off his glasses and shined them on the hem of his t-shirt. "You aren't my best friend—SCRAP is. But you're a close second."

"'A close second.'" Finn smiled, but it was a sad smile. "Thanks. I'll take it." He shut his eyes again and leaned back in his seat. "Tell me about more dinosaurs. Tell me everything you know."

Edison happily obliged. He leafed through the sauropod section of his book, extolling the power of the apatosaurus' whip-like tail, but when he looked back up at Finn, he found him asleep, chin to chest, hair hanging into his face.

Edison stood and pulled his roommate's blanket off the bed, enduring the excruciating feel of fleece on his fingertips, and draped it over Finn's sleeping form.

CHAPTER 44
UPPER CRUST

Wharton Academy was buzzing with activity. It was the academy's annual Open House event, meaning that the parents who paid good money to pawn off their children on this prestigious school would finally be forced to spend time with them for an entire weekend.

As the recipient of the Good Fortunes Scholarship, Finn had received a care package, delivered to his dorm in honor of this event—a basket full of summer sausages, aged cheeses, and three meal vouchers to Upper Crust, an exclusive Italian eatery nestled into the heart of Wharton's campus. Finn extracted a note from the lavish basket and read it aloud to Edison, who had unscrewed the cap of a glass jar in the basket and was now popping gourmet olives into his mouth.

Finn read the note, sure he was nailing an imitation of the headmaster's car-salesman voice: "*Finn. We hope you and yours have a terrific time at Wharton Academy's Open House! Sincerely, Headmaster Bruce.*"

He shook his head; Headmaster Bruce had either forgotten what had earned Finn his spot at Wharton, or the man simply didn't know what else to do for the orphan on Open House.

"What am I supposed to do with three vouchers?" Finn muttered, more to himself than to Edison as he tossed them back into the basket.

"You should use them to eat." Edison shrugged, shoving another olive into his mouth. "Three times."

They both raised their heads at the sound of a knock on the door.

"My parents." Edison attempted to straighten his tie. "They want me to have dinner with them, and something they refer to as 'quality time.' At Upper Crust, actually. You can go with us if you want." He threw a look at Finn's gift basket. "You can use one of your vouchers."

Finn shook his head, the idea of imposing on Edison's 'quality time' not appealing to him. "Nah. I'm good. But thanks."

As Edison disappeared out the door, Finn ripped open a package of fancy crackers and smeared one with artisanal French cheese.

It had been a few weeks since Truth or Dare. Finn still had dreams—dreams of Oscar's rheumy eyes and swollen hand, cut with images of a totaled Volvo—but they were shorter and less intense now. And his knuckles, while still ponderously sore from punching the arbitrator even after all this time, were at least beginning to go into their "yellow" stage of bruising. It wouldn't be long until they were healed completely.

Finn looked down at the half-empty sleeve of crackers in his hand. He was *eating*. He was hungry, for the first time in a long time. He grabbed his guitar by its neck and settled the body over his thigh. As he began to absently strum a few chords, he stared at the window, which was shut tight all the time now; snow counted as precipitation, so Edison had waived his "two and a half inches" rule.

Finn's stomach complained; the French cheese and crackers hadn't been enough. His eyes traveled to the gift basket and settled there.

Italian food could be pretty good right about now.

Setting his guitar back against his dresser, he rose up, plucked one of Bruce's meal vouchers out of the basket, and shrugged.

Finn trudged across the Wharton Gardens, hands stuffed into the pockets of his green army jacket. Snow fluttered down from the sky like white feathers against black velvet, illuminated by the Victorian street lamps that dotted the Wharton. Tiny flakes stung his face in pinpricks of cold and melted away into his skin.

Lyrics from Counting Crows' "Long December" did laps through his mind as he passed the gazebo. December was a month of memories for most people, and typically of the joyful variety. Finn's were different. December was the month he'd pulled that Bird's Eye View flier off the bulletin board at Guitar Haven. It had been the month his parents died. He felt that tide of grief creep up and began to lick at his ankles, and he backed away from it.

Your past is stealing your present. And if you aren't careful, it'll steal your future, too.

Snow had collected on top of the gazebo in the Wharton Gardens, making it resemble an igloo on stilts. Finn stopped and stared at it a minute. It was rare that he looked at it in the daylight.

Everly was at his side every night out here, materializing like some kind of snow goddess in a black pea coat to sit and listen to music with him in patient silence. He still had feelings for her; he knew that. Sometimes as he looked at her regal silhouette in the dark, those feelings would surface out of nowhere, punching through his haze of despondency for but a moment before disappearing again. Everything he knew he felt for her had been buried beneath layers of guilt and grief, and he didn't know how long it would take to dig out from under it. He'd felt nearly numb these past few weeks, but he counted it as a small mercy: Everly had a boyfriend, anyway. It did him no good to think of her as anything other than a friend. That ship had sailed...he'd seen to that himself; he'd launched the damn thing.

He dug his hands deeper into his pockets, drawing closer to the bright lights of the Promenade, the social hub between Kingsley Tower and Raine Manor. There weren't actual rules keeping Aion Hall students from attending this watering hole for the upper class, but the high prices and hard looks kept the riff raff at bay. Finn fingered the meal voucher in his pocket.

The Promenade had undergone an extravagant transformation for the winter holidays. Finn blinked up at the lit trees which were on full display for the wealthy parents. He located Upper Crust and admired the impressive facade of Tuscan stone ribbed with dark, wooden beams. Even from here, Finn caught the authentic scents of gourmet wood-fired pizzas. As he approached the heavy, wooden door at the front entrance, a greeter looked at him as if he had sprouted two heads before begrudgingly ushering him inside.

"Good Evening, sir. This is Upper Crust." The maitre'd, dressed in an expensive suit, said the words as if he wanted to be sure Finn hadn't taken a wrong turn and ended up here by mistake. He looked down his nose at Finn's sneakers, then up at his crooked tie, visible under his green army jacket.

Finn stomped onto the carpeted floor to shake some of the snow off. "Table for one, please."

The maitre' d's scoff scraped the air. "This is *Upper* Crust, sir," he repeated.

Finn produced his meal voucher from his pocket and placed it on the walnut greeting table. "Table for one, please," he said again.

The maitre'd pinched the voucher with two fingers and turned it over, his eyes falling to the place where Headmaster Bruce's loopy signature authenticated it. An expression of disappointment passed over his face before he looked up at Finn with a forced smile. "May I...take your...coat...sir?"

"I'm good." Finn returned the man's fake smile with one of his own. "But thanks for asking."

The man snapped his fingers, and a server ushered Finn to a small corner table next to the double doors to the kitchen, giving him a terrific view of the waiters as they came and went. It was clear they wanted to keep the Unfortunate out of the way...somewhere unobtrusive where he couldn't spoil the appetites of their elite patrons.

"This food had better be worth it," Finn said under his breath, feeling the familiar heat of a dozen disapproving stares. Across the room, a woman shook her head as she gave him a once over. As she whispered something to her ancient husband, Finn propped his elbows up on the table. The woman gasped and vanished behind a leather-bound menu.

Finn smiled to himself. This could be kinda fun.

He drummed his fingers on the table and scanned the room. Because Wharton didn't want to inconvenience the wealthy parents of their students by confiscating their technology, the ban had been lifted for the weekend. The room was a sea of heads bent low over glowing screens, and conversation was spare. Finn had to laugh to himself; the students of Wharton finally had a chance to reconnect with their parents, but they were more excited about reconnecting with their phones.

As Finn's eyes continued to sweep the room, they snagged on a familiar face. Valerie sat with a stern-looking couple at a table next to a stone fireplace on the other side of the dining room. As their eyes met, Valerie's face lit up like one of the Christmas trees out front. She pushed herself to her feet, arm slicing through the air in a frenzied wave, as if trying to hail a taxi.

"Finn!" she practically shouted. Several irritated patrons stared and shook their heads. Finn smiled and waved back, but Valerie didn't stop—she was beckoning him over. Finn rose from his lowly table for one and wove through the tables across the dining room.

"Oh my God. I'm dying here," Valerie hissed in his ear when he reached her. She tugged his arm until he slumped into the chair next to her. "You're staying," she whispered out of the side of her mouth, her eyes pleading. "I'm in Hell. Help me endure it."

Finn stifled a laugh with his fist. Before he could object, Valerie turned to the couple across from her, who had to be her parents. "Mom, Dad, meet Finn. He's my team member in the Young Historians."

Valerie's father, a man in a three-piece suit with hair that was clearly dyed, rose and shook Finn's hand, eyeing him warily. Her mother stood and shook Finn's hand as well, nearly re-bruising his knuckles in the process. She wore a power-suit with a little too much shoulder pad.

Valerie's mother reseated herself and took a sip of water. "Charmed. Tell me—is this Young Historians Club particularly demanding? We were just talking to our Valerie about maintaining her grades. She earned an unacceptable score on her Molecular Chemistry exam, and we're wondering what might be to blame."

Out of the corners of his eyes, Finn saw Valerie bow her head. "I got a *B*, mom. Besides, it's an advanced class."

Her mother pursed her lips. "Yes, well, Konrads do not get *B*s."

Valerie cast Finn a look of misery and he jumped to her aid. "My dad always joked that 'Cs get degrees.'"

Mr. Konrad narrowed his eyes. "And what does your father do, son?"

Finn felt himself deflate. Valerie opened her mouth to speak for him, but he spoke first. "He's, uh, gone."

Valerie's mother tilted her head to the side. "Oh, are your parents gone on holiday? Where do they winter?"

It was Finn's turn to bow his head. "No. I mean...they're dead."

Valerie winced, and the table lapsed into uncomfortable silence until Mrs. Konrad cleared her throat and changed the subject, reaching across the table to pinch some of the fabric on Valerie's dress between her fingers. "Is this your Dolce?"

Valerie nodded with clear apprehension, seeming to know this question wouldn't be followed by a compliment.

"You should've worn your Prada—the one with cap sleeves that we got you in Italy last year," her mother opined. "It's more flattering. Makes you look like you have more up top."

As Valerie's face went a shade of scarlet that rivaled the marinara sauce on her father's pasta, Mrs. Konrad turned her attention to Finn. Her eyes roved over his green army jacket. "And who dresses *you*, dear?" She shook her head and scoffed. "Good Lord."

Finn felt his mischievous spark return. "No, Mrs. Konrad. Good*will*." He dipped a piece of baguette in olive oil and bit into it with gusto. "Like it?"

Valerie clamored for something to say. "How's Daniel?" she blurted. A thick silence followed, punctuated only by the sound of clinking silverware from the surrounding tables.

The Konrads exchanged a fraught glance before Valerie's mother answered. "He's...the same as he's always been."

"You should have brought him," Valerie said, eyes fixed on the surface of the table. "I would have liked to see him."

Mrs. Konrad offered an almost apologetic smile across the table to Valerie before throwing a self-conscious look at Finn. "*You* know what he's like. It would have been more work than anything else."

Out of the corner of his eye, Finn watched Valerie arch an aggravated eyebrow as her jaw tightened. He wondered who Daniel was, but when Mr. Konrad promptly changed the subject to an upcoming trip to Saint Tropez, he figured it was best not to ask.

He took a long swig of water. It was impossibly good—infused with berries or something. His eyes wandered around the room. He spotted Edison nearby, shoveling baked ziti into his mouth as his parents fruitlessly tried to engage him in conversation. Other kids in the restaurant were reporting the year's accomplishments to their parents as if they were reading stock reports to investors. Yes, Finn was definitely an outcast here. He was different. But maybe that wasn't such a bad thing.

As he scanned the crowd his eyes caught a flash of white-gold hair. Everly was sitting a few tables away. His stomach somersaulted. She was beautiful, as usual, wearing a tan sheath dress beneath an understated black cardigan and a classic string of pearls, her already pigmented lips played up with the barest hint of red lip color. Next to her, Nick Dain wore a sleek suit and a confident smile. Arm sprawled possessively around the back of Everly's chair, he was laughing, head thrown back, with an older version of himself. Mr. Dain was clearly a former athlete as well, being in tremendous shape for an older man.

Everly made polite conversation with Nick's mother—or more likely his step-mother, based on her age—she didn't look much older than Everly, or maybe that was just compliments of Botox. Arm candy—that's what she was to Nick's dad, and that's what Everly was to Nick. Finn hoped Nick would choke on the piece of bacon-wrapped asparagus that was halfway to his mouth.

Everly's mouth was smiling, but her green eyes weren't. Finn's gaze landed on her hands; her knuckles were white as she twisted her cloth napkin, and as he watched her bite her lower lip, he knew she was nervous. That was her "tell." Nick didn't know that, but Finn did. He buried the mingled feelings of regret and jealousy that rose up from his stomach like bile.

He remembered that Everly didn't have parents here, either; the two of them were perhaps the only ones in the room in that unfortunate situation. He felt a twinge of longing and tried to meet her eyes, but Everly's gaze didn't make its way to him.

Finn turned his attention back to his table, determined to ignore that side of the restaurant for the rest of the night, and found the Konrads berating a waiter who was trying to take their order.

"Really, this place used to have a better selection." Mrs. Konrad's voice dripped with condescension. She folded her hands on the table and tilted her head to the side, blinking rapidly, as if she had something stuck in her eye. "Where do you get your lamb? Is it imported?"

"And the wine selection is sub-par," Mr. Konrad added. "Had we known, we would have brought a bottle from our personal collection—a Château Cheval Blanc or an Ornellaia, perhaps." He listed the labels loudly enough to be heard by several other tables.

The waiter issued a deep bow. "Forgive us, Mr. and Mrs. Konrad. Perhaps I can see if the chef is willing to prepare you something custom." The waiter turned to Finn, eyebrows raised in expectation, pen poised above his notepad.

Finn squinted at the names of the sumptuous Italian dishes that were scrawled elegantly into his leather-bound menu, none of which had prices listed. He smiled and took another sip of rich-person-water as he looked up at the waiter.

"So....no onion rings?"

CHAPTER 45
HIDE AND SEEK

As Professor Moskowitz sat behind his desk, waiting for the Young Historians to arrive to their next mission briefing, his mind was steeped in guilt. Guilt for what Finn had endured during that ruthless game of Truth or Dare. Guilt for the other team members who had been forced to watch the spectacle play out. Guilt at ever having offered the team this spot in a competition that he hadn't fully understood—one that had warped into something sinister and appalling in the two decades he'd been absent.

He felt his intestines twist into a cramped knot as his mind flashed back to the look Everly had given him in the observation room. Resentful. Distrustful. Mordecai was, of course, compelled to pull his team from the competition right now, but that was impossible; they had signed contracts. Contracts he himself had urged them to sign. What had he done?

As he lowered his head into his hands, he remembered the meeting of the timekeepers that he had barged his way into. He had advised his team to be smart enough to control their emotions during their interviews; in a game like this, emotions could only be used against you. But he had not done the same. The knot in his stomach tightened.

Fool.

Follow your own advice.

He held the phonographic record in his hand that held their next challenge. His outburst to the timekeepers could potentially have made things worse. Only when he opened this envelope would he know how *much* worse.

As the door swung open and Wharton's Time Team entered the room, the professor let out a slow, self-regulating breath; at least they were together this time. Their last meeting had been fraught with palpable, unspoken drama, but the old man supposed the last challenge had supplied some much-needed perspective.

The professor watched Finn as he took his seat. The boy looked beleaguered, as if he'd lost a lot of sleep and weight, but not conquered in the way Moskowitz had feared; Timekeeper Vandecraft had tried her best to break him, but she hadn't counted on the ability of his teammates to put him back together.

The professor sighed, his stomach wrenching as he took in the wary looks on both Everly and Valerie's face. "I need to apologize." He turned the phonographic record over in his hands. "To all of you. But especially to you, Mr. Mallory."

Finn lowered his eyes to his hands. "You don't have to do that."

"No," the old man rose to his feet and made his way around his desk, "I do. These are not the Time Trials I believed I was signing you up for. I fear I've made a grave error."

"Then let's not compete. Let's just take that stupid record and break it in half." As Everly's scowl deepened, the professor felt himself wither a bit under her gaze.

"I'm afraid that's not possible." The professor shook his head. "You all signed the contract, and there are consequences for refusing to comply with its stipulations. Consequences from which I can't protect you."

317

"What do they think they're going to do—sue us?" Finn raised his eyes from his hands and settled them on the professor.

Valerie scoffed. "I'll put my parent's lawyers over theirs."

"Monetary consequences are the least of things." The professor averted his eyes to the window and softened his voice. He lapsed into silence a moment, attempting to drum up the courage to say the words that would paint a complete picture of what the team faced. This was a detail the professor had thought would be irrelevant to his team, and thus he hadn't divulged it, but now he had to, and he braced himself for their reactions. "Those who refuse to complete the Time Trials are exiled."

"From Wharton?" Valerie spat. "They can expel us for quitting a competition?"

"I didn't say 'expel,' my dear. I said 'exile.'" The professor kept his eyes on the windows, not yet ready to face the expressions of his team.

Out of the corner of his eyes, he saw Everly rise to her feet. "What does *that* mean?"

"Arbitrators will take you to a desolate location in an undisclosed period of time," Professor Moskowitz sighed as he forced his gaze to meet his granddaughter's, "and they will leave you there."

"And then what?" One of Everly's eyebrows shot up. "You just...live there? I can't believe we've never talked about this! What happens if you stay in the past?"

"You typically die there." The professor bowed his head. "They usually send you somewhere far away from civilization. Sometimes they send you so far back that there *is* no civilization. In any case, exiled society members are forced to live out their lives as tourists."

"Tourists?" Everly took a step backward. Her voice was a whisper now. The anger in her tone had been replaced by fear.

"It's the term for someone who lives out the rest of their natural life in the past." The professor closed his eyes and pinched

318

the bridge of his nose, inwardly pleading that his granddaughter refrain from asking for more specifics.

Instead, it was Finn's voice that piped up. "Is that even possible?" The professor was taken aback at what looked like a shine of fascination in the boy's eyes.

"Well, yes." The professor clasped his hands in front of him. "You lived part of your life on the *Titanic* for the first challenge...you just didn't spend very long there."

"But how can you just *stay* there?" Finn leaned forward on his elbows. "Wouldn't you catch up to the present and...change it?"

"Time moves the same in the past as it does in the present. You could feasibly bend time to five minutes ago, but a second in the past is the same as a second in the present. You would always be living in a fantasy. Only the present is truly real."

"It might not *feel* like that..." Finn tilted his head to the side, that look of quiet fascination continuing to play over his face. Everly studied him, brow furrowed.

"I suppose our reality is what we make it," the professor nodded. "But what has happened has happened, and nothing you do in the past, no matter how long you stay there, will change that fact, whether it feels real or not."

"Excuse me." Edison had removed his glasses and was holding them in one hand while subtly rocking in place. "If you were to bend time to five minutes ago, wouldn't you run into your former self? Wouldn't there be two versions of you?"

"No," the professor answered. "There is only one version of you that can exist at a time. The past version of you doesn't really exist—it's just a glimpse—and thus it is overridden by your present form when you travel back in time. The short version is that there are no duplicates, and the pen that is writing your story in this 'book' of time is the only thing with actual ink."

The professor and his team fell into silence then. The old man watched his granddaughter make a study of Finn's face, which still bore the expression of quiet reflection that it had taken on at the mention of time tourism. Edison replaced his glasses with a shaky hand.

Valerie's hands were balled into fists, her nostrils slightly flared. "So, we're stuck. We've established that." She rolled her shoulders in an aggressive shrug. "Go on, then—open the envelope. Let's just get it over with."

The professor's chin rose and fell in a deferential nod as he withdrew the phonographic record from its sleeve. For the third time this year, he set it in place on the turntable. The Grand Timekeeper's smooth voice poured out, but Professor Moskowitz couldn't help but notice that some of his trademark ebullience seemed dampened somehow.

"Greetings, Wharton Academy, and welcome to the third game of the Time Trials! It was an unfortunate end to the last challenge...but disqualifications do happen. Rest assured that the rules and regulations placed forth by the Historians' Society are there for your protection and for that of all who compete.

This brings us to our next challenge. What do you do when it is not others who need the saving, but yourselves instead? Perhaps this next challenge will tell us, for the game that has been selected is Hide and Seek."

Professor Moskowitz felt the room spin around him as the blood drained from his face. His knees began to buckle, and his hand instinctively found the edge of his desk to steady himself.

Hide and Seek: the most dangerous of all challenges in the Time Trials. How was this possible? This game had been drawn last year, and it was an unwritten rule that the timekeepers made every effort to vary the challenges. It had seemed impossible that it would be drawn again this year, and yet...

Vandecraft's vicious smile flashed through Moskowitz's mind. *"It's reality you want? Let's make it real, then."*

She was simply delivering on her promise, and it was all the professor's fault. He made his way behind his desk and sagged into his chair as the Grand Timekeeper continued.

"Hide and Seek is a game in which children hide in creative places from one who is designated the seeker. The children attempt to remain hidden for as long as possible without being found in hopes of being the last discovered. If the seeker is unable to find those hiding, he or she eventually calls, 'Olly, olly oxen free!' and those left undiscovered may reveal themselves, ending the game.

"In the Time Trials, Hide and Seek is a game which is rife with excitement, adventure, and danger. Your team will be dropped into a perilous historical situation and forced to grit it out for as long as possible until your Command deems the situation unsurvivable and is forced to pull their chain. The team which is able to outlast the others will be declared the winner and will be one step closer to victory. After an undisclosed period of time, if teams are still left standing, the Historians' Society may deem to declare 'Olly, olly oxen free' and end the challenge.

"The only question that remains is where you will be hiding. The first world war was nicknamed 'The Great War' because it was supposed to bring peace to the world for good. Because of technological advancements such as machine guns, mustard gas, and armored tanks, this war was fought in an entirely new way than those before it.

"You will be dropped into 'No Man's Land,' a patch of battered earth between two opposing trenches, prior to a particularly vicious skirmish between German and French troops. Your job is to last as long as you can, but please remember, as always, your safety should be the most important concern. Wharton is currently tied for the lead and we look forward to seeing what this team has in store for us. Good luck."

Professor Moskowitz sat in frozen silence as the record continued to spin, pop, and garble, long after the Grand Time-keeper's voice had faded. It was only when he felt the heat of his granddaughter's green gaze that he rose to his feet and removed the record from the turntable.

"Hide and Seek." As he struggled to find his next words, the weight of the guilt he bore pressed upon his chest and made it difficult to breathe. His eyes dropped to his Oxfords.

"It's bad, isn't it?" Edison's deadpan delivery didn't disguise his fear as his rocking grew in intensity.

"It's..." The professor's eyes slowly rose from his feet.

"It's something we can handle," finished Valerie, placing a hand on Edison's shoulder. "The *Titanic* felt overwhelming at first, and we handled it, didn't we? Vale might have taken the last challenge, but we're all proud of how Finn took the lead in Truth or Dare." The professor felt his stomach sink. Valerie was trying to hide her fear behind false bravado in an attempt to put her team at ease, but there was a slight tremor to her voice.

"Perhaps we should start with the basics," Edison suggested, looking at Finn out of the corners of his eyes as his rocking slowed. "What are the rules of Hide and Seek?"

"Yes," stammered the professor. "Of course. The basics. Well, it's much different than Marbles in that you are looking to save *yourselves*—not past peoples. The Time Bender will take you into the past, but it will be programmed to return to the present as soon as possible—as soon as you have disembarked from it."

"Wait a second," Everly interjected. "The Time Bender leaves? How are *we* supposed to get back?"

"The object of the game is to survive for as long as you possibly can," the professor said. "There are teams who have lasted for only minutes but there are also teams who have lasted for weeks. Your goal should be to find a 'sweet spot' where you and your team can bunker down in safety for as long as possible." The old man took a deep breath and expelled it slowly. "They will drop you into a spot that will not be easy to escape from. You can attempt to make a run for it, but they will have accounted for that when they choose where to drop you, and options will likely not be plentiful."

"If there's no Time Bender, how is there still a Command?" asked Valerie.

"Whoever takes on the role of Command will be *part* of this challenge—just not housed in the Time Bender. And only Command's chain can be pulled to bring you back to the present. It is a critical responsibility." His eyes drifted from Edison's face to Valerie's. "It will have to be one of the two of you, as the Rules of Trials states that team members must alternate as Command. Everly took the role on first, and Finn served as his own Command in Truth or Dare."

"I'll do it." Valerie threw a protective look at Edison, who didn't object.

The professor tried to cut Timekeeper Vandecraft's smile out of his mind but it grew back like a malignant tumor.

Was this his punishment for daring to question the time-keepers?

He watched his team as they left the room to begin their preparation research at Wharton Library. Valerie led the way, her chin lifted in an attempt to exude her usual confidence. Edison followed, his fingers flicking the guitar pick fidget cuff that his roommate had made for him. Finn was next, a boy so convinced he was undeserving that he couldn't see his own worth. And finally, Everly. His own flesh and blood. Last year, Hide and Seek had cost the Halls of Ivy Prep a team member.

Would one or more of these children meet the same fate?

CHAPTER 46
INTO THE FIRE

Valerie pushed the series of buttons that lowered the glass door of the Time Bender. In a few seconds, the team would play the most dangerous game that the Time Trials could offer.

And they were entirely unprepared.

For a week now, Valerie had put the team through "basic training." She had them crawl through muddy snow, practice diving into holes that she had dug herself and kept the group holed up in Wharton's library for study sessions each night, but she knew none of this began to scratch the surface of skills they would need in order to survive the Western Front.

For the first time in Valerie Konrad's life, she was truly scared. It wasn't just the incredibly high physical stakes of the challenge that frightened her—it was the state of her team. Finn had been through hell in the last challenge, where he'd watched Oscar die, a thing he attributed to his own failing. Everly's nerves were shot: she was equal parts angry at her own grandfather and fiercely protective of Finn, who she obviously harbored feelings for, though she wouldn't admit it. And then there was Edison. What would a challenge like this do to Edison? Flashing lights and whirring gears were bad enough—but gunfire?

But it was this or exile.

Valerie would never show her fear, of course. Especially not today, when it was her turn to act as Command.

"Receiver check." The team activated the receivers in their ears and confirmed that they were working. Edison had been fitted with a noise cancelling function for the jump and rested in a comfortable silence. Valerie watched him for a lingering moment and remembered him the last time he'd been in that seat, writhing around, hands over his ears. His receivers would help him prevent another episode during the bend, but they would become a liability in No Man's Land, where the team would need all of their senses functional to survive. Valerie narrowed her eyes.

He's so much like Daniel.

She shook her head.

Focus.

"Launch, we are secure and awaiting your coordinates." During the first bend, Valerie had been so excited, her heart beating in wild anticipation of what was to come—an adventure that promised danger, but also reward. It was different this time. There was no reward, even if they won; the curtain had been pulled back during Truth or Dare, revealing the Time Trials for what they truly were, and there was no unseeing it.

This was all made worse by the fact that Professor Moskowitz had all but disappeared after it had been revealed that they were playing Hide and Seek. Valerie had understood what he was doing when he had stepped back before their first challenge; he had been letting them figure out their own way, and it had worked. This, however, felt less deliberate. In the past week, the professor had looked like a deer frozen in the headlights.

"Coordinates received," Valerie stated, wearing a mask of confidence. "Launch, we are ready to make the bend."

The assembly of gears above began spinning faster, stockpiling the energy needed for the jump. Valerie tuned out the discord and collected her thoughts. As soon as the bend was complete they would need to exit the Time Bender as quickly as possible. The machine was programmed to bend back after it had sufficiently cooled down, and the jump produced a dangerous amount of heat within short range of the bend site. Once they were free of that frying pan, it would be into the fire.

The team had preprogrammed both German and French uniforms into their pocket watches, as they would be dropped into "No Man's Land," the neutral space between trenches, and they didn't know which side they would encounter first. No Man's Land might be the length of a football field or it might be the length of ten—it constantly changed as the war dragged on, both sides scrounging and sacrificing for mere inches of progress. The sides would take turns charging at one another and blowing each other to bits.

The one thing the team knew was that this place would be laden with danger of all sorts. There would be sniper rifles and machine guns pointed in both directions. There would be curled tentacles of barbed wire emerging everywhere, designed to snare men and make them easy targets. There would be unexploded shells littering the field of battle, quietly lying in wait, and there would be bodies. So many bodies. As strange as it was, the bodies are what scared Valerie the most. It was one thing to study photographs of the dead from the safety of her dormitory in Raine Manor; it was another thing to watch men choking for breath on their own blood.

The sensation of weightlessness violently slung Valerie from her thoughts. Bright blue light blasted into the Time Bender as the teammates floated helplessly in their leather restraints. The window went black and gravity showered into the machine, slamming them back into their seats. Valerie rubbed her temples for a moment, trying without success to massage away the excruciating pounding in her head.

She snapped into action, quickly pressing the sequence of buttons which would open the door. She knew that they had about ten minutes before the Time Bender would make the bend back to the present and they didn't want to be anywhere near it when it did.

"Let's get moving!" she shouted to the team, plucking out Edison's modified earpiece so that he could hear the command.

The lower door unfolded and Valerie ran out into the blackness. Her feet sunk into the ground as her skin absorbed the cold of the night. Having forced the team to prepare for this moment by crawling through practice fields for weeks, she immediately identified the heavy smell of mud. This smell was mixed with a number of other odors; the sulphuric musk of gunpowder, the bitterness of iron, and...death. It was everywhere; the putrid stench of decay hung thickly in the air, seemingly woven into the night mist. The promise of the bodies she had so feared infiltrated the very air she was breathing, but lurked just out of sight, waiting to be discovered.

"This way." Valerie picked her way into the unnatural quiet of the night. It bothered her that it was so silent; she had imagined the front as a place of constant explosions, where the rattle of gunfire never stopped. The silence of this place was almost worse.

Finding a sizable crater in the earth, she ushered her team into it. Finn, Everly and Edison slid in as Valerie tried to make sense of the quiet.

Everly's eyes were wide beside her in the trench. The girls had tied their hair into tight buns which would be concealed by the projections of their wetsuits, and they both wore no makeup; any sign of being female would certainly stand out on the Western Front. Valerie had even suggested cutting their hair for this challenge, but Everly had balked at that.

"We're a safe distance from the Time Bender." Valerie kept her voice quiet and even. "We shouldn't move until we have to...which probably won't be long from now."

Everly nodded and sank back down into the mud. A loud, metallic groaning startled the group, but it was only the Time Bender doors drawing closed. The machine began to rattle. It was surprisingly quieter from the outside than it was on the inside. Suddenly, the machine was enveloped in a blue energy, and the muddy area surrounding it seemed to pinch together slightly. The machine warped and blinked into the blue light, and then, in one violent flash, disappeared altogether. The team could feel the intense heat from the bend even from where they were hiding. The machine had left a crater of its own in its wake. What had once been mud had baked to solidity in one violent instant.

A series of bright projectiles ascended into the sky, leaving trails of orange embers floating back to earth behind them. The projectiles floated like glittering stars which had been nailed into the night, flooding the battlefield with light and leaving the team dangerously exposed.

Valerie knew what these were and what they meant: they were bright flares which hung in the sky on parachutes, a sign that the timekeeper's promise of a "vicious skirmish" was about to be kept.

CHAPTER 47
EXPOSED

Soft whistles sounded in the night, followed by a tidal wave of screams as thousands of boys and men began charging from somewhere. The team attempted to discern which direction the screams were coming from, but it was proving difficult.

Concussive blasts of erupting ordinance ripped through the tense night air and shook the ground, while explosions carelessly scattered earth into the night, peppering the team with a confetti of indiscriminate debris. Artillery shells screeched through the air as the sound of the surging soldiers escalated steadily. Next to the team, the earth ruptured from a violent explosion, and Finn instinctively dove onto Everly, shielding her from the torrential barrage of rubble that rained down upon them, holding her tightly to the ground.

The descending screams of the soldiers were drowned out by a storm of gunfire, which erupted from all directions. Bullets, glowing red from the heat of being projected through the barrels of savage machine guns, hissed above the team in ruthless search of their targets. A soldier folded over into the crater in which the team was hiding. He slid lifelessly into the mud, his uniform so soiled that it was impossible to determine whether it was German grey-green or French blue.

Valerie clawed her way to the top of the crater. She steeled herself before stirring up enough courage to pop her head up before quickly ducking back down.

"We have to move *now*!" she screamed to the team. "We can retreat with the French army!" She activated her wetsuit and was blanketed by a blue uniform, which the holo-cloth had accurately caked in mud. Finn rolled off Everly, but unconsciously kept a protective arm around her as he activated his wetsuit. Valerie pointed which way they would go, her voice drowned out by the deafening sound.

She crawled through the mud, winding her way through the remnants of a barbed wire fence. She rolled nimbly to the burning frame of a small tank—long out of use, but excellent for providing cover.

A whistle sounded and the French began to retreat back to their own trenches. The flares in the sky had burned out and the lifeless world returned to darkness, save for a multitude of fires, which feasted hungrily in the night. The chaos of the retreat provided an opportunity, and Finn and Everly made it to Valerie in a quick scurry.

"If we can make it to the French trenches, we can put the front behind us," Valerie shouted, everyone's hearing having been shot away during the last bombardment, including her own. Her eyes darted between Finn and Everly. "Where's...where's Edison?"

Finn's heart sank as he looked at Everly, whose green eyes had gone wide. Valerie grabbed him by the shoulders and shook him. "You *left* him?" Her face was a mix of rage and abject horror.

Finn pressed the bottoms of his palms to his eyes, a groan rolling out of him. He'd assumed Edison was right behind him, but the truth is, he hadn't even turned to look. He'd been more

concerned about Everly beside him. Edison was likely still in the crater, covering his ears, paralyzed by the sounds of the gunfire...
...alone.

A surge of nausea almost dropped Finn to his knees. He could see Oscar's face in his mind, his lips rapidly purpling.

"Please, don't leave me."

An image of Edison followed—in their dorm, contorting his long, clumsy fingers over the frets of Finn's guitar in an attempt to play a C major.

"You're not my best friend...but you're a close second. You talk to me like a person."

Valerie's face was a mask of disgust as she opened her mouth to say something, but the sound of a falling artillery shell cut her off sharply. The explosive concussion of the nearby blast scattered Finn's thoughts and disoriented him before a fresh eruption of gunfire forced him to scramble for cover, diving behind the decomposing body of a horse. He curled into a tight ball as bullets whistled overhead. He waited for it to pass before peeking above the putrid body to ascertain where he was.

In the moments when the explosions in the sky afforded bright flashes of light, Finn made out a figure in a black bodysuit wandering aimlessly.

Edison.

Relief washed over him, draining away his panic and replacing it with adrenaline. Edison was alright. But he wouldn't be for long if Finn didn't get to him.

As Finn rolled over the horse's body and sprinted toward his frazzled roommate, his eyes caught movement: soldiers in muddy, grey uniforms beginning to quietly emerge from nearby trenches. Finn tackled Edison. Together they tumbled into a deep crater, the German soldiers approaching swiftly, rifles at the ready. Knowing that they had seconds, Finn frantically flipped open his pocket watch and scrolled through the presets.

When the German soldiers poured over the crest of the crater, they found him dressed in a friendly, grey uniform, his head donning a spiked, Imperial helmet.

"We're all clear here." Finn's articulator manipulated his voice into perfect German. The soldiers nodded and continued to comb the broken landscape for survivors. They hadn't noticed Edison in his black bodysuit, partially obscured by mud.

Finn activated his earpiece. "Valerie," he said in a hoarse voice, "I have Edison, but it's going to be difficult to move him. He's in bad shape."

"What do you mean, 'bad shape'?" Valerie's anger hadn't receded—that was apparent, even through Finn's earpiece. "Is he alright?"

"He seems to be." Finn's eyes darted over Edison as he knelt down next to him in the crater. Sitting this close to his roommate, he could feel Edison's heart beating impossibly fast, like a bird's. "He's just in shock. The noise, I guess. We won't make it to the French trenches—it makes more sense for us to go to the German lines. They're about thirty yards away."

"Stay with Edison. I'll switch uniforms and make my way to you three."

"Wait," said Finn, suddenly queasy. "Three?" He shot to his feet. "Everly isn't with...you?"

"No!" Valerie fumed. "Wasn't she just with *you*?"

Finn's eyes darted around in the darkness, searching for Everly as Edison rocked in place at his feet. The sky lit up with another explosion and Finn's heart sank as his eyes landed on a huddle of German soldiers.

They were surrounding something.

No, not something...someone.

In the midst of the huddle, long blonde hair spilling out of her cap and cascading over her shoulders, was Everly.

CHAPTER 49
THE SPOILS OF WAR

Everly's screams pierced the air as she was dragged into the trenches. She twisted against the hands that held her, but she was no match for six men.

"They have her!" Finn shouted into his earpiece. "They have Everly!"

"What?" Valerie cried. There was a brief silence. "Stay where you are," Valerie finally managed. "I'm making my way there, but we can't keep splitting up like this!"

A primal anger, unlike any he had ever experienced, consumed Finn. He felt like a piece of saltwater taffy, stretched thin enough to break. If left alone, Edison was in imminent danger. But so was Everly. Finn's mind spun, the agony of the decision he was forced to make twisting into his gut like a dagger.

He couldn't hear her screaming anymore. Panic shot through him, bringing him sudden clarity.

"Forget that," he growled. "I'm going after her."

"Finn," Valerie's voice was impatient, "I'm Command, and I'm ordering you to wait. If we split up—"

Finn turned off his earpiece, ripped it out of his ear, and stuffed it into his wetsuit pocket. He dropped to a crouch beside Edison.

"Listen," he panted. "You have to stay calm. Valerie's coming, but you..." he threw a look in the direction where he'd last seen Everly, "you have to try to keep it together, okay?"

A flare above reflected off Edison's glasses as he nodded.

"I'll be right back." Finn took hold of Edison's shoulders and looked him in the face. "I promise, I'll come back for you. I'm sorry. I'm just...I'm sorry."

His heart accelerated into a frenzy, dumping more adrenaline into his system. He was wasting time—time that Everly didn't have. He sprang to his feet and tore toward the trench into which he had seen Everly disappear, tumbling in blindly, eyes flashing in search of her.

The high, dirt walls were fortified with sandbags and the ground was littered with discarded tin cans, cigarette butts, and empty liquor bottles. A prayer book with a tattered ribbon page marker sat atop a battered crate. Finn nearly tripped over a man who was slumped against the dirt wall of the trench, a red stain quickly spreading across his leg as he was tended to by a medic.

"*Mein gott,*" the man groaned through gritted teeth. "*Töte mich einfach.*"

Having ripped out his earpiece, Finn didn't know what that meant, but he figured it wasn't exactly an expression of joy. He steadied himself against the wall before pushing his way through the crowd of muddy soldiers, stepping over a number of other men who had been wounded in the recent skirmish.

A gaunt hand reached out from the mud, and gripped Finn's leg. Finn looked down to see a young man who was clutching his stomach with his other hand. He couldn't have been much older than Finn himself. The boy whispered something in German as blood spilled between his fingers like water breaking through a levee.

"*Hilf mir.*" His watery eyes pleaded as they stared up at Finn. "*Hilf mir.*"

Finn's gut turned over as he reached into his pocket to find his earpiece. But his fingers closed around something else instead. He let his fingers dwell on the cat's eye marble—Ebba's marble.

He's already dead, he reminded himself as he looked down at the bleeding soldier.

Everly isn't.

He could see her eyes, staring at him in the garden under the light of the streetlamp. He could hear her voice in his head. "*Your past is stealing your present. If you aren't careful....*"

"It'll steal my future, too," he finished for her.

He tore his leg loose from the soldier's grip and splashed through the mud. "I'm sorry," he murmured.

He pushed his way past another crowd of men who were huddled in a semicircle against the wall of the trench sharing a cigarette. When he broke through that crowd, he found what he was looking for.

A pack of men were crowded into a sizeable dugout which had been carved into the far side of the trench, seemingly gathered around something of interst. They were crammed so tightly together that Finn couldn't see around them, but he could hear their gruff voices.

He scrambled to restore his receiver to his ear and turned it back.

"What have we here?"

"Stand back! Finder's keepers."

"Wait your turn—you'll get a look at her in a minute."

"A woman? In uniform?"

"I'm more interested in what's under it."

There was an explosion of laughter before someone asked, speaking as if they were looking at a unicorn, "How in the hell did she even come to be on the front?"

The reply made Finn's skin crawl: "Does it matter? She's ours now."

Finn's eyes cast around in desperation, finally coming to rest on a short trench shovel. His hands closed around its handle as he took a step towards the crowd of men, seething with rage. His eyes continued to scan the interior of the dugout and found the men's rifles, which were leaning against the dirt wall. There were six men in the room, and they all had guns. A trench shovel would be no match for that. Even if he managed to grab a rifle instead, Finn would still be outnumbered, and he'd only manage to take out one or two before they took him down.

No, attacking them would be the worst thing Finn could do; they'd make quick work of him, and Everly would be left to whatever depraved plans they had for her. If he really wanted to save Everly, he couldn't act on impulse. He would have to keep a cool head for once in his life. No sudden, poorly-thought moves.

A few of the men moved to the side enough to allow Finn to finally catch sight of the object of their interest. Everly was still dressed, fortunately, but she wouldn't be for long if Finn didn't think fast. Her frightened eyes scanned her captors, widening in sudden recognition as they snagged on Finn's as he lurked in the background.

If she screamed now, all would be lost. But Everly was too smart for that; Finn saw the terror drain from her eyes as he pressed his index finger to his lips and began scrolling through the presets on his pocket watch. He found "World War I: German Lieutenant" and selected it.

Finn's uniform revamped itself, two rows of buttons emerging from a thick, clean overcoat. As a peaked cap materialized over his head, he assumed his most confident look, his arms folded and his face stern.

If something freaks you out, look at it.
Face it.

He cleared his throat softly and drew himself up to his full height, chest puffed out, hands clasped behind his back, waiting for the boorish soldiers to notice his presence. Slowly, the soldiers began to turn, nudging each other to make it clear that they were being watched. Six pairs of eyes took note of Finn's lieutenant's garb and exchanged a nervous glance.

"Those in authority have first call on spoils of war." Smooth, flawless German poured out of Finn's mouth. "You'd do well to think twice before opening a parcel that's meant for another." The calm manner in which he spoke shocked himself, as inwardly he was screaming obscenities.

The soldiers regarded him with apprehension.

"Forgive us," one of them grunted. "We didn't realize she belonged to anyone."

"She belongs to me." Finn crossed his arms. "A prisoner of war. Cunning, this one. I'm not sure how she slipped away, but I thank you for returning her to me."

Everly looked up at him from her place on a pile of sandbags, cheeks streaked with dirt, chest heaving as she tried to regulate her breathing.

Finn could read the questions in the soldiers' faces. Sixteen years old was not too young to be on the fields of battle in 1917; to be a lieutenant, however, was another matter entirely. The soldiers were undoubtedly skeptical because of Finn's obvious young age, and there was no possible way that they didn't find Everly's clothing and even her mere presence on the battlefield suspicious. A woman had no business in No Man's Land and everyone knew it. Finn needed to get these men out of here before they became brave enough to question him.

"Again, we meant no offense," the soldier said, running a wary hand through his whiskers.

Finn fixed the men with the most condescending, authoritarian look he could muster. "Don't let it happen again," he snarled. "Back to your posts—all of you. I'll have you reported."

The men collected their weapons and scrambled out of the dugout toward a different chamber, some looking humbled, others looking dubious.

As soon as the soldiers were out of eyeshot, Finn flew to Everly's side, kneeling beside her, frantically scanning her for injury. "What did they...did they do anything to you?"

Everly, still stunned and pale, shook her head in a silent 'no,' and folded into Finn's arms. Her heart, rapid from fear, hammered against him through their wetsuits.

"Valerie was right," she murmured. "I should have cut my stupid hair for this."

Despite the circumstances, a laugh escaped Finn's mouth. It came out like a gasp. His arms were still around Everly's waist, her body pressed up against his, the scant light from the overhead oil lamp casting a soft glow over her face. Even in a trench, she radiated.

He'd been in a haze for so long, but now he could feel something—heat and honesty. For the first time since that city sidewalk, little seemed to stand between them, and it wasn't only because of the holo-cloth that was shellacked to both of their bodies. He looked into the liquid green eyes of this girl who never seemed to jade, no matter what life dealt her. Unlike him, she didn't go bitter, or wall, or retreat, or hide under false armor. Emily Neil had been right about one thing: it wasn't easy to understand what Everly saw in him. But if the two of them could get out of this trench alive, someday maybe he could live up to whatever image she had of him.

He raised two fingers to her mud-daubed cheek. "If something had happened to you..." He didn't finish the sentence; his words hung in the air. He felt his breath begin to come faster as Everly took hold of his face and brought hers closer. His mouth searched for hers in the feeble light, but it didn't find it.

"Edison's down!" Valerie's voice came in over their earpieces, panicked and urgent. "He's been shot!"

Just as Finn and Everly heard her over their earpieces, a scrambling sounded above. Everly relaxed her grip on Finn's neck and he cautiously left the dugout, pulling himself up to the ground above the trench. There was a figure there, dragging something dark, drawing in heavy breaths.

"What's wrong with you? How could you?" Valerie was a dark shadow supporting Edison, who was still wearing the black, inactivated bodysuit. His right shoulder bore a circular wound that was erupting with a staggering amount of blood. Everly scrambled out of the dugout, and she and Finn helped ease Edison down into the trench. Valerie sprang down next. As soon as her feet hit the ground, her fist shot out and smashed into Finn's eye.

"What the hell, Valerie?" sputtered Finn, voice cracking as he backed away.

"You just *left* him there," Valerie fumed. "Like he was nothing."

"What was I supposed to do?" He threw a look at Everly, who had eased Edison to the ground and pulled his head into her lap. "They took her. If I hadn't gotten here when I did—"

"He just walked right into the gunfire!" Valerie had drawn right up to Finn, her face inches from his. "When I found him, he was bleeding, unconscious...and by himself!"

Finn's hands flew to his head. "I had to make a choice! It wasn't exactly easy, okay?"

"Valerie, we can fight when we get home—just pull the chain!" pleaded Everly, who was watching Edison slowly lose color in his face as she put pressure on his shoulder.

Finn felt an overwhelming surge of soul-crushing guilt and indignance, blended together into one crippling brew.

My fault.

Will it ever stop *being my fault?*

Valerie reached for her pocket watch, but when she looked up, her face was a mask of panic. She felt around desperately but came up empty. "It's gone," she stammered in disbelief.

"What?" Finn scowled as he rubbed his eye.

"My pocket watch." Valerie struggled to keep her voice steady. "It isn't here."

"That's the only way we can get home! You're Command—it's the only chain we can pull!" sputtered Everly. "Edison's losing a lot of blood. I'm trying to slow it, but—"

"It could be anywhere out there!" Valerie began to pace the trench. "I was crawling all over, and who knows when the next offensive is going to start!"

"I'll go look for it." The words sprang out of Finn's mouth without hesitation; it was his fault Edison was shot, but wallowing in his failure wouldn't get them anywhere.

"You'll never find it." Valerie collapsed onto a crate and lowered her head into her hands. "It's probably covered in mud. You might never find it, and you'd be risking your life every moment you were out there."

Everly's face was waxen as she looked up from Edison, whose lips were going pale.

"If I don't take the risk, we *all* die." Finn climbed the wooden ladder to peer into the darkness, but turned around to look straight at Valerie. "Just...let me make it right."

Valerie opened her mouth as if to say something, but thought better of it and closed it.

Finn turned to face the battlefield again. Devastation stretched as far as the eye could see. Small fires dotted the landscape. Finn's eyes fell upon some spiraled barbed wire, sharp and sinister, waiting for an unsuspecting soldier to stumble into it. His mind instantly likened it to something he recognized, something he'd seen many times before: excess guitar strings. Whenever his dad had changed strings on his guitar, there would always be excess string sticking up from the headstock. Some musicians clipped the surplus string, but Trent Mallory didn't; he'd curled it instead. "It looks cool," he'd said. "Doesn't it?"

Finn shook his head. It was stupid to think of music now...

...wasn't it?

"Hey." He scrambled back down the ladder, a flame of hope sparking to life in his chest. "Valerie. What did you say that music app was called?"

"What, Time Tunes?" Valerie threw him an irritated look over her shoulder as she tended to Edison. "Finn, seriously, now is *not* the time."

"No, listen." Finn shook his head, stooped next to Valerie, and grabbed her by the shoulders. "We can *use* Time Tunes..."

Valerie's face scrunched up as her eyes searched Finn's. "...to find the pocket watch!" she finished. "That's genius!"

Finn smiled. "You play the music, I'll go find it."

Valerie nodded. "Play 90s alternative," she said into her earpiece. Her mouth was a wry twist as she looked at Finn. "If anyone can find it now, it's you."

Grinning, Finn hurled his body out of the trench, glancing back at Everly, who bit her lower lip as she watched him go.

I can save them.

Finn belly-crawled through the mud, passing the body of another dead horse. He pushed past the smell and tried to focus on what he could hear. He listened carefully for recognizable music, but he was met with nothing but eerie silence.

He crawled on, past the charred remains of what had once been a grove of trees, now reduced to a cluster of scorched sticks. As he crawled, Finn pitched forward, face-first, into a puddle of muddy water. He cursed quietly, spitting it out in disgust. Still no music. But he did hear a rattling; he raised his eyes to a mass of barbed wire and realized it was moving. He narrowed his gaze: there were people caught in the wire, struggling fruitlessly to free themselves, like moaning flies snared in a web of steel. Finn felt a shudder pass through him as he pushed on.

He had been crawling through the mud of No Man's Land for perhaps a minute when he finally heard something—it was tinny and minute, like percussion being played by a rodent. Encouraged, he crawled forward in the direction of the sound.

As it grew louder, Finn could discern a voice—small and incomprehensible, but singing to a familiar melody. He crawled furiously, feeling his fingernails bend back as he clawed at the muddy earth beneath him. His arms flew to his head and closed over it as the ground began to rattle, as if he were sitting on a fault line that had just ruptured. Several aftershocks followed. The faint sound of the music was now obscured by that of a distant bell, mingled with what sounded like a bicycle wheel spinning with a card caught in its spokes.

Finn froze. Valerie had put the team through enough research for him to know what that sound was: gas rattles. They were how soldiers warned each other of an impending gas attack, and gas meant the potential for another offensive. He had to get them out of there—fast.

There was another set of explosions behind him and Finn jumped to his feet, knowing that the gas from those explosions would be close. He crouched behind the stump of what was once a tree, one hand clamped over his nose and mouth as a hissing sound joined the muffled music.

He cast a quick glance behind him and saw it—mustard gas, rolling behind him like dry ice at a Halloween party. It was only as the vapor rose up and passed through the moonlight that Finn could see how yellow it was.

Hit with the heavy stink of onions, Finn rolled forward, belly crawling over bodies in order to outrun the gas. Remembering that the gas was heavy, designed to sink into the trenches and force soldiers to expose themselves or die, Finn edged his way up a small mound, hoping that it wouldn't disclose his location to the soldiers who were surely scanning the darkness for easy targets.

Adrenaline coursed through him. He couldn't lose track of the music. He surged forward through the mud, slipping and sliding in the direction of the sound. His eyes fell upon the silhouette of a tank.

Bingo.

He remembered Valerie ranting about one earlier in the trench.

And suddenly Finn could hear more than just a beat—he could make out words. Lyrics. Kurt Cobain, screaming about feeling stupid and contagious, beseeching the listener to entertain him.

Finn slapped the mud in victory as the music got louder and clearer. Nirvana. "Smells Like Teen Spirit." You couldn't get any more "90s alternative" than that.

He could hear the chorus clearly now.

Apparently, the French soldiers could hear it, too. From the blackness, a burst of machine gun fire erupted, tracer bullets igniting through the night like angry fireflies. Finn curled into a ball behind the charred tank as bullets pinged against the tank like golf ball-sized hailstones slamming against a tin roof. The muddy earth around him exploded as bullets ripped into the landscape.

The onslaught stopped for a moment while the gunners swapped in a fresh belt of ammunition. Finn's ears were ringing, but in the moment of peace, he could still hear Cobain's voice screaming about 'a denial' from Valerie's pocket watch, louder than ever. He scrounged around the base of the tank's skeleton with greedy fingers, numb from the cold mud.

Near one of the treads, half submerged in mire, was Valerie's pocket watch.

Music poured out of it: the refrain of the song—the word "hello" repeated over and over again, as if greeting him. As if summoning him.

Without hesitation, Finn slid forward, plucked it out of the sludgy earth and scrambled to get back behind the cover of the tank.

A bullet whizzed to his left, close enough to push his hair to the side as it blasted past him. He slammed his back against the tank and laughed in relief, feeling the impact of a fresh barrage of bullets pummel against the metal on the other side like a jackhammer.

As the last chords of the song whined to a finish, Finn grabbed the chain and yanked it three times.

CHAPTER 50
SILENT TREATMENT

When the team reached the Historians' Society medical bay, they all had injuries to be treated. The most serious was Edison's, of course, and he was whisked away immediately by a team of strangely dressed doctors. Valerie had an assortment of scrapes and cuts from crawling around in No Man's Land, and one of the gashes on her elbow would need stitches. Everly had bruises on her arms, shoulders, and neck from being dragged to the barracks. Finn was the least injured, his most significant injury being, ironically, a fairly nasty bruise around his right eye.

Finn, Everly, and Valerie found themselves in the same white room that they had been taken to after the last challenge. The doctors had a bit more repairing to do this time, but ran the same strange tests that they had during the first visit. One of the doctors waved a silver wand over Finn's head and frowned while listening to a large pair of earphones.

Just as before, the doctors made a silent exit and were replaced by Philomena Vandecraft, who walked with more pep this time to the stainless-steel table at the far end of the room. She wore the same black dress as before, but sported a different colored cloche hat—chartreuse.

Finn, Everly, and Valerie took their seats and waited for the timekeeper to begin, but she seemed content to simply bask in awkward silence. Her eyes, however, betrayed her excitement.

"Will Edison be alright?" Everly finally asked, her face still streaked with mud.

Timekeeper Vandecraft folded her hands in front of her. "Yes, dear; he was only shot in the shoulder. His injury looked worse than it actually was." Her eyes flicked to Finn. "Tell me, Finn Mallory, what inspired you to make the decision to abandon one team member for the other?"

Finn felt his eyes flare.

Wow. Right to the chase.

He glanced at Valerie before answering. "I had to make a call. Everly was in the most danger." He pictured the six soldiers man-handling her into the trench and bristled all over again. "I mean...stuff was imminent."

"I see." Timekeeper Vandecraft's chin dipped in a nod. "And your romantic interest in Everly Caldwell...did that have anything to do with your decision?"

Finn felt his heart stop dead in his chest. He flashed a look at Everly, who met his eyes briefly before biting her lip and staring down at the table. Finn kept silent; denying it was futile.

The timekeeper cocked her head to one side. "I always wondered why you chose to swim with sharks instead of ranking your teammates during Truth or Dare. At first, I figured you did it to avoid having to rank yourself last, like our poor, ill-fated Oscar Clement—may he rest in peace." Vandecraft smirked. "But now I wonder if it wasn't more to avoid ranking her *first*." She tapped the side of her cloche hat in mock thought.

Vandecraft let her eyes trail to the empty spot where Edison would have been seated. "To be honest, Finn Mallory, now I'm not even convinced that you would have ranked *yourself* last."

Finn glared at the timekeeper. How dare she suggest that Finn saw Edison as expendable?

But was she right? The moment Finn had seen Everly's blonde hair spilling out from under her cap, he'd had to fight to remember that Edison was even there. Vandecraft's words swirled around in his mind, obscuring the truth like black ink in water.

"He shouldn't have been shot." Valerie's voice was steely. She threw a look of disdain in Finn's direction. "He shouldn't have been *alone.*"

Of the many emotions Finn felt, anger surfaced first. Hadn't he saved Everly? And hadn't Vandecraft said that Edison would be alright? Finn was used to being wrong, but this time he felt he was at least half-right.

"I had to make a call, Valerie," he repeated, struggling to keep the umbrage out of his voice. "Are you saying it was the wrong one? Either way, someone was going to get hurt. What, do you think I *like* this?"

"You should have waited for me to get there." Valerie was on her feet now. "What if Edison had taken a bullet to the head instead of the shoulder?"

"Well, he didn't!" Finn surprised himself by jumping to his feet to face her. "He got shot in the *shoulder*, remember?" He ran a hand through his hair. "Look, I hate this, okay? I hate that I had to leave him, hate that he got shot...I feel bad enough without getting raked over the coals."

His shoulders rose and fell as he tried to catch his breath, only then noticing Everly's hand tugging his arm, urging him back into his seat.

Philomena Vandecraft watched the exchange play out with a flicker of excitement in her eyes. "And you, Everly Caldwell. What do *you* think about Finn's decision?"

In the brief silence that followed the timekeeper's question, Finn thought of a hundred things Everly might say. Maybe even she would throw him under the bus. Tell him he was wrong. Selfish. Negligent. That she wasn't his to protect.

But Everly didn't say anything. When Finn looked up from the table, she was giving Vandecraft a look that could burn a forest to ashes. Instead of trying to produce an answer to the loaded question, Everly simply folded her arms and waited for the next, defiant in her silence.

"How disappointing." Timekeeper Vandecraft pouted sarcastically and rose from her seat. "The silent treatment might work for this interview, but based on the dynamics I've witnessed here today, I would say that you still have plenty to discuss." She got up and gathered a small stack of papers. "Bear in mind that you still have a challenge left, Everly Caldwell. Do try not to get captured this time?"

She sashayed out of the room, winking a grey eye as she did.

CHAPTER 51
TIMEKEEPER

As his team was enduring their interview with Timekeeper Philomena Vandecraft, Professor Moskowitz eased himself into a chair in Timekeeper Garridan's simple office. The walls of the room were mostly bare, save for a white flag, printed with the Historians' Society's logo and pinned behind the Grand Timekeeper's stainless-steel desk. Proud, steel bookshelves, which housed binders and books of rules and regulations stood on either side of the desk. Beyond that, the room was quite empty and utilitarian, a stark juxtaposition to Moskowitz's busy classroom, which was littered with a fire hazard of historical treasures.

"Mordecai!" The Grand Timekeeper walked in and took his seat behind the desk. His typical Cheshire cat smile was painted on his face, but it straightened as he took in the professor's solemn expression.

The professor knew that this conversation would be a tricky one; the Grand Timekeeper wielded tremendous power and there was still a game left to be played. He feared his last outburst had earned the teams a trip to the Western Front and hoped that a more private meeting might reap better results.

He kept his voice quiet. Even. Deferential. "Grand Timekeeper, I hope that my speaking to you doesn't result in further retaliation against my team."

Grand Timekeeper Garridan folded his hands on his desk and sat a bit straighter. "Things were difficult to watch today," he nodded slowly, "but you know there is inherent risk in the Trials— just as there always has been. The boy will be fine, Mordecai. Our doctors are excellent."

Moskowitz was, by nature, a patient man with a slow fuse; however, he found himself having to carefully temper the anger and frustration in his voice when he answered. "And my granddaughter? When will *her* scars heal? If Finn hadn't made the choice he made..." he felt heat rise to his face, "...those lecherous fools..."

"You allowed your granddaughter to participate in the Trials, just as you allowed your own daughter to compete in the past. You have only yourself to blame for that."

The old professor bristled for a moment, then sank back into his chair. Garridan was right.

"These Trials are not the ones in which my daughter competed. If I had known..."

Garridan sighed. He rose from his chair and faced the bookcase. "Mordecai, I respect you. You are a wise man. But I have been here from the beginning. You, in contrast, have been absent from the Trials for two decades. Things evolve with time, and the Trials are no exception."

Professor Moskowitz looked down at his hands, knowing the truth and finally allowing himself to fully reckon with it. It was he who had accepted the invitation for Wharton to compete in the Time Trials and it was he who had offered the chance to compete to these children. What had he expected them to say when he had offered them those contracts? When he had offered them the chance to travel through time?

"Look." Garridan softened his tone and turned to face the professor again. "You are a member of the Historians' Society and that buys you some respect. There have even been discussions about inviting you into the deeper circles of the society. There is much you don't know, and many of us feel that you bring a unique perspective which might prove valuable for a timekeeper." He drew in a breath as if trying to collect courage with it, and then expelled it. "I want you to be our Mortal Compass. Our fifth timekeeper."

Professor Moskowitz looked up, shocked into silence by the offer.

"I know what you will ask." The Grand Timekeeper reseated himself. "And you already know the answer: the Time Trials *must* be finished. The consequence for those children, should they choose not to participate, would be exile, and none of us wants that. If your team secures a victory I can see about removing your granddaughter from an active role for next year, but that's all I can offer you." As he studied the professor's face he made a soft clucking sound. "Mordecai. You know this is more than fair."

Professor Moskowitz issued a reluctant nod before he stood to leave. To argue would accomplish nothing. Securing Everly's safety was perhaps a start.

"Say it out loud a few times tonight," Garridan smiled, dramatically spreading his palms in front of him in the air. "'Timekeeper Moskowitz.'"

CHAPTER 52
FANTASY

Finn shoved the microfiche card under the lens of the reader, and microscopic words flooded the screen. His fingers hesitated over the "zoom" button.

Did he really want to know?

He'd almost done this dozens of times since the *Titanic* challenge, the image of Ebba Andersson's porcelain face and green eyes replaying in his mind over and over as she offered him the cat's eye marble in the palm of her hand. Finn had saved Ebba when he'd saved the ship. But had he *really*? What had really happened to the Andersson family that fateful night in 1912?

"What's up, Tellerville?" A voice behind him interrupted his thoughts, his fingers still hovering above the "zoom" button. He turned to see Nick Dain leaning against one of Wharton Academy's tall bookcases. The jock looked slightly uncomfortable amongst the books, as if he were allergic to knowledge or something.

The lacrosse player's eyes widened. "Daaaang." He sucked in his breath through his teeth in an audible wince. "That's one hell of a shiner."

As Finn's hand traveled to his eye, he threw Nick an ironic smile. "Yeah, well, you should've seen the other guy." He scanned Nick from head to toe and arched a questioning eyebrow, waiting for Nick to get to the point—to make fun of his hair or his shoes, or make some crack about food stamps. But instead, Nick pulled up a chair next to him. He straddled it, sitting on it backwards, his muscular arms resting on the back. "I, uh, need your help, Tellerville."

Finn's eyes cut from side to side. "With...?"

Nick sighed and looked down at his hands; he looked lost. Finn felt bad for him for a fraction of second before remembering that he hated him.

"It's Everly." Nick's smile faded. "I have to find a way to get her back."

"Wait, what?" Finn felt his face scrunch up in confusion. "'Get her back?' I thought you two were..."

Nick scowled. "She dumped me, okay? After Open House." He threw an embarrassed glance around the library, as if afraid others might hear. "I mean, she was weird for weeks before that, too." His voice trailed off before he found it again. "If we're being honest, it's like she was never really into it. She was there...but not really."

Finn felt himself flush at the memory of Everly's body pressed up against him in the trench, and the assertive way she'd pulled his face toward hers. She'd been single this whole time? Seriously?

"Anyway," Nick continued, his eyes meeting Finn's, "I figured you might have some insight. You know, on how to get through to her. Maybe make her reconsider..." His face hardened. "...since she spends so much time with that stupid club of yours." He lowered his voice to a whisper. "Please, man, I'm desperate. I've dated a ton of girls, but she's the only one I've ever really liked."

Finn didn't realize he was smiling until the lacrosse player slitted his eyes in anger. "You better wipe that smile off your face before I make your left eye match your right."

Finn lifted his palms, quietly enjoying the desperation in Nick's voice. "If you want to know how she feels, maybe you should just ask her."

The pallid face of a mousy librarian appeared around the bookcase, arms crossed. She pressed a finger to her lips and issued a loud, "Shhh!" She uncrossed her arms only to wave her index finger like a windshield wiper. "This is a library, gentlemen, not a boxing ring." Her small frame shuddered in indignation before she turned on her heel and disappeared.

Nick swore under his breath and got to his feet. "Listen, I'm onto you, Tellerville. I know you have a thing for her. You think you're one of us now, hanging around with Everly, but you're living in a fantasy, man. You'll never have a chance with her. You'll never be more than a charity case. She *pities* you." His voice grew louder. "I've waited around for Everly for three years. Girls like her end up with guys like *me*." He smirked. "Maybe someday I'll let you take out our trash or trim our lawn or something."

The bug-eyed librarian reappeared around the corner, the chain on her glasses quivering as she shook her head. "Mr. Dain, I'll not tell you again!"

Finn smiled coolly. "Do you mind?" He gestured behind him at the microfiche. "Kinda busy here."

Nick cast a final, wrathful glance over his shoulder as he was led out of the library. Finn watched him go, unable to get the corners of his mouth to relax out of that smile until he redirected his attention to the microfiche reader and the tiny words that were displayed across its screen—words that would tell him whether Ebba Andersson had lived or died.

He drew in a deep breath and pressed the "zoom" button, squinting as the words grew larger and closer. It was a list of the dead, and he inwardly prayed he wouldn't find the name Andersson on it.

His eyes scanned the screen. First Class. Second Class. No... Ebba's family had been Third Class.

Finn kept scrolling, until the surnames of the third-class dead stared back at him in alphabetical order.

Abbing...Abbot...Abelseth...Ahmed...Ali...Allum...

Finn's heart sank into his shoes.

...Andersson.

He pressed his eyes shut before opening them and forcing himself to read the detail next to the name.

"The Anderssons were third class passengers bound for Winnipeg, Canada when the vessel sank. The entire family— Anders and Alfrida and their five children—Sigrid, 11, Ingeborg, 9, Ebba, 6, Sigvard, 4, and Ellis, 2, were lost to the ocean. Their bodies were never recovered."

Finn's hands scrambled to turn off the machine. He jerked the microfiche card out from under the lens, his heart thudding under his stupid Wharton tie.

Why had he looked?

He had been carrying that blue and green cat's eye marble for months now, letting his fingers dip into his pocket to graze it whenever he needed a bit of courage. It had been a confidence booster—a reminder of what he was capable of—that he had saved the *Titanic*. That he had saved Ebba. That for all the people he'd lost in life, he'd saved *some*one. He'd basked in the glow of it...let it fill him up when he felt empty.

Now what?

Finn had always known that their challenges didn't change reality—that whatever good they were able to pull off in the past was nothing but fantasy. And until today, that had been good enough for him.

He looked past the stacks of books toward the door where Nick had disappeared.

"You're living in a fantasy, man."

Finn looked down at his sneakers. Maybe Nick was right, but it didn't matter; he may not have truly saved Ebba, but he'd saved Everly.

And he'd almost kissed her to boot.

CHAPTER 53
A GOOD HURT

Edison was at a routine appointment for his shoulder, and Finn was taking full advantage of the chance to play guitar. He'd chosen one of the loudest, longest songs he could think of: "November Rain" by Guns 'n' Roses. The song was nearly nine minutes. He strummed with fury, he picked with intensity, he flung his hair around like a rock star. He sagged to his knees, letting sweat roll down his face to his neck. Days' worth of pent up energy came out of his fingers onto the strings.

Valerie's mad at me.
Edison's shot because of me.
Vandecraft targeted me....
But I saved Everly...
I did. I saved her.
I...like her.
I think...I think she likes me.
Why?
Why does she like me?

A knock at the door. Loud. Insistent. Aggressive.

Finn scowled, stalked to the door, and threw it open, heart still hammering, fingertips still pulsing. His eyebrows jumped when he saw his visitor.

"Valerie." He dragged an arm across his forehead, pushing away some damp, limp hair.

"Ew, why are you so...sweaty?" Valerie's lip curled as she threw him a look that was half amused, half accusatory. "Never mind, don't answer that."

Finn scoffed. "I'm playing *guitar*, Valerie. Jesus."

"Sure." Valerie rolled her eyes and looked past him into the room. "Anyway, are you gonna let me in or what? I'm going to get frostbite from holding this thing." Finn's eyes dropped to her hand; she was clutching an ice pack that was almost as sweaty as he was.

"Yeah, I mean, I guess, but Edison's not here." He opened the door wider and let her in. He watched Valerie's eyes rove over the walls to his Nirvana poster and swerve to the picture on his bedside table of his mom and dad as teenagers, the year of Finn's conception. His parents were wearing the height of '90s fashion, his mother in heavy eyeliner and a crushed velvet baby doll dress with combat boots, and his dad wearing blue flannel and a Mudhoney shirt. They were sitting on the hood of a Volvo. The very car they died in. Finn ran a hand through his sweat-logged hair, suddenly self-conscious; even Everly hadn't been in here.

"I know he isn't. That's why I came."

Finn snorted and leaned on the ladder to his loft. "Are you gonna hit me again?" When Valerie didn't answer, he smiled. "Have you considered a career in MMA? Because you should."

They lapsed into silence.

"Here." Valerie shattered the quiet as she handed Finn the ice pack, the cold making him gasp as it hit his fingers, which were still throbbing from his frenetic picking. The guitar solo in "November Rain" was no joke. "This should help with that. For what it's worth, at least your shiner makes you look tough."

358

"Thanks," Finn muttered, watching Valerie check the cleanliness of his desk chair before lowering herself into it.

"I'm sorry I punched you." Valerie looked at the ground as she spoke. "I'm not saying I was wrong, because I wasn't—but *you* weren't necessarily wrong, either. I know you were in a tough spot." Before Finn had a chance to speak, she pulled something out of her handbag. "You left this in Moskowitz's class. It fell out of your bag or something."

Finn looked down at the book. *The Spectrum: A Book About Autism.*

"Thanks. I thought I lost this." Finn turned it over in his hands; he'd been getting overdue notices for weeks now.

Valerie looked at him intently. When she spoke, her voice was uncharacteristically soft. "You should try *The Autistic Brain* by Temple Grandin. I've read it three times."

Finn narrowed his eyes but didn't speak, because somehow he knew if he didn't, she'd keep talking.

She did. "Part of the reason I got so upset was because it was Edison."

"Yeah, I know." Finn sighed. "I screwed up—we've established that. He got shot because of me, and I get to live with that. So—"

"No. There's more." Valerie drew in a deep breath and let it out slowly. "You know...Edison, he's like my brother."

Finn nodded. "You guys are close. I get it."

"No." Valerie's reply was quick and exasperated. "Just...shut up and let me finish, okay? I mean...he's literally like my brother. Daniel." She stood and moved to Finn's bedside table, picking up the picture of Finn's parents, looking at it as she spoke. "Daniel has autism, but he's not nearly as high-functioning as Edison. He's barely verbal. We knew he was different right away; as a baby he didn't smile or babble, and by four he hadn't said a word. But I learned how to communicate with him. How to calm him when he had meltdowns." Valerie looked up from the picture. "Anyway, you met my parents."

"Yep. Class acts, both of them." A short, derisive laugh escaped Finn's mouth. He affected a deep, throaty voice in imitation of Valerie's father, "'Is your lamb imported?'"

Valerie threw him a rueful smile. "Well, as you can imagine, they like things they can control, and Daniel's autism isn't one of them. They put him in a group home as soon as he turned seven. They barely visit him, or mention him, even. I think they're embarrassed by him." She set her mouth. "I think they'd like to forget him, actually."

Finn looked at his feet. "That sucks, Valerie." He remembered their first meeting of the Young Historians, and the way Valerie had instantly taken to Edison. He thought of the way she protected Edison but also got annoyed with him and gently ribbed him. Almost like...a sibling.

Valerie nodded. "I know. I wish they'd given me a chance to really know him, you know? I wish they'd let me love him, even if they can't." She was quiet a moment before she spoke again. "When I met Edison, it made me feel like I had another chance. Like protecting Edison is a way to protect Daniel. Makes me feel like I'm taking care of my brother."

Finn wasn't used to seeing Valerie vulnerable. It was like seeing a fish fly. He combed his mind for the right words, but he didn't have time to find them, because Valerie spoke again. She looked back down at the picture in her hands. "You look like him, you know. Your dad. Same hair, same stupid smile."

She set the picture back down and made for the door, but before she left, she stopped. "Hey, Finn? I don't know what happened to your parents. I know you lost them, but...that doesn't mean you don't have a family." She smiled. "The professor once told us we were family, and we are. You, me, Edison, Everly." She squinted at him. "Do me a favor, okay? Just...let your family love you. 'Cause we do." As if suddenly realizing the high sap factor of her words, she punched him in the shoulder. "Families don't work if you push them away, dumbass."

Then she was gone, leaving Finn with the sound of her footsteps on the stairs and a sore shoulder to add to his shiner. He raised her ice pack to his eye and winced; the cold bit him and made him squirm, but it also felt good at the same time—kind of like Valerie's words.

It was a good hurt.

CHAPTER 54
MAKE BELIEVE

Professor Moskowitz turned over the envelope which held the assignment for the last Trial of the season, running his fingers along the edges of the paper. Two of the more dangerous games had already been selected, but the professor knew that any of the games could be made perilous when their details were created by *these* timekeepers.

Timekeeper. The old man studied the crimson logo printed on the front of the envelope as he recollected the offer that Grand Timekeeper Garridan had made to him after Hide and Seek. An offer to become the fifth timekeeper—the "Mortal Compass" for the Historians' Society. Moskowitz felt his heart flutter at the thought, despite the fact that he willed it not to. Were he to accept this position, there were so many questions that he could finally have answers to. So many wrongs he could right.

But then he heard his granddaughter's scream in the ear of his mind as she was dragged into the trenches by a pack of eager soldiers. He fidgeted with his old fingers as he stared at the door in anticipation. When he had learned that his team would play Hide and Seek, possibly because of his own foolish outburst, the old man had frozen. Panic had set in, supplanting all the advice and wisdom he would have liked to have dispensed to his team on the cusp of their penultimate challenge, a thing for which he felt an abiding, soul-crushing guilt.

How could he even consider this promotion? Better to run. Get his team through the teeth of this last challenge and never look back.

As the door opened, the professor forced his restless hands to fold in his lap. He smiled as he regarded the four students who filed in—together this time.

Valerie helped Edison take his seat, his arm still awkwardly cradled in a sling. He had lost a concerning amount of blood by the time they had returned to the present, but luckily the damage inflicted by the archaic bullet was more superficial than anything. He had been required to stay in the hospital wing of the Historians' Society headquarters for a week after the competition to be properly monitored; a trip to the hospital was forbidden, of course, as the extraction of a 1917 bullet would lead to plenty of unwanted questions.

Edison hadn't been alone, however; while there were rules about the other players staying, forcing Finn, Valerie, and Everly to reluctantly board the private jet back to Wharton Academy, there were no rules pertaining to SCRAP. The little robot stayed by Edison's side throughout his recovery. The head nurse looked at him with reproach at first, regarding him as a nuisance, but in the end, she took quite a liking to him.

"Welcome back." The professor felt a sharp pang of regret pierce him at the sight of Edison's sling. "How are you doing, Edison?"

Edison offered a one-shoulder shrug and looked at the professor impassively. "I am alive."

"Indeed, you are." Professor Moskowitz laughed.

"My parents are upset with me," Edison added. They'd had to lie to Edison's parents about how he was injured, as the sling was impossible to hide. The story was that Edison had wandered onto the Wharton Archery range, where he had accidentally been shot with an arrow. Headmaster Bruce was dismayed, particularly concerned about the optics of the situation, but as archery was a sport, it was quickly forgiven and swept under the rug.

"I'm afraid *I'm* the one they should be upset with." The professor sighed as he got to his feet and moved in front of his desk, closer to his team. "I should have never asked you to participate in the Trials." His eyes dropped to the floor. "This is my fault."

"Don't start that," Valerie said. "We read the contract and we signed it. We knew the dangers."

Everly raised her eyes, but said nothing.

"How many people get to save the *Titanic*?" smiled Valerie, looking at Finn.

"Or take a left hook from Valerie Konrad?" Finn quipped back.

Edison offered a silent nod.

"Well." The professor released a deep breath. "Be that as it may, I must apologize for my lack of assistance as of late. I panicked, and you deserve better from your mentor." There was an awkward silence after which the professor added, "You had important parts to play and you played them beautifully. It was me who forgot to be a part of the team this time."

"I don't know about that." Everly's green eyes drifted to each of her teammate's faces. "I'm not sure *I* was an asset to the team. I'm the one who got captured. If I hadn't been, Edison probably wouldn't have been shot."

"Nonsense." The professor shuddered at the memory of his granddaughter disappearing into a trench. "Every challenge is different. Your leadership in the first challenge led us to victory. Valerie's leadership was invaluable during this one, when mine was absent. And Finn has a tendency to go rogue and save the day..." he

364

stopped and stared at Finn with quiet intensity before adding, "At some point, maybe I can thank you for what you did out there, son."

Everly looked at Finn and then quickly redirected her eyes to the floor.

"And Edison," the professor finished, "You are the glue that holds the team together."

Edison watched the professor for a moment, expressionless. "It's not easy," he said with a straight face.

"So," Valerie smiled ruefully. "I take it we didn't win."

"No," the professor confirmed. "We did not. All the teams were sent to different parts of the same front and Vale Academy was able to secure the victory. They had played this game before and were able to use that to their advantage. The Neil twins figured the safest place to hide was actually in the most *dangerous* place; they never attempted to leave No Man's Land. They found sufficient cover and simply waited."

"What kind of cover?" asked Valerie, always ready to hone her game.

"Bodies," said the professor. "They hid under bodies and pretended to be dead themselves. People don't tend to waste ammunition on the dead."

"So, do we have our next challenge?" Valerie leaned forward on her elbows.

"We do." The professor held up the familiar sleeve of a phonographic record. He positioned the record on the gramophone and let the needle drop into place with trembling fingers, hoping the assignment that awaited them would be survivable.

"Greetings Wharton Academy! While you forced to withdraw from your Hide and Seek challenge, you survived to see another day. It is our hope that some important lessons were learned, even if the challenge did not result in a win."

Professor Moskowitz bowed his head, sure that last line had been intended for his ears.

"*As it stands, Vale Academy has amassed two impressive victories by thinking outside the box and playing to win. Wharton is on the board with one win, though it was quite a 'titanic' victory. A win by The Halls of Ivy Prep or Wilmington Prep might not win them the Time Trials, but it would earn respect.*

"*We are excited to present you with our last challenge to see the ultimate results: Make Believe! The game of Make Believe is a favorite amongst little boys and girls. Using the power of their imaginations, children can reinvent their worlds in any way that they see fit. They can become anyone and they can do anything.*

"*In the Time Trials, the game of Make Believe offers you this chance. It is the only game in the Trials which grants you the choice of where and when in time you will go. Your mission is to change the past in the most significant way possible. We want you to use this as a chance to make the world 'better.' When all teams have completed their chosen tasks, they will present their changes to the panel of timekeepers for evaluation and grading. This challenge is a subjective one, and we look forward to seeing the ways which Wharton's Time Team can change the world. As always, remember that your safety is of the utmost concern.*"

With that exceedingly ironic statement, the Grand Timekeeper's voice vanished and the machine popped with static until the professor picked up the needle and turned it off.

"So how bad is it *this* time?" Finn ran a hand through his hair and raised his eyes.

"It's not." The professor smiled. "Make Believe gives us the power to decide our own fate. It's a mental game more than anything."

"So, we choose the event..." said Valerie slowly, "...we change it in some way that makes the world 'better'...and then we just come back and we're done?"

"Well, you have the interview at the end," reminded the professor. "However, it will not only be with Timekeeper Vandecraft this time—the other timekeepers will be on the panel as well. Be that as it may, Timekeeper Vandecraft's opinion will still weigh heavily, as she was your designated timekeeper for the other challenges."

Valerie scoffed. "So, we don't stand a chance in hell."

"Maybe that's a good thing." Everly looked at each of her teammates' faces.

Valerie curled her lip. "How is anything with that woman good?"

"Because," explained Everly, "if we win, we automatically get the 'honor' of competing again next year. It's why Vale is back after last season's victory. Do *you* want to play this game again?"

Valerie shuddered. "I think I'll join chess club or something. Good call, Everly."

"Why don't we just throw the challenge and do some sightseeing?" Finn shrugged. "Let's just see a stegosaurus and pull our chain when we're done." He stole a glance at Edison, whose eyes brightened under the lenses of his square glasses.

The professor looked at Finn over the top of his chrome spectacles. "I would advise against that. Remember, the council will still have your fate in its hands. Your effort must at least have the appearance of being honest or there might be repercussions. The Society does not like to be mocked."

"What if there's a tie?" asked Everly.

The professor nodded. "It's a possibility. Because of the current score, a tie is the best we can do. In that case, we would most likely move to a tiebreaker. A final challenge. The tiebreaker would in all likelihood be something with definitive results—a game like Marbles or Hide and Seek where the winner is clear."

"The Halls of Ivy Prep got 'invited' back after a second-place finish," reminded Valerie.

"But it was after an 'impressive performance,' remember?" Everly drummed her fingers on the top of her desk in thought. "So, let's not be impressive. We need to do something that doesn't stand out and then lose."

Valerie nodded. "But we can't just lose it outright. It has to at least look like we tried."

"Losing is harder to figure out than winning." Finn smiled.

"The other schools are probably going with something obvious..." Everly mused.

"...like killing Hitler or something," Valerie agreed.

"Exactly. The ridiculous part of this challenge is that the world isn't going to get better from any of this. If you kill Hitler or save Martin Luther King Jr. or something obvious like that, great. But when you 'turn the page,' what did you really change? Nothing. I think the other teams are going to do very impactful things in the past, but they won't actually change anything in reality."

There was a brief silence that was finally broken by Finn. "So...what do we do?"

"We do exactly what everyone else will do: the obvious thing— something heroic and noble," Everly said. "Nothing ventured, nothing gained. We'll have to pick a target that doesn't offer us any real danger, so killing Hitler is out—sorry, Valerie. We'll also have to prepare for it just like we would anything else. They have to think this is a sincere effort."

"I can make flashcards," smiled Valerie, ignoring Edison's audible groan.

"Alright," Everly slapped her hand against her desk. "Let's get to the library and study. Losing doesn't just *happen*, you know."

Valerie turned to the professor. "Any advice for us?"

Professor Moskowitz smiled and looked the group over. "Not this time." He let himself out of the classroom, leaving the four students behind.

The team stood to leave, regarding each other's injuries, all incurred during the last challenge: Edison's sling, of course, was the most notable. Valerie's stitches were out, but she still sported some bandages on her legs from cuts she'd gotten from barbed wire in No Man's Land. The area around Finn's right eye was still a bit yellow where Valerie's shiner had once been, and some bruising could still be seen on Everly's neck and collarbone.

"I wonder how many people are wondering why the Young Historians Club looks like hell run over twice." Valerie laughed and turned to Everly. "How did you explain all your injuries to Nick, anyway?"

Finn instantly looked away, but Everly watched him out of the corners of her eyes. "I didn't need to. I broke that off a long time ago. It just wasn't...making sense."

Valerie's mouth lifted into a smug smile as she gently escorted Edison out of the room, leaving Finn and Everly alone.

Everly looked at her feet. "I never actually thanked you." She looked up into Finn's eyes. "For what you did for me, back in that trench. If you hadn't gotten to me when you did—"

"I know." Finn half-smiled and looked away. "Forget it. Seemed like a good time to do something right with regard to you."

Everly studied his face. His eyes were clearer now than she'd ever seen them, but they still held a trace of their original sadness. She reached out and let her fingertips graze his, feeling a tremor pass through her. She waited for him to say something more—to close the gap between them, but he didn't.

As the two of them walked side by side to join their friends in the library, something still stood between them—an invisible wall. These past few weeks had chipped away at it, but its vestiges stood firm. As Everly watched Finn beside her, hands in his pockets, she wondered: what would be the thing that finally collapsed it? What would finally scrub his eyes clean of that sadness?

The two of them passed the Wharton Gardens, where they'd spent so many nights. Everly remembered the night Finn had made his admission to her, about his parents. About what he'd believed he'd done. Even after all he'd done right, he still didn't feel redeemed. The deaths of his parents, and the part he believed he played in it, was the original wound, and unless it was healed, that wall would exist between them forever. It would exist between Finn and everyone he knew until he reckoned with it. Looked at it. Faced it.

The snow had melted and the beginnings of leaves were starting to make an appearance on the once barren trees in the Wharton Gardens. The gazebo had even been lacquered with a fresh coat of paint. Spring, the season of renewal, wasn't yet here, but it was imminent. Everly could feel it.

Finn had saved her back in that trench, and now it was him that needed saving.

CHAPTER 55
STUFF TO SAY

Finn's head pounded as he heard the gears above decelerating to a slow, soft purr. This was the last challenge and he was ready to get it over with. The team had studied for hours in the library, devising a solid plan to foil the assassination of Abraham Lincoln. They would make their way to Ford's Theater in Washington D.C. on April 14, 1865 and expose John Wilkes Booth before he could shoot the sixteenth president of the United States. Just like their *Titanic* challenge, they had exact times and details to work with, which would make this task fairly easy. Sure, Abraham Lincoln would still have been assassinated when they returned to the present, but they would lose the challenge for lack of originality, and the Society would be satisfied with their modest show of effort.

Finn mentally reviewed the notes in his head. He was assigned to the door of Ford's Theater with Valerie, where they had planned to stop Booth before he could even enter the building. It would be very difficult to gain access to the Presidential Box, so they'd have to catch him early and distract him somehow. Finn knew to watch for a shifty-eyed guy with curly black hair, dark eyes, and bushy eyebrows.

Finn's thoughts were interrupted by Everly gently urging him to exit the Time Bender.

"Come on, Finn." She stood in the porthole, beckoning, green eyes fixed on him alone. Finn waited for Edison and Valerie to get up as well, but they stayed seated, making no move to unfasten their leather restraints. Neither of them would look him in the eye. Finn freed himself from his seat and followed Everly out of the humming machine, casting a bewildered glance back at them.

As he emerged from the porthole, he looked around him, confused. This place didn't look anything like what he was expecting. They had planned to arrive at their destination at night, just prior to the showing of *Our American Cousin*, the farcical comedy that Lincoln would attend, but there was still light in the sky.

Finn furrowed his brow. The Time Bender was surrounded by weeds and tall, dry grass, and several yards away he saw a deteriorated car with broken windows and a flat tire. He did a double-take.

A *car*. A Firebird. In 1865.

He frowned. Something was wrong.

He spun around to face Everly. "I think there's been a mistake. We have the wrong coordinates or something." His eyes fell upon the broken chain link fence that surrounded the lot in which they were standing, trash and debris caught in it like bugs on a car's grill. His stomach somersaulted as a feeling of sudden recognition began to set in.

"Everly...what is this?"

"Finn," Everly gently grabbed his wrist. "Look at me."

Finn tried to focus on Everly's green eyes, but the surroundings were becoming more and more familiar, and he couldn't stop his gaze from wandering out to the road beyond. It was a road he knew...a road he had walked many times. An abandoned shopping cart full of garbage was tipped over across the street. "I grew up here," he murmured.

Everly's voice was feather-soft. "I know." Finn continued to throw his gaze around, disoriented as he felt Everly take his pocket watch and began to spin the dial. Instantly, Finn's wetsuit transformed into a pair of jeans and a flannel worn open over a vintage t-shirt.

"Finn, listen. We don't have much time," Everly began. "The Time Bender is set to return to the present in half an hour; we actually have it idling." She swallowed hard, as if struggling to keep her voice steady. "It's early December, three years ago, and your parents...they're home. What you do in there..." she raised her hand to his cheek to guide his face to look in the direction of the duplex in which he had once lived, "...is up to you." It was then that Everly's voice broke. She paused and looked down in an obvious reach for composure.

"Maybe you want to use this time to get closure...say the things you always wanted to say if you'd had the chance." Tears were streaming down her face now and she smeared them away with the back of a hand. "Or maybe...maybe you'll want to stay. Your life here would always be a fantasy...it would never be real...but maybe it would *feel* real, like you said. Maybe that's enough." She looked him directly in the eyes. "Reality is what you make it, right?"

Finn's mind spun. Everly Caldwell was standing a few yards from his childhood home, and she was crying. Before he could gather his thoughts or decide what to focus on first, Everly turned abruptly and walked back through the tall weeds toward the Time Bender.

"You're on the clock now, Finn. You need to go."

Finn walked out of the vacant lot into the road. It was dusk and the air was heavy with the oily, metallic, industrial smell he had come to know as home. The Volvo was parked out by the curb, unharmed, the bumper covered in stickers, just as he remembered it. The windows of the upstairs unit were two dark squares; Mrs.

Cole, their grumpy upstairs neighbor, was probably already asleep. In the bottom unit, the windows were lit, the sun-bleached curtain and rusted bars blocking Finn's view of its occupants.

Finn drew in a deep breath and tried to steady his rapidly beating heart as he walked toward what had once been his home. He could hear a faint sound even before he reached the door: a guitar being strummed. The timeworn floorboards groaned under his feet as he stepped onto the porch. The paint on the duplex was peeling, the grey wood beneath exposed. Finn placed his hand on the doorknob, resting his forehead against the door for a moment, trying to collect himself before he opened it.

The door was unlocked. Finn pushed it open and was instantly hit with a familiar smell which could best be described as a blend of coffee grounds, incense, and laundry detergent. His eyes swept the dated couch, the pilled cushions, the knicked coffee table, and the water-damaged corner to the right of the kitchen doorway.

It was exactly as he'd left it. Not a thing out of place.

The strumming was coming from the kitchen. Finn could see the neck of the guitar, and the hand gripping it, the fingers of which were sliding expertly along the frets. Breathing deeply, Finn approached the kitchen doorway. Its frame was marked up and dated from all the time's Finn's parents had measured his height against it.

Trent Mallory looked up at his son, a smile instantly springing to his face. Finn felt his throat begin to close up and he fought it.

"Shark Finn! Did you eat yet?" Before even waiting for a response, Finn's father stood up and set his guitar down, resting the headstock against the kitchen table. He narrowed his eyes and moved toward his son, a look of amusement and curiosity dancing on his face. He reached out a hand and ran it over Finn's chin.

"Is that...stubble?" He burst out laughing. "How did I miss that? I swear, Sarah, they grow too fast. It happens overnight." He shook his head and wrinkled his nose good naturedly. Finn's hand rose to feel his own chin; he hadn't even thought of that. So much time had passed since he'd lived this life. When he'd last seen his parents he'd been only fourteen...now he was on the cusp of seventeen.

Finn's mother sat at the table wearing her Coffee Pot uniform. A rectangular badge was pinned to her polyester dress: "Sarah." She looked up from her checkbook, which she had been focusing on with a steepled brow. Her face relaxed and she giggled...a laugh like bells.

"Stop it, Trent, I think you're embarrassing him."

Finn studied his parents' faces wordlessly, unable to string a sentence together as he took in every detail of them: every line, every expression, trying to preserve it in his memory.

"Hey." Trent's face lost the goofy smile and softened as he lowered himself back into his chair. "You okay? You look like you've been places. Like you've got stuff to say. Why don't you sit down and tell us what's on your mind?"

Finn pulled up a chair between his parents and sagged into it. "I'm..." His eyes darted between their expectant faces. "I just wanted to say...I'm sorry. I'm so sorry." He shut his eyes. "You can't know how sorry—"

"For what? If this is about the other day...." Finn's dad waved his hand in the air, guitar pick still pinned between his thumb and middle finger.

"No." Finn opened his eyes and leveled his father's stare. "It's more than that. I know you gave up your lives for me. *Because* of me."

Finn's mother shook her head as he spoke, but Finn talked over her frown. "I wasn't planned, I know that. And if you hadn't had me—"

His mother's hand found its way to his cheek. "Don't say that." She brushed some hair out of his face. "When you were born, we took a detour." She shrugged. "And detours turn into adventures." She sketched a smile. "You're our adventure, Finn."

Finn's father nodded. "If I could do it over, I'd take the same road." He sighed and stretched his legs out under the table. "All that matters now is your future and what you make of it." He leaned closer, eyes roving over Finn's face. "I swear, you really do look older today. Wiser. I'm proud of you, kid."

Finn's eyes wandered to the kitchen counter—to the ancient toaster on the chipped, laminate counter, the oil stains behind the range, and the peeling wallpaper above the cabinets. This had been his life, in all of its tumbledown familiarity. This was home. And it could be again.

He could stay. He could live out the rest of his life here, in a fantasy. He could make it up to his parents, and prevent that fateful night from ever happening at all, just as he'd done in so many dreams before. He could press "rewind."

His hand dipped into his pocket and grazed his 1912 cat's eye marble, and as it did, he saw Everly's face in his mind, tear-streaked and beautiful as she stood with him in the knee-high weeds.

All that matters now is your future and what you make of it.

Finn's dad had taken up his guitar again and was now absently playing the opening riff to "Hunger Strike" by Temple of the Dog, staring up at the ceiling, legs crossed at the ankles.

Finn shut his eyes, and in the ear of his mind, Everly's words swam and mingled with those of his father's.

"Your past is stealing your present. And if you aren't careful, it'll steal your future, too."

Yes, he could stay.

Or...

His mother's voice cut through his thoughts as she walked to the freezer and pulled it open. "You know, you never answered whether you'd eaten. Want something? I think we have a frozen pizza in here somewhere."

As she rifled through some bags of frozen peas, Finn withdrew his hand from his pocket. "You said it looked like I've 'been places.'" He swallowed hard. "And I guess I have..."

He stood, and his parents looked at him in expectation. Trent's fingers grew still on the guitar strings and swirls of white mist drifted out of the open freezer.

"...but I also have places to go."

His mother smiled, head tilted to the side. "Okay." She chuckled and let the freezer door fall shut. "Be careful out there." She threw an arm around her son the way she always did before he left the house, but this time, Finn held on, memorizing the feel of her and the lemony, all-purpose cleaner smell of her uniform. He felt a lump form in his throat.

Trent dragged his pick over the strings and spoke through his strumming. "We'll be right here where you left us." He winked and redirected his eyes to his fingers as they picked, strummed, and slid, humming as he did.

Finn turned to leave, but cast his head over his shoulder once more to take in his parents—the streaks of red in his mother's hair, the freckles on the bridge of her nose, the way she knit her brow in concentration as she moved about the kitchen. The holes in the knees of his father's jeans, the lopsided smile that matched his own...the way he whispered the lyrics under his breath as he played his guitar.

Finn felt the lump in his throat dissolve. "I know," he murmured.

Everly sat amongst the dandelions with her knees drawn up to her chest, eyes darting between her pocket watch and the direction in which Finn had disappeared. There was a very real chance that the group of four that had come here tonight would return to the present as a group of three. She may have just seen Finn Mallory for the last time. There were only a few minutes left on the clock before the Time Bender would return to the present, and Everly was mentally preparing for a new reality.

She had planned this, she reminded herself. Finn deserved the chance. He deserved the opportunity to finally get some peace. To feel redeemed.

She glanced at her pocket watch again. *Five minutes.* She released a slow sigh but looked up at the sound of her name.

Finn stood with his hands in his holo-cloth pockets, the corners of his eyes crinkled with his smile. His warm brown eyes were a bit misty, but they looked contented in a way she had never seen. That haunted look was missing, replaced by a look of calm and decisiveness. He strode toward her and bent down, taking her hands and pulling her to her feet.

Everly started to say something, but her words were lost as Finn tipped her face up to his and kissed her. He kissed her in a way that made up for the other times he should have—all the times they'd been interrupted, and all the times he had been too wrapped up in his own anxieties. For a rare moment, he did not think, deliberate, or worry—he just pressed "play."

"You came back," Everly said against his mouth.

Finn shrugged. "Yeah. I guess I did." He smiled dryly, arms still locked around her waist. "Figured I lived in the past for long enough."

There were only two minutes left on the clock when Finn and Everly climbed back into the Time Bender. Just before ducking into the porthole, Finn stopped; he withdrew something small and round from his pocket and hurled it into the tall weeds of the vacant lot.

CHAPTER 56
REAL

Timekeepers Keenan Wakefield, Maverick Doherty, Philomena Vandecraft, and Dashiel Garridan wore their most formal of clothing and matched it with their most serious of faces. With their heads bedecked with vintage hats, their odd and eccentric leather clothing, and their dramatic boots, they were a sight to behold.

They had all reviewed the footage for each team extensively, of course, but the real test would come in the interview. It was in the interview of games like Make Believe that teams found true success or failure. Philomena Vandecraft, who had been assigned to this team for the three prior challenges, had promised her fellow timekeepers that Wharton Academy would not disappoint in this area, and so far she had not been proven wrong; Grand Timekeeper Garridan had never seen a team go so personal in a challenge like this.

The doors to the great hall opened and Finn Mallory, Everly Caldwell, Valerie Konrad, and Edison Pellegrin walked in for their official interview. They took their seats at the large, rectangular table, opposite the four timekeepers.

Grand Timekeeper Garridan rose from his seat and presented the team with his most respectful of bows. "My congratulations on having completed the last challenge of the year, and my respect to you all. Wharton has been a most interesting team to follow. Your propensity for unconventional tactics has been delightful. My deepest regards to your mentor as well..." he raised an eyebrow, "...he is *certainly* one to keep a close eye on."

He smiled and clapped his hands together. "So. Onto the formalities. This interview is your opportunity to explain your decisions to this panel of timekeepers. Answer carefully, as this process is a delicate one. The truth should come before all. We are not interested in what your *mentor* wants us to hear—we are interested in what *you* have to say. Be genuine, and you will go far. Let us begin."

He sat down and waited patiently for the questions to start. Timekeeper Vandecraft stood up, her grey eyes electric as always. "Obviously, you made an interesting choice today. While most of your competition were risking their lives to accomplish feats of heroism, you chose to brave the urban streets of...Tellerville."

She turned to the other timekeepers. "Not the safest nor the finest of neighborhoods, I'll admit, so it did take *some* courage to go there." The other timekeepers chuckled while Philomena studied Finn with intense eyes.

"I'm curious," she asked innocently. "Finn Mallory, was it *your* idea to use this technology for such a...noble cause?"

The timekeepers' laughter ceased, and Finn felt the blood rush to his face as they stared at him in expectation.

Before he even had a chance to speak, Everly's voice piped up, speaking for him. "Finn didn't know anything about it. We made the decision as a team."

Timekeeper Vandecraft's face stretched into a contented smile and Everly realized her mistake immediately. The timekeeper had seen the footage. She had *seen* Finn's surprise. She was, as Edison put it, probing for weakness, and she had not done so in vain.

"My, my, child." The timekeeper feigned surprise. "When you say 'we' made the decision as a 'team' do you mean everybody *except* Finn? He is part of the team, after all...is he not?"

Everly looked down at the surface of the table.

"You never answered the question," pointed out Timekeeper Wakefield, trying his best to make himself useful. "Why did you go so personal on this? How does that accomplish the goal? Timekeeper Vandecraft is correct; it does look like an excuse to..." He wiggled his fingers in the air, grappling for the right word.

Philomena had it for him. "Have fun," she smiled. "An excuse to play with the parents and get a little kiss?"

Everly seethed with anger and Philomena could smell it on her. "Well," she corrected herself through a satisfied smirk, "I guess it wasn't a *little* kiss."

The timekeepers snorted and averted their eyes, but Philomena kept hers, unflinching and grey, on Everly.

"What did you want us to do—kill Hitler?" Everly's voice was steely. The timekeepers snapped to attention, watching Philomena eagerly as if they were fourth graders on a playground about to witness a fist fight.

Vandecraft cocked her head to one side as she retorted. "Surely preventing the Holocaust is more important than 'Shark Finn' getting to talk about obscure grunge bands with his 'musician' father, don't you think?"

Valerie stood, knocking her chair backward to the floor. It was a miracle that she had lasted this long. "Killing *Hitler*?" she snorted. "Yeah, we thought about that for two seconds before we realized how stupid of an idea that is! Doing that doesn't change anything in reality. You said to make the world better."

Grand Timekeeper Garridan rose to keep order, but Philomena quieted him by placing her hand on his arm. "A 'stupid' idea?" Her eyelashes fluttered coyly. "Why, whatever do you mean, Valerie Konrad?"

"We kill Hitler, we save Lincoln, we create world peace, who cares? What does that solve? What is this, a high school homework assignment? What are we supposed to do with that, write a blog?"

Philomena Vandecraft seemed perplexed for a moment, but fired back quickly. "And giving this orphan his parents back for a few minutes? How does *that* change anything?"

Everly rose to her feet. "We saved the *Titanic* but it's still at the bottom of the sea, isn't it? You said that you wanted us to change the world for the better. We did that. We made *his* world better." She looked at Finn and softened her voice. "At least it's real."

Philomena Vandecraft sat down in defeat, with no questions left to ask. But she stared at Everly, her grey eyes sparkling with satisfaction. The other timekeepers nodded in approval.

Vandecraft hadn't been lying: Wharton did not disappoint.

CHAPTER 57
YOU'RE WELCOME

Wharton's Time Team waited in their prep room for the interviews to conclude and for a decision to be rendered by the timekeepers. Valerie set forth a steady stream of cursing as Everly rested her steepled hands against her forehead, attempting to make sense of what had just happened.

It had felt so good to put Philomena Vandecraft in her place in front of the other timekeepers, but there was something about Vandecraft's smug look at the end which didn't quite settle right with her. Finn had silently assessed the situation, remaining quiet throughout the heated exchange, and Everly was beginning to realize that his silence might not have been for the reasons she had originally thought. When the timekeeper had attacked him so viciously, Everly had assumed he didn't have the strength to fight back, but she was slowly seeing that it was because he didn't feel the *need* to fight back; Finn was different. He was contented somehow. At peace.

"I think we made a mistake," Everly sighed. "I think *I* made a mistake."

"Don't be silly, Everly," said Valerie, still seething. "You destroyed her up there. The other timekeepers were totally on your side."

"Isn't that a bad thing?" asked Edison robotically.

The group turned to look at him.

"What do you mean, Edison?" Everly asked.

"We were supposed to *lose* today," Edison reminded them.

"Oh, we're *going* to lose," Valerie assured him. "We're total losers."

"You're sure about that?" pressed Edison, pushing his thick glasses up onto his nose. "You were very convincing. Your arguments pretty much told them why we should win. She beat us at our own game. She wanted to lose that argument and she did."

Valerie and Everly exchanged a somber look as the arbitrator came in to alert the team that a decision had been reached. They followed the black clad man into the main warehouse and took their seats next to Vale Academy. Their school banners hung proudly above them and the audience watched with bated breath.

Finn shot a glance at Emily Neil, who gave him a slight nod before assuming her cold glare ahead. The timekeepers walked forward and took their seats. A hush came over the oddly dressed spectators as they waited for the final verdict to be announced.

Grand Timekeeper Garridan stood and waited patiently for absolute silence. He smiled warmly, his smooth voice attempting to hide his utter excitement. "The Historians' Society has long lived by the saying 'Veritas Filia Temporis,'" he began, basking in the gravity of the moment. "This year, our Time Teams have certainly done that slogan proud, finding truth in unexpected corners of history!" He paused as the society members clapped in appreciation. "It has fallen upon the High Council of Timekeepers to deliver a decision for the game of Make Believe. This is no easy task. The stakes were high and the teams all made compelling decisions."

As Felix Winkler poised his pen over his notepad and the camera crew directed their lenses toward Vale and Wharton, Everly looked up to find Philomena Vandecraft appraising her with her cold, grey eyes. The timekeeper smiled at her, letting Everly know the verdict before it was even read. Edison was right: Vandecraft had *wanted* to lose that debate in front of her peers. She'd known what buttons to push, and Everly, wanting to protect Finn, had fallen right into line.

"And so," the Grand Timekeeper concluded, snapping Everly from her thoughts, "we had to ask ourselves—in the game of Make Believe, what is real and what is not? We believe that one team was able to show us the answer." He paused for dramatic effect before bellowing, "Wharton Academy!"

The crowd roared in applause as Everly felt a knot grow in the pit of her stomach. Flashbulbs popped and Felix Winkler began to move through the crowd with his microphone at the ready as the Grand Timekeeper urged the audience to silence with his excited hands. "And so we have a tie between Wharton Academy and Vale. The council has conferred and we will not award a winner for this year."

The crowd went silent.

For a moment, Everly thought that they had dodged a very dangerous bullet.

Until...

"We shall have *two*!" The Grand Timekeeper threw his arms up in elation. The unexpected result excited the crowd into tossing their odd hats into the air, like high-school seniors at a commencement ceremony. Spectators standing near Professor Moskowitz slapped him on the back and pumped his hand in congratulatory merriment as he forced a brittle smile and shrugged his shoulders weakly.

In the midst of the excitement, Timekeeper Philomena Vandecraft found Everly's eyes and mouthed a silent, "You're welcome."

ACKNOWLEDGEMENTS

There are many people without whom this book would not have been possible. First, we're endlessly grateful to the team at Tiny Fox Press, Jennifer Wallace, Galen Surlak-Ramsey, Markella Wagner and Madi Holler. Thank you for believing in our vision for the book and its characters, and for taking a chance on two eccentric, married school teachers and their first book.

Secondly, we'd be remiss if we didn't thank each other, for the late-night/early-morning, caffeine-fueled brainstorming sessions, the days scrawling plot maps on the dining room window in Expo pen, and generally being each other's resident sounding board, critic, and "Wonderwall." Without the dynamic between us, the Time Trials never would have made it out of our heads and onto the page.

We thank all the teachers we ever had who inspired us not only to be teachers ourselves, but to be writers, as well as all the students who have passed through our own classrooms, from whom so many pieces of the book's characters were drawn. Much of Finn's idealism, Everly's cool grace, Valerie's fiery assertiveness, and Edison's cerebral genius were harvested from the dozens of students we've had the privilege to teach.

We're incredibly thankful to our family, friends and colleagues who beta read for us when our book was just a clumsy, fragile, newborn thing. Thank you for your time, your kindness, and your belief.

We thank our two sons, Declan and Ezra, for providing us ample opportunity to stay young, curious, and spry, never letting us get too comfortable in one spot (we mean this literally; life with these two means seldom sitting down). They are our two greatest adventures and our proudest creations.

Lastly, as one of the book's major themes is "found family," our final "thank you" is to those who have served as "found family" to either of us throughout our lives—those who have accepted us without reservation, baggage and all, no matter how heavy. You likely know who you are.

About the Authors

Jon is a high school English teacher, Magic the Gathering enthusiast, and Buccaneers fan. A native of Atascadero, California, Jon graduated from Cal Poly San Luis Obispo.

He enjoys thrillers and horrors, and world-building is his favorite part of writing. Jon is a the "pantser" of the duo—he likes to jump into stories and see where they go!

Dayna teaches fourth grade. When she isn't writing, she's reading historical fiction, gardening, or stewarding their family's Little Free Library. Born and raised in Los Osos, California, Dayna graduated from San Francisco State University. Her favorite part of writing is developing character arcs and relationships. When writing, Dayna is the "plotter" of the pair—she likes detailed outlines and playing with permeating themes and symbols.

Website:
mcconnellwriting.com

Twitter:
@JonMcConnell20
@dayna_mcconnell

About the Publisher

Tiny Fox Press LLC
5020 Kingsley Road
North Port, FL 34287

www.tinyfoxpress.com